Now
Silence

NOW
SILENCE

A Novel of World War II

Tori Warner Shepard

SUNSTONE
PRESS

SANTA FE

No personalities or characters in this narrative, except for public figures, should be traced to any particular person or persons, living or dead. This is a work of fiction.

Sunstone books may be purchased for educational, business, or sales promotional use. For information please write: Special Markets Department, Sunstone Press, P.O. Box 2321, Santa Fe, New Mexico 87504-2321.

Book design | Vicki Ahl
Body type | Adobe Jenson Pro ❖ Display type | Odine
Printed on acid free paper

Library of Congress Cataloging-in-Publication Data

Shepard, Tori Warner, 1939-
  Now silence : a novel of World War II / by Tori Warner Shepard.
     p. cm.
  ISBN 978-0-86534-596-6 (softcover : alk. paper)
  1. World War, 1939-1945--New Mexico--Santa Fe--Fiction. 2. Santa Fe (N.M.)--Fiction.
I. Title.
  PS3619.H4545N68 2008
  813'.6--dc22
                          2008016513

Published in

WWW.SUNSTONEPRESS.COM
SUNSTONE PRESS / POST OFFICE BOX 2321 / SANTA FE, NM 87504-2321 /USA
(505) 988-4418 / ORDERS ONLY (800) 243-5644 / FAX (505) 988-1025

This novel is dedicated to David with love

And with deep admiration to Lynn Stegner
And humble gratitude for the strength
of the 1,800 New Mexicans captured at Bataan

Foreword

During the first half of the twentieth century, Japan converted itself from a closed, self-contained agrarian group of islands to a major industrial and commercial country supported by vast shipping lines. Divinely guided by their Emperor, the Japanese people considered themselves to be naturally superior and to justify their need for more resources, they rallied behind a belief stemming from their glorious founding myth called *Hakko Ichiu* that meant "Universal Brotherhood" or more pointedly, "The Eight Corners of the World under One Roof." Citing *Hakko Ichiu*, the Japanese initiated and justified launching what amounted to a holy war by attacking China and then joining the Triple Alliance with Italy and Germany to back their move to dominate the entire Pacific.

They continued their bold conquest with a surprise attack at Honolulu's Pearl Harbor on December 7, 1941, sending 160 fighter planes in each of two successive bombings virtually crippling the US Pacific Fleet and destroying 188 planes. Eight hours later, the Empire launched a second surprise day-long attack on the strategic US Army Air Field in the Philippines. This thorough bombing virtually devastated the Pacific-based American Air Corps at a time when the Americans were fully engaged combating the Germans in Europe.

The Philippine Islands, ceded by Spain to the US in 1898, were key to the Imperial Army's assault upon Australia. A week later, the Japanese launched their pounding of Luzon, the main Philippine island, by bombing the harbor to finish off the US Navy and then coming ashore with well-supplied trained troops aimed for Manila.

Because of Pearl Harbor, America had declared War on Japan. President Roosevelt delivered the declaration in his "Day of Infamy" speech, causing such national hysteria that the impact of this second obliterating attack on the Philippines was lost. Not until Roosevelt's Year-End Speech did the President assure the impaired Pacific forces that "the entire resources of the United States" would be committed to defending the Philippine Islands. Meanwhile, the Japanese had stealthily surrounded the islands with a full-scale blockade.

General Douglas MacArthur, the US Commanding General had severely misjudged the intent of the Japanese to attack and now, his planes and ships crippled, he ordered his ill-prepared 320,000 combined US and Filipino troops to defend the Philippine Islands, petitioning for immediate supplies and support from Washington in order to save his islands.

Having spent part of his youth there, General Douglas MacArthur was obsessively loyal to the Philippines. His father had been the Military Governor of the Islands and now in 1941, he, the most decorated officer of World War I and a military hero, was in command. As a holdover from the Great War's Gentlemen's Army, MacArthur kept a stable of thoroughbred cavalry horses during a time when swords and horses were giving way to artillery and tanks. Adding to his lack of preparedness was the fact that the armaments on hand for defense were World War I surplus used mainly for training the Philippine Scouts. Because of the out-of-date supplies, MacArthur's soldiers were put to defending the beachheads on Luzon and the Bataan Peninsula with obsolete equipment. The lack of food and medication alone had ruinous consequences.

Shortly after the crippling raid on Clark Field, MacArthur abandoned Manila to the Japanese, declaring it an "Open City," hoping to prevent an overwhelming loss of both civilian and military lives at the hands of the well-equipped Japanese bombers. This abandonment allowed the Japanese free access to the city. MacArthur then dispatched the balance of the 80,000 men to reinforce the diseased and starving army of General

Jonathan Mayhew Wainwright IV on the Bataan Peninsula guarding Manila Bay while he removed his own stables and 4,000 men to his command post on Corregidor, a heavily fortified island the size of New York's Central Park guarding the entrance to Manila Bay, the finest anchorage in the Pacific.

However, this war was waged from the air, and were it not for the fortified safety of the Malinta tunnel at the US Garrison on Corregidor, MacArthur and his islands would have fallen far sooner. The quarter-mile long tunnel on "The Rock" into which MacArthur and his family withdrew was a ventilated underground fortification with electricity, water, flush latrines, cold storage, and a fully equipped hospital. There were enough rations stacked inside to supply twice the number of men there for 180 days. Joining MacArthur, his family and staff on the well-supplied Rock were Philippine President Manuel Quezon and his wife. Meanwhile, the food rations for General Jonathan Wainwright's troops commanded to defend the beaches from any Japanese landing had been cut to less than half, as Roosevelt continued to promise MacArthur the necessary reinforcements both in supplies and additional troops.

A scant two weeks after the Japanese had destroyed the US air defense at Clark Field, on December 22nd, backed by 80 Japanese Naval ships, Lieutenant General Masaharu Homma waded ashore with an additional 43,000 fresh troops primed to take the American Island Territory. That the Allies fought against the enemy's superior war machine until April 9, 1942, demonstrated their extreme courage. They held out while MacArthur played for time, banking on the President's repeated assurances that supplies and reinforcements were indeed on the way; while Roosevelt had promised Churchill those very resources for the defense of Europe. Not the Philippine Islands.

Stalling, the Allies—both Filipino and American, some Dutch, Australians and British—held out in the jungles, most now ravaged by malnutrition, malaria and dysentery. Still, they managed to stack up large enemy casualties and by early 1942, they were forced to resort to scrounging food, even eating the livestock of the cavalry which reportedly included MacArthur's prized horses. Hopeful for the promised supplies, they made do equipping themselves by lifting ammo, stashes of tobacco, tins of food and medicine off the bodies of dead Japanese.

In an attempt to spare his people's lives, Filipino President Quezon proposed to Washington that the Philippine Islands be immediately granted their independence from America and the islands declared neutral. He envisioned that his plan would effectively cause both warring forces to be withdrawn. He could then disband his standing Philippine Army and cause all hostilities to be called off.

Roosevelt rejected Quezon's proposition outright and insisted he and his people support the "American determination and indomitable will to win."

Meanwhile, successive waves of Japanese planes battered The Rock where the 4,000 men, Quezon, MacArthur and their families were sheltered sustaining only minor casualties. The Japanese were again reinforced with more troops while the malaria-riddled Americans bivouacked in the jungles on Luzon and the Bataan Peninsula were out of food and quinine. Desperate, they realized there were no supplies on the way and that they had been declared expendable. Wainwright may have seen it before MacArthur had.

By February 22, 1942, the Japanese had taken Burma, Borneo, Guam, Sumatra, Singapore, Java, and Hong Kong. They had invaded Timor and bombed Darwin. Next to fall was the Philippine Islands and without fresh troops and supplies, General Wainwright could no longer hold out against them. Where were the promised supplies?

Then for good measure, the Japanese bombed Pearl Harbor a second time.

At this point, Roosevelt capitulated. MacArthur was enraged when he received the order for a full surrender to the Japanese—he would never hand over the Islands to the enemy. He vowed to die in the defense of the Philippines. Meanwhile, Quezon and his family together with the Philippine War Cabinet were ordered evacuated, and on February 22nd, the President of the Philippines and his entourage boarded the submarine *Swordfish* for asylum in Australia. His farewell gesture was to place his signet ring on MacArthur's finger with these words, "When they find your body, I want them to know that you fought for my country." His wife, Jean, together with young Arthur MacArthur, insisted upon remaining with him there. So he handed a large package with his valuables to Quezon for safekeeping in Australia. The package was marked for preservation for the MacArthur legal heirs.

The following day, on February 23rd, Roosevelt ordered MacArthur to make his escape to Australia rather than be taken as the Emperor's war prize.

As an officer, he could not refuse an order from his Commander-in-Chief. But his loyalty was to the Islands and believing that he had been given no choice, MacArthur resolved to resign his commission and become a civilian so that he could defend Corregidor as a civilian and a volunteer. While setting about to tender his resignation from the United States Army, Roosevelt notified him that he was to head up the Philippine Relief Force being organized in Australia in order to recapture the Islands from the Japanese.

MacArthur agreed, counting that he would head up an important force. Three weeks later, on March 15, 1942, MacArthur, his wife, his four-year-old son Arthur MacArthur and his Chinese amah joined his staff to follow the Philippine President Manual Quezon to Australia on a dark night in heavy seas. They were given one-in-five odds for survival.

Four worn PT boats were the only available craft since the *Swordfish* had already departed with Quezon and his party. Well after the photographs and press release with the general's famous, "I shall return," the MacArthur party boarded these boats and left in the dark protected from enemy radar by the twenty-foot waves. The Japanese General Homma, seeking the glory of MacArthur's dead-or-alive capture, dispatched part of a full destroyer division in pursuit.

The day following his escape came the headline news from Tokyo: MacArthur had "fled his post."

But MacArthur survived causing his men in the field to be openly contemptuous over his leaving them with an Air Force without planes, a Navy without ships and an Army without weapons, food or medicine. They reviled his having come only once on January 15, 1942, to inspect their dire conditions on Bataan, and his having abandoned the hoarded food on Corregidor to the enemy. No longer did anyone believe his continual proclamation, *"Help is on the way. Thousands of troops and hundreds of planes are being dispatched. The exact time of arrival of the reinforcements is unknown.... No further retreat is possible. If we fight, we will win; if we retreat, we will be destroyed."*

A month later President Franklin Roosevelt awarded MacArthur the Medal of Honor, reinstating his status of hero in spite of his inaction and failure to defend the Philippines, not to mention the open contempt of his men.

Newly promoted Lieutenant General Jonathan Mayhew Wainwright IV became the Allied Commander of the Philippines with orders from MacArthur *never to capitulate to the enemy.* But in order to save lives and stave off starvation and disease, on April 9, Wainwright surrendered his surviving 70,000 troops in Bataan to the Japanese, finally acknowledging that the promised reinforcements and supplies would never arrive.

The Japanese had succeeded. The Empire had over-run the entire Pacific in six months.

By June 1942, the entire 320,000 combined Allied Forces were completely surrendered and all but the Filipinos taken prisoner by an enemy unprepared to take any burdensome prisoners. However, Jonathan M. Wainwright, trusting his soldiers would be fed and the Geneva Convention honored, turned himself over as the highest-ranking American POW ever taken prisoner. During his brutal captivity he remained angst-ridden over what he considered his sole responsibility: the decision to surrender his men to the Japanese. So wearing a conical coolie hat and herding goats he worked alongside the other prisoners in the fields until 1945, when Russians liberated him with the other POWs from a prison camp in Manchuria.

During Wainwright's imprisonment, MacArthur wrote a slanderous and cruel memorandum to Army Chief of Staff George C. Marshall insisting that Wainwright be denied a Medal of Honor, calling him a coward and an alcoholic. He was not alone in this opinion, but MacArthur himself was a questionable hero, still widely scorned for abandoning the Philippines. His own Medal of Honor was considered fraudulent because, unlike General Wainwright, he was never near the front lines. He was, in fact by the time of his award, comfortably celebrated as the Hero of Australia while his starving men were abandoned and brutalized.

1
Florida, February, 1944

Phyllis slowly pulled herself free from the same damp sheets she had passed out on a few hours before. Her head was heavy, her mouth like sand but the time had arrived. She took a long breath and dropped her hand over the black receiver, anticipating the ring. *This whole ordeal had taken long enough.*

But her nightmare had been exact, and now was the time.

For several nights running she'd been overwhelmed by visions of the crash. Blood red and violent with the sounds of snapping, cracking bones. She had heard the hollow reverberating thunder of high-speed metal striking metal. She could smell the explosion from the motorcycle's gasoline and see how the smoke hung heavy in the air, illuminated by flames flickering like snakes' tongues searing the acrid paint and exploding the tires. She could also taste the chemical cinders, the very soot and its biting sting.

"Are you certain it's Russell?" she asked.

"We have notified his wife. She gave us your number." Dispassionate voice.

"Wife?" Phyllis' bile rose.

"She agreed to allow you to identify the body."

"The divorce is almost final," Phyllis protested, knowing all concern was absurd now. The time for divorce was past.

Phyllis replaced the receiver on the hook. She had forgotten to ask where the collision had taken place. It did not matter. If she took her time he would have been scrupulously gathered up (if not reassembled) before she steered the Lincoln Zephyr down the winding road along the bluff toward Lake Worth. No doubt he had been hurled free of the flames, unconscious and beyond suffering. Still, it was hideous; she needed to be spared the small details.

It was a shame that Russell's lame-duck wife Anissa had been brought into it. She was clinically crazy—coo-coo. She lived with a cult in New Mexico where they truly believed that a ten-foot tall Saint Germain was close to ending this war with Germany simply by brandishing his blazing purple sword. It was altogether too apparent that, in spite of her militant certainty, the War expanded to cover both hemispheres, annihilating everything in its wake. No power on earth had been able to end it.

Anissa should have been locked up years ago.

Had she been as calm as she appeared, Phyllis would have been able to return to her dreaming-sleep for more information. But more than information, she'd dream of leave-taking and farewells, of his final torn embrace, where she in turn would promise to cherish his memory and ask him if he had suffered very much. She would have smothered his face with kisses, allowing him one more chance to tell her how he adored her before he faded to black, a movie trick announcing an important scene shift.

Instead, because she knew he expected her to, she rose and peeled off the wrinkled sheets and the clothes she'd slept in last night, to dress herself for the role of the bereaved. As she checked her face in the bathroom mirror, she took pleasure from her green eyes and thick Rita Hayworth shoulder-length red hair; steadying herself now, she labored a deep breath for the dance ahead, beginning with the police questioning.

Fumbling, she spit on the mascara brush in its mirrored box and applied coal black to her lashes, purposely smudging under both eyes for effect. Next, she dabbed pancake makeup over her freckles, while the realization flitted over her that this death brought both grief and a giddy income.

She applied lipstick to mask her thin-ish lips. Grasping that she was an heiress jerked her heart alive. She was both confused and gratified when Russell's crash was confirmed. Death's croupier had now pushed the chips to her corner. Forget that women were always whispering about her, heaping nouns on her: whore, a piece of baggage, chippy, trollop, slut, doxie.

Now they'd have to add, *"residual beneficiary."*

On stage without a script, she contemplated how she wanted to be seen. Repeated nights of bloody dreams had prepared her role, put her beyond shock. Except for a small tremble in her right hand, she was composed.

She was the main attraction and he could not be legally dead without her witnessing signature. So said his wife; so said the officer. Everyone would have to wait patiently. So flipping on another light in the bathroom, she peered into the mirror taking her time. There was no rush, either at the precinct or at the morgue.

The force of his death would come to pound her a day or so after she had returned home from the morgue. And in the disorientation that is either caused by or is—in fact—mourning, Phyllis would make a bewildering choice.

Afterward. Not before.

Now, in the early dawn of his death-day, she took her time, conscious that Russell's spirit stalked the house, watching her, proud of the only woman he'd ever loved, proud of her youth. She moved through the new sun's pink light to his favorite chair in the library and there she took repeated deep breaths with her eyes closed in order to see him more clearly. When she saw him, he seemed upset.

"Why?" she asked him.

Silence and a grim dissatisfaction on his fading face was his last decipherable response to her.

Later, she gave up and let him rest.

Aware of her newsy appeal, she returned and concentrated on the mirror and made her face up for interviews. For the past hour, she alone owned title to the house. She owned the art and paintings, the 1939 Lincoln Zephyr and the Cadillac convertible on blocks to preserve the tires. Everything was hers except the lumber operation in Dawson Creek and the motorcycle which was unsalvageable. She smiled as she combed through her thick hair and she studied her face. There would be a stringer for the *Palm Beach Times* slumped somewhere at the precinct primed and ready to jump up, popping a barrage of blinding shots at her. So she studied her face again, never hurrying.

Murine, she thought, then changed her mind. Red eyes were essential. By the time she entered the white lights of the precinct, her hand was again steady.

"Well, yes, he had been drinking." She had intended to admit only that much, hoping the officer was not slyly accusing her of matching him jigger for jigger, night after night, or—the thought struck her suddenly—that she had sent him out to fetch *her* some more rum.

"So, he drank a lot normally?"

"I asked him not to, but you know how it is with men in wartime. I can't get his attention these days. Not a kiss, if you understand what I mean." So saying, she emphasized the wrong thing.

"It's the war and all this waiting for D-Day," she added. "Not me."

"Lady, how much had he been drinking?"

"Enough to run dry, to go out for some more." She straightened her spine, ran her red fingernails nervously through her hair and took a deep breath. She needed him to note in writing that she, Phyllis MacAndrew, was not tipsy. Not this time.

She caught herself ruefully pursing her mouth to lob a counterattack. "But you know it wasn't his fault, you know that, don't you?" The officer glanced over at her and lit a cigarette before he spoke.

"That he hit a parked truck like a Kraut dive bomber?"

"Are you telling me the truck had no lights?"

"That's right, Ma'am. It was parked by the side of the road. The driver was sleeping. It happened after midnight."

"So he'd turned off his goddamned lights, did he?" She was starting to color. "I hope to God that jerk has insurance."

"I hope your fancy boyfriend has insurance."

"We were going to get married. I have a ring, see?"

"Yes, Ma'am." He blew out a breath. The ring was expensive.

"Where is he? I want to be with him."

"I wouldn't advise it. Color of his eyes?"

"Greeny-green. Like mine."

"That's him, lady. We got the right one. His wife said to call you. She's in New Mexico." Phyllis reeled—that was an unnecessary second slap in the face. For a few moments, she said nothing, remembering how just the mention of his cult-addicted wife Anissa rankled Russell, sent him into a tailspin, uncoiling him.

Phyllis relished picturing her own rendition of the scene: Officer to Anissa: "I'm afraid I have painful news for you."

Anissa to Officer: "Painful? The world has been waiting for justice! He'd been begging Saint Germain to strike him down because of sin—sin, alcohol and vulgar music." Anissa was a fanatical member of the Chicago-based I AM Movement where she and several hundred others did daily battle against liquor, meat, sex and war.

Phyllis' heart was heavy as she sensed Russell's ghost hovering somewhere above the weary group in the early morning precinct, being battered by his impossible wife. Whatever the issue, Anissa was right and Russell was wrong. And now he was dead wrong. Let Anissa and her Saint exult; Phyllis was certain they were in fact gloating themselves silly in their muddy small town a thousand miles from nowhere. They were so far off the beaten track that they were perfectly safe saying whatever they wished: not even the Japanese nor the German planes could reach them while they printed inane books, passed out misleading pamphlets and ranted on and on, disapproving of simply everyone and everything surrounding the war. They lashed out against bombs, bullets, whisky, cigarettes, adultery, dancing, meat and the Andrews Sisters. Who knew what else they would latch onto?

Roosevelt needed to declare them anti-American because it was the war that had spurred Americans' craving for tobacco and alcohol.

And their fanaticism against dance tunes. Certainly, the I AMers were unpatriotic, undermining the national morale because music was the war's voice and even promiscuity had its soothing place. Anissa and her sour believers went wholly against the grain. They alone waged their own war within the greater war.

From his anteroom in the sky, Russell must have seen Anissa's self-congratulating elation since he had died before she'd signed the divorce papers. That was surely the reason Russell had appeared to her so upset and agitated—he was still trying to throttle Anissa. The task now fell to his residual beneficiary; she was equal to the task.

"Where in God's name did you take him? Please officer, tell me where he is!" Her voice cracked, tears swelled. She snuffed them back up into her sinuses and coughed. It was urgent that she quiet his remains— only she could ease his turbulence.

"Morgue, Ma'am. You gotta fill out some papers, like his wife said. She figures you can identify his clothes." This third uncomfortable mention of Anissa, his soon-to-be-divorced crackpot wife, was painful. Phyllis tried to erase the woman from her mind but she could not.

His blood-sucking wife, this distant specter, was a pampered *millionairess* who relentlessly upped the ante by refusing to sign the divorce papers and righteously hurtled names and insults at both Phyllis and Russell which, if you must know, Officer, she wished to state for-the-record, caused Russell more agitation, more anxiety and misery, forcing him to drink, yes…forcing him to drink. You have witnessed the pitiful results, Your Honor. She virtually murdered him. And then there were his children, by one of his wives, the First Mrs. Barclay and another child too, a hazy girl somewhere. Half French.

Step aside, ladies. All you who are slated to muster out when the Third *Mrs. Russell Watson Barclay* ascends to preeminence—all to be slashed from your privileged "Next of Kin" status. But for this tragic unforeseen event.

Let them all rot in Hell.

In the meanwhile, thank God, the reason the reporter and the wags looked at her accusingly was that Russell had had his lawyers sign over as much of his property as he was able to in Palm Beach County before the divorce; he told her that she was the only woman he'd ever loved. The ink was barely dry.

And it was true. He had never really loved the others. How could anyone?

He sang to her.

Had he ever sung to them?

Only she, the new Mrs. Russell Barclay-elect. She was his consort, she was his inspiration, his consolation, his movie star; he took her everywhere with him, set her up at The Breakers before moving her into his winter home in Lantana. He treated her like a queen because she was his adored redhead Scottish lassie, and he was her rich Yank.

And in West Palm Beach, Florida, she went to the hairdresser, had manicures, and he took her shopping, promising her the moon when his divorce was final and even more than the moon as soon as the war was over.

His house—now all hers—was filled with paintings, books and memories. The sunlight filtered through the French doors which led out onto the lanai overlooking the gardens where the lawn fell away down to Lake Worth. She lounged in a wicker chaise under the gnarled sea grape aware that an occasional submarine was cruising the Inland Passage south to Miami. She felt personally protected by the superior American Navy. And she was grateful not to be in gloomy Scotland because everything was bigger, brighter, better in the States.

In early 1944, Roosevelt was slowly lifting the rationing that had been incredibly austere just a year earlier. Sugar could now be had but decent Scotch was still impossible to find because, she had heard, that cases and cases of the lovely stuff were stockpiled in Cornwall for the invading Allies' pleasures. Phyllis knew she'd have to wait for the end of the war to see Scotch again. She missed it more than the meat and butter.

But she knew and everyone knew that D-Day was imminent, huge *Life* magazine photos of the accumulation of men, armaments and ammunition were not just published, they were flaunted: *Just take a gander at this, Krauts. We'll get every last bloody one of you.*

She gloated along with the Americans, clinking her highball (a distilled-in-the-USA rum), saying things like ATTA BOY, and A-1 and GEE-WHIZ. She felt blessed to be an American now and no longer just a refugee from her viper's nest of a home in Aberdeen.

"Okey dokey," she said and took a sip, shuddering at the dark memories around her Scottish family in Aberdeen.

A short year before, in need of a job and out of cash, she had found herself in Canada where the Canadian National Railway had deposited her: Dawson Creek, Mile One of the Al-Can Highway, the Trans-Canada to Alaska super road. Finding work wasn't difficult to come by as even the Canadians had sent their prime men to fight for freedom. On the second day, she had been taken on as a receptionist for a small town lawyer named Bailey in Dawson Creek when Russell pushed through the office door on serious business. It had been a muddy spring in 1943, "The Road" (as they called the Al-Can Highway) had been completed to Big Delta, Alaska. By this time, the men had all been moved north, leaving a wake of abandoned road equipment littering the muddy countryside.

The place looked derelict and the pay wasn't great. Then in he came.

She remembered glancing up when Russell strode over to her desk, breezing past three disheveled workers who were seated along the walls, obviously waiting to see the same man.

"I need to see Bailey right away," he demanded.

"I'm sorry, sir," she said slowly, taking note, for he was clean shaven, an alien here in Shit-Creek Canada where razor blades were unknown. Both the town and the men had the look of utter collapse; the residue of men working the lumber camps rarely bathed.

The Road had been completed, 1,590 miles in eight months and eleven days—an incredible feat for National Defense. When it was over, 10,000 troops had scrapped their mess tents and bulldozers and had moved on. The bone yard of kinked refuse they left behind was a veritable semblance of the war—hostile, rusting and dangerous. Chucked supplies that had been double-ordered; the wastage was huge. Blankets burnt, road equipment driven off precipices, kerosene heaters bulldozed under while prefabricated huts had been set afire. Dawson Creek was now a ghost town of empty barracks and flattened campgrounds. A parts yard for scrap metal. It was the picture of war.

When the road dust settled, Bailey's legal business picked up steam—bankruptcies, and wills. Prostitutes and thieves now piled into his cramped office. He'd been the one to spot the advantage of owning a lumber camp to feed The Road. Highways always require nearby lumber, and government checks did not bounce. He didn't have to look farther than the closest trout stream to find backing for such a profitable enterprise. Russell Watson Barclay stood midstream in his waders with a good head on his shoulders and money in his pocket.

Bailey had found his mark.

"He knows me. Tell him Barclay is here. Get on it, please. I'm in a hurry."

"I do not believe you have an appointment, Mr. Barclay."

"All hell's breaking loose at the camp. Bailey and I own it, fifty-fifty."

"Please have a seat. These others have appointments and you will simply have to wait your turn, Mr. Barclay." She guessed he might be forty, not quite old enough to be her father. His younger brother, perhaps, and she smiled at the thought. He might even be a naughty uncle.

"Miss…"

"Phyllis."

"Phyllis, I need Bailey. I need him now, on the double." He must have been impressed by her hair. Back in Scotland red hair was not exceptional but everyone here in Canada commented on it. But she was done with Aberdeen. Now she needed a new pasture.

"Please have a seat, as I said." She stopped midsentence because his eyes were a leaf-green color, greener than her own.

"It won't be long," she added, suddenly moved to placate him.

"If he cans you for this, for making me wait when, as I said, all hell is breaking loose in camp, the cooks walked out, the men all laid down their tools…" he paused for a reaction and got none.

"As I said, I guarantee you're going to get fired and that you're going to need a meal, so I'll take you out for a steak. Let him know I'm here. Please, Phyllis. Be sweet now."

Then he added. "If not, I'll see that you're fired."

She was young, twenty-one, and she had not run up against privilege before. Not in this manner, at least. He had turned it into a contest. "Just take a seat, sir," she said.

"I'm still buying you dinner." And so he sat down, staring at her, muttering to himself. Eventually, his turn arrived and he strode past her, his back straight. As it turned out, he had been a welterweight champion at Princeton when Dempsey and Tunney were stars. That alone accounted for a great deal.

Both he and Bailey emerged from their conference quite agitated as they passed words between themselves regarding the burgeoning strike. Barclay then called across the now empty waiting room, "What brings you here to Dawson Creek anyway, Phyllis?"

"Asthma," she replied, leaving off the part about lacking the fare to make it all the way to Vancouver. That and the unpleasantness over an affair with Roger, a married man in Aberdeen. Her past year's history teacher, in point of fact.

"I'm ready to make good on my promise," he said, aware that she had not yet been sacked.

"Find a replacement for her," he advised Bailey well within her hearing. "If you can."

For dinner, he took her to the only restaurant in town. It had a single sign in the window, so it was called the *Help Wanted* and it was little more than a truck stop for the lumber trucks. Everyone always needed help. But the cash for slinging hash was low, and what women were there were all prostitutes. A dollar a minute, easy pay for something that wasn't even work. The men chose between lumberjack and soldier. The women opted for whatever paid quickest.

She noted that it was likely Russell owned the only tailor-made clothes in the entire province.

"This is an unhealthy place for asthmatics," he observed, pulling a silver flask from the inside pocket of his tweed jacket. She explained that by 1940, asthma was epidemic in the British Isles. Strong men who had never suffered before now became stricken and were summarily declared unfit for the service. If they had the means, they were instructed by their doctors to seek quiet places in which to restore their health.

"Most of the chaps from Aberdeen chose Canada for being English speaking and not a direct target. Pearl Harbor rather changed everyone's mind about the States." She thought she sounded intelligent and informed.

"So, Great Britain is now suffering from a sort of massive asthma attack?" he laughed.

"It is a good idea to leave, actually. The children, as well, have all been sent off but more for safety than for health. If anyone has a relative somewhere else, they pile them up with all the young ones."

"No one could accuse the children of cowardice, certainly not," he agreed.

"Canada sounded so romantic," she admitted. "The Mounties, too." British Columbia reported more men than women in a smoldering world where most men were at one front or another—a promising place to find a suitable man for a young twenty-one-year-old woman. A lassie with red hair, fleeing her mother and intolerant Aberdeen, a place too stiff for a girl with play and ambition.

"Have you been through a winter here?" he asked, signaling to the waitress.

"I arrived only days ago. It's been only muddy, muddy and cold."

"Nothing like Scotland. I've been grouse shooting there several times in fact."

"Do you think they will bomb Aberdeen?"

"Probably, if they take London like they did Paris. Are you so afraid of the Jerries that you'd seal yourself off in this godforsaken little lumber town?" He pulled out a pack of Chesterfields and offered her one. She nodded and accepted a cigarette with awkward formality.

"This is as far as I've gotten. The trains are full to spilling over. I've not made it to the coast. I have a cousin in Santa Barbara but that's America. She said they'd had an oil refinery bombed by a Jap submarine." Shoving her emptied water glass forward, she accepted three fingers of Scotch from his flask. Sipping, she tried to think of something intelligent to say but failed. He, on the other hand, seemed to be remembering something from the distant past, maybe connected with Santa Barbara, or America, she could not say. But she knew he was most certainly an American, and a gentleman.

When the waitress slumped over, he ordered both of their dinners without offering Phyllis a choice. "Two sirloins, rare, please," he stated.

She had not seen decent tweed since she'd left home.

"You want to help the war effort, do you not?" he asked, breaking the silence. She wondered if he was trying to proposition her. Lately, men begged her for sex, saying that they were about to die. *One last…Please.* Before he was sent to the front, even Roger begged her for relief from his anguish and overwhelming terror of battle. She offered him the solace his wife could not and he said she was an Angel of Mercy and gave her his ration of cigarettes.

It turned out badly and Mum threw her out.

She examined Russell closely. "Certainly, I want to help the effort," she said. "My brother was killed a year ago. My only brother." She stared squarely into his green eyes as she spoke, anxious that he pay attention to her, respect her.

"My mum was devastated," she said. "I, too."

He moved his left hand to cover hers. For a while, both were silent.

"See this?" he held up his right hand. His thumb had been mangled; his second and third fingers had been joined so that they resembled something fleshy and pliable.

"I'm Four-F because of it, so I came to pitch in on the Al-Can highway to do my part for the effort. As things got underway, Bailey and I bought the Dawson Creek Lumber Camp. It's the only show in town now, that and the great fishing and hunting."

"I thought the Al-Can Highway had been completed. Somebody said it was a complete marvel, that it's as great an achievement as the Panama Canal."

"And they are right. I was an engineer from Princeton, that's how I came to work on the highway. Bailey was Johnny-on-the-spot and came up with the lumber camp at the very start. We did The Road in eight months, start to finish. So, I'm back to fly fishing before I leave."

"Leave? To where?" she asked, trying to quiet a sound of alarm ringing in her ears.

"Back to Florida for a quick trip until it gets too hot, then I'm back here again."

"When does it get hot?" she asked, relaxing some.

"Soon, but I'm here finishing up with the lumber camp now that The Road is operating."

"Why? What's the purpose of it? It leads from nowhere to the very Styx." she said, her voice lowered for effect, her interest in him was rising with each sip of Scotch.

Not surprisingly, the young girl would come to have a comfortable feeling about highways that led over the horizon. In fact she grew to count on finding that all roads would lead directly away from Rome, not back to it.

"Inland airstrips. The Road gives us an inland supply route out of reach of the Japs. We've got mobility, so to speak."

"My aunt has seen the conning towers off Santa Barbara. She's actually seen the Japs' submarines with her own eyes. Everyone is terrified."

"We're ready for them," he assured her and took a deep swallow, closing his eyes as the Scotch burned its way down his throat. He held his glass with his left hand.

"You shot off your own finger?" she asked, shaking her head.

"It was a hunting accident. The safety was off. I always keep the safety off. It's far better that way. One day my gloves froze on the barrel. I was climbing over a barbed wire fence and the damned thing went off."

"An accident," she reconfirmed, looking away from his face as the waitress placed their identical steaks before them.

He got her quite drunk, or she managed to get herself pie-eyed, one or the other. But he was a gentleman to the end and drove her safely home, skidding through the mud. The next morning, when she slogged in to work late and groggy, she felt both enervated and defensive. Who was he to accuse her of cowardice, fleeing her country with the first threat when he'd put his toe on the trigger and blown his hand to bits with his shotgun just to avoid the draft? Four-F indeed! She had seen right through his story and he had attempted to seduce her after he'd gotten quite tight, and they'd kissed, long and lingeringly. She was not that sort of girl, however.

When she asserted this, he laughed.

"I want you to know that I really am asthmatic," she told him when she looked up from her desk in the two-bit lawyer's office to find him standing before her. Again he was in no mood to mind the queue, and she found him less attractive that morning than the night before. Her summation was affected by her own hangover. Surely his head throbbed as well because her own pulse pounded in her ears.

And he seemed down but he smiled, and suddenly Phyllis was

mesmerized by a vision of herself being courted wearing glamorous clothes in a place without mud. She, his leading lady with the arresting red hair. He, always the gentleman in excellent tweeds.

She felt Russell's hangover, she felt his attraction to her, and it made her feel momentarily like a queen.

"You may be an asthmatic if you choose. I think you're a great gal," he said, smiling at her, squinting. What a bloodshot charmer! And last night with a drink in his left hand, she had been taken by him; he was debonair, intelligent, fit, strong and pitifully, lamentably misunderstood. He'd had a terrible go with wives and now he hoped he'd learned his lesson. He was badly in need of a pure-hearted girl, like herself.

He told her how sweet and nice she was, not selfish and spoiled like the others.

It was clear then that he was to be her fast ride out of Dawson Creek.

When he said, "I'd be happy to teach you how to shoot; that is, if you don't already know how," she accepted.

The gun fit her perfectly. A Churchill 29" side-by-side ladies shotgun he'd had lying about.

And he was handsome and rich. And because he found her fascinating, she was.

The lumber camp was only the beginning. He had properties down in the States.

And now, he was being held at the Palm Beach County morgue, being chilled on a slab, waiting for someone to poke him and say, Yes, that's the one. That's him, all right.

His death was another chapter. Her grief was incremental once she grasped that she was wealthy in her own right, she preened, certain that the bank account bestowed both wisdom and a lifelong contentment. When she spoke, crowds would quiet, attending to her thoughts. The world would bow to her. She felt powerful and beautiful, the owner of a fine house with rolling lawns and lantana bushes, two cars and a library. A library and the elegant shotgun. Hers was a new delirious future spreading before her like a highway to the horizon.

The pity was that Russell got sacrificed in the process.

Mum and Dad—they're the sorry ones now. She knew that her aunt would pass on the news in a letter to be sent immediately by air to Aberdeen. The news of her acquisitions would set her above their scorn now, in spite of how her small-minded mother continued to rebuke her, insisting she'd tainted all of them—the family—forever.

And yet, when she thought of him after the morgue ordeal, the theater went dark. She no longer felt his presence. It must have been that he no longer thought of her, buoying and transforming her as always into an alluring being. She was just his lonely redhead now, money in her pocket for the first time. Still she knew that she was more than that, more than the fictional creation of a dead man. How was it that he had left the earthly plane so hastily and not stayed to communicate with her, to encourage her?

To call back his memory, as a legacy, she assumed his hatred and vigorous revulsion for his former wives. Pledging herself as a living memorial to his presence, she fanned the coals of his disgust. Feeling the same tightness in her chest, and his frustrations, she set out to vanquish every woman he'd ever slept with. She owed him that.

But Anissa was the primary target and like a true warrior, she studied the enemy. In his library she accumulated every photo album he had, stacking them on the dining room table.

Obsessed with his past, she filed through old photos and barely paused to examine the ones of his first wife and three children. She yearned to know everything possible about Anissa. She cared less about how his first wife dressed, about how she crossed her legs in what silk upholstered chairs and held her iced tea. Her focus was Anissa, the second wife.

Everything surrounding this last one both mesmerized and repulsed her. There she was, a blonde skier in gabardine pants in St. Anton, Austria, with her wary smile. Then again, photographed often in bars wearing hats with barrier cocktail veils that might burst into flames from cigarettes, or at the very least prevent her from sipping martinis. Anissa in her cocktail veils, little black dresses, beauty parlor hair and manicures before she threw it all over and joined the I AMers, swearing eternal sobriety and abstinence. Anissa, whose flesh-eating lawyers had pecked away at poor dear Russell, tormenting the both of them.

Phyllis could not take her transfixed eyes off her pictures. Later she pulled back from the table heavy under the stacks of albums and rose to fetch Anissa's engraved shotgun with the walnut stock, and vowed never to relinquish the Churchill. It was far too fine. Let the lawyers make demands.

Phyllis coveted the grand shotgun she held in her hand, delighting in the perfect balance of it. Possessing the enemy's weapon gave her its intrinsic power. Primitive tribes knew that shooting the enemy was weak, but that eating the enemy gave cannibals great force and vigor. Nevertheless, she acquiesced to simply possessing the gun rather than being served Anissa's brains simmered in the cup of her skull. All she in fact needed to overpower the woman was the gun and it was solidly in her hands. The lawyers might well make their demands, nothing would come of them.

Anissa, the legal bereaved widow, did in fact call again regarding the matter of her shotgun, but she was a day too late.

2
Allied Prisoners of War Camp, Cabanatuan, Philippine Islands, 1943

P
vt. Melo Garcia and Pfc. Arsenio Lujan slumped back on the patch of shaded dirt next to the Cogan grass, confused and debating what to type. In their cracked unwashed hands they held four blank postcards doled out by the Red Cross with the instructions that they were to *type* their messages in fifty short *simple-to-understand* words—personal matters only—no mention of the Japs, prison conditions, or the war. Type only. Both prisoners were twenty-one years old, both from Santa Fe, New Mexico.

"I should tell 'em about my dysentery?" Melo muttered. "How the Gook guard smashed my hand for not doing what he said in Japanese?" He glanced across the baked dirt grounds of the prison camp to check out the line forming outside the American central control office. From the hopefulness of the men in line, he guessed there was more than one typewriter inside. "I don't understand goddamned Japanese."

"Only tell 'em you're alive," Senio said. As for being alive, there were still close to 1,300 POWs from New Mexico among the 9,000-plus Allied, non-Filipino captives in the muggy latrine-stinking jungle prison camp. The Japs let all the Filipino natives go free and only used the white men for hard labor.

"Don't waste words. If they get the card, you're alive. But you got to type it in English. No Spanish. Only typing."

"Me and Mamacita talk Spanish."

"Can't say you're starving, they'll scratch it out. Nothing about the food." For *lugao*, watery rice soup, they boiled one pound of carabao meat to feed 50 large men, 200 pounds for 10,000. Then after they boiled the carabao to mush, they threw in moldy rice and the men dubbed it Tojo water.

"How many words is it to say how we followed the smell and found Ricardo Mares dead under the infirmary floor? Dysentery and cerebral malaria, like all us suckers here in Cabanatuan…"

"Yeah, she always liked Ricardo. She'll be real upset, but that's prison conditions. So you can't say that." The mistake had been not knowing that Ricardo was dead until he was too far gone not to report. Had they known, his rations would never have been passed up. They'd have been shared, or gambled and parleyed uphill into something better.

"So I'll tell them Ricardo didn't make it and we got a Red Cross package at Christmas and the Nips copped most of the Old Golds and the Chesterfields and stashed 'em in that shed along with all our mail sacks and we're going crazy out-of-our-minds to get our mail."

"No can do. You can say thanks for the vitamins in the Red Cross boxes. Your beriberi almost went away—that's personal. Maybe you should say you lost your brother Franque at the start of the Death March?"

"No question I should say that. And about my dad being tortured to death at Camp O'Donnell? How they pounded nails into his skull?"

"No, say he didn't make it—but *nada mas*," Senio insisted. If the useless interpreters suspected anything sneaky, the sorry bastard would be singled out, beaten, the cards burnt.

"Just didn't make it? Who are they kidding anyway—these Gooks can't even read English. They'd just as soon behead you for saying something fucking nice about the fucking rice."

"Your mama knows about Franque and your dad—for sure everybody already knows," Senio muttered matter-of-factly, too weak to stand the impact of grief. "Doc Matson said he turned over all their dog tags to General King since he's in charge of everything American."

"General King is a pile of squirrel turd like the rest of the idiot officers. They don't do jack shit," Melo said. "So I'm gonna tell her how you saved my ass on the Death March and when we get back to Santa Fe, LaBelle and me are gonna get married."

"Tell your Mama I saved your sorry ass more times than even I can count." Senio held his own note cards in his hand, debating when to stand in the long sun-stroke line for the typewriters. "She owes me a load of tamales."

"I'll tell her, if I ever get my turn at the typewriter." However many typewriters there might be in the American central control shack there would never be a supply of good ribbons. Several thousand emaciated men continued to form a line outside and Melo looked up to see if they had moved forward even an inch. Hard to tell, by this time the men all looked alike—skin burnt, shaved heads, scrawny, bony, skinny, emaciated, lice-riddled stooped bodies with torn rags for clothes. *Fundoshi*, g-strings made from old sacks tied with string. Makeshift shoes. If Melo had a hard time telling one from the other, the Japs stopped trying. Mostly they treated the white prisoners all the same (viciously) with their eyes on a few badass standouts like Senio and Melo.

"And I'll tell my Mama that you and me look great in the g-strings we made and we are now real prisoners of war, not captives."

"Not that it makes any difference," Senio said.

"Like hell. It means we can get the Red Cross boxes. The Geneva Convention says we have to be paid each month and we get to send letters home."

"So Geneva says we have to type the letters?"

"The Nips say that it has to be typed and just nobody tell the truth."

"So how can anybody tell the truth about what this war's like, anyway?

"Just lie. Everybody lies," Senio said. "The Gooks probably lie too."

"Fucking right, it's all lies and stealing food to stay alive."

"There's bags and bags of letters from home locked up and rotting in that store room and they won't let us at 'em. Hell, I'd give up chow for three days if I could just get my mail."

"Yeah, I wonder what it's like Stateside now. I don't want to hear anything bad that happened in Santa Fe. I can only take so much."

"Everybody's real fine there. They're safe and sound in the piñon trees. No bombs, no Nips, no war, no nothing. Nothing ever happens there. It's like it's hidden."

"But it's still dirt poor. Just Indians sitting on the Plaza trying to sell stuff and catching chickens for enchiladas and tamales, plenty of rice and beans though."

"Don't say rice."

"Yeah, right. So, you think that LaBelle is still a virgin?"

"Was she a virgin when you and me left with the National Guard?" Senio asked.

"Technically?"

"Yeah, technically."

"No, not even technically."

"You got your own answer then. She'll never be a virgin again. It's all over for her."

"She better not be making it with someone else. Maybe she went back home to Colorado."

"All's you need to do is get your letters from the store house. Your answer's right there, Melo old buddy."

"Shit."

"Shit is right."

"Shit"

Santa Fe, New Mexico, February, 1944

Anissa always knew what Nicasia, her next door neighbor, was wearing that day. In her black dresses, she was fixed and unchanging. Her hair was pinned in a bun—never let to stream down. She was a slight, modestly dressed mother of a fallen soldier as well as the wife of his missing-in-action father. And she was the mother of a Bataan Death March survivor, dressing exactly like the other bereft women in their aspects of mourning and she had, with them, grown sorrowfully prayerful. Their numbers were large in such a small town and they had a faceless similarity, one to the other.

Anissa, though, appreciated Nicasia's great sparks of watchful kindness and her grace. Nicasia listened to everything she said with a sharp purpose, trying to comprehend new facts, always ready to step in to soften tragedy when it arose. Her eldest son, Franque Garcia, had been killed at the outset of the Bataan Death March, and the telegram assured her that he'd died a hero's death. She'd been informed that Faustino was missing she had not received the black-starred telegram. That small detail opened a shaft of possibility, she dreamt that the Faustino Garcia rumored dead was another soldier with the same name. Nothing, no mail had been received from the American soldiers after their surrender to the Japanese in April of 1942. After that, dark and empty silence.

Nicasia prayed and fasted for the end of the war when her remaining son was shipped home alive. She cherished her youngest son Melicio Garcia's life over her husband's and more than her own. Two years before when the shattering news arrived of the surrender, LaBelle, his novia, the woman who he'd promised to marry, moved in with her to wait out the war. He was their last hope; only he could make the world reasonable and whole. LaBelle said Melo was her destiny; for his mother, Melo, gave her life purpose.

"I can't stand this war any longer," Anissa had shrieked the day before when Nicasia ritually appeared at her doorway, tamales in hand. She threw down the *New Mexican*, the only local newspaper. "Death, casualties and that damned Roosevelt again."

Nicasia could but nod. Each day she came, hoping to hear that the War was almost over, the news to feed her beating heart. There never was a war that did not end sometime.

Every day, the war. All day, they ate and breathed the war and its blaring talk. The American public received waves of unreliable information. Overstatement was the norm. No one had the facts, and if anyone knew the truth, it was "rephrased" for the greater American morale. Roosevelt warned against exaggeration, repeating again that the war would be long and difficult but reinforcing the government's constant censorship by holding back such facts as the Doolittle Raid on Tokyo in 1942, and the penal conditions of our POWs surrendered to the Japanese.

All real news leaked out from unauthorized sources. And it was often a year late. The American Red Cross tried to keep up with the deaths of their *hitos, tios, maridos, abuelos* and *amigos* but the Japanese Red Cross refused to cooperate. When reported, the names of the war dead (culled from the town's 900 conscripted soldiers) were proclaimed to be heroic deaths, but were in fact useless wastage from starvation and jungle disease, not war doings. Their lives were lost through wanton neglect, some of which was the result of governmental deceit. Their sacrifice brought no one closer to freedom or the coming Golden Age.

Anissa had read the last entirely credible report aloud to Nicasia stating that the Empire itself was starving and out of gas and oil so, as a last resort, the Japanese were shipping the POWs from the Philippines to work as slaves in the coalmines of the Japan's home islands in a last ditch effort to eke out fuel for the desperate war.

Anissa continued to read aloud saying that those men who were still alive and fit for work had been crammed into the holds of the Hell Ships headed north in zigzag paths fleeing the US Naval bombers above water line, and the American submarine torpedoes below. Both the Japanese and their prisoners were targets on the same boat, starving and fleeing fire from the US. *The New Mexican* quoted escaped American prisoners saying the conditions on board these ships were far worse than the Bataan Death March, even more disgusting.

War was chaos; confusion and lies on all sides. But these new reports of packing the POWs, shoulder to shoulder without food and water into the holds of the Emperor's remaining rust-buckets rang true.

And the part about being helplessly attacked by the Americans even truer.

Now, her neighbor stood quietly dressed in her worn black dress with another plate of tamales in hand. Only her neighbor Anissa seemed to be able to sort the facts out of the long paragraphs, so Nicasia arrived bearing some gift in exchange for Anissa's close readings of the printed news.

"God damned Roosevelt!" Anissa had summarized the day before.

So the war raged on and heartbroken widows stood helpless to do anything but pray. Rocks and talismans were traded, dirt was blessed. Rumors of stronger saints and more powerful Deities spread, and women crowded shrines. Powerless, they begged for help. The more contemptible the enemy, the more extreme were the prayers and offerings.

Yet there was hope. It came from an occult national movement called The I AM Presence that Anissa subscribed to, a religious group claiming to have direct revelations about the unfolding of a promised Golden Age. Edna Ballard, the founder of the I AM Movement and herself an Ascended Master, moved her printing press and offices of the million person strong Movement to Santa Fe during the war in order to further the I AM belief in the Divine Presence of God's consuming Violet Flame. Anissa, properly outraged by the Nazi Evil, joined the Movement in Chicago and followed Edna's move to proselytize, vowing to practice chastity. Next to the power of God Himself, Anissa and the movement believed in Jesus Christ and their wondrous Ascended Master Saint Germain, whose promises to end Evil itself were irresistible.

Even Nicasia trusted Saint Germain to guard and keep their small town safe. It was an I AM fact that death was powerless in *La Villa Real de Santa Fé de San Francisco de Assis* because of Saint Germain's protection and His Purple Sword.

But His Protection only extended to the city limits. Good things like piñon fires and roasted goat were stored for those who stayed safe inside La Villa Real de la Santa Fe. Because of Saint Germain, Anissa had repeated over and over, everyone in Santa Fe woke each morning unharmed, and she preached that under His Dominion no child in the town had yet contracted whooping cough or chicken pox.

"But what about the Japs?" Nicasia had asked timidly. There were actual Japanese in town, internees who were forcibly held in the town's Alien Enemy Internment Camp for national security. In a hasty move immediately after the attack on Pearl Harbor, all Japanese were rounded up and held in internment camps, their rights removed. The 2,000 men behind the guard towers off of West Alameda Street were protected too by the same magic spell that protected the original Spanish families. It was said that none of them took sick—but two died of old age. Or remorse, which was allowable.

"They should have committed *hara-kiri* out of guilt for their Emperor's sins," Anissa agreed. She would have supplied them her shotgun, if it had been in her possession.

Even though the Santa Feans were protected from physical disaster, the 20,000 souls who lived there suffered deep anguish. One in every four households had been stricken with war losses, their sons and relatives dead, wounded and imprisoned. So their families grieved and prayed to any saint who would listen.

Anissa urged everyone to invoke the strongest power, The Great I AM Power. "Saint Germain will bring His Pillar of Violet Singing Flame to heal your sorrows." She then pointed out that all Catholic Novenas, Masses and Good Friday Penances had been useless to end the unjust war; the war America had been dragged into through evil and lies. What had the Christian Catholic God done that could match the protection from the Violet Ray?

"Saint Germain has kept the enemy off shore," she called out. "Not your Yahweh." The cloud of protection over Santa Fe was all the proof anyone needed. The old Gods had failed, the new ones were alive and throbbing with power. Saint German was their hope.

"When it's the right time, The I AM Presence will blast his Circle of White Lightening and simply end the war," Anissa had described the power of the Violet Ray to Nicasia so many times, over and over. And she was so convincing that for Melo's sake, Nicasia had given up meat and took to passing out I AM literature on the Plaza.

The following morning, earlier than usual, Nicasia stood by the open door holding a bowl of bread pudding, and called out again, "*Señora?*"

No answer, but Anissa glanced up from her ever present distress over the printed news thinking she'd heard shuffling footsteps outside her open door. She had grown accustomed to these early visits and to the delicious meals Nicasia brought when she timidly asked if the paper had any good news. Meaning of course, news of her youngest son, Melo. She rarely ever called him Melicio.

He and his brother Franque had been conscripted into the war with the other boys his age because they had joined the National Guard. The Great Depression was not quite over and in 1939 the only work was government work. So the young men and their fresh-out-of-school buddies joined the Guard to learn to shoot and ride horses for money and glory at Fort Marcy. John Wayne cast both Melo and his brother as extras in his *Santa Fe Stampede* when, without discussion or agreement, the National Guard became the 200th Army Artillery and Santa Fe's Federalized sons were shipped to Clark Field in the Philippine Islands with few supplies and little training. Faustino, Nicasia's husband, followed them later when he signed up the days after Pearl Harbor, December, 1941.

"Anissa? *Señora?*" Nicasia stood straining for a reply. There was no audible response from the adobe room. Peering into the darkened room, Nicasia could easily make out Anissa lying on her daybed under the woven wool coverlets, prostrate, presumably overcome with her usual anger at the war. Anissa appeared to be emotionally stricken but then she always showed very strong feelings about things, a rare trait for a Gringa.

Nicasia passed over the doorstep quietly. Anissa rested in the front room, beyond which was the kitchen and beyond that, a bedroom and a bathroom. She tiptoed farther into the darkened house, fearing that Anissa was now depressed over devastatingly bad news which might involve her own family. Nicasia knew, in fact they all knew, that the men from Santa Fe had been setup by Washington as lures for the bullets of the Empire of the Rising Sun; they were given nothing to defend themselves with while Roosevelt lit Churchill's cigars and gave the British everything they asked for. Even after the attack on Pearl Harbor.

Surely Roosevelt had known that the enemy was gearing up for war when he casually requisitioned these boys from the Santa Fe National Guard and assigned them a new name: General Wainwright's 200th Army Artillery. They were sent to the Philippine Islands (named for King Phillip the Second of Spain) because of their mutual Hispanic heritages. The two distant penal colonies left over from the 16th century spoke the same antiquated Inquisition Spanish and this made them brothers. In the beginning, it was good times for all of them.

But eight hours after Pearl Harbor, boys and men of Santa Fe were bombed, strafed and eventually abandoned to the enemy. April 9, 1942. They were handed over to the Japanese four months after the sneak attacks on Pearl Harbor and Clark Field, needing the food, medication, and shelter due them as human beings. Trusting that the Empire would adhere to the Third Geneva Convention regarding prisoners of war, they were surrendered by their officers in a blundering effort to save lives by asking for humanitarian aid.

The Japanese were staggered by the Americans' ignoble surrender. Their orders were to kill the enemy, not to take them in and bed them down. They had no food to share. Where were they to find enough extra food for 55,000 non-Japanese speaking guests in a war they had waged for their own badly needed rice and oil? The Allies may have been starving but the Japanese were stretched thin. It was imperative that honorable prisoners fall on their swords and kill themselves. But this massive defending army arrived with their hands out for food.

MacArthur walked backwards on his beach toward an awaiting landing craft, talking to the movie cameras. "I shall return," he intoned during his close-up, the words slipping like honey out of his lying mouth. This was how he abandoned his men to a brutal enemy, affecting every home in Santa Fe.

MacArthur was given the Medal of Honor and became the toast of Australia. Lamb chops and lager.

For the morale of America, he asked that information regarding the Death March and the prison conditions be blacked out. Only positive news should be broadcast. But in time, stories from one source or another leaked out, causing the town to seethe, suffer and despair.

Nicasia carefully picked her way over the balls of crumpled newspaper lying on the floor. Anissa had undoubtedly read the headline saying how Roosevelt's dark angel, MacArthur, had personally given the order to have all Japanese ships sunk. How he had approved killing the remaining American Prisoners of War being shipped from the Philippines, the islands he had abandoned.

"*Puedo?*" Nicasia asked again after she had crossed the threshold and placed her plate on the coffee table next to her neighbor. Anglos were difficult. You had to ask permission even to bring them tamales; otherwise they called it *barging in*. But Nicasia actually loved this strange woman from Chicago who rented her Tia's house and paid every month on the first day, even if it was a Sunday. She respected the blonde lady who had twice climbed the Eiffel Tower and could read stories in French, and she was honored to clean for her occasionally, because she learned such interesting things. She did not need the money; the $10,000 death benefit she'd received for Franque sat untouched in the bank. And she had been offered her husband's $10,000 when they said he was missing in action. To accept it would equal an admission.

"*Entra*," Anissa said, coming alive. "I was reading the goddamned newspaper again and it made me positively sick to my stomach. I had to stop reading and now I can barely move, it made me so ill." Anissa was about to repeat Roosevelt's last orders.

Nicasia rarely argued with her intriguing neighbor. The woman had been to the university, she knew important people. It was worthwhile listening to such an intelligent and rich woman. "Go on," she said, agreeing to be sick herself.

Anissa read the editorial aloud, "*Eschuche.*" Then she paused because the article was padded with backtracking and speculation. The truth was hidden in the patriotic rant.

She put the paper down. "It says, basically, that our flyboys are now bombing and sinking the Japanese ships carrying our POWs to Nagasaki. Our Navy is murdering our own American prisoners of war."

"No!" Nicasia's hope for Melicio foundered; her eldest, Franque, had been bayoneted by the Japanese right at the start of the Death March. A year later, she had heard that her husband Faustino had been tortured to death or that he'd gone missing but she knew nothing more and hope see-sawed in and out of her shallow sleep. She feared each day that she might receive the telegram, or his dog tags.

As for who was winning and when it would all be over, Anissa had brought her slowly around to seeing the hidden truth—that all Allied propaganda was lies and confusion. No one was winning yet.

Anissa had said, "No one ever knows a goddamned thing." That was the only truth anyone could believe. Censorship itself was propaganda, everything about the War was managed and controlled.

"It's not the Gooks this time, you see?" Anissa explained.

"Uncle Sam?" Bile rose in Nicasia's throat. She was about to vomit.

"For once, the Japs must have marked their POW ships, not with a red cross, but with words in their own language." Anissa shook her head in outrage, and continued without taking a breath. "You think our idiot men ever made the smallest effort to learn a few characters, to translate the most urgent signs?"

"What should the writing say?"

"It had to say, *Prisoners on Board. Do not Bomb.*" Anissa shrugged in total disgust and turned to her neighbor. "The whole mess is here in today's editorial." There were tears in her eyes.

"It's called 'friendly fire,' meaning that we murder our own."

Nicasia wept as well. She was too weak to respond.

"It's like abortion—worse even than slaughtering babies," Anissa reasoned and the older woman nodded. "Maybe it's just the same. Friendly fire is like how you feel about abortion. Just a fancy word for getting people out of the way."

"Pray with me," Anissa said. "Ask Saint Germain to grab those Army-Air Corps pilots out of the sky and protect both Melo and his *compadre*, Arsenio Lujan." The two women knelt on the floor, heads down, weeping.

After a while and in a clear singsong voice, Anissa began the invocation:

> *In the name of God, the Beloved I AM Presence, and in the Name of the Beloved Ascended Jesus Christ, I AM the Strength, the Courage, the Power to move forward steadily through all experiences, whatever they may be, by the glorious Presence with I AM. I AM the Commanding Presence, the Exhaustless Energy, the Divine Wisdom, causing every desire to be fulfilled. Serene, I fold my wings and abide in the Perfect Action of the Divine Law and Justice of my Being, commanding all things within my radiance to appear in Perfect Divine Order.*

At the end, there was pause for begging and pleading. Both women silently formed their supplications. Nicasia implored, weeping, beseeching for the life of her remaining son, and in exchange for his life, she renewed her vow to abstain from sex and meat. Anissa, accustomed to chastity, asked for a peace larger than simple peace from war. She prayed for the death of Evil Meat-eaters, Drunks, Idiots, Mussolini, Hirohito, Roosevelt, Hitler and Russell L. Barclay. (Why not?)

"You must trust, *Querida*," Anissa said, putting her arms around the stooped shoulders of the older woman, "that all you asked for will be done by the Violet Power of Saint Germain and by God Victoriously Accomplished."

"It will be done," Nicasia said. "God Victoriously Accomplished."

"Amen."

"Amen."

Late that night when the moon had set, Anissa received the phone call from the West Palm Beach Police precinct. Unable to stifle her excitement, she lay in a thrilled swoon of abundant reward on the hand-hewn daybed that served as her living room couch. Russell was gone! She felt that she'd been granted wings. Her wavering faith had been fortified and she thanked her God Victoriously Accomplished and the Seventh Ray fifty, if not one hundred times, over and over.

All she had done was to pray to the Resplendent Essence and as a personal favor, a sure sign, It had swiftly removed Russell from her arena. The thorn in her side had been excised *just-like-that!*

Now she could count on spiritual peace and the transfer of some war bonds and his half of the lumber camp. They were hers to dispose of as she wished. She would hand them over to Edna and Guy Ballard and The I-Am Presence for the furtherance of the Power of Truth.

She knew Russell had signed away his Florida love nest; the whore was welcome to it.

Her heart beat wildly. Russell's death was part of an irrefutable mounting sign that the Surrender would come soon. Now America was getting ready to accept the Ascended Masters and their God-gifts of Light, Life and Love. And her ordained mission was to spread the glorious word on the Plaza to mankind and thus make it manifest. One by one, handing out brochures with the pictures of a ten-foot tall Saint. When the Glory came, it would come through the agency of Saint Germain, the same Saint who had orchestrated Russell's sudden death—the unmistakable sign of His Benevolence.

But this sign that she had just received, which she interpreted as the message of certainty that the war was at an end made her momentarily wistful. She'd have to pack up to return to Chicago. Changes would flow, like having to leave Nicasia before her son returned. She'd miss welcoming him back.

At the end of the war, she would go to her home with the dock on Lake Michigan but it would not be a homecoming. There would be no triumph to it, no welcome.

The I AM Presence in Santa Fe too would begin to decamp. Waiting out the war in Santa Fe had suited all of them well. She'd miss the place. Would anyone here miss her? For centuries now bands of immigrants had come and gone, leaving only a small imprint on the isolated town. Between the wars, fervent German ladies arrived with the intention of imposing serious culture on the place but they too returned home like the retreating tide. Texans as well. They came and went, came and went, leaving empty handed. But the town endured. Unchanged. Poor. Recalcitrant and still speaking their antique Spanish, a town more Mexican than American.

Cabanatuan Prison Camp, Philippines, 1944

Tokyo Rose says the war is over," Senio whispered to the POW standing on his left at the morning *Tenko*—part drill, part headcount as well as three hundred and sixty degrees of bullying and torment.

"Says who?"

"Scuttlebutt." The Bamboo Telegraph was fast and heavy with rumors of the final battle, but a month later the war was still not over. One low voice said MacArthur was coming back with beef, planes and aircraft carriers. Others said he was already in the jungle with ammo, cigarettes and chocolate. Sometimes the men who went off on work details in Manila came back whispering what they had learned from the Filipinos—that the war was almost over in early 1943. They whispered that The Empire's Zeros "were being shot out of the sky faster than the Japs could build them. They heard that the Nips were being forced to relinquish the Pacific, that the Americans were new getting even.

But Tokyo Rose said it was all lies. She broadcast that the Americans had already surrendered.

More rumors passed, saying that, island by island, the Allies were strafing the Rising Sun and sinking one Japanese ship per day, every day. And that liberation was right around the corner.

But the war was not over. It would take a total of three and a half years to force Tojo's Army to its knees and bring the POWs home. By the end, the number of surviving American and Allied prisoners was a pathetic thirty-four percent. The survival rate of POWs in German Camps was ninety-four percent.

Pfc. Senio Lujan banked on the one-in-three odds that he would make it back home with Melo Garcia, his *vato*, alive. Times were when he'd been beaten unconscious by some screaming guard's rifle butt for not saluting fast enough, that he considered maybe we wasn't going home after all. The Japanese were brutal, attacking even their own their own enlisted men when they weren't off abusing the whites. Any reason was reason enough, *Bushido*, the Samurai's code. They could do anything they wanted to their humiliated captives. By and large the guard/overseers were both sadistic and bored, so torturing POWs afforded them some small diversion in a camp where no one wanted to be. Like the POWs, any Jap seen fleeing would be shot.

The men called the overseers by their given English names. One, Pig Vomit, had his eye on Senio and clouted him with his rifle butt given any chance. He'd beaten Senio so badly one time that Senio lay mercifully unconscious on the bare dirt by his split-toed shoes while Pig Vomit continued his frenzied job, trying to break what was left of his jutting ribs.

"Pig Vomit, Pig Vomit, look over here!" Melo shrieked and other prisoners joined in the chant. The overseer stopped, confused, and looked about for the cause of the uproar. Melo with some help from the doctor was able to slink in and drag Senio away from under Pig Vomit's squint-eye. The name stuck.

Prison Camp had been structured so that the only protection the men had from the Japanese was supposed to come from their own officers in some legal orderly manner. None of the other 3,000 (too many) officers in camp would have lifted a finger to help an enlisted man like Senio. Officers just sat on their cans playing gin or solitaire in the shade. They even refused to filch fresh vegetables for themselves by working in the vegetable garden.

But not Doc Matson. The Doc knew how to trick an overseer into letting a prisoner go. One time, he offered him a cigarette, another, he pointed to the sky. Once he started irrationally screaming and the overseer paused long enough for the victim to escape and fade into a cluster of POWs. The GIs considered Doc special, the only officer who was not totally useless.

"What happened? *Qué pasó?*" Senio asked Melo hours later when he regained consciousness. Senio was a bleeding mess.

"Pig Vomit hammered you from behind. No warning. Americans give warnings, first. Not these bastards."

"Gooks say it's *Bushido* to shoot a guy in the back." Senio had been on the outside of the group of men, doing nothing, walking away from the roll call when Pig Vomit brought him to the ground. All the Japs screamed the word *Bushido*, meaning that the white men are expected to fall on their honorable swords—the only good prisoner is a dead prisoner. That's *Bushido*, a code that glorified death.

Right now, it looked like Senio was going to pull through. "Thank the Doc for me, okay?"

"He's a good guy."

"If anything, I've got a major grudge against the other officers," Senio started in. "First they surrendered us and they asked the Nips for taxis on the Death March for chrissakes."

"They've got it made, playing gin rummy while we're dying of starvation and dysentery thirty a day. An officer bite the dust? He'd have to be really stupid." Melo agreed. "*Tonto.*"

"Yeah, for me, I got no respect for the Nips generally and the officers specifically. *Samo-samo.*"

Melo muttered, "Me, too," and he was right. At Cabanatuan there were 3,000 officers who by the Geneva Convention thought they could not be made to work like the 6,000 slave grunts had to. They were assholes, first-class college-boy assholes, but they got what was coming to them because the Japs didn't play by the Geneva Convention.

"So they're supposed to make the rules for the Americans in camp."

"Rank does not mean shit in fucking MacArthur's war."

"You hear that General Black asked General Masaharu Homma if he could have a room at the Manila Hotel?"

"So, what'd he say?" General Homma was mean, the top *honcho* over the 320,000 surrendered troops.

"He screamed somethin' high and squeaky in Japanese. He's still trying to figure how MacArthur escaped and left all his three hundred and twenty thousand men without a pot to piss in."

"Tokyo Rose says no problem, the war is over. Japan won. Everybody's out of rice. They won because Roosevelt's out of rice. Everybody in Washington's out of rice."

"She's full of chickenshit."

"What happens to us if we lose the war? I mean, what will *really* happen?" Melo knew the answer. He didn't have to ask.

"They save their lousy rice and just machine gun us, standing in graves we dig ourselves."

"What happens if we win?"

"Same thing. They want us dead so we won't rat on 'em."

"When do you think that'll be?"

"Another month, maybe."

"Shit."

"You know it. Shit"

"Worse than shit."

3
Santa Fe, New Mexico

S till devastated that Roosevelt would fire on ships carrying POWs, Nicasia awoke at dawn the next morning with a strong hunch that her prayers might have been answered; that God Victoriously Accomplished was hard at work. And she waited impatiently to hear it first hand from the Señora. This time she came with a small stack of *empanadas* made the traditional way, with lard, flour, suet and raisins. If necessary, she would lie, saying that the lard was just butter. Out of respect for the I AMers who weren't supposed to eat meat, she tried not to use suet but nobody could get butter.

Voices, animated voices flowed out from Anissa's front room. Nicasia paused, holding the bowl lightly in her hands as she squinted to see if Anissa had a visitor. She always brought food because Anissa was no cook.

Nicasia hesitated, trying not to breathe, as she listened and heard Anissa talking rapidly. "*Á quien?*" There was no one there. No one visible, and all she could pick out was Anissa herself clearly in a state of ecstasy or divine madness, one or the other. She was spinning and although it was confusing, Nicasia convinced herself that something astounding had indeed occurred and being good news, it had to be about Melo, so she quietly entered and paused out of respect.

She knew, because Anissa had told her, that saints would appear if you meditate, even the Virgin Mary might come, especially if you used the short cut—spinning. When she spun and grew dizzy, she could see the saints even more clearly. It focused the attention.

Nicasia still hesitated. Anissa was talking to herself and spinning with her arms flailing in a state of total jubilation. She spun with such concentration that she didn't notice Nicasia's presence, and she continued singing, exclaiming and spinning, just missing the stick furniture. She had explained it before to Nicasia as "Divine Possession" which was, as she said, a very good thing.

"*Señora? Puedo?*" Nicasia didn't want to disturb her, but it was clear that Anissa was blissful in her trance and was probably receiving messages from an Ascended Master somewhere out of sight. Wonderful news. What if it was something about her Melo, starving, twenty-three years old and still holding on to a thread of life?

"*Por favor, dimè?*" She pushed the empanadas forward, needing to be informed. It was too important not to.

"Of course, Nicasia, come in! The Purple Flame has come into my life. Our prayer is answered!" Anissa fell backward onto the daybed, clutching at her excited heart and kicking her legs. She was out of control. The news was rapturous enough to seize her with tremors.

Nicasia, filled with joy and desperate to thank St. Germain, did not know how the prayer had been answered. She tried not to seem selfish. "*Señora?*"

"I can't believe it! I cannot believe how incredible Saint Germain in His Wisdom and Mercy is." Anissa said. Then she stopped thrashing her legs and sat up to receive the dish of little pies.

"Thank you." Her feet tapped a hurried dance. Her attention skirted over the small suet packages, for she still pulsed with electrifying Supernatural Energy.

"Señora, please?"

"Yes, Nicasia. It is astounding."

"Melo *mio?*"

"No, *Querida* Nicasia, I am so sorry. My *esposo*, Russell Barclay, my rotten drunk husband. I wasn't even his first wife."

"He is coming home?" Nicasia had to ask, because Anissa rarely mentioned him. She had always presumed the worst—that mercifully he had not even survived the first day of the Death March. Early death was considered a blessing by Padre Sembrillo because the dead were now at peace, resting in Jesus' bosom.

"No, not at all. Quite the wonderful and amazing opposite."

"He died without pain then?"

"Right as rain."

"I am so sorry," Nicasia said, moving to embrace the grieving widow. "You didn't tell me he was a POW."

"Russell? Oh my god, he wasn't a POW, he was a goddamned drunk, and he drank alcohol, ate meat and kept a whore. Even the dirty Nips would have turned their backs on him."

"It is bad to speak of the dead in this way," the probable widow of a war hero said, the stricken mother of a lost son. She still wore her son Franque's dog tags that clinked together with her other medals of the Blessed Virgin and Saint Christopher as she held the bowl with the empanadas out, moving them to the table near the wood-burning cook stove.

"It's okay. Saint Germain flattened him. You remember when I prayed; we prayed together, you and I, just yesterday? I was about to sign his divorce papers, hoping never to see him again in my life when, I can't believe this, he died just like that!" She snapped her fingers and pinched herself for luck. "I'm giving whatever I get out of him to Edna Ballard for our Saint Germain Foundation in Chicago."

"You have a big house in Chicago, no?"

"Edna Ballard said to lock it up and walk away. It wasn't that easy, but that's what I did."

Anissa understood that Nicasia could never have done such a thing. She was just the latest in a succession of Garcias since the late 1600s to have been born and still be living in their familial adobe. If she gave it up and walked away, she would have been a lonely exile, walking the riverbanks, weeping like *La Llorona* the legendary witch, screaming for her lost children. Like her men, she would be ragged skin, an empty form, a draft animal, servant to inhumane masters. Her house with the tomato-colored geraniums in the south window was too important to leave. The heritage of it alone was enough to bring Melo home.

How often had Anissa explained how it happened that Edna Ballard had been called by her Saints to lead the I AM followers from Chicago to live out the war among these fixed, rooted people? Edna Ballard and her husband Guy were the founders of The I AM Presence Movement. They were avatars calling down the Ascended Masters to oversee the unfolding of the coming Golden Age. Anissa, skeptical, leery and educated, had joined them in Chicago because to her mind, at least, they made some sense in a brutal world gone mad with destruction. The Purple Sword was the logical solution to the vicious return of the world war cycle.

She showed her devotion by giving up meat in that city of abattoirs, going on the wagon and refusing Russell sex because he was undeserving. Phyllis was not his first dalliance and in fact, there was a girl-child somewhere, the daughter of someone's French nanny. Of the three mortifications, abstinence was the most appropriate.

"You did not love your husband, even in the beginning?"

"Of course, I did. I was mad for him in the beginning. I was too young to see that he was a lady's man, a man who could not keep his pants buttoned, ever."

"Was he in the army, *pues?*"

"God no, they wouldn't even have him, considering what he'd done to his hand. So clumsy he shot off his thumb. An accident years back. I mean, he was Four-F long years before Pearl Harbor happened. And he was devastatingly attractive to women, that was the problem."

Nicasia let her talk.

"You know how it is with men who drink. It traps them. His day has passed and my bet is that his mistress, a chippie named Phyllis, was about to dump him as well."

"A chippie?"

"*Una puta.*"

"Saint Germain let her live?"

"She was not on the motorcycle with him. He died alone. Too bad he didn't take a Japanese with him in the name of freedom and bloodshed. No, Saint Germain didn't even rid the world of the whore, Phyllis. We might as well keep this just between us. I don't want people to think I'm a mean person, even though I am right. Just say that he's part of the war dead."

On the following day, the newspaper carried a posed photo of Roosevelt seated at his desk wearing his same toothy smile. Nicasia was outside when she saw Anissa come out and bend down for the paper lying on the wooden planks of her portale. Although it was not in the local *New Mexican*, the news that Russell L. Barclay had gone to his great reward bounced door-to-door throughout the town. That Anissa's husband had died was met with disbelief because no one believed that she had ever been married. She was so difficult. And she could not even cook.

Cabanatuan Prison Camp, Philippines

Because the POWs captured by the Japanese were reduced to sorry animals, Senio jaundiced to a yellow the color of a carrion crow's beak, became part fox, part raccoon. To stave off starvation, he had mastered rat-like cunning. Out of quinine and food, MacArthur and his generals had surrendered, thinking to save the lives of their severely weakened and under armed 320,000 Allied troops. Wainwright compassionately handed over his men in Bataan because of his misconception that the Japanese were well supplied with a great deal more than rice. The bitter truth was that with the help of the guerrillas, the 12,000 Americans might have better survived being abandoned in the enemy-controlled jungles. So since April 1942 when his battalion had been surrendered to the Japanese, Arsenio Lujan, Pfc., 200th Army Artillery from New Mexico stole food for himself and Melo.

For their part, the Japanese were unprepared to take any prisoners; and anyone allowing himself to be captured was a despicable coward, deserving whatever treatment was meted out. To their astonishment, an overwhelming 70,000 men had surrendered and the Japanese forced them—12,000 Americans among them—to walk the sixty-eight miles to the train for a ride to the inadequate barracks at Camp O'Donnell because they did not have vehicles enough to do otherwise. The world knew those sixty-eight miles as the Bataan Death March.

Of the 12,000 Americans, 5,000 died on that four day march. One corpse for every twenty yards of road. The Japanese maimed, mutilated and murdered the thirst-crazed, starving POWs. Anyone who broke file was bayoneted, those who stumbled were eviscerated and ground under by the thousands of feet still coming. During the worst of it, Senio dragged Melo to keep him up. This was the kick-off for their brutal three- and-a-half year fight to stay alive.

Senio's adrenalin-fired outrage over the emasculations, disemboweling, decapitations, amputations, starvation and disease he acutely witnessed on the Death March quickened his survival strengths. He and his best buddy, his true *hermano*, Melo Garcia, vowed to keep themselves alive first; then to bring as many of the 1,800 men from New Mexico home as possible. They looked out for each other, and not just against the Japanese, but against other prisoners. Men formed tribes, banding together because the odds that a loner could survive were a nasty 500 to 1. Survival depended upon an unquestioning solidarity. Within a battery, it was impossible to imagine a man stealing from another, or Senio ever stealing from a New Mexican.

Theft from a Japanese was not theft, it was called liberating. *Samo-samo* for the insufferable British snobs in camp and ditto from the filthy, selfish Javanese Dutch. Pillaging whatever the Texans had was good sport, while the Texans in turn victimized the Damn Yankees.

Senio and his blood brother Melicio Garcia protected their sick buddies. They stole or scrounged food often hiding it crotched in their G-string *fundoshis*. They washed clothes and guarded gear for their buddies in sickbay. They stole, and stolen money bought Black Market quinine and canned food enough to delay the steady number of deaths—one more corpse every two hours. Of the dwindling 9,000 Americans in Prison Camp, 2,500 were now buried in shallow graves. Without medicine, malaria and all the diseases from starvation and filth—diphtheria, pellagra, and dysentery—ran unchecked. The camp reeked of infection and shit from the slit trench.

Melo had been hit hard on the Death March and was going downhill fast only to be pulled through by Senio's anger. Other times Senio thought he was the one going to cash in, forcing Melo to rally. But Senio was wily. Wilier than the rest.

Senio gambled for anything from a handful of rice to a future Red Cross box. Men even bet their next meal. Maybe the loser would never have to pay, maybe he'd be dead, maybe the Red Cross boxes would not come, maybe the war would be over. Senio worked the system and mastered it, so he pulled Melo through.

What loot he got, he hid in ceilings, under floorboards, buried under rocks in the yard. Only the Japanese side of the prison camp had electricity for lights at night, so shrouded by a moonless dark, Senio liberated food and pinched cached rice grain by grain into his mouth, reaching down under the floorboards where it had been stowed. The two Santa Fe buddies fed each other.

Until someone ratted and the guards saw the few small pieces stuck to his chin. Then everyone in their group was beaten and left out in the hot sun without food or water for twenty-four hours. After that, Senio and Melo groomed each other like chimpanzees and when one slept, the other guarded.

Rule for Survival: *Trust only your buddies, suspect everyone else. The enemy is everywhere.*

The hot blood in Melo and his Santa Fe buddies stood them in good stead. They were quick-footed and dark-eyed, mostly handsome with a dose of Arab fire. Of necessity, thieves and undercover operators, most were beaten less by the Nips because they were less white. Their people had been prisoners from the Spanish Inquisition, prisoners isolated for in New Mexico and the Philippines, hardened to exertion and weather. They knew survival, absolute loyalty and dark fierceness. An-eye-for-an-eye, they were unafraid of cruelty. And they were quick to administer justice.

When Senio said, "that dog has to go," he was right. One of the British officers had actually carried his pedigreed dog with him on the Death March.

"It's no good having a dog here," Melo said. The Limey solidly refused to share the dog's meat with starving enlisted men. Certainly with not Melo or Senio.

"So who does he pay for the meat?"

"Somebody who can stomach English people," Senio admitted. No one liked them—the pompous blokes turned over Hong Kong and Singapore right at the start. Hardly put up a fight.

When it came to slitting the dog's throat, Melo made Senio agree to wait past dark to avoid the beagle's eyes.

"Skin it like a rabbit," Tivo suggested, thinking the *quan* was another stringy monkey. Primitivo Lucero laid claims to being a cook at La Fonda Hotel back in Santa Fe before the war. He knew a bag of tricks with food and he could create a feast just talking about cooking.

Senio made two long slits with his knife, preparing it as he was instructed, hoping that, like a rabbit, the carcass would slip easily out of its coat. Just two long incisions.

But no, the dog's skin had to be hard-cut into strips and jerked off—a messy affair leaving a lot of bloody hair stuck to the dirty carcass.

They called it *quan* and *quan* was anything good, everything rice was not. Any crowd, sensing *quan*, gathered like hungry gnats. The word came from something similar in *Tagalog*, a regional dialect of the Philippines, and it translated into something like *whatchamacallit*. This dead dog qualified as *quan*, and a pan was filled with red palm oil for frying.

No emotion crossed Senio's face while he simmered the dog that had been given meat meant for starving American enlisted personnel. He served the pet in small portions, each piece with teeth-fouling hair. Some men went away truly disgusted, but there were plenty who wanted a piece, including the men from New Mexico's 200th Army Artillery who ate with their eyes closed trying to pull dry dog hair from their mouths. They said it tasted like possum.

"Bloody cannibals!" the British screeched at them in their exaggerated accents. Senio sneered. He didn't know any Englishmen he liked, but Melo said he had met one who was okay.

"We'll be back tomorrow night and bloody skin you alive!" they shouted vowing revenge, catching their shallow breaths between the last words.

Melo nudged Senio and they pulled a Scotsman over. Senio and the Americans liked the Scots and the Scots liked the Americans, so they asked the Scotsman to deliver a simple clear message, a tipoff to the Brits not to mess with either of them. "Tell him this: we're the ones who drank the dead guy's blood."

"We ate his fingers," Melo said. Everyone had heard the story that had circulated just after the end of the Death March when the men were most crazed with thirst and starvation, but no one knew if it was true. The rumor said someone in camp had cannibalized a freshly dead man in one of the steaming hot train cars at the very end of the Death March. No one knew who would stoop so low as to drink blood.

"We did what we had to do. Melo and me were dying of thirst. Plus, starving." They told the story over and over until they believed it themselves.

"Pass it on," they told the bloke from Glasgow. "Tell the assholes we did it. It was us."

The Brits did not return.

The survival rate for New Mexicans in prison camp exceeded that of all other tribes because of their abiding sense of what worked and what did not. When Senio gambled, he won. When he stole, they all ate. It had always been like that in Santa Fe. Love, pride and a strong heritage of hands-on justice. And the justice was based on tribes. Cowboys against the Indians, Spanish against everybody, macho Spanish with long memories and old vendettas.

4
Santa Fe, New Mexico, 1944

"Señora Ballard hates the president and he hates her," Anissa informed Nicasia that morning.

"*Claro que si*," she replied. Many people hated him. Republicans, isolationists, and the followers of Edna Ballard. They were given to shouting how vile the president was to anyone who would listen. The rest of the country loved him enough to re-elect him four times.

"I'm going down to the Plaza today. *Ven conmigo?*" Anissa asked, and received a willing nod.

Edna dubbed Santa Fe, the small town with its dirt streets, "the Golden Temple of the Sun" when she exhorted all her devotees to leave Chicago and move there with her. If Santa Fe was not golden, at least the sun in its pure blue sky played its part and the influx of devotees paid higher rents than anyone else for small charming mud houses. It was, as well, out of the reach of Japanese bombers on the Pacific and the Germans on the Atlantic, and it was so poor that no one would have marked it for plundering or pillaging.

Four hundred years earlier, the Conquistadors reported it to be one of the fabled Seven Cities of Cibola, the cities of pure gold, but taking a closer look, all they saw was mud and mountains. No wheels, no steel, no written language. A subsistence economy, natives happy to trade for shells and feathers.

Edna, claiming her husband was an Ascended Master, overlooked the dust and the burros bearing stacks of faggots on their backs and assured her followers that the little town was solidly under Saint Germain's Protection. And it appeared to be so.

Further, it was the perfect place to honor Saint Germain, beseeching him to cleanse the world of evil with His Purple Flame. The 7,000-foot altitude alone seemed to elevate Edna and Guy's proximity close enough to hand-deliver the prayers asking to purge America of the Infidel and to allow the coming Golden Age to unfold. Santa Fe became the wartime sanctuary for their ten-foot-tall Saint with His purple robes and His upraised Blazing Sword. He was proclaimed more effective than reluctant Jesus and his shy mother with His Might and Purple Power. So billows of prayers rose to his feet.

This Marvelous Saint was worthy of prayers; He looked the part.

And too, His consort, The Goddess of Liberty on her island in the center of New York Harbor: She shared the desires of their Cosmic Master, and it was known that She loved Edna Ballard as well, and hated Roosevelt.

While the blanketed Indians bent over their turquoise and silver displays on the other side of the square, reconsidering the promises of their own gods, Anissa proclaimed her Saint and gave out His pictures hand-to-hand in front of La Fonda Hotel. This was a war where the promises of your Deity mattered, that and the size of His Weapon.

Any day on the Plaza, Anissa's voice rang out clear, calling for recruits."Saint Germain says President Roosevelt is an agent of discord and depravity and as a sign, he has been struck lame. The president is in agonizing pain and yet he will not step down. Four terms now." The end of suffering only required a few more signatures. A dollar in the basket.

"Roosevelt killed my husband and my son Franque, Roosevelt." Nicasia, a beans-and-rice Catholic, echoed. She'd seen the light. The truth was that any other Saint was paltry compared to Saint Germain, and now she pressed printed sheets of I AM literature on passersby from her corner of the Plaza. But in her heart of hearts, she never shook her old church ways. She rang carillons of bells, sent prayers throughout the cosmos, and quietly kissed the hems of any passing saint who could bring Melo home.

Through the legal system, Roosevelt had cut the I AMers off from the postal system saying that they knowingly published untruths. Fury was unleashed against him for this as Edna's followers fought back.

Anissa called out, "Edna Ballard says Roosevelt will go to hell."

"Oh Lady, cut it out!" a man wearing a business suit remarked in passing, but when Anissa turned pursue him, he was swallowed by the crowd.

She continued to preach. "But now Roosevelt has killed more people—including the Japanese—than the Nazis have. He continues to bomb POWs, and the bastard thirsts for more." She waved a fist in the air. Then she started in on alcohol, war, meat and popular music, and worked back to her usual pitch against Roosevelt and his mannish wife.

The daily paper printed articles reporting their own abhorrence of the I AMers—and by natural extension, Anissa and Nicasia. The locals joined the fracas calling Edna a meddler and urging her to move her flock to the station platform for the overnight train back to Chicago. Wars within a greater war. Fires inside clouds.

Anissa, defending Edna Ballard, redoubled her efforts. And in a fit of moral superiority, she even called her late husband's house to notify Phyllis that she might as well keep the blasted shotgun. Guns, in fact, were a worse offense in the I AM lexicon than both meat and liquor. But probably not sex.

The phone rang and rang deep into the Florida night. But too late.

Phyllis herself had had a change of heart. If she'd apologize, Anissa might be guaranteed the return of her gun. And Phyllis, when she came to a decision, rarely wavered. Russell had always said that she was a girl who stuck to her guns.

With only four gallons of rationed gas per week, and not a prayer of ever being able to purchase a rail ticket, she had already set out from West Palm Beach on her bicycle, a Schwinn. Santa Fe was over 1,500 miles away and Phyllis saw no reason the trip to deliver the hand-chased Churchill side-by-side should take more than seven weeks. Thirty miles a day seemed perfectly reasonable, more when she could coast downhill.

Anissa's phone call would have made no difference to her. She had made up her mind.

Florida

Even when she slept, she felt observed. Hidden eyes watched her as she made pin curls of her profuse red hair. Gossips screeched about her as she smoothed her hands over her breasts beneath her lime-colored silk nightgown. The town wags picked her to shreds. Russell heard them and bought her French gowns and silk stockings, not for her birthday, but just because... He was a gentleman. His final gesture had been the house.

"I had no idea about it," she'd said. In his new will, she was the residual beneficiary.

"He did it secretly without my knowledge." But she had known. He'd told her he was thinking of doing this. Reminding him of it was tedious, but her timing had been good. Any more delay and she'd have been right back where she'd started, grateful for a desk job in Dawson Creek.

She knew how Anissa reviled her. Ahh, Anissa had the Sword of Saint Germain up her ass! Bloody woman! Still legally married, she'd been his primary beneficiary and had retained her huge house on the lake, plus the war bonds and the lumber camp. That camp might have been Phyllis' anchor-to-windward. She would have kept it and sold the Florida place when the goddamned war was over and the going prices for winter homes bounced back. In its way, Dawson Creek was more like Scotland—without her horrid family.

Florida was too dull for her—too much selfishness and trivia.

The rich winter people flooded south from the Industrial Giants, fencing themselves off against the prehistoric, bigoted Floridians. They came mindlessly hating all the Niggers and *Cubanos* who had the bad luck to occupy that flat swampy peninsula, appended as it was to the United States like an uncircumcised penis.

They certainly never came for each other, for they caviled and complained against each other as well—they only came for the sea which was exquisite. The sea, as it washed over the reefs, its color turned green, like her own green eyes. And it stretched out as a beckoning thoroughfare before her, past Greenland and on to a heroic welcome in Aberdeen, and the newly enlightened Scots. Scotland always welcomed prodigals with money in their pockets. It would again.

She paused in her assessment. If her mother apologized, must she forgive her? Phyllis knew darkly that as a baptized Christian she was obliged to offer forgiveness to any bloody creep who was contrite. But forgetting? She might never forget, who could? Who would not harbor ill feelings? However, if her mother's apology was sincere, Phyllis would be required to extend some form of moral forgiveness to her puritanical mum. The whole dark and starving neighborhood was puritanical, drawing the line across sex, nothing else.

No line through drinking yourself into a foul humor every night and when the small matter of Phyllis' being fugged by her history teacher was found out, they all went berserk. That such a small pleasure was blown out of proportion pointed out how stuffy and intolerant Scotland was. Here in the States it has been her experience that you had plenty of permission to sleep around but not with a Negro. Being high-minded, she found that a failing.

The ground was still fresh on Russell's grave when she had called his sister, Doris, for reassurance about her inheritance. And Doris gave it readily, insisting that Phyllis keep the money, even implied—of all things— that she'd earned it. She used the word, *services*.

"Try to forget about Anissa. Just keep what was given to you and be glad. It's rightfully yours." So Phyllis accepted what Russell had wanted her to have and tried not to fancy that the lumber camp should have been hers as well.

Money became her; it seemed to make her brainier even though she thought she had been endowed with sufficient and amazing attributes. So she dressed the part of a widow—ring, pearls, hair done, high heels. Still, no one telephoned. No one wrote notes to her. The mail she received was on legal-sized paper with letterheads and rosters of associates' names, some dead, some still living.

The neighbors had forgotten their courtesy.

Phyllis' heart rushed when a personal letter in her Aunt Marjorie's tight penmanship finally arrived, asking after her well being and sending months-old news from Aberdeen. Her aunt in Santa Barbara again encouraged her to come and stay. "Yes, I'd be more than happy to find you a place here. I'm so sorry to hear about Russell's passing over. I know that you were fond of him." Phyllis, with a three-minute egg timer placed by the phone, called to thank her for being such a brick and to lay out her plans.

"Family is family!" Marjorie exclaimed. "I hate to take up time on an expensive call but you must hear me out. Your plan is absolutely daft. You'll not make it even the first quarter of the way."

"You don't know me very well," Phyllis retorted. "I'm determined to get there on my own. Texaco advertises friendly stations with clean restrooms never farther apart than forty miles or so and if I need a safe place, I'll jolly well rely upon the Texaco Man Who Wears the Smile. I can't see any other way."

"I beg you not to do it. Just wait a few more months; they say it will all soon be over. You can then travel comfortably by train. Why won't you please just wait a few months?"

"Because I'm planning to bicycle," she replied. "If the war ended today, the trains would be even more jammed with the returning soldiers." What choice did she really have? Hers was only an "A" sticker on the windshield of the Lincoln Zephyr and of course she had no access to public transport; she was a visiting civilian. Further, she had no contacts in the

States other than Aunt Marjorie who had taken a position with a family, nannying their two adopted children.

That was the sum total of her choices.

Dawson Creek was a closed book.

"Certainly, your young niece may join you with the children!" merrily said their mother who was given to avoiding the nursery altogether. "You can all picnic at the beach."

Phyllis had heard tales about this family and how comfortable the house was and how sadly plain the children were. Especially since the mother was a great beauty. It was quite a fright, really. Any reputable adoption agency would have taken pains to actually match the children to the parents. Surely, in the case of this family, a respectable agency would have seen fit to find children other than Little Dickie and Sally. But Marjorie had said that the family had scrimped by not going through an accredited agency and had dealt directly through a local lawyer. They had been too Scotch; they had been foolish. Cutting corners made things bleak, dreary. She was reminded again of Aberdeen.

"But come along, if you must. You'll be taken with the weather and the place and, while the children are young, they have a certain appeal. They are obedient, and I for one will welcome the company. Here, we spend long hours at the beach."

Then she added an abrupt reversal, "I'm returning to Aberdeen the very moment this bloody war is over. So do get here soon."

"You are no longer concerned about Japanese submarines?"

"Certainly not. Not now!

Phyllis sighed and lit a cigarette. For the moment then Santa Barbara was as good a destination as any, so she packed only the necessities for the trip ahead, sadly lingering in the house on her last night. It was only meant to be their home during the winter—summers were to have been spent at Dawson Creek fishing and shooting in the cool air of the Peace River Valley, and now, sadly, spring was approaching. If Russell had lived, they'd be readying things for Canada. That choice had been preempted by Anissa.

Her passing moods insisted that the more she abhorred Florida, the more she was certain she would adore California, even if the children were deficient. And halfway between here and there lay Santa Fe, if one drew a reasonably straight line.

As she wandered through the house, badly needed rum in hand, she caressed the paperback mystery that still lay open on the dining room table where Russell had left it. She needed him. There had been so much that was wonderful about him.

She moved the book next to her rucksack to be packed. Her last shrine to him was now just his side of the double bed, where the crease of his head was still in the down pillow. If he were still alive, she maintained that she'd stay and never leave, but he wasn't alive, and to be decent, she finished the work at his desk, paying an unpaid claim from the corner grocery store before she stashed the checks on top of his book near her rucksack.

Turning the bottle upside down, she sucked out the dregs of the rum, then launched on a nostalgic tour of the house once again. She had everything set out, including the paperback. She folded the death certificate and put it next to the checks. Now that everyone was made aware of her plans, she hoped to astonish the local wags with her arresting courage— setting out to bicycle her way 2,500 miles to be with her aging spinster aunt. She hoped her decision made them all feel bloody weak and uninteresting by comparison. And she had told them it was a charitable plan.

There had to be another bottle of rum on one of the shelves. Ahh. Next to a bottle with a few inches in it, she discovered several packs of Chesterfields.

The clothes she planned to take were Russell's, left where Russell had hung them—his worn khaki shorts, a few matching shirts with pockets for coins, plus her lipstick and the zinc ointment, as well as ready cash for the first phase. She set out his pith helmet for protection from the sun. What she was not taking would be locked up and put away, but not for too long considering Florida's mildew and how others were laying claims to everything she'd been awarded.

She poured herself the last of her new rum stash in a highball glass and dropped the bottle in the garbage. There was no ice left.

When she wasn't being clawed over by the Palm Beach matrons, she was being hounded for money. Even the maid demanded severance just for coming once a week to wash up. She appeared after the funeral with her hand out, holding back her own key to the house as a form of ransom. Bloody woman had forced Phyllis to change the locks on the house, needing to safeguard Russell's golf trophies and the carefully boxed collection of heirlooms. Things like a stein from Princeton and the photo albums of the three children from his first marriage to Jean, and diaries.

Later she might want to befriend his children whom she'd never met, using these heirlooms as bait. She would speak of how their marvelous father adored her; she would exonerate herself. She was not a cunning slut, she was an adventurer, and there *was* a difference. She had been cruelly misjudged and she would be vindicated—later, after the war.

After the war, she knew they'd all adore her.

She lit a Chesterfield and lowering herself into the chintz couch and continued talking to herself, making plans, memorizing the words of her script for a future spontaneous encounter.

"I can well imagine that you and your brother and sisters share a misconception about me."

But she had taken the money, fair and square. She would have been a loving stepmother to them, had their dear father not died in the sudden and unfortunate accident. She wept at the poignancy as she pictured their stunned silence as they looked her over approvingly; she planned to wait a few seconds before resuming. "I've saved some precious items for you which I'd always planned to bring when the war was over." It would certainly be a sad but rewarding scene.

She envisioned herself driving to them in her Lincoln Zephyr and personally presenting these gifts. Then, having been welcomed into their different homes, she'd return to Scotland and have the car shipped. Or France, she could go to France. She hoped she'd be able to manage all of this soon.

She polished off the last of the rum and lay on their double bed, weeping over the sheer heartrending picture of her being friendless and in an empty house. The clothes had been laid out, and when she shook herself awake the historic next morning she grasped his khaki shorts and tearfully climbed into them, right foot first. After placing the small things that she was to take next to the flaunted, broadcast bicycle, she bolted the doors to the house and buckled back through the house to double-check the locks.

Her eyes fixed on the shotgun in its leather case.

With a resigned sigh, she shook her rum-addled head and pulled her arms through the straps of the heavy and carefully packed rucksack. Next, she pulled her right arm through the strap on the leather shotgun holster and tried to center it before pounding the pith helmet down over her thick hair. All that remained was to throw her leg over the high bar on the second-hand Schwinn and push down, right foot first, to begin her newsworthy expedition.

She would return the gun only if Anissa apologized.

Once she left the gravel driveway, the first short section was downhill from the house with its lovely view. If she'd forgotten something, she refused to return back uphill to fetch it. She carried a wad of cash. She had a bank account. She could do whatever she fancied. And for the next 2,500 miles, she chose (chose and elected) to make a noble statement.

Anyway, Florida was not her sort of place. The people were too ghastly rich, too spoiled. She was not like that, never had been. She was still the genuine loving girl that Russell had fallen in love with, and it was time she was simply allowed to be herself—a fierce beauty who incidentally held no prejudices against people for their skin color. The only thing she found offensive in others was stupidity. She had a nose for that. Otherwise, she was as benevolent as the next person.

As she set off, she formulated her inalterable goals. One, to get from A to B; Two to get Anissa's goat; Three, to demonstrate her stamina and devotion to Russell's memory, who was of course watching altogether too silently but with amazement from his perch on high; and Four, to be free of the self-righteous women who were trying their best to sour everything she'd been rightfully given. (Mum among them.) Five, possibly to move eventually to Capri. She'd heard it was lovely with a blue grotto and cosmopolitan tastes.

"You won't make it even to Tallahassee!" Richard Frenzl, the banker, said when she withdrew cash in ten dollar bills.

"You certainly don't know me." And each time, she reiterated this: to the bitch next door, to the postman, to the sour-puss clerk in the tackle shop, to the radio repairman and certainly to the conniving and grasping housekeeper Russell was too timid to fire, she had to repeat herself. "No one knows what mettle I am made of." Pedal, pedal.

So she had mounted the bicycle and left the Lantana house overlooking Lake Worth, quite aware of herself as a glamorous heiress in a Technicolor movie and wishing she could see the glimmering shards of her own dazzling charisma as she passed. "You don't know me. I do not back down."

Every car slowed—some hooted. At first, she waved back gaily, holding the bicycle as steady as she could on the gravelly shoulder of the roadbed. They admired her, *Hubba Hubba!* She ought to have put a sign on the back of her shirt: California or Bust.

Within the first hour, pedaling along roads she habitually drove, she realized that her outfit was ludicrous. She looked like a Great White Hunter off in search of a lost herd of elephants. Whatever had possessed her?

And she had waited too close to noon to start out. The morning temperatures were already in the nineties. The more she struggled under the blazing sun, the less she enjoyed bicycling.

But she had stick-to-it-iveness. Russell had admired that about her: Phyllis did not waffle. Not only did she damn well do what she said she would, she was who she said she was. For the present, she had plenty of time to ruminate about her virtues. She was young, and she believed she had a charming bonny accent, and she felt that her beauty weakened men and aggravated women. She told herself that she was a star, that the world was her oyster.

But perhaps she would be wise to stay off of the major roads and head off for the green cool kudzu that covered and protected the abandoned trucks and barns of the families now torn apart by war. So many vine-tented farms had been abandoned by their men drafted away in the fight for freedom. So she turned to where the scarlet hibiscus grew, to the lantana and away from the oleander medians. She told herself to change directions.

She had started out on the South Dixie, pedaled over to Lake Worth Road then west, heading for the Florida Turnpike. Carefully folded in her shirt pocket was the map gone soggy now, and she was too bushed to swing off the bicycle and fight her slipping pack to trace out a tree-covered cooler route. She did not feel free and liberated; she was not as she had imagined herself, coasting down hills, the wind in her hair and a broad smile on her face.

Bugs hit her teeth if she parted her lips, they speckled her neck.

The late February air was heavy, a steady wind swept off the Atlantic at her back, drivers honked, convoy trucks that ground past at 'victory speed' forced her from her steady path to the side of the road. War Bond billboards mildewed in the humidity. Burma Shave. Swamps.

Barely two hours of searing sun and still looking even more and more like a drenched freak, she was on the verge of collapse. She could no longer fight the shifting pack and shotgun on her back, so she gave up and searched for her first overnight stop. Of course, she had planned to rely upon the soothing comforts of the advertised, clean, well-equipped Texaco stations for short breaks in her journey, and at night, to sleep in small, scrupulous Swiss-run tourist inns which must exist.

But now having turned to go along the inland route, she toiled past stinking motels thrown up for truck drivers and the railroad workforce. On her first night at a Y in the road, she bought a roadside meal for a dollar and in a rundown room shared her bed with cockroaches. All through the humid darkness, the trains clacked past whistling into the night, rocking GIs from their poker games by swaying them to sleep while Phyllis swatted flies, sweating naked under musty, line-dried sheets.

The following day was the same: under a shade tree adjacent to a stream and even doused with D.D.T., she was driven away from her midday exhaustion and earned rest by a million hungry mosquitoes. At most she had come forty miles in two days. Her tires melted on the asphalt and it was not yet summer. She went another sodden mile, trying to outrun the ravenous swarms at her back. Bugs by the millions, hatching young and hungry everywhere in the kudzu, under the sugarcane plume grass. What had made her think that a tree-lined road would be pleasant?

Forsaking her green dream of a ride through the countryside, she turned east again toward the Dixie Highway, retracing her way. At least the motels would be adequate winter fare for pale women from Detroit and their pneumonia-riddled sun-starved children. So what if people stared at her and whooped and yelled as though she was a deluded runaway.

She didn't care anymore. She turned back and was actually surprised to stumble across her first Texaco Station on a connecting road to the coast. Delirious, she pulled into it. The promised Texaco smile floated above great moons of underarm sweat staining the proprietor's careless uniform. His doughy face changed to a leer when he noticed that she was completely alone. Then he saw the shotgun. Not a .45. So he turned down the radio and stood closer to her.

"'Bout the most I can do is pump your tires, Miss."

"No, thank you," she said, out of breath, ready to faint. She tipped the bike sideways and let it fall, too tired to throw her leg over the bar, too exhausted and discouraged to return the smile.

He owed her something, something that had been promised in the slick, half-page Texaco advertisements. A cool place to rest in the shade, some pampering. Hospitality. Maybe even a Coca-Cola.

She was pointed in the direction of the clean bathroom where she was repulsed by the sight of the piss-stains under the toilet seat still up from the last hundred men who'd used it. The dried urine on the floor flaked yellow and sticky from the one-hundred-ten-percent humidity. She found an unwrapped roll of toilet paper and tore into it. One essential rationed during this war was toilet paper. Kleenex too had gone the way of great puffin. After she used some and helped herself to more, she replaced it on the sink and returned to confront the same proprietor with his eager idiotic look.

Now, he turned up the sound on his radio. He tapped his foot to the sound of "Chattanooga Choo-Choo," bobbing his head, never taking his eyes off her. Raising her voice, she announced, "I think you had best clean up the bathroom."

"Don't expect women in here too much nowadays. Rationing's loosening up though. We get more gas." She gave him a weak nod, took a deep breath, and exhaled. His shirt said, CLYDE.

"It's bloody hot!"

"You're not from here, I can tell," he said, congratulating himself on his close observation. She defined herself by not having a drawl as she addressed him as though he were her servant.

"I'll be needing a place for the night, if you get my meaning." What she meant was, *clean, fit for a queen.*

"Now, lady, my wife'd blow me sky high!"

She gave him a hollow laugh and in the end, he directed her to a house owned by a widow-lady who let out rooms. He reached in his shirt and scratched his belly. "If you don't mind waiting, I'll take you by there." He winked. "I can show you a real good time."

"You are quite mistaken. I'm not that sort of girl." Drained and discouraged, she readjusted her rucksack, checked Russell's gold Bulova watch on her wrist for the time, centered the shotgun case and hefted her weary leg over the bar to set out for the widow's place.

"No more than three miles, and most of 'em's flat."

Three miles took over an hour. She was dehydrated, fatigued and in a very dark humor. No one to blame but herself. There are canals and rivers enough in Florida, she could easily have taken a canoe and gotten halfway to hell, farther than riding this goddamned bike. Bloody fool that she was. Florida was crisscrossed with options superior to pedaling a bike.

"My word, ain't you a sight!" Mabel Sue said, hands on hips, an apron over her cotton dress. Phyllis could barely speak.

"Clyde," she uttered.

"Don't I just know it? He called and said you wanted a room for the night. That'll be two dollars, but breakfast comes with it."

"Anything," Phyllis said, hefting herself off and kicking down the stand. The packs on her back had shifted, pulling her to the left. The first to come off was the shotgun, which prompted a whistle from Mabel Sue.

"Mighty smart. A pistol's easier to haul though," she said, cocking her head to note that her foreign guest wore a sopping, stained shirt. "I got a Bendix. That'll be fifty cents more for the electricity." The room was clean but the pillow looked sour and the mattress lumps cast deep shadows under the chenille spread.

Phyllis was past caring.

She lay down, closed her eyes, and prayed for rescue. Russell owed her that much. Why in the hell had he let her do this? Why had he made her the innocent victim of those harpies and ex-wives who had literally driven her from her own comfortable home? What she had thought to be her own decision, was not. The bitchy neighbors had driven her out. She had been manipulated. Russell would have been distressed to see her now.

Jealousy, it all boiled down to jealousy. Even Mum. Well, it figured. More than one jungle species was known to turn against its own. There you have it—jealousy. Russell had given her the house and all the others received were poisoned apples. Well, one day, they'd all croak eating those apples. They'd kick the bucket, be tossed into a pauper's pit.

"Jest one more thing," Mabel Sue said, appearing in the opened doorway without knocking. "If you turn on the lights?"

Phyllis opened her eyes slowly and squinted in the direction of the voice. "Yes?"

"Well now, I couldn't say I'd advise it because of the bugs." Phyllis swung her head toward the open window and saw that the screens had been removed. "Moths to a flame, like they say."

"Right," she agreed. "I don't think I could stay up late enough to even switch on the light." Unending Wartime Daylight Saving—sun forever.

A war with no night, no moon and stars. The blazing sun never dropped beyond the horizon any more. When it did, it popped right back.

"Any chance of finding a bit of supper here?"

"Care for a lime Jell-O salad? Some chipped beef on a bun?" Phyllis moved her head, faintly nodding. She was too bushed to quibble. "Fine. Another dollar?" Phyllis, being Scottish, was frugal but this woman was stingy-mean. She lay back pitying herself.

Mabel Sue was a case in point and reminded her just how much she disliked the native people here. Their stupid lazy accents made them seem inferior, unlettered, certainly unambitious and uninteresting. Phyllis weighed her low opinion of Mabel Sue's dim brain against the facts, but given the present situation, she'd have to admit she'd been outsmarted. In the infernal hour it took her to pedal from Clyde's station to this appalling house, Mabel Sue had craftily removed the screens, turned off the hot water and set some green Jell-O slime in a mold to pass off as dinner. The bar of soap was a mere sliver. The wretched towels were mildewed.

She'd been outsmarted by the Floridians, all of them. All of them women.

Miserably, Phyllis gave up and fell into an exhausted sleep, not even opening Russell's half-finished paperback that she'd dropped in her sack. The chipped beef dinner had been spitefully placed on the night table as she slept with a bill for the dollar. Flies covered the chipped beef.

5

She fled the next day after a breakfast of eggs and ham. Coffee but no tea. No milk. No sugar. Even the blacktop leading back to Highway One, the North-South road, looked hopeful in spite of the wind from the Atlantic. Over the dreary next days the few motels she stayed in smelled like Cuban whorehouses. Sweat and sperm on the damp sheets, damp because everything was damp where the heavy air sank, and she was sure even the angels wept, making the humidity worse. How did she know what a Cuban whorehouse smelled like? It smelled like this.

At the end of an insufferable week, with her clothes sweat-stained and wadded into her rucksack, she pulled into a roadside joint and settled herself in a dinette booth, utterly discouraged. With a quick swipe, she availed herself of yesterday's mangled newspaper from a chair, and then ordered two poached eggs on toast. On the front page of the paper Churchill and Roosevelt posed, promising victory followed by eternal and endless peace and prosperity. She and Russell loved both of these men. She trusted them to save Great Britain. Everyone did.

"Hiya!"

She looked up to see a boy too fresh to have seen combat, dressed in a starched Navy work uniform, two green stripes on his sleeve. He was clearly harmless and callow as much as he irritated her by sitting opposite her without encouragement.

"Mind if I come on board?" he piped out. She gazed wearily up from her reading to find him already seated. "I seen the bike outside."

"I take my meals alone," Phyllis replied, vaguely contemplating another twenty miles or more while the morning was still on the cool side of a hundred degrees. She was committed, far too far down the road to simply turn back and reappear hangdog on the oleander sidewalks of West Palm Beach with some face-saving excuse.

"Are you in training, Ma'am?" he asked, jutting his chin toward the bike outside the window.

"For what?"

"I dunno, the Olympics if they ever start up again?"

"It's not only the war, it's Hitler himself. What a pig, walking out of the stadium like that just because Jesse Owens was not a white. He's a moral outrage; I don't care what color Owens' skin is. He had won four bloody gold medals!" She spoke clearly and intelligently for the benefit of the impressionable sailor. "Hitler!"

She returned to her paper, scanning for more news to fire her blood. "Now, if you don't mind."

"Buy you a cup of coffee?" he pressed. "I feel just the same as you, Ma'am." As she only nodded and kept to her paper, he continued. "Where're y'all headed?"

"If you must know," she said to the young man so fixed in place. "I am bicycling to California because I can't get a seat on the bloody train."

Awestruck, he exhaled. "California! My CO's from San Luis Obispo. He says it's real great there." She stared at him. Of course the young fellow had a CO—he was probably buried under a pyramid of commanding officers. And this fact gave her a friendly thought.

"We're stuck here waiting to ship out for D-Day," he added.

"Hey Sailor, since you seem to be glued to that bench, may I ask a favor? I need a place to stay. A safe place for a lady."

He could not have been more than eighteen years old, but he seemed genteel. It was good that he had only just joined up near the end, even though the prospects were not good for coming back from D-Day in one piece. Roosevelt's latest fireside chats delineated the stomach-turning calculations of the sacrifice of one million casualties required to feed the coming rout.

"Sure, Ma'am, a place to live?"

"No, no. Just for a night or two."

"Aww, Ma'am, that's a snap. I'll get you a room in the billet in the officers' *VIP* guest quarters. The base, the Naval Station at Mayport. It's real nice, a fine kind of place."

"Yes?" she said, congratulating herself for this rescue. She had come close to 190 miles from Melbourne, laboring with her pack, and fighting both the ocean breezes and the slipping shotgun holster. "But I'm not military, not even a Yank."

"If I can't fix it, Commander Johnston can. The Air Corps are all on two-hour alert, antsy to get going. He could use some fun."

She put her paper down and beamed at him. That was exactly what she needed—fun. Not *Hubba Hubba*, not whistles and catcalls. She needed to be treated like a lady, to be pampered and admired and shown a good time. Manners and civility had been rationed with gas—that much was patently clear.

"I've got a Jeep outside. I'll give you a lift." His nametag said "Halsey." Was there a remote possibility that he was a nephew or some distant relative of Fleet Admiral Halsey's? Perhaps the officers kept him as a pet and gave him leeway simply because of his name. They had chosen well for he was a very sweet well-mannered boy.

"What's your first name?"

"Buddy, Ma'am," he told her.

"Aren't military vehicles off-limits to civilians, Buddy?" she asked.

"You best give me that gun. It's just ten miles from here, so take your time, and finish your coffee. I'll throw your bike in the back," he answered brightly. "I can handle the flack, Ma'am. Don't worry about me. Maybe in that hat, they'll think you're British. You look it."

"I am."

When he drove up to the guard post, Buddy stopped the Jeep and pulled her bicycle down, steadying it for her to mount and ride through the gate. "Jess follow me, Ma'am. I'll take care of everything." Phyllis removed her pith helmet, tried to smile and raked her fingers through her sticky, wind-blown hair.

The Shore Patrol in his khakis stood at attention, "Sir?"

"This lady's a guest of the Lieutenant Commander's. She's being assigned a room for the night." Phyllis straddled her bike and nodded while he dealt with the guard. It was clear somehow regulations were that she'd have to ride to the officer's billet on her own, but he'd go behind, her pack and shotgun in the Jeep.

"Sir!" the SP said, looking directly at Phyllis. Not smiling, he pointed the direction with his bayonet. "Down and to the left."

Buddy grinned at her and nodded.

She wanted him to know that she very much appreciated what he was doing for her as she lifted her right leg over the chipped blue bar. "You really seem to know your way around."

He nodded. "Yes, Ma'am."

As she pedaled through the camp, she passed by hundreds of sailors who broke formation to hoot and whistle. Her Jeep escort followed in her wake. Their petty officer yelled "Attention!" to his troop, but he gave up, craning to watch too as she passed, before he signaled young Buddy over for debriefing. Men in battle were never horny, but behind the lines they were desperate with erections.

"*VIP* guest quarters, sir," he said. "Personal friend of the Lieutenant Commander's."

"In that case, I order you to put her in your Jeep and drive her there," said the petty officer. "That's an order, Sailor."

"Yes, Sir!" And Buddy saluted against his Navy cap. The Gentlemen's Navy knew the difference between protocol and gallantry. Other branches of the service did not.

"Thank you so very much," Phyllis said regally as she climbed into the Jeep while her bicycle was re-loaded into the open back for the duration of the short drive. Smiling warmly, she laid a hand on Buddy's shoulder. He smiled back at her with the respect due a friend of his mother's, or a maiden aunt. Did she look old enough to be his mother? she wondered. She was just twenty-three but the bicycle ride had done her no favors.

When she was taken into the long low building, she removed her helmet and conducted her own reconnaissance. Everything was standard Army-issue. There was metal furniture, and couches with indestructible brown vinyl upholstery thought to conjure up the comfortable memory of leather. In the center of the entry was a metal desk with a seated WAC listening to *The Warsaw Concerto* through the static on the radio. The air was humid and smelled of mold, tobacco and booze. A small rotating fan blew at her, clicking like a metronome and adding to the temporary atmosphere of the billet. When the walls were pulled away, nothing more valuable would have been lost than the echo of men's voices and footsteps, the odors of their soap and liquor. It smelled like home in Aberdeen on a Sunday morning with the overflowing ashtrays and dregs of leftover booze.

"I understand you might have a room for the night?" Phyllis addressed her.

"We're pretty full, Ma'am." She seemed to require nudging, some authority to hang on. "On Red Alert. Everyone confined to base."

"Lieutenant Commander Johnston," Phyllis said, dropping the name Buddy had mentioned while gazing fixedly into her eyes.

"Mrs. Johnston?" the WAC asked.

Buddy appeared behind her and boomed out, "She's the Lieutenant Commander's sister, Miss Johnston." He stood at attention. "She's a Powers Model. She needs her own personal quarters."

"Thank you, Buddy," Phyllis said, pleased with his intervention. "Yes, I hope that will pose no problem."

"Two nights, no more." And then Phyllis was handed a key. "The Naval Air Corps is on two-hour alert," she repeated. Phyllis smiled to demonstrate that she was not only respectful of this serious condition, but on behalf of the British Isles, she was grateful.

"Of course, if they get called out, you can have the whole place to yourself. It'll be you and me and the radio." For returning the WACs curt smile, she was handed a key. Out of the corner of her eye, Phyllis spotted a handsome man standing apart, waving to get her attention. She nodded but the man stood his ground, wanting her to come closer to him.

"A Scottish lassie?" he asked, nodding to her as she approached and Phyllis noted the deep tan of a very good-looking Ensign. She touched her face and then tried to smooth her hair as she smiled at the man. He moved closer, too close, as though she were his captive. "You're Scottish?"

"Aye," she answered, looking at him, doubting the Lieutenant. Commander might have a Scottish sister.

"I've been over there—a flyboy. I'm in flight school here. Back and forth."

She wanted to assure him she'd been hearing about the preparations for the invasion for two full years. Certainly she felt large gratitude for she had seen pictures of the gigantic war stores for the attack; and it wasn't just herself who was thankful but her brother who had been killed. And that she'd lived in a castle.

"We need you," she said. "We cannot go it alone."

Until this last push, the Americans had only fought in small-scale battles; now the Yanks were ready to send a million men into bloody combat using the crushing weight of American power and armaments. Words could not express the gratitude and relief of the British and French. Mum too. The whole Allied world was waiting for a moonless night with perfect seas, waiting for the go-ahead to launch the invasion. For the present, the Wehrmacht was bunkered on one side of the Channel, the Allies on the other. At night they'd batter each other from the air.

"We'd be lost without you," she said, grateful tears forming in the corners of her eyes. "These are frightening times."

"You're lucky to be Stateside. It's real rough over there," he said. She nodded in agreement. "They have almost no food left," he said.

All the more to thank these Yanks for. The British under constant German barrages had suffered severe damages and shortages three years before the United States even thought to cut back on sugar. Her Aunt

Marjorie went on and on about it in her letters, listing the family's mounting deprivations. They had made some parsnip wine and said, indeed, it was quite close to champagne if you close your eyes. (Not bloody likely!) And there was that mock haggis: a little bacon rind, some oatmeal, a leek, vegetable water and some bicarbonate of soda. Oatmeal could always be had, they said, nothing else.

There were children in grey-skied England who had never even seen a lemon or an orange because the Bosch had such a grip on the Mediterranean, blockading the fruit; even onions from Brittany were shut out. Children were given Tums and cough drops—there being no candy to reward them.

Other shortages had been in force there since 1939, when the Japanese occupied the rubber plantations in Malaysia, cutting off the material for new tires, forcing chemists to seek a substitute for rubber with no results in sight. In a direct response to Pearl Harbor, the Allies physically embargoed gasoline to Japan, forcing the enemy to convert to coal. Tit for tat. War is hell.

Slowly, rationing in the States took on a life of its own. Even when it was only a token, the Americans felt that rationing was the one Lenten observance that might precipitate the defeat of Evil. Anissa, for her part, welcomed rationing with a zeal. And she steadily maintained that abstinence alone could pull in the victory.

During most of 1943, all pleasure driving was prohibited. In the United States, sugar, butter, meat, and paper were always scarce—but never a jot on the scarcities in Great Britain where even eggs, needles, carpets, combs, hairpins, pots and pans, nursing bottles and nipples were impossible to obtain, not to mention blankets.

"My poor Mum is still drinking victory coffee," she added and studied him to see if he knew how ghastly the filthy ground acorns boiled in water tasted. "First razor blades, then buttons, now, they say, it's shoelaces." She took a breath and smiled again. From her breast pocket, she withdrew her bright red lipstick and looking squarely at him, she applied it to her mouth, pressing her lips together. "How do I look?"

"Like a dame," he said, smiling. "What's your room number?"

She looked at the tag on the key and showed it to him. He grinned and made a mental note.

"Count on me to buy you a drink. The bar opens at five p.m. sharp. I'll buy you a steak dinner too." He shouldered her rucksack and shotgun.

"Travellin' light," he said. "We call these knapsacks."

"I have a beastly headache," she replied, part of which was true.

"I don't think your bike will be safe outside, even if this is the base."

"I'm certain it'll be just fine," she said and made a move to proceed down the hallway, passing the line-up of sequentially numbered rooms.

"I have a frightful headache," she repeated. She did not in fact look her best, and she wanted first to meet the Commander before she slipped out with an Ensign, no matter how appealing.

"A Scotch should set you up," he offered. "I'll be in the bar, waiting. Name's Walter." There was a playful glint to his eye and at the word Scotch, she brightened up. The Quartermaster General had requisitioned the world's allotment of Scotch (not to mention the bourbon they seemed to like so much) for military use, and blissfully that supply was now within her grasp. She'd heard that it cost a buck a bottle in the PX but you needed an ID card. Phyllis smirked because she was now about to land a friend in the military with privileges.

Possibly more than one, if the Lieutenant Commander panned out.

Walter left her to settle in, setting the door so that it was unlocked.

She was relieved to be alone and glanced around the plain but functional room, finding there were no surprises. She spied the ever-present, perpetually makeshift and boring blackout/air-raid curtains over the metal-framed windows. Hardly homey, there was a bureau against one wall with a mirror over it, a double bed with a lamp on the one night table. A wicker chair sat shoved under a serviceable battleship-gray metal desk. She fixed on the door to what appeared to be the shared bathroom and went to open it, knocking first. The toilet seat was up, the door to the next room wide open. Was she expected to share the bathroom with a man? Even if he was an officer?

Locking the door on the opposite side, she went through the medicine cabinet and discovered a bottle of APCs – army issue aspirins. Swallowing three, she cupped her hands under the faucet for water and peeled off her sweat-soaked clothes to stand in the warm shower as long as the hot water held out. The APCs took hold and numbed her skull. So relieved, she tossed off a small prayer of thanks to the God of the Britons for her extreme good fortune. The same God who would save the Queen had saved her as well. Perhaps Russell had paid her a call and asked for a helping hand?

Dripping, her hair wrapped in a hand-towel, she perched on the bed and, lying down, fell exhausted into a spiraling sleep under nothing but a sheet in the muggy southern room. Later she kicked off the sheets.

At five o'clock, the sounds of happy-hour exploded down the hall on schedule in the BOQ Bar and Lounge. The jukebox jumped in as Walter rapped on her unlocked door and received no response. He entered and whistled quietly at her nakedness. She did not stir. Surprised but helpless, Walter left as she, dog-tired, slept on.

He returned later with both her bicycle and an erection but still she did not stir. So he shook his sorry head and headed down for a drink.

Songs like *Mairsey Doats*, *Rum and Coca Cola* and *Mexicali Rose* colored her dreams subliminally. This war, like a Hollywood production, was permeated with songs. By dawn, in the creamy half-light, she groggily saw her bicycle resting on its stand over by the wall of the room, and wondered about it. She remembered leaving it at the entry.

Suddenly she became aware of another person in the room. In a panic, she looked up and saw a man wearing only briefs standing over her with an amused look in his eye.

"Buddy told me to look after you," he said.

Her heart was pounding. "You're quite a sight!" he said.

"What the hell are you doing in my room?"

"The door was unlocked. So..."

"That's a rotten lie."

"You are welcome to check for yourself," he said. Because of the twinkle in his eye, she smiled. He was one of the good-looking cheerful Yanks, so confident like the rest that with their superior munitions, their never-ending supply of armaments, pontoons, fighter-planes, tanks, food and tailored uniforms, certain they, he as well, had all but defeated the Germans well before any planned invasion.

D-Day, the final curtain, was days away, although no one knew the exact time or place. D-Day would end it all. They'd be rolling in clover over the White Cliffs of Dover. There'd be champagne for everyone, fireworks, tickertape parades down every Main Street, medals of honor, and wives with tears streaming down their ecstatic faces. Someone had penned inspiring words to the war's theme song, the *Warsaw Concerto*, telling how the diseased Germans took Poland, reinforcing the purpose of the war.

But the war lingered, outrages and casualties mounted. It was March 1944. Honor and justice had yet to triumph. It was only a matter of time before D-Day.

"Do you always parade about in your underwear?"

"Mostly men here," he said. "Just checkin' in on you, see if you need something..." his hand was on the door. He made a slow move to leave.

"Please come back." It sounded like begging. "You'd best be Lieutenant Commander Johnston." She patted the place next to her on the bed. "I'd like to thank you."

"Jimmy, call me Jimmy," he said, locking the door behind him, peeling off his skivvies. He lay down beside her. She kissed his chest, and moved to kiss his neck, reaching down to find him.

"I haven't brushed my teeth," she said. It had been so long since she'd been made love to, she melted into him with a deep longing, pulling him onto her and combing his shoulder with her teeth. She ground her turmoil into his chest. She tried to climb inside him and out the other side.

"You are beautiful," she said, not breathing.

He could only succumb. When he was rigid, she took his cock and pushed him deeper into her. She felt bottomless; he could fall into her for miles. She raked his back with the nails of one hand, the other holding his balls. And he in turn caressed her body, slowing her frenzy. At the end he held her head in his hands, pulling on her lips with his mouth, thanking her.

All men begged Heaven for a ride such as she, a siren piping the troops into battle. She was a gift. Buddy said she was a dish, he was right. She was a banquet.

Mired inside her own yearnings, she moaned with pleasure for the satisfaction of her lust. Not caring much who he was, what she needed was a man, any man. And she was generally difficult to satisfy. Finally, she was worn out, straining for air. He stroked her, taking time to calm her, teasing the soft skin of her breasts, her face, and trailing his hands over the strength of her legs.

Likely he was married. All officers were and without their wives, well? And she was short one train ticket to the coast. And a bottle of Johnny Walker.

"I am a widow," she said. "It's been two months." She related how a convoy truck driven by an eighteen-year old recruit hit her war-hero husband in the deep black of night and that there would be a court-martial.

"Heads will roll," she assured Jimmy, hoping he was not connected to the Adjutant General's Office.

He remained silent.

She kissed his collarbone.

Again and quickly, he turned to make love to her. "I am sorry about your husband." Then he pushed so deeply into her that she almost screamed out. Afterwards, she thanked him both for listening to her and not offering to assist her legally. Passion and justice are polar opposites.

"Most of the time, I prefer to take care of myself," she whispered.

"I have no doubt of that."

"Where are you from?" she asked as he pulled his arm from under her and began to drift away into a satiated sleep. "Do people ever call you James?"

"California," he said slowly.

She smiled. *How lovely.* She closed her eyes, content and relaxed. Just then the bathroom plumbing gave out a harsh lead pipe banging and she heard the pounding of water in the shower and a door slamming. The officer sharing her bath had been roused by their mating howls. The time was 0548, almost reveille.

"Stick around," Jimmy said, pulling on his skivvies. "I'll show you a good time." He kissed her neck, smiling at her. "I want you to stay." And he quietly left for his own room down the hallway.

Why not? Of course she'd stick around for a fine man who might help her. She'd sleep with him of course but she hated the word "fuck," even if everybody used it, day and night. Mainly she wanted a good time, like he promised. And an allotment of Scotch.

When the shower had been freed up, she pulled herself off the bed, washed and dressed to go to breakfast, hungry for all the butter, bacon and eggs the US Navy could provide. Dressed again in Russell's wrinkled khaki shirt and shorts, she passed through the lobby and was completely taken aback to find Jimmy waiting for her, seated in one of the government-issue metal armchairs.

Crushing his smoke in the ashtray, he rose to greet her. And he was magnificent: tall, shaven, scented and in full whites with three gold stripes on his shoulder boards.

"I've called an orderly to come for your clothes."

"Really?" she said, staring at him. "I'll need my things."

"Yes," he agreed, "but please stay tonight."

"I must get back on the road. I have to get to California and I have twenty-one hundred miles to go! You surely understand."

Taking hold of her hand, he said, "If you stay with me for a few nights, I'll pull strings and get you on the train."

She knew what he meant. "I don't have anything proper for dinner."

"My orderly will see that you are taken to the PX. You might find something there."

"Okay," she said and smiled. "I'll stick around."

Back in her room, after a huge breakfast, the Commander's orderly knocked on her door. It was Buddy.

"Hiya," he said. "Everything ship-shape?"

"Have you been sent to take me to the PX?" She owed him a great deal—the room, the Lieutenant Commander, the Scotch, everything.

"Yes Ma'am. Commander Johnston gave me this for you." It was an envelope filled with crisp new bills—thirty dollars, enough to buy whatever she pleased. Not to mention cigarettes, Clark Bars, toilet paper and booze. She had plenty of her own cash, but she accepted the gesture as her due.

"Well then, shall we go?" she grinned at Buddy and took his arm to the Jeep and the PX and returned with a new pair of slacks and a silk shirt, plus some other incidental sundries in a brown bag. "I want to thank you."

"All in the line of duty, Ma'am."

"I'm grateful to you for helping me out."

"I figured it was getting too hot to ride a bicycle across Alabama, Ma'am."

"If everything works out, I'd like to give you my bike. It's a man's bike. Would you like it?" Things metal were rare. She'd had a hell of a time just finding a serviceable bike—everything steel went to the war effort scrap pile to be melted down and reborn as a Sherman Tank.

"Mighty kind, Ma'am. But I don't know when I'd ever use it. I'm hoping for a sports car at the end of all this."

Having complied with his commander's instructions and wearing a silly grin, he left her back at the officer's guesthouse and took her laundry. Any God-fearing Christian which Buddy no doubt was, being from the South, would have to grasp that he was pimping for his CO, slow as such realization might be.

"I'd still like to give you something," she said, watching him back away shaking his head, muttering something to himself.

Later, there was another knock on her flimsy door. "Are you

decent?" Off duty now, Jimmy was still in his whites, bearing a carton of Chesterfields, a bottle of Haig and Haig Pinch and come to take her to the bar. The sight of him weakened her.

"I need you," she said and sat squarely on the bed, unbuttoning her silk shirt. He sighed, belted out a laugh and locked the two doors to the room.

For her, time and again, nothing equaled the thrill of the first time. She lived for the seduction and the desperate need. She had cut her teeth in Scotland on how to hike her skirt in a school closet, smothering screams of triumph. His, hers, theirs. This morning had been tremendous but now that her panic and urgency had faded, she'd let him take the lead and maybe she'd stage fewer troubling noises. The thrill of the chase ends in a mountain of trophies. Neither of them asked for more than that.

"I can stay longer if you'll help me find a ride to Santa Barbara," she reminded him when he had come and was bathed with their musk. She had left a hickey on his neck. When he rolled off her and onto his back, she leaned across the bedside table and yanked a pack of cigarettes open.

"Smoke, Commander, Sir?"

He smiled at her as she placed a lit cigarette between his lips and noted on his watch that it was 1700 hours and the bar was now open for business. Happy Hour—time to get dressed. He reached for his pants, the cigarette smoke stinging his eyes.

Male laughter and music started to pound the fragile beaverboard walls of the temporary building thrown up by the Seabees. The smoke from the packs of Camels and Chesterfields billowed out from the bar and the jukebox rocked with songs like Perry Como singing the German love song *Lili Marlene* and Kay Keyser crooning *White Cliffs of Dover*. The officers on alert were eager to riddle the Nazis with bullets, anxious to stand right there on top of the White Cliffs of Dover and spit in their damn Jerry eyes. "Play it again!"

Fresh out of colleges, primed to fight for God and Country, they were all on alert, and confined to the base. Drinks were two for a quarter, and he offered to bathe her in Scotch while she was still dressing to join the officers. When she was ready, he led her solemnly to the bar. She glowed, feeling utterly glamorous, if not established for her wartime effort. The young Ensigns swarmed her for there was not one man in the entire building who had not heard how she was putting Room 14 to good use.

They belted out their victory song from *The White Cliffs of Dover* for her.

"I saw the movie last month," she said as the song ended. "Irene Dunne, Peter Lawford, Van Johnson, Roddy Barness."

"At ease, men," Jimmy told the pack. "Look but do not touch." She was property of the Lieutenant Commander for his sole comfort and amusement.

He owned her for the night. His alone. For morale's sake; for the effort.

"At ease!" he said.

She tipped her highball toward them and said, "Thanks for the song. To Victory!"

"Yeah! To victory!" they called, backing to a safer and safer distance. The Dame belonged to the Commander, boys. There were other women seated at tables with their husbands—wives, some quite elderly, wives of other Commodores, but in the bar, there was only one. Home at last, she thought to herself. She had risen above earthly toil for the night.

The conversation buzzed as Phyllis enraptured the men with her redheaded possibilities, more dramatic because of her thickening accent, as she embellished her own noble suffering after her twin brother's death and Russell's "friendly fire" death-by-stupidity (an army truck and its driver) and her concern over the pending trial. "He had worked on the Al-Can Highway in forty-two," she said.

"When this damned war is over, I'm going home to Aberdeen." To a man, they lusted after the plucky widow.

"War is hell," they said in her defense.

Jimmy, their Commanding Officer, tried to change the subject by recollecting how he had met Admiral Nimitz and of his confidence in the Pacific Campaign.

"Is your orderly, Buddy Halsey, related to the Fleet Admiral?" Phyllis interrupted with the question she'd put out of her mind earlier.

"Turns out, he's not. But he's a fine boy," Jimmy said. More drinks, smokes and interesting stories went round the room. "He's loyal to the death."

And one by one, the Ensigns had the floor.

"Here's one that beats all, Sir. I don't know if you've heard about the German pilot? It's in the *Stars and Stripes*." And he reached for the military newspaper to show the headline: "Rouged German Airman."

"So it says that our boys captured this Luftwaffe creep. He had waved hair, lipstick and painted fingernails. Painted toenails too."

"Fags! Queers!" the men hooted. Someone hit the *Lili Marlene* button again on the jukebox. The laughter continued and the conversation rose, peppered now with frightening stories about the bestial Japanese. They weren't even human, they lived to die, they lived in trees; they were rat-like and too tiny even to qualify for the US Navy.

"I've got one for you," Phyllis said, well into the mood. "One of the POWs from the Bataan Death March, under censorship, wrote his mother and said that he was just fine and that they were being well taken care of by the Japanese and not to worry at all and that he loved her. Then he added a P.S., suggesting his mother might soak off the stamp and give it to his younger brother for his stamp collection." The men were silent; they'd heard this one before and they encouraged her, nodding with their mouths open. It was great having a dame around.

"When she removed the stamp, she saw written under the stamp, *they have cut off my tongue.*"

Jimmy put his arm around her. "It's not true," he said. "Prisoners don't need stamps for the Red Cross mail pouch." She stared at him; she hated the Japanese, hated them more than the Germans, because they were vile little apes who killed for the sake of killing. Still, she'd heard this story more than once circulating around the States; there had to be some truth to it. She tapped out a cigarette and three men leaned over with Zippos to light it, as the music pulsed under the roar of bar conversation.

"I'm so glad it's not true," she said, although she had fancied the story. Out of the corner of her eye, she caught Walter strolling in.

"Thank you," she called out to him, waving to invite his attention. Seeing himself out-ranked, he merely shrugged and smiled.

"He brought my bike in from outside last night. Lovely of him," she said, holding out her glass. "I need a refill. Please, Jimmy."

"Baby, you can have anything your little heart desires." Immediately, she saw herself on her back in a berth with Jimmy on top, rocketing across Louisiana toward the golden state of California. Humping their hearts out. The delicious two-backed beast.

"I want you," she whispered to him. "Over and over."

"First a steak dinner and then back to work," he promised her. She inquired whether the Navy was going to pack along all their booze and meat when they were ordered to ship out. Or would they leave some tailings behind?

"Please ask if I might not have a bottle of Scotch to take along with me on the train? Just in case."

"I'm sure going to miss you," Jimmy said when she heard the knock on her flimsy billet door the next morning. "Here's Buddy to take you to the station."

"Here's looking at you," he said, taking the small tumbler of stale Scotch from the night table and raising it to her. He kissed her, said she'd be in safe hands now. She knew that he on the other hand might not make it back. Last night, before they had made love, he danced her to *We'll Meet Again*, stepping lightly at first, then slowing to an imperceptible sway, burying his face in her hair.

Into his ear, her eyes closed, she sang that drunken truth of wartime tears. "Don't know where, don't know when." The exact songs tens of thousands of strangers were singing to each other that same night in 1944.

6

Ready to board the train with the ticket taped to the official-looking package in her hand, Phyllis grinned. She had a berth, she was set up, and she was ready to swing. She was indeed a soldier of fortune; she had it made in the shade; she was bold. Eyeing the passengers, she passed down the aisle between the rows of bench-like seats intending to turn the whole train upside down. The only known cure for a broken romance was fun. Men by the hundreds swarmed the cars along the platform.

"Y'all have a fine, safe trip, Ma'am," Buddy had said as he handed her the carefully wrapped package from Army Intelligence marked "CLASSIFIED," a ruse which gained its courier the berth. And the berth was small recompense for her time and attentions—all Jimmy's idea. The package weighed two pounds and when she had asked him what was inside, he had said, "Silver Bullets." She glanced down at it and held it to her heart asking that it be protection against forces even more predatory than she.

The tide was turning. If they could see me now, she sighed. Mum, the whole lot of them.

"Buddy, you've been bloody wonderful to me," she said in a low voice, and then looking at him, she suddenly realized that Buddy considered her a whore, and she wanted to tell him that when he grew up, he'd understand. War had its own rules.

Silently, he handed her the Churchill side-by-side.

The Streamliner's undercarriage spewed steam, impatient to move off. Everything was threateningly huge, oversized driving wheels, blackened encrusted connecting rods. From the windows men called out good-byes to tear-streaked women while those on the platform barked orders. This moment had importance, everything now was urgent and exciting.

Porters gave directions and watched an ambulance backing down the platform after loading a soldier on a stretcher into the Red Cross car directly behind the engine. The special car that had been fitted out with shelf-like bunks, shunting the purple hearts to the V.A. hospitals spotted across the country.

"Just remember to change trains in Albuquerque. The Santa Fe will get you to L.A., and then you get on the Pacific Daylight going north," Buddy had repeated and when she reached out to embrace him, he had jumped back.

"Orders are that you keep the package with you at all times, now," he said then and turning abruptly, he bolted to his parked Jeep.

Suddenly irritated with him, she turned to board the train, the box in both hands.

The train blew a long whistle and lurched backwards a foot, then ground its enormous wheels against the track, its great weight pulling the cars west off to New Orleans. She was jolted inside the first car and staggered before steadying herself to pick her way toward the back of the train. The soldiers, drunk and reeking of sweat and beer, were sprawled across the seats in the passenger cars, some playing poker, other sailors feigning sleep with their bucket hats over their faces. While there were indeed a few reading, they could hardly concentrate because of a boisterous cluster around a 101st Airborne Pfc. playing *Chickery Chick!* on his harmonica. The men crowed out this song, another of the inane wartime hymns like Ella Fitzgerald's "*I just lost my bubblegum.*"

As Phyllis wove down the aisle, the harmonica stopped and they all whooped catcalls. When the small tinny harmonica introduced another ditty, one by one the car full of men belted out, *Mairzy Doats*, waving for her to chime in.

It was her due—all the men singing to her, rocking with the rhythm, shouting out the song, all urging her to join in. And she did.

They loved it. Sixty men, perhaps more, applauded and hooted for her, occasionally turning their bawdy attentions to a scowling WAC in a corner with a book.

"Shut-the-hell-up," the WAC bellowed back at them, while Phyllis was taking her bow and inching farther down the aisle.

"You shut up!" a marine retorted; the men showed no signs of letting their high spirits drop.

Phyllis looked at the blighted, high ranking woman, wondering if the men had been this way since boarding in Miami and waved a cheery hand at her which was summarily ignored. A thirty-year old lieutenant gazed at her fixed and unblinking the entire time then he stood up and joined in the chorus, focusing on her. Phyllis watched his face intently during the song. His nametag said Barnes. He smiled back and when she nodded to him, he winked.

She wanted to ask him why he, an Army Air Corps officer, was in a cattle car packed with unruly, horny enlisted men, but she was interrupted by a large seaman pulling her by her arm into the fray as the train gained momentum.

"Welcome to Operation Train Ride!" *Hee-Hah!* They called out. *Clackety-clack,* the train rolled off well past the backyards of Tallahassee, headed toward the Gulf where cooler air would sift through the open windows and wash away the unavoidable reek of pure male in the car. A well-aimed bottle sailed overhead and directly out a lowered window.

"Dead Soldier," said a GI. "So-long, Buddy!" These men were reckless.

Another leaned into her. "I got a hard-on up to my armpits," he whispered as she drew nearer. "Help me, please Ma'am!"

"Hey you, keep your pants on," she said and a burst of laughter erupted around her. She didn't laugh at him, because she and the Marine shared a bond: they were both on leave and ready to ride and so far she felt fortunate to be a stowaway on their train. Hadn't she pitched her pith helmet sailing it off over the blacktop from Buddy's Jeep and abandoned her bicycle? With these men and on this train, she was launched into a new adventure—the horizon-crawling roads fanned out and away.

And she was pining for sex too. She wanted Jimmy so much she had a cramp between her legs thinking of him. She had better try not to be a silly schoolgirl over the gorgeous married Lieutenant Commander, wanting him just because he was not there. The *clickety-clack* pulled her back to the present where she found herself rocketing a few miles closer to California hoping for the best with Aunt Marjorie. *Home is where, if you have to go there, they have to take you in.*

Holding onto the backs of the seats, she moved slowly through the car.

"Where-ya headed, Miss?" a Marine ahead in her line of approach asked as she continued unsteadily along the rows of seats where the ashtrays overflowed.

"California!" she exclaimed and took a deep reassuring breath acknowledging her gratitude for being off her hard bicycle seat and in this car with men presumably ricocheting down the rails returning *from* or headed *for* battle. All credit to Jimmy's pull that she now couriered the well-marked National Defense "CLASSIFIED" packet and got a berth that was not hers. And in her pack she had yet another bottle of Haig and Haig Pinch and a carton of Chesterfields.

She moved on hoping to reach her own Pullman before some inebriated war-fatigued man pulled her into his lap and planted a sticky kiss. There was never any danger though because the Yanks were all talk and no action. They ducked when push came to shove. Like Buddy. This much she knew was true.

Notwithstanding the presence of a lady, the men's songs were lewd for the most part; they swore and carried on about chickenshit this and chickenshit that.

Working her way past feet, boots, trash and bodies, she got halfway through the next car before a man did a double-take, calling out, "Hey

Ma'am, where you going with that shotgun?" He looked at her hand and not her ass.

When Russell had told her, "*This is a rifle, this is a gun. Day number one: boot camp. The rifle rested on your shoulder, the other hung low.*" She thought it quite amusing. Now it was an inside joke.

The next car of men ran *Mairzy Doats* into the ground, fewer and fewer coming in on the choruses, fun's fun but poker is poker. She passed on to the third car and walked purposefully through it, tempted to go back to ask the poor blighted WAC to join her for a cup of tea when the stinking men grew truly unbearable. She made it through the last car of sprawling, crawling, itching and twitching enlisted men, closing the metal door with its rubber gaskets behind her to enter the peace of the Pullman.

She imagined she would of course share a compartment with one other person and later when she left for the dining car, the porter would make up the upper and lower berths with ironed sheets and soft blankets. This was where she belonged.

The doors to the compartments were lettered on either side of the narrow aisle and through the glass upper half of the doors, she could see passengers. Beyond them were windows open to the countryside zipping past. Only a few door curtains had been pulled for privacy. At the end of the car on a small chair a Negro porter wearing a dark blue uniform rested, his face in the newspaper. She hailed him by waving and flashing her ticket so that he rose to show her to her compartment. After he knocked on the door and opened it, he held out his open hands ready to receive the elegant shotgun holster which she handed over. Next, he indicated that she should give him her backpack and her "CLASSIFIED" paper-wrapped packet as well. But she pulled the box to her chest.

"No, thank you," she told him. "Orders are that no one may touch this. Sorry, but thank you." She slipped him an extraordinary amount, a five-dollar bill which he acknowledged with a polite nod and an extreme smile.

"I'll be needing your services later," she said.

A Bird Colonel shared her small room; he was Army—a

paratrooper pin on his collar. Noting that a lady had entered, he made motions to stand but she held out her hand and shook her head. She smiled at him as he sat back and she riffled through her rucksack until she pulled out the paper bag with the Chesterfields and the unopened fifth of Scotch. The Colonel gave off a soft whistle at the sight of her supplies, settled now on her seat. Her cabin mate was old, physically spent and certainly married.

"Please don't get up," she said, and lifting her finger, she indicated that she certainly did not want to bother the Officer who struck her as being utterly exhausted, perhaps even in pain. She moved to leave again looking for a W.C.

Swaying with the train, the package in hand, she moved through more Pullman cars, opening and closing doors, hoping for the ladies' toilet to refresh her makeup, cover the freckles and try to comb her tangled hair. After the last heavy door, she stumbled into the smoke-filled club car, a crammed swaying vault of booze and officers. Only one bathroom on the entire train was given over to ladies and she found it next to the lounge. Placing her hand on the knob, she turned her head in time to spot Barnes, the Army lieutenant from the first car, close flanking her. She smiled at him, taking in the wings on his collar.

"I'm Roddy Barnes," he said when she came out, combed and made-up again. There was something out of place. He seemed old to be a wartime lieutenant. By the end of the war, even young boys had enormous ranks and ratings, the Air Corps especially.

"Phyllis, er, Barclay." The widow Barclay put out her hand. "I'm hand carrying my husband's ashes."

"You were allotted my place in the Pullman car," he said.

Her eyes widened. She looked him over slowly, essaying whether she'd been found out.

"Brass requisitioned it. Said they had a VIP requiring a berth."

She looked properly chagrined by sticking out her lower lip.

"It's an honor, Ma'am. I'd like to have a wife myself to do me proud when the time comes." She gazed at him silently assuming by this that he was unmarried as she searched for something memorable to say.

"He's going to be buried in the veterans' cemetery in Santa Barbara."

"You from there?" he asked.

"He was from Santa Barbara. I'm headed there first."

"Sorry to hear about this. I know it's hard. What front, if you don't mind me asking?"

"North Africa," she said simply. "First day of battle. Mind terribly if we not talk about it?"

"Of course," he said.

"I have a Purple Heart myself. Didn't hurt all that much."

"Oh my god, I'm so terribly sorry!"

"I'm getting off in Albuquerque. Two more nights. It's an honor to turn over my berth to you," he said.

"That car... I'm so sorry you have to ride in that animal cage." Turning, she clutched the packet closer. "Would you mind terribly coming with me?"

Happily, he lurched behind her though the narrow corridors, one compartment after another, until they reached what had formerly been his.

"Here," she said. And when he entered, the other passenger, the weary Bird Colonel, glanced up from his reading and greeted them with a look of delighted relief as he stood to put out his hand.

"At ease, Roddy, I've been expecting you here."

"Yes, sir, I gave my bunk to this widow lady. Happy to do it." He offered a slow salute.

"Nice of you. Get some rest though. We need you sharp and on your toes," the Colonel said without any more detail.

"Yes, sir." Both men smiled.

"One of the few who actually hits the target. A real Ace, few like him and few like him," the Colonel informed Phyllis who stared at him, confused. "That's a joke. He's one of our best. Seventeenth Bomb Group, that's saying a lot."

"Thank you, Sir," Roddy said. Phyllis reached down to pull the bottle of Haig and Haig Pinch from the brown bag and extended it toward him.

"Please distribute this as you see fit," she said after checking for any sign of disapproval on the Colonel's face.

"I am grateful for your berth," she said, offering Barnes an apologetic smile, sorry he had to ride in that boozy car listening to the men's continual carping about officers and all the chickenshit heaped on them.

That was one characteristic of this war—chickenshit. Ninety percent of the three million US soldiers would never see combat; they worked in offices, or pushed supplies around getting buried under chickenshit from the drill sergeants. If they weren't singing about it, they were railing against it. She guessed that only ten percent of the men on the train had any combat experience at all and those were now wounded lying in the Red Cross car, stacked in bunks. The rest were drunk in the cars being pulled behind them down the track.

"Don't pay me no never-mind," he said. "Here's lookin' at you." He gestured with the bottle in the direction of the Colonel, then Phyllis—both gave him a nod, so he pulled up a stool for his seat and rang for the porter to bring glasses, with ice.

"Tell me about your missions," she said, settling into her tall-backed seat, flirting. "You getting back from Europe?"

"Firebombing Tokyo most recently. Orders are to bomb everything that moves. Washington wanted a debriefing, so now I'm going back to Kirtland for my plane. Brass says to sink every ship in the Jap Navy, anything still floating."

"Ready for the assault on the Empire itself. Roddy's under Doolittle's command. He's that good," the Colonel said, obviously at home with man-talk.

"What've you got now, boy? Seven or eight more victories?"

Roddy grinned. "Nine that I've counted." If the enemy plane had been seen going down, it became a hit. Eddie Rickenbacker had 26 victories but the tally had a huge margin of error. Sometimes, the downed planes just got up and came back at you.

"If you've got a plane, why are you on the train? You should have flown your fighter plane to Washington!" she insisted. *What was the matter with everyone in this war?* Muttering, she helped herself to a shot. Why could she not have been given someone else's berth? Why had they made this hero ride steerage on a train? It was more of what they all referred to as chickenshit!

"Chin-Chin," the Colonel said softly to her. "Smoke 'em if you got 'em," and he pulled out a pack of Camels. Roddy clicked his Zippo open and all three bent towards it, cigarettes squarely in their mouths and their eyes closed.

"Plane's down for repairs. I brought Ernie Pyle back for leave—he's from there. It worked out." Ernie Pyle was the newspaper correspondent who wrote of the grunts in the Pacific trenches; Ernie brought the war home to America, but Phyllis knew nothing about him because she followed the war in Europe.

"You must fill me in on this fascinating person," she said, raising her glass.

"He's a great man, a great writer," the Colonel said.

"You can say that again," Roddy said. "Ernie's a great guy. He rode right next to me, laughing and talking all the time. He was the one who suggested that, since I was in Albuquerque, I get a new pin-up on my nose cone done by Vargas."

"Who might that be?" Phyllis shook her head, trying to recollect if she'd even heard these names. Where exactly was Albuquerque? A place to change trains.

"Vargas is an artist. Paints famous pin-ups. It's a way to decorate your B-Twenty-Five."

"I'm going to take my leave," the Colonel said, setting his glass on the floor. "Here, Flyboy, you can have my seat." And with a knowing wink, he lurched off for the club car where he'd join men his own rank for drinking.

"Nice man," she whispered as Roddy moved into the vacant seat, glass in hand. Phyllis kicked off her shoes and stretched her feet across his knees,

"May I?" she said, glancing up to ask for permission to board.

"Does a plane have wings?" he said and rubbed her feet with his free hand, caressing them.

"I've missed having a man," she said, making her challenge sound like a confession.

"That's just A-Okay with me, Ma'am." He chuckled to himself, "Anything for a widow…" There was the joke about widows—all of 'em horny and great looking. So, the joke went like this: There was the five-fingered widow who begged guys to wank off. They owed it to her. The five-fingered Widow would never give you syphilis. Widows…you gotta love 'em all.

"I need a refill," she said. "And another cigarette."

An hour later and pretty drunk now, the Colonel reappeared at the door to announce that he'd waited in the lounge car until he'd been given a table for three. "Follow me," he said, staggering off ahead of them, opening doors which they closed behind them. Phyllis trundled the two-pound parcel careening through the cars to dine with it on her lap. After dinner when they returned, the berths were made up. The sheets were so tight you could bounce a quarter off them, the corners hard turned. Her shotgun and rucksack were carefully placed at the foot of her lower berth.

"Come back later," she whispered to Roddy. She pushed the "CLASSIFIED" box in beyond her pillow.

"Won't be long. My buddy the Colonel's about done for." And true to expectations, the older man crawled fully dressed up into his berth. And rocking with the train, he rolled onto his back and fell fast to snoring.

"You left the door unlatched," Roddy whispered, climbing through the curtains. His clothes were practically off when he slipped in next to her, too drunk to get hard without energetic help. She hunched over him, and began licking him, tasting his sweat, sucking on him silently. Then, kneading his balls, she began to wildly nurse his penis until it was almost hard, she mounted him and rode him mindlessly, faster and faster, outrunning the train. As she worked over him, her mind raced, forming lists of other men and how much she savored the first times with them, the chase, and then their own mindless surrender to her.

Spent, she rolled off him, and they collapsed in each other's arms, needing to sleep off a surefire hangover. They slept the few hours until dawn outlined the curtain.

"Ahh, my God!" Roddy said, sitting up. "So soon?"

But it was still early and Roddy was grateful for the train's wretched clatter and jerking that gave him leave to fuck right under the Bird Colonel. Grateful for the Haig as well. Astonished that his assigned place in the berth was on top of a redhead with a thick accent who slept with her toes next to her husband's ashes. Life held unaccountable offers.

Reluctantly he pulled on his pants and stumped back to the bullpen of sodden men splayed this way and that across their seats. He nodded to the WAC who was awake and reading, trying to steady her reading matter against the continual pitching of the train on its uneven rail bed. He took his seat and looked out the window. Water.

"Louisiana," he announced to no one and waiting an hour or more, he stood to return to Phyllis who was propped up comfortably in bed on her pillows, gazing out the window at the passing countryside. The Bird Colonel was now gone and she held her breakfast tray on her lap.

"You only have to tell the Porter that you are sick and he brings you whatever you wish in bed," she said.

"You hardly look sick," he said. "Hung over, maybe."

Later, when the train's rhythm changed, the side-to-side banging subsided and the sway of the screeching, metal-on-metal grew strident, the wheels slowed to pull the train into the huge New Orleans station.

"One hour!" called the porters.

"Stretch our legs?" he said and they turned to leave the car. The Colonel stayed behind and closed his eyes in the sudden quiet. All he could hear now were distant voices.

The men filed off to the USO, staffed by young girls who poured Kool-Aid and passed out box lunches for soldiers as their part of the effort. The men gratefully headed for showers and to make phone calls, while in the vast lobby, Roddy signaled to a grunt and handed him a five-dollar bill.

"Two big bottles of rum, one for you, GI. One for me."

The soldier punched his thumbs up, and quickly remembered to salute, clucking, "Yes, sir!" It was his lucky day.

In the swirling center of the detraining soldiers, Phyllis and Roddy, still half drunk, were swept away. Drowning in their sexual thirst they stood like parting lovers, pressed into each other, tongue kissing, tasting. She licked his teeth catlike, drinking him in, oblivious to the gathering audience. She pulled deeper into him. "Fuck me," they both said at the same time.

As the train rolled west, Phyllis passed the time pouring Louisiana rum and having her cigarettes lit with the clicking Zippo. That night, now completely rum-sponged, they had plied the Colonel with booze. After dinner Phyllis stood outside their compartment waiting as the porter made up the berths. Roddy stood apart down the aisle and stared through the windows, the countryside was dense and black. A moon the color of shells shone through clouds. Telephone poles sped like wickets past the windows.

"Sleep well," she had wished the Colonel as he climbed up the ladder to his berth. Phyllis had waited for the snoring to commence and when he had hit a solid rhythm, she poked her hand out the door with a hi-sign for Roddy who silently tip-toed into the compartment.

"Kilroy is here," he said and they resumed: Fuckety-fuckety-fuckety-fuck in rhythm with the train on the way through Texas and beyond.

He could do better, she thought.

"I just need to get to know what you like," he said, "and less hooch."

"Yes."

After falling into a drugged sleep, Roddy woke with a start and an urgent thought. "Why not get off with me, short of Santa Barbara. I'll arrange a military burial for your husband." He'd forgotten she'd said Russell was from Santa Barbara.

"In the morning," she said, pushing the package deeper inside the berth again. "We'll talk about it in the morning." And she tried to remember why she'd said Russell had to be buried in California. No reason except that Marjorie was there. For the next few hours, they tried to sleep, unconsciously monitoring the Colonel's throaty wheezing over the clatter of the train.

"I promised I'd scatter some of his ashes in the Pacific too," she whispered with a parched cotton mouth sighing as he kissed her neck. She turned to avoid his mouth as he continued kissing her, his breathing quickening.

"Being with you has been wonderful," she told him this not to entice him, but to end this round.

At dawn, they waited again and as soon as the Colonel, less and less steady now, climbed down, Roddy crept out wearing his clothes from the night before. The observant new porter knew when to bring her breakfast— baked apples with whipped cream.

"If you stay with me in Albuquerque, I can easily secure a place for your husband in Santa Fe's National Cemetery. It's a nice spot on a hillside with views of the Sangre de Cristo Mountains," he said when he reappeared in her compartment dressed and convincingly red-eyed as if he'd had a miserable night in his assigned seat. And he wasn't hung over.

"Lovely," she said, smoking a cigarette in bed with her coffee. Still slightly tipsy her thoughts were random. It all seemed so gay, like a huge party. For the moment, she did not want Roddy to step off the train and walk off into the sunset. Too much like Jimmy, too much like Russell. She couldn't weather more abandonment. She needed a home where she was admired, that much was true. She wanted things of her own in a place of her own.

Meanwhile, she was riding a train.

He returned again later, when the cabin had been restored to its daytime order to find the Colonel, re-installed in his uniform, reading the paper and facing Phyllis who showed the effects of her excesses—cigarettes, rum and adultery. Her lips appeared to be even thinner from dehydration. Still, she was game—up for good times.

"Good morning, Sir," he said to his superior.

"At ease, Lieutenant." He sat.

"I've actually got to deliver this gun to a woman in Santa Fe," Phyllis said as if talking only to herself. Roddy stopped trying to read the back of the Colonel's newspaper in order to understand what she was saying.

"The shotgun, yes? You never said anything about somebody in New Mexico," he said. "That's my home state."

"It's just that this gun belongs to her and I could easily take it to her and, well? Weren't you saying something about doing that?"

"You mean, you'd detrain with me, and we could go up, do the burial, find your gal and hand over the gun and …"

"Why not? I could say I was train-sick, could I not?"

The Colonel put down his paper to evaluate the two of them, one of whom he knew as an officer and therefore trustworthy. The other was a lively unaccountable stranger with her husband's ashes in a box marked "CLASSIFIED."

"I'd just need to exchange my ticket. It can't be that difficult since I've already got one?"

"Run that by me again?" he said.

"What if I say I'm bloody sick as a dog? Get off this train and take another in about a week?" She stared at him carefully. "I've already informed the porter twice that the train's infernal jerking makes me quite ill. He'd let drop that his orders were to bring breakfast in bed if the passenger was ill. So, I became ill and he's under orders."

"You dames!" the Colonel said. "I've spent a good half of the morning in the dining car waiting for someone just to bring me something, anything, while you've been sitting pretty right here in bed?" He folded his paper and nodded at her with amusement. "It only takes one redheaded broad to outmaneuver the Joint Chiefs of Staff!"

On the third day, the overloaded train pulled into the sand pile called Albuquerque where a cluster of men shouldered their gear and swung off. Phyllis, bearing her package, climbed down, trudging behind First Lieutenant Roddy Barnes, US Army Air Corps ace fighter pilot, who carried his bags, the Churchill 20 gauge shotgun and her rucksack, as he walked down the platform in search of the transportation to Kirtland Air Force Base. He told Phyllis to keep an eye out for a large, canvas-topped personnel carrier with seats spanning the sides of the bed.

They passed an ambulance where a unit of medics with their stretchers outside the Red Cross car waited to transport the wounded as soon as the baggage carts and passengers cleared the platform. Their assignment was to relocate the men to either the V.A. Hospital at Kirtland or to Bruns Memorial Hospital in Santa Fe.

The oversized olive drab vehicle was parked outside the adobe terminal, and a tall volunteer with the Red Cross, wearing a light grey uniform, climbed down from the driver's seat. She held a cardboard sign stapled to a stick which she waved urgently at the service men. It read: Kirtland AFB and Santa Fe.

"Here it is!" Roddy called. Unsteady on her legs, Phyllis exited the station building, feeling the effects of the rum and the train and holding onto the package for support. She scanned the desert town and saw a hot sun in a clear blue sky as Roddy, carrying her things, prodded her in the direction of the truck. He stopped to ask how she was doing.

"Fine enough, considering," she replied, though in truth she was in shock from having clearly made the wrong choice of places. Here everything was dusty brown, and so forlorn that the train should have sped up, not stopped. It was the sort of area that asked to be a bomb test site.

She regretted giving up her ticket to Santa Barbara and she looked at Roddy, accusingly.

He stopped, put down both his gear and her shotgun, and then took her into his arms. She felt like crying, and she did not want him mauling her.

"It's the most God-awful place I've ever seen," she said, pulling free.

"You'll like Santa Fe, though. Snow-capped mountains, piñon and juniper trees. I promise you'll like it there."

"This place is bloody ghastly. Scrappy and poor."

"Your husband will be pleased. You'll have to trust me."

He tried to kiss her again but dropped his hold when he heard the stern welcome, "Good afternoon, I am Anissa Barclay, Red Cross volunteer. How many of you for which destination, please?" She waved her clipboard in the direction of the truck and when she noticed the English leather holster, she gave it a blistering glance then, in a state of confusion, turned to count her passengers.

Phyllis who had been mired in self-pity, not listening, not paying attention, missed her first shot at the target.

7

Santa Fe, New Mexico

Late on a star-filled night, Anissa returned the "Deuce n' Half" troop carrier to the motor pool and sank into her own two-door Ford for the drive home, chagrinned to have only made off with a forty pound sack of flour for Nicasia. It had been an extremely long day and her arms ached. Thirty-five miles an hour was the legal speed and she had signed up to careen the enormous multi-geared vehicle from the mountain town at 7,000 feet down the steep La Bajada grade to mile-high Albuquerque. It was already close to noon when she waved the cars she'd blocked past her on the single lane, potholed road. Her usual assignment was to meet the train in Albuquerque, pick up military passengers and deliver them to Kirtland Air Force Base, stopping first at the base commissary and next the Gross Kelly Warehouse before heading back. She had plenty of room in the back for anyone thumbing a ride up to Santa Fe.

Anissa signed up to be a Red Cross Volunteer once a month and was convinced that she could help the effort by maneuvering the two-and-a-half ton truck for a supply run since few of the local women drove at all. This, however, was far less effective against the cruel Empire than the time well spent personally passing out pamphlets on the Plaza, saving America from Evil.

Nicasia was entitled to sugar and meat from the Base Commissary having a son in the Army but she had no way to get the sixty miles to Albuquerque. Fortunately, Anissa made it her business to fill her list each month and when she pulled up, the Pfc. saluted and signaled for her to pull over for loading other supplies to be shipped to Santa Fe, allowing her time to bolt into the commissary with Nicasia's list. She discovered that the Commissary was waiting for another shipment of sugar and meat. So, lacking sugar, she threw in a sack of flour for the widow who had lost two men to the Japanese.

Her rage came to a head at the warehouse dock, where she watched men loading supplies of staples, canned goods, and bulk rice for the Japanese Internment Camp onto the truck assigned to her. Hours if not days following the bombing of Pearl Harbor, all persons of Japanese extraction were rounded up, told to bring one suitcase of their belongings and summarily imprisoned. Large families were allowed to stay together, although the locations were barren and forbidding, often in the stables of racetracks across the country. The Internment Camp in Santa Fe was for Japanese men only, older men who were born in Japan and considered a threat to America. In 1943, to have 2,000 Japanese under guard in a multi-cultural town of 20,000 began more a curiosity than an outrage, attracting little attention but by 1944, when Anissa noted that bags of sugar had been set aside for the camp, she was furious. How was it, she demanded, that they were privileged to have ample sugar and meat?

Slowly, it dawned on her how she was in fact actually aiding the "Other Side" by running supplies to the *dangerous enemy alien* internees locked behind the fence in Santa Fe. No sugar for Nicasia, plenty for the Gooks.

Her patriotism suffered. Not only sugar, but other rationed items to this country-club prison had been piled onto the back deck of her truck. This, in the name of National Security? Why not send them right back to where they belonged—hiding in caves on the death-trap islands of Iwo Jima, Saipan, Pelaliu?

She decided to leave the supplies on the parked truck. She would do nothing more for the bunch of whiners. For, every time the sniveling internees had the slightest complaint, they telegraphed the Spanish Embassy in Washington DC, demanding to have a neutral observer arrive in order to enforce the terms of the 1929 Geneva Convention. The bleating little weasels had gotten a copy of the Convention and printed up 1,200 copies in Japanese, and here Anissa was, volunteering to drive a truck across the night desert with all their favorite delicacies. Food she could not have for herself. Not that she was greedy for sugar, but she had her principles.

Her arms trembled from the exertion of driving the truck as she quietly walked next door where Nicasia dozed, confident of finding beef and sugar on her kitchen table when she awoke the next morning. A light had been left on in the kitchen and the house was still.

"I'm back!" Anissa announced in a loud whisper, setting the flour sack on a chair.

Nicasia shuffled to the door wearing a hopeful smile, wrapped in her flannel granny gown, remnants of worn lace around the neck. The old widow stretched her shoulders and tried to wake up, looking not at Anissa's face but at the extra sack of flour.

"No sugar?" she asked.

Anissa shook her head. "Tons and tons of it, all for the slimy toads in Jap Trap. Rice, too. I've never seen so much stuff. I don't know but there's about two thousand men there." Anissa was in no mood to pander to the Aliens.

"You went to their camp?" Nicasia knew full well how Anissa felt about the enemy aliens, but her old Uncle Procopio was one of the watchtower guards and he insisted that he liked them, said they were polite men. After tolerating their presence for two long years, all hell had broken out when everyone in Santa Fe learned what the Japs were doing to the boys from New Mexico. After the explosion, things simmered down and now there was just a sullen détente between the town and the Japanese internees.

The truth finally came to light when three American POWs had escaped from Cabanatuan Prison Camp in the Philippines and made it to Australia to seek out MacArthur. They gave firsthand accounts how the Japanese were sadistically torturing our POWs after they had been surrendered in April 1942 on Corregidor. By their accounts, the prisoners had been taken in groups of 500 and forced on the Death March. They detailed how even more died of starvation, disease and vicious killings from the sadistic overseers. MacArthur and his top brass decided that demoralizing information of this nature should not be let out.

But a story this violent could not be stifled and, in spite of the national wish for secrecy, the world press printed their testimonies word for word. The news took fire overnight. And the town of Santa Fe, her sons in inhumane captivity, turned vicious and stormed the camp, demanding bloody retribution and fomenting to tear the older Japanese internees limb from limb because they were Japanese. Reason enough. An eye-for-an-eye, the time-tested concept.

They screamed that their men had been shanghaied into the war. That their sons, mere boys who were in the National Guard had all been taken away, moved to Texas, renamed the 200th Army Artillery and then sent to the Philippines with out-of-date ammunition. Now, the Japanese must be forced to pay with their own lives.

This news fanned the New Mexican families' despair and hatred for the Japanese making it well and good that the FBI had seized these enemy aliens and imprisoned them. As the loathing exploded, the internees asked for more barricades. In Santa Fe, the 2,100 elderly Japanese men cringed to see thousands of enraged New Mexicans carrying guns, axes, and stones outside their barbed wire fencing.

"Just go home," the Camp Commander said, addressing the screaming throng. "If you harm these prisoners here, the Japanese will show no mercy and enact greater reprisals on your own POWs."

What greater horrors existed? As if the Nips had not already done their merciless worst—water torture in which they shoved a hose in a prisoner's mouth, or up his ass and bloated him like a balloon before they stomped him to death, smashing hands with hammers, and systematically starving men to death.

"Send these bastards back! Get our boys home now!" LaBelle lead the chanting.

When the mob was forced to disperse, an uneasy standoff between the camp and town was jimmied into place. Hatred infused the heavy air like smoke and LaBelle no longer concentrated on railing against MacArthur. Here in Santa Fe, she could look directly at the enemy, aching to scratch their eyes out with her long nails and Procopio, Nicasia's uncle who worked at the camp, refused to work as a guard until the town settled down.

LaBelle, both comfort and plague, had saved Melo's three postcards from 1941 and 1942, saying that they were waiting for reinforcements and supplies. They were out of food, he had written, and they were told to hold out with rusted ammo left over from the 1914-1918 war. Months after the attack on Clark Field they held out waiting for the promised reinforcements that never arrived.

Then, surrender and silence.

Some called it a slaughter, pitting improperly armed boys against an overwhelming number of men pledged to die for their emperor. MacArthur couldn't get away from the mess fast enough. On April 9, 1942, the Allies surrendered 320,000 Filipino and American soldiers to the Japanese.

The three escapees stated unequivocally that the Japanese expected that each surrendering soldier would require only a trench burial and that MacArthur was in Australia suppressing publication of the abuses suffered by the Allied POWs.

"They're yellow-bellied Japs, so send 'em back!" LaBelle rallied wildly against the "enemy aliens" residing in Santa Fe and against the fathers and cousins of these men here who had bayoneted our boys when they passed out from dehydration and the shits.

"Hey, hold up!" Nicasia's Uncle Procopio had a great respect for the gentle men behind the wired fences. "These men are not our enemy."

"You know what their people do to our guys?" she demanded, slapping his shoulder. She knew now and they all knew that the Japanese shot entire groups of prisoners, New Mexican sons and lovers, ten at a time. Always groups of ten. If just one member of a ten buckled from brutalities, the Japanese beheaded the others with him. Beheaded them slowly in a practice they called "meat cuts."

"Not these sad sacks," Procopio said. "Stop calling them *yellow-bellied Japs.*"

"Okay," she said, sneering. "Have it your way, I'll remember to call them *crumbum* Gooks, then."

"They have rights," Procopio said. "Some of them have sons fighting in Europe for us."

"Cut me some slack," she said. Showing her exasperation with the sixty-year old man.

Procopio from his vantage sitting in the guard tower at the gate of the internment camp and was made very aware of the internees' rights. By the Geneva Convention, each prisoner was to be given adequate living space, and served three meals a day weighing over 5.298 lbs. Add to that two hours of visitation a week and immediate medical attention.

If they worked, they had to be paid.

"Is it a goddamned hotel in there?" she shrieked at Procopio, so he shut up and refused to tell her that the skinny small men had painted the Rising Sun on the backs of their undershirts and made illegal *saké* for the Emperor's birthday. Or that they were within their rights to demand a visit from the war-neutral Spanish Embassy each time something was not well managed.

"And you of all people must have heard just what that prissy Spaniard demanded?" LaBelle challenged.

"Hey, LaBelle, get a hold of yourself. There are bunches of things that needed fixing," he told her, hating the fights she always started.

"To hell with them in that country club." LaBelle begrudged them their vermin five-hole golf course. Who cared if the entire Jap Trap grew fidgety with "barbed wire fever?" What about the twenty-acre vegetable garden—not to mention that chicken house?

They sold their vegetables and eggs to the Cash and Carry Grocery in exchange for beer and then they traded stuff to Bruns Hospital for fish. The FBI arrested one Japanese businessman in Bolivia who said he'd never missed a meal since he and sixty other Bolivian/Japanese were seized and handcuffed in La Paz. They were allowed to take one suitcase each as they were driven ("dragged," they reported) from their homes to the plane, onto the ship, to the train and given meals in Fred Harvey's Alvarado Hotel, then trucked up here to Santa Fe, not missing one goddammed meal. Three squares a day!

Both LaBelle and Anissa would starve before they'd eat their enemy-tainted beets.

Nicasia's Uncle Procopio got along especially well with the Bolivian-Japanese; they spoke Spanish, slipped him supplies and gave him golf lessons. But LaBelle turned a deaf ear to him and honed her two-inch nails.

Grieving for her son and her husband left Nicasia too weak and empty for hatred so she left all that for LaBelle and Anissa to heft, often wishing they were quieter about their feelings.

"Uncle Sam gives them everything they want." Anissa railed.

"The Japanese must pay for their treachery," LaBelle had said, pacing Nicasia's house, breaking crockery. Nothing was too terrible for the slant-eyed scum who held Melo in chains. His last postcard came seventeen months after the one before and it repeated that he hoped to marry LaBelle when he got home and that they were waiting for the food promised by MacArthur and his yes-man, Wainwright.

This disgusting news of the Death March flushed LaBelle and the rest of her God-fearing community away from any possibility of prayerfully accepting The Will of God, much less brotherly love. Now, together with LaBelle, all the citizens of Santa Fe found it intolerable to live in a town, ten percent of which housed a camp of subhuman aliens staring you in the face, drinking your beer, eating meat and requesting fresh fish. Two thousand of the 20,000 people lived under the rules of the Geneva Convention having to be paid and not be forced to work. They ate royal amounts of food, bought cigarettes, and sucking on rice candy, sat back reading Oriental scribble books while Santa Fe's boys starved and worked as forced labor for the enemy aliens' Emperor in the jungle without medicine, clothes or tools.

Not all the news had been blacked out. The news of the 200th surrender had been revealed within days after the fall of the Philippines. Everyone read that MacArthur had left. They learned too that he was awarded the Congressional Medal of Honor.

As soon as she read the accounts, LaBelle, Melo's *novia*, had packed herself up and ridden the train from Trinidad on the Colorado border to wait out the war with Nicasia, her mother-in-law-to-be. But the death lists were slow to come and it was months before Nicasia had been informed that she'd lost her first son, Franque. Nothing official confirming the loss of her husband had been received to date but in her heart, Nicasia knew…

She had not yet heard about the Death March and its repulsive circumstances. It was kept under wraps.

That night with her bag of flour, Anissa was even more enraged over Jap Trap as she entered the quiet, dark house and put the sizeable sack on a chair. Carrying forty pounds was easier than steering the "Deuce n' Half."

Nicasia put her finger to her lips, "Don't wake LaBelle."

"It's unforgivable that we have to deal on the Black Market to get what is hand-delivered to them. My God, look at me! I even drove that truck miles and miles with stuff for those Nips." Anissa pounded her chest like a sinner.

"I quit! I'm never doing another Red Cross run," she said. "I feel like a sympathizer." She studied her long-suffering neighbor. Nicasia made an effort to practice acceptance, a virtue Anissa rejected as ineffective and possibly immoral. LaBelle, if she were awake, would roll up her sleeves and side with Anissa, pushing the heat up to boiling.

"I fell asleep," Nicasia said. "I was waiting for you." She turned on another light in the kitchen and without making any sound she went to her small shrine in the corner and re-lit a votive candle.

In the *nicho* hollowed into the adobe wall near the darkened fireplace, framed hand-tinted photographs of men were illuminated by wavering votive candles; Melo's picture was the most prominent. He wore his artillery uniform and his hat sat loosely on his close-shaven head. Anissa was aware that Nicasia's love for this, her last son, was so fierce that she'd sacrifice anything for him. But she'd have to fend off LaBelle if she ever attempted to get close to her son at this point in time.

LaBelle's loudness also stood between Nicasia and the greater world outside her doorstep. She took up a lot of space. How Melo had fallen for her was a mystery. Opposites attract.

"Don't wake up LaBelle," Nicasia said again and sat down.

"Believe me, I wouldn't think of it," Anissa whispered.

"I got an envelope today," Nicasia said quietly. "It was addressed to Faustino Garcia, Santa Fe, New Mexico." She pulled a dog tag out of her nightgown and Anissa took it and held it to the light. The tag was made of steel and read, "Faustino Garcia, PVT First Class," with his serial number and Blood type O. By physically holding the tags, Nicasia's last hope that there had been an error in lists of the dead died. Without the tags, she held a splinter of hope that there was more than one Faustino Garcia; that it was the other who had been tortured and beaten, dead from unspeakable pain. In her heart, she felt the truth but privately she fanned the tiny flame that her husband, the real Faustino Garcia, lived hidden in the jungles, helped and fed by friendly natives.

"There was no message, just this." She took back the tag.

Anissa went to the depleted fifty-year-old and wrapped her throbbing arms around her. "I am so sorry, so very sorry." The old woman sobbed, shuddering with grief. Since the bombing at Clark Field, her dark eyes had lost their fire. She knew her losses would be early ones.

"Have you shown LaBelle these tags?" Anissa felt that LaBelle should return to her family in Colorado and foment against the Japanese from there. Her loud protests made the war even more unendurable when Nicasia needed quiet now for her grief.

Nicasia shook her head slowly.

"You could tell her you need to be alone."

"Can you drive us to Chimayo tomorrow?" Nicasia asked. The Santuario in Chimayo represented prayer itself and it was a place for the lame to leave their crutches, for the blind to see their first light. It was a holy place where the Blessed Virgin traded penances for prisoners' lives; a place with a deep pit in the floor where pilgrims dug the healing dirt with their fingernails and walked away, rejoicing over answered prayers. Nicasia understood that pilgrimages were one step towards saving the life of Melo, or lightening his sufferings.

Anissa scorned the Santuario twenty-five miles north of town. It only guzzled three gallons of gas *id y vuelta*; but gas was not Anissa's real concern compared to the empty myth of the place. Chimayo was nothing more than stories and legends. Anissa felt that the Heavenly Catholic Bureaucracy was entirely too meek, that it had no grit.

"LaBelle will want to come too," Nicasia said quietly.

Anissa was only half listening. Weakened by the solidity of Nicasia's enormous grief, she realized refusing to go to the shrine was heartless. She knew that The I AM Presence of the Archangel Michael and his Legions of Power and Protection were the ones with the power to soothe Nicasia. That the pilgrimage to this weedy shrine was feeble.

The Christians were hopeless saps, hadn't she said it? Their God was clearly ineffective; He could not distinguish between the German Catholics, the Irish Catholics, the New Mexican-Catholic-since-the-Inquisition Catholics and the Italian Catholics. Look what he did to the French Catholics. It was a religious outrage. It was the SAME GOD for everyone on each side of the Maginot Line.

"Yes, of course, we'll go whenever you want," Anissa said wearily. "And with LaBelle, if absolutely necessary."

The last time she had agreed to take them, LaBelle refused to kneel quietly and unobtrusively. She had stood instead, and in a loud voice demanded immediate results from God. Well before this excursion, LaBelle had taken Anissa on fist-to-fist regarding her I AM beliefs, sneering at them. When and if they crossed paths on the Plaza, she was openly hostile to Anissa's proselytizing, now face-to-face with her own God, she was unabashed and borrowed some of the I AM methods, mixing her orders to

God with veiled threats of purple swords and fiery wrath. And LaBelle had every evidence that her bullying worked because she heard "voices" telling her that Melo still loved her and that he was alive. So she stomped her feet and waved her arms in triumph as though she had her own Purple Sword.

Anissa found her irritating and offensive. Still, she agreed to drive the two in the face of their God's languid silence. She maintained that understanding His Will took guesswork.

"If you really need to bring her," Anissa repeated, walking out, shaking her head.

As she dragged herself next door in the cool mountain dark, she realized how much LaBelle's turbulence disturbed her which led to how LaBelle mirrored the chaos of war, and last, she admitted to herself the truth of her own loneliness. She suspected that Nicasia needed LaBelle's presence just to buffer the hollow sound of an empty house. It was a high price to pay. She hoped that at the end of the war she might have a private word with Melo about the seriousness of marriage, and of choosing carefully. And she hoped he'd thank her for her neighborly concern.

The three postcards had been the only sign of his survival. The rest was rumor, confusion, speculation and nightmares. If a card ever came through the Red Cross, it was full of lies, but it came as a tangible sign that there had been life at the point of origination. Melo sent none after the surrender. Now there were Faustino's dog tags in an envelope. What the hell did MacArthur think? That they'd never find out anything? Was MacArthur burning their letters to heat his headquarters in Australia?

LaBelle had been around town before the war but after the surrender, she turned dead serious and assigned herself to Nicasia, never having been invited.

She was still on deck almost four years later when the Red Cross alleged that thousands of POWs were being sent to Japan as slave labor. Then devastating eye-witness accounts came forward reporting how a US Navy Submarine had torpedoed the Death Ship, *Arisan Maru*. Seven

POWs had managed to escape having watched the Japanese lock the hatches over 1,800 American POWs. They were horrified to witness the Japanese row themselves off to safety in near empty lifeboats as the ship drowning the POWs sank.

Compared to the Hell Ships, the seven men reported that the Death March was a day at the beach. The prisoners on the *Arisan Maru*, and on any of the several death ships, died daily, packed into airless, stifling holds of rusty listing ships, standing shoulder to shoulder, awash in rocking tides of shit and vomit, victims of the enemy, now targeted by their own Navy.

But it was the eyewitness report of the inhumane and senseless drowning of the 1,800 that turned the stomachs of the world.

The New Mexican printed the testimonials of the seven who had escaped, word for word.

If it could be called prayer, LaBelle now ordered God to get Roosevelt cracking. She prayed that the American Flyboys spare whatever ship carried Melo to Japan, giving him a fighting chance for life. She hoped that that the submarines would leave him alone too. And she joined the Bataan Relief Organization, sending letters to Washington.

Then marching around the Plaza, a tray in hand, she offered a free tamale to anyone who purchased war bonds, while she ranted on and on about injustice and brutality. She was hell on wheels. And she was loud.

"Must she to come to Chimayo?" Anissa asked.

On the Plaza late the following morning, Anissa was dressed in gleaming white as she passed out her I AM pamphlets to a huddle of serious-looking women standing on the corner wearing dark city clothes. Older men wearing clothes too funereal for a shimmering Santa Fe March day waited close by for their transportation to arrive and bear them off in cars with shaded windows. Anissa locked eyes with an amiable but weary lady and extending her hand, she wove towards her wearing a confident smile.

"Excuse me, Madam. I'm Anissa Barclay with some welcome news about the war-to-be-swiftly-ended." This caused an abrupt end to whatever concern the four ladies had been discussing.

"I'm Nannette," she said, pressing Anissa's hand in a courteous way peering back through rimless glasses. She smiled hesitantly while her three travel companions turned to listen.

"My news is that God Victorious will soon end this war. The signs have come."

"How fascinating," Nannette said with a soft Germanic accent, hopefully Austrian.

"Here," Anissa said, handing out the pamphlets that featured a blazing sword held by purple-robed Saint Germain, his head haloed, his face sweet. "You can read here about the Empowering Sacred Fire that will bring peace to the physical plane of earth through the Breath of our Mother/Father-God and Archangels." Anissa held the gaze of Nanette's tired eyes.

"When?" Nanette asked. "How?"

"Soon. By fire," Anissa said. "An All-Encompassing Sacred Fire which will lift you from this three-dimensional world into the Fourth Dimension." All four ladies turned to face her. Not only did she have their complete attention, but they seemed interested in her science.

Anissa indicated that they could follow her and as they turned to do so, a professorial man came up to them and said, "It's late," while pulling off his Burberry raincoat.

"We're waiting for transportation to take us to our destination," he added as a courtesy.

He too joined them in following her past the tethered burro across the narrow street to take a seat on one of the four benches under the elms facing the corner where their designated transportation was expected. Their interest gave Anissa a boost and she was more eloquent than ever as she delivered her speech about the I Am belief in God Victoriously Accomplished.

"Just repeat the word, *Vanquished*, and it is made manifest." Her eyes gleamed.

"You believe that God is actually listening?" Nanette asked.

"There is a Sacred Unity of Everything." When Anissa chanted, it sounded like a mantra, a prayer.

"Unity?" Burberry said. "Fusion."

Anissa reported, "Everything will seem coincidental."

Five people watched her closely, nodding.

"Last night, for instance, I happened to be at the station in Albuquerque and I had been overcome with the memories of my antique Churchill shotgun, a gift from my father. It was there! Being brought to me by a man I've never seen before in my life. Never met."

"You are sure it was yours?" Nanette asked, losing interest.

"There is only one. Mine. Once the idea of the holster and the shotgun was in my Heart Flame, the thing itself appeared. You would probably call this coincidence."

"So he handed it over to you?" Nanette said, looking away.

"He will," she said. "He will bring it straight to me."

The European lady thanked her and turned to move off.

Anissa caught up with her, saying, "I am trying to describe how one's thoughts become manifested in reality. How the All-Encompassing Sacred Fire will end the war."

"Here it is! Here it is, finally!" A man ran across the street to pull the group together. "You might say I made them come just by thinking of them?"

Yes, she nodded. "Exactly."

Three matching gray Fords were lined up on the corner opposite La Fonda Hotel, where the fleet of cars regularly appeared, picking up passengers wearing formal city clothes. Passengers who were not told of their destination, never given maps. Perhaps they were simply told to arrive dressed for work.

Even the newspaper had blacked out the name of the place that attracted such an unlikely stream of folk. Whatever happened—accidents, multiple births—happened in a place with no name, simply somewhere north of Santa Fe. More arrivals pushed in, coming in larger and larger groups all headed north to the place without a name.

But Anissa knew. She had been informed directly by Dr. Oppenheimer, the dashing Mad Scientist, where it was and what they did. Knowing made her feel powerful and she wished to tell these people what she knew about them and what they were to accomplish. But Oppenheimer, the genius behind it all, asked that she not. He preferred to tell them himself.

Nanette beckoned to her. "I'm so pleased that someone has faith that this war will end."

"Have a pleasant ride." Anissa waved to them. She couldn't reveal that she, who had eschewed meat, sex and alcohol in the name of The I AM Presence, had not only been offered but had accepted a martini from the devastatingly charming Oppenheimer at John Levert's dude ranch. Or that the suave Dr. Oppenheimer had brooked National Security to tell her about his secret mission. Or that almost everyone in Santa Fe County had figured out they were headed for the deeply rutted road leading to the high mesa and the Los Alamos Ranch School.

She understood that once there they'd be working on the astonishing secret contraption and drinking martinis with Kitty Oppenheimer and her popular husband. And that she too was justified in tippling a martini or two in support of the war's end.

In parting, she reminded Nanette, "Remember that the Divine Will of The I AM Presence will manifest anything you conceive of. Just ask for it."

"I'd like to be able to go straight back to my grandchildren in New Jersey," Nanette laughed, gazing at Anissa's face as though fondly reminded of her own daughter.

Anissa pictured Nanette's white clapboard house surrounded by mock orange near Princeton.

"I'll be here when you come back to town. Hurry back." She waved to the three cars pulling away from the curb, sorry that Oppenheimer seemed to be stalling, unable to simply get on with the business. But the handsome scientist guaranteed that his invention would end the War in the Pacific. He said it was huge and big things take time.

"Your secret is safe with me," she told him quietly, sucking on the olive from her empty glass. Dr. Oppenheimer was an extremely attractive man, tall—taller than even she. And he had a gleam in his eyes for the ladies. Remembering this conversation, she smiled as she watched the cars pull away. That last martini had been particularly intense.

A clock near the hotel said noon; so reluctantly, Anissa turned slowly to walk home where Nicasia was waiting. She was in a state of elation having found an entire group of educated people extremely receptive to the Transformational Power of the Divine Flame, and not the usual crowd of immovable dunces who used the Plaza as their personal entertainment space. Only the realization that she was soon to face LaBelle for the drive to Chimayo knocked her from her pleasant cloud.

The Santuario at Chimayo was an impoverished small-town Lourdes minus the freezing streams of pure spring water. A dry desert shrine, the best it could offer was the earth that healed, the sacred dirt. And that grainy, sandy earth resided in a small chapel off the main altar of the church. A large inventory of crutches, baby shoes and silver *milagros* hinted of the power of the dirt.

Could the dirt bring Melo home? she mused, walking up the hill to Nicasia's small house.

But someone, probably meaning well, had mailed Nicasia her husband's dog tags—so not even Mother Mary could bring him back. He'd been killed, and no sprinkling of the consecrated earth could reverse this fact. The Japanese had created disastrous situations, but they so far had not stolen the prisoners' tags. However, none of it made any difference because Anissa knew that this coming visit was more perfunctory for the Roman Catholics than effective. Nothing more than show, she determined that if it really "worked," Nicasia and the other widows and mothers would have bodily stationed themselves inside the church, refusing to leave.

She did not want to make the requisite sign of the cross over her heart and on her forehead with the sacred dirt, the dull dry dirt of the

Santuario. Certainly after the life-transforming Power of the Sword of Saint Germain, miserable dirt, even if it was Healing Dirt was paltry. But for Nicasia, she'd have stayed on the Plaza. But for Nicasia, she'd refuse to drive LaBelle.

"I've always known in my heart that he was dead, I knew there was only one Faustino Garcia. My heart knew he was dead last year, even if the telegram with the black stars on it never came." Nicasia said, seated on a folding chair under the one dried-out tree in her front yard where she had been waiting. LaBelle was nowhere to be seen.

"I'm so sorry." Anissa deeply meant what she had said. "Who mailed them?"

"No one. They just appeared."

"Are you ready?"

"LaBelle is doing her hair. She'll come soon. You have the gas?" Nicasia asked. Anissa nodded. "Five gallons."

When LaBelle finally thundered across the yard, they loaded her into the back of the two-door Ford and pulled onto the dirt road.

"How are you, LaBelle?" Anissa said.

"So-so," LaBelle said when she settled down. As always, she was only focused on Melo and her manicure. Her visit to Chimayo was only to aim arrow-like requests for her *novio* at God. It never occurred to her to add names of the other POWs. She never muddied the waters, never threw a fake punch.

Anissa started the car and ignored LaBelle, driving north without conversation.

They were no more than ten miles out of town when Anissa saw the three identical cars, empty and pulled over to the side of the road. It was all very poorly managed, this secretive conduct.

"See that?" Anissa said.

Nicasia nodded.

LaBelle said, "Them?" Groups of people stood about, smoking and stretching their legs.

"Yes,"

"Every day across the Plaza from Woolworth's, I seen 'em. You think they care about the war? Never one tamale." The faint rasping of a nail file was heard from the back seat.

"I know what they're doing," Anissa said. "You remember the road we passed a few miles back, the San Juan Ranch?"

"Mister Levert's ranch," Nicasia said and she looked into the back seat to see if LaBelle knew what they were talking about. She did not look up, so apparently she was not interested to know about the famous dude ranch that attracted people from all over. Or about how Procopio had made himself useful by delivering vegetables and eggs there from Jap Trap.

"Where?" LaBelle's nails were being honed for close combat.

"Back there," Nicasia said. Even though the ranch was stable-proud, known for fine horses and long sunrise trails, it was the lively bar that attracted most people. The martinis. Once there, Anissa had bent her rules and would have leapt again if the great doctor had beckoned.

"Never heard of it," LaBelle said.

Anissa shot her a glance and continued. "Oppie, the scientist, he goes to the ranch all the time. He said they have a huge military facility where the boys' school used to be and they're manufacturing submarines. Top Secret. He told me himself."

"How do you know all of this? Procopio never told me nothing," LaBelle said.

"I know Oppenheimer. He comes to the big Gringo Fourth of July party. We eat hot dogs. The things they used to call wieners. Oppie's always there."

"Roosevelt is stupid," LaBelle said. "They should make submarines near water."

"Can't. They still have that black-out zone along both coasts. Pearl Harbor can happen again. Why do you think they built the Al-Can Highway?"

"Your crazy scientist said so?"

"He did."

"*No me importa*, I don't care," broke in Nicasia who had been lost in her own thoughts. "There's nothing they can do to help anybody. My Faustino is gone, my son Franque. It's too late for submarines."

All of a sudden LaBelle leaned forward from the back and placed a gentle hand on Nicasia's shoulder, allaying small parts of her misery. "There, there," she said in a soft voice.

Anissa turned to peer at LaBelle and the car veered. She pulled back into the center of the road and continued to drive north.

When they drove through the small, chile-growing village surrounded by mountains, they parked next to the Santuario and, entering the church, they genuflected before opening the gate in the altar railing. Rounding a corner, they ducked to negotiate the shortened doorway leading into the shrine with its sacred healing dirt. Everything was there as before, and *milagros* of legs, lungs, eyes, hearts and wombs covered the ceiling nailed in catacomb-like patterns. There were testimonials pinned everywhere—, the residue of miracles, tangible mementos to quietly answered prayers. Notes of gratitude for the mended bones of "worthless sinners" and typed words from walking "worms of the dust" who had survived polio. Empty shoes had been left by those whom the Lord had plucked.

Nicasia came there to pray as she smeared her tear-stained face with His grainy earth. She prayed aloud to her own Quiet God to reassure herself that He was not asleep. And in Melo's name she used His sacred dirt gratefully; the dirt that was His gift. Here, in His presence, she would never betray His Almightiness with Anissa's powerful God Victoriously Accomplished, the God who was about to destroy the enemy with Circles of White Lightning and Sacred Fire. In times of true grief, Nicasia came home to Jesus and his Virgin Mother while LaBelle paced, looking upwards with fierce eyes.

"Give him back!" LaBelle ordered, trying to rout God from the sack.

Anissa remained silent, watching. The Santuario was Nicasia's place, the ritual home of all Good Friday pilgrimages, begging each war-year for the safety of the POWs. She, with hundreds of faithful, walked through the freezing night abiding the cold just as their sons and husbands were enduring torture, dysentery, starvation and thirst—all those same sufferings that even Jesus had taken upon himself so that on Judgment Day, His Father God would open the Gates to the Garcia's Heaven first to Faustino and Franque. Then they would all lean down for Nicasia and Melo.

At dawn every Good Friday, Father Sembrillo, the aged parish priest at the Santuario, would raise the host, a sun against the pink clouds clearing in the East, and pronounce the words, "This is my body." And the assembled penitents replied, "Have mercy on us."

"I prayed for my men like I always pray at Good Friday," Nicasia said, back in the car. "Jesus answered me. He took Faustino to His Heart two years ago; He raised him from the Japanese sewer into His Golden Heaven up high beyond pain and suffering. That's when Faustino started coming to me in dreams. He told me he was finally at peace. And Franque is with him. They went together."

"I know." Anissa drove in a fog of sadness, sad for Nicasia and other true widows. Sad for the long drawn-out deaths of their men and the millions who mourned them.

"And Melo is still alive," LaBelle said. "I got the word."

"Let's hope so," Anissa said.

"They pounded nails into Faustino's head before he died." LaBelle added fuel to an already blazing fire. "But they ran a bayonet through Franque at the start."

"They are at peace," Nicasia said, unable to recall how she heard the story of what happened to Franque during the Death March. How he was left groaning in pain, lying in the line of march, while files of prisoners, goaded by bayonets, tried and failed to step clear of him. It seemed she had always known this story since the day her first son was born. Her bones knew the story.

Closer to town, Anissa broke the mood of deep sorrow and grief by mentioning the whore, Phyllis. "Russell's doxie is here."

"¿*La puta?*" Nicasia said. "The woman who stole your husband, Russell?" LaBelle seemed interested too; she'd heard all about it and was ready with her nails to shred the tramp's flesh.

Anissa's deep pleasure with how Russell's death had been staged by Saint Germain hoisted her mood and she added more details about Phyllis.

"She didn't take him away. She picked him up. There's a big difference."

"And? *Pues?*"

"She is hanging around here like a ghost. I know her spirit is getting closer. She wants something."

"What could a ghost want? More men?"

"No, she wants to return my gun."

"Let her try. *Ojalá que trata,*" said LaBelle with the stiletto sharp nails. "We'll get her first."

"I hear she only talks about herself, otherwise she's boring."

"So, we'll shut her up," LaBelle again.

"She's all yours," Anissa said. LaBelle was welcome to get a hammer lock on the chippie. "You may call the shotgun yours if you'll take it back to Colorado." Two birds with one stone.

8

Albuquerque, New Mexico

In the airless box of a room of the Kirtland BOQ in yet another officer's guest quarters, Phyllis found herself disgusted with both Roddy and Albuquerque. She wasn't even hungry for breakfast. Her goal was to win Anissa over by introducing herself as a worthy ally. She counted on its being quick and easy, considering that Anissa and her vulnerable cult appeared to be able to swallow almost anything. It should take no time at all.

But Anissa was sixty miles away in Santa Fe and at present, Roddy was still coated with sweat, positioned on top of her, ready to come. She would wait him out and then talk. Soon. Only a few more minutes. Seconds now. One thousand, two thousand…

She was anxious to revert to her original plan—California. Meanwhile, she considered what failing to confront Anissa meant, and she was left with an empty feeling of unfinished business and of being misunderstood. Since she was here, she would spend a day, return the shotgun and put it all to rest. She'd be glad she had.

Anissa, religious as she seemed to be, would apologize out of divine fairness and a sense of justice.

Roddy had finished and rolled off, gasping for breath with his eyes still closed.

"May we leave now?" she asked.

"I said you'd like Santa Fe," he told her, getting out of bed and heading to the shower. He gently reminded her how confusing she could be at times.

"Sometimes I don't even know what makes you tick."

She knew she was a chameleon, at once arrogantly demanding then the needy girl, and back again; sometimes she was thin-lipped, pursing her mouth, but when she was drinking Scotch she was daring with ready laughter. Of course, Roddy wanted to please her but his footing was shaky. He must have suspected he was not a satisfying lover.

"I never said you'd like it here in Albuquerque."

"Well, I don't," she said and reached for a Chesterfield, not bothering to pull the sheet to her breasts. He reached down to the night table and took a cigarette, lighting it for her. When the cherry on the tip was well set, he passed it to her between his first and second fingers. It was too late. She preferred lighting her own. But by the time she sat up, he was sucking, setting it.

"I absolutely hate it when you do that," she said. "It's soggy."

"Sorry Babe. Come on, get dressed. I'll requisition a driver to take us up. The road's been straightened. Used to be it took all day." The 23-turn switchback had been bulldozed, converted to a major two-lane highway, blacktopped now for important military defense use. But why? She had asked. It led from a sandpit, which was Albuquerque, to the end of godforsaken nowhere.

"So?" She concentrated on smoking. Not on getting up. "It's getting hot."

"You're lucky it's not real summer yet. It'll be more comfortable up there, you'll like it." He pulled on his khaki pants, buttoning the fly all the while watching her as she drifted in and out of focus, like the tides, once in—eight hours later she was out.

"Last night, you said you wanted to return the shotgun, and to talk to the director of the cemetery." He tried to keep his voice even and slow.

"Yes, no," she said. "I should have sent the gun up to Santa Fe with the Red Cross volunteer. I don't know why I didn't just put the gun on that truck with an address. How many people live there anyway?" Phyllis supposed it could not have been more than in West Palm Beach, a handful of people with their houseguests. Ask anyone and they would very likely know Anissa Barclay. Why hadn't she thought of it?

"Sure, but you couldn't have just asked a Red Cross volunteer to take your late husband's ashes and bury them, could you?"

The box sat squarely on the dresser, accusing her of neglect.

"Why not?" She closed her eyes and took a deep pull on the cigarette, then removed a fleck of tobacco from her front tooth with her tongue. "I think perhaps I'll just take him with me to Santa Barbara." She knew the package held no ashes. She could say that someone had sucked out Russell's ashes, like blowing out an eggshell. She hardly cared: it was all a prop, the costume of a courier. And, it amounted to a pre-paid ticket to the coast.

Was she drunk when she agreed to get off the train with Roddy?

And the gun was part of the stage gear too; it was her letter of introduction to a retraction from the Imperial Self-Righteousness: Anissa.

"Yeah, sure the chances are good that people know her," Roddy said, bringing her mind back to the topic at hand. "Probably find her at the La Fonda Bar, having a drink."

"Anissa doesn't drink." Phyllis was certainly not interested in introducing them. Anissa was hers alone.

Why even involve this man in her life when the romance was doomed; the sooner Roddy flew off, the better. She needed a man who could stand up to her. Roddy was just a flyboy from the dunes; she deserved a prince. Either the prince or his three uncles with the gold, frankincense and myrrh. Not Roddy for godssake.

"Then she's the only Anglo woman not at the La Fonda Bar. We can ask the telephone operator—maybe she has a phone," he said and she sensed he was pushing her—impelling her to do things his way.

"She does have a phone." Phyllis felt that she knew everything about Anissa. She'd made a study of her by eavesdropping and perusing the photo albums. Even though Russell never loved her, the Rules of Love dictate that there had to have been something appealing about Anissa in the beginning.

"Operators know everything."

"I only wish she drank," Phyllis said, putting her feet squarely on the floor, beginning to pull herself out of the sheets.

"If we could have a drink girl-to-girl, and smoke, we could be friends." She stood up, her red hair matted; her body musky with Roddy's sweat.

"I know what you mean," he said and moved to kiss her on the shoulder. "I know just what you mean." There was a certain protocol to smoking and drinking; it made strangers into friends and then into lovers, *Just one more*. It was drinking and smoking that made them equal. In the end, he insisted, it gained women the vote.

Standing, Phyllis took a deep drag and put the cigarette out in the ashtray next to the sealed package on the bureau before she went into the bathroom to shower. When she emerged, wrapped in small white towels and smelling of Ivory soap, she smiled sweetly but looked away and took another cigarette.

"I'll buy you another carton," he told her. "Base commissary's around the corner."

"Lovely," she said, still not looking at him. She was reveling in how the very act of holding Anissa's shotgun gave her power over her rival. She moved to pick it up, holding it like a baby to her hunter's chest.

"Are you okay?" he asked. "You've changed your mind about taking your husband's ashes to the National Cemetery there?"

He had redirected her thoughts, causing her to picture herself holding the box at the cemetery, standing over an open grave, the color guard bugle wailing, everything dressed with American Flags. The final trumpet mourning *Taps* sets the mood of resolution, as the beautiful widow raises the container over her head pouring a stream of pebbles and wine corks into the hole. What would she say?

What would Roddy say?

"Oh my," everyone would say. "Oh my!"

Roddy would believe anything she chose to tell him. They would be human remains if she had said they were. Half of the Western world believed in Transubstantiation—ordinary thing to lofty being. The other half of the world believed in matter going the other way. Man to slug.

"I wish I knew what you're thinking," he said. "Are we taking the box, or not?"

"Not this time," she answered. The next hurdle was the gun. And avoiding Anissa who would certainly reveal that Russell had not died in Sicily. (Or had she said Africa?) She had been drinking too much lately. She was forgetting things.

He came up to her and kissed her neck. "I know it's hard," he said. "Please tell me what you want to do."

"Thanks," she said, still concentrating on Anissa. What she knew was that Anissa yelled (blasting Russell with accusations on the phone) and that she was certainly quick with insults (she called Phyllis a whore-doxie) and must be given the chance to apologize, to take it all back. Anissa needed to show her finer self. Phyllis determined that Anissa in her heart-of-hearts yearned to be a fine person, that she wanted a high place in that hierarchy of Saints she doted on.

Instead, she said. "I think I'll dry my hair in the sun."

"Of course," he said, dressed now in his khaki uniform, his shoes tied, ready to leave. "I'll go down to get those cigarettes while you dress."

"You are a sweet man," she said. As she pulled on her wrinkled clothes she suddenly knew how things needed to be. Roddy should stay behind; she should take the Jeep alone.

When he returned, she was seated again on the bed. Her plan was useless; she'd have to scrap it for another day.

"Roddy darling, could we just take a small tour of the countryside and I'll take in Santa Fe when you're on duty?"

"No need, I've asked for more leave," he said. "To be with you." He smiled as he tossed the carton of Chesterfields onto the bed next to her. This, at least, pleased her. She reached for the box, ripped off one end and opened a new pack.

"How about some coffee and donuts?" he said.

"Let's get the lay of the land first. I need to buy something to wear.

What do people wear in this dreadful place?"

They took the shotgun but left the "CLASSIFIED" package on the dresser walking out into the astounding sunlight to find the waiting Jeep. She squinted, adjusting her eyes to the light, nodding toward the Jeep. In her mind was one priority—she needed warrior's garb for the shotgun ceremonial; she had to be superbly dressed. Photos were in order,

"Let's find the finest dress shop in this godforsaken place," she said, breathing out smoke, walking quickly as though she could escape over the horizon and be done with the gritty treeless place.

They approached the driver who sat in the open Jeep reading the *Stars and Stripes*, engine off. When he looked up to see them a few feet off he threw down the newspaper and bolted out of his seat, saluting.

"At ease, Private," Roddy said, returning the crisp salute. "The lady and I have R and R in Santa Fe."

"At your service, Sir."

"Take the day off," Roddy said, hopping into the driver's seat. He jiggled the worn silvery ignition button as the driver helped Phyllis into the open vehicle. The windscreen was up, but the Jeep was open to the sun and a breeze ruffled Phyllis' still-damp hair as they sped off for their first order of business. Battle dress.

In a dress shop on Central Avenue, he insisted on buying her a turquoise broomstick skirt trimmed in silver rickrack and a blouse to go with it. "It's what everyone wears here."

"Are you sure this is how people dress?" she asked, staring in disbelief. The outfit managed to accentuate her breasts and it was too hot to wear something tailored, even the slacks and silk shirt from the PX would be soaked in sweat by the time they arrived in the promised land. She grimaced at herself in the mirror while the sales lady stood behind clucking.

"You'll just love it. You wash the skirt and then tie it to dry with lots of string on a broomstick," the clerk offered proudly. Phyllis stared at the ghastly clothes. At least she could pull the blouse low off her shoulder.

"Now you need a *concho* belt," Roddy told her.

"I have my own money," she said, reluctantly selecting a Navajo silver belt with large stones. So dressed, they climbed back into the Jeep and gunned off under the blazing sun.

"I don't think you'll like Anissa," she told Roddy as they sped across the flat landscape. "She's a stick in the mud, no fun."

"Tell me your connection again?"

"It's her gun. Russell asked me to get it to her just before he was shipped out. It was the last thing I promised him before he died in combat."

"That's wonderful of you." Again, he stressed how he hoped to have someone like her to honor his own memory; she accepted his compliments with a nod.

"Here," he said, handing her some zinc ointment. "This sun will fry you." When she smeared it on her face, it stuck to her skin like a bandage.

"How long is this drive?"

"No more than three hours," he said, hoping the trip would give them time to talk and time for her to make herself more clear. Sharing cigarettes made it cozier, but a radio in the Jeep might have made the silence less heavy. The drive promised to be tedious, given her mood.

"Did you bring water?" she had asked. The only conversation.

"The canteen is in the back."

Hours dragged until they came to a rise and the distant snow-capped mountains appeared deceptively close. Before the 10,000-foot peaks lay nothing but a stretch of vast flat brown prickery dirt.

"Miles and miles of oblivion," she said, reaching back, lapsing into another interval of brooding, neither listening nor speaking.

"Penny for your thoughts," he had said, dismayed at her rudeness, her refusal to pay attention to him.

"You won't fancy Anissa," she replied.

He'd heard her the first time. "She disapproves of drinking, smoking and sex. She's a member of an impossible religious group called the I AMers."

Phyllis had been considering how to approach Anissa. She should have phoned first.

Finally when the Jeep crested the 700-foot rise at La Bajada the distant town was revealed—so many clay lumps tumbled at the foot of the Sangre de Cristo Mountains. Roddy had been correct. This town looked interesting, a secret place. Off the beaten track. In its own way, it was camouflaged. A hidden place.

Once they pulled into town, Phyllis brightened. It was cooler and the town had an older charm, all one-story small-scale adobe cottages. By the time they'd wound through small streets and arrived at the Plaza more and more people appeared. There the buildings were two-story, the hotel on the corner of the square-block park had three and at the end of a central street sat the cathedral. Groups of people dressed in Western get-up were milling on the sidewalks while the older women, dressed in black, seemed to keep their own company by holding each other's elbows.

One huddle of men struck her as being wholly out of place—five men, all around thirty years old, wearing three-piece suits and wingtip shoes. They observed her with interest from their shady corner across from La Fonda Hotel as Roddy parked the Jeep.

"They look like undertakers."

"Mormons is my bet." Roddy cut the engine and Phyllis ran her fingers through her hair and looked about hoping to make short order of her mission. She had been prepared to announce, I'm looking for a cold, self-righteous forbidding woman named Anissa Barclay hoping to bring the men in suits closer.

Close by and handing out free pamphlets, Roddy noticed a striking woman dressed in white. "She'll know."

Instinctively, Phyllis reached into the back of the Jeep and brought up the encased gun, holding it to her chest for protection and wary that the natives spoke no English. She might need sign language so she set her face in a pleasant smile. She was astonished when the pamphlet-bearing woman suddenly bolted across the potholes and ordered, "Put down that gun!"

The pack of suited men turned in interest. Every Western movie told Phyllis that these men, dressed as they were, did not belong there. Vultures in the hen house.

Phyllis flashed with resentment. "Don't you dare," she barked.

"Madam!" Suddenly, Anissa stopped where she stood. Before she continued how life and death were entirely in the hands of God Victorious and his Saints (not men and their whores), she glanced at her own monogram.

But Phyllis had recognized her immediately. Stepping out of the Jeep, she fully expected to be embraced.

"Phyllis," she said. She had traveled far; she should be welcomed. For chrissakes, Jesus always got a glass of water when he came through towns.

If Anissa was caught off guard, she did not show it except that she caught her breath before plunging in. Roddy moved to stand by Phyllis, his hand out expecting to be introduced.

"I called to tell you to keep the gun. My weapon is the Blazing Purple Sword of Saint Germain." Several passersby looked away wearily. Anissa was more predictable than the 300 advertized days of pure sunshine.

Phyllis stared at the strong, unflappable woman facing her, "You called me after I left on my bicycle?" She stressed that word, bicycle. She deserved a hero's reception. "That was over three weeks ago."

"You are a fool."

"Roddy, may I present Anissa."

The introduction did not interest her, so Anissa threw back her shoulders ready for her next volley.

"You could have mailed the damned shotgun. Keep it, yes, keep it. You are a whore. You are a slut."

Anissa had obviously prepared for this meeting, Phyllis had not.

"Predators like you need guns," Anissa said.

A crowd slowly gathered. Anything here was a public event—there had been good and bad blood on the Plaza since the early 1600s. Mountain men, trappers, Spanish soldiers, gamblers, miners, merchants, politicians, priests and railroad men—everyone hardy and adventurous had come onto the Plaza dragging some history behind them. What they said, whatever they did was quietly observed and became imbedded in the ever present memories of the nearby silent Indians wrapped in trade blankets whose minds were slates four centuries long; their daily gaze missed nothing. Stationed under the long portale on the Plaza, they listened, bent as they were over their handmade wares

They watched the white men because the white men required close scrutiny.

Phyllis, backed by Roddy, was surrounded by a loose odd-lot audience of more men than women, and the street opinion awarded Anissa the first win. After all, this was the Plaza where notices were affixed to the light poles, vendors sold tamales, Paco peddled firewood from the back of his burro, women visited on the benches, young men fought for dominance (or over a girl), and Anissa passed out pamphlets, while LaBelle got into hot political arguments pedaling her win-the-war tamales. Arguments flitted like flies.

And Anissa appeared to have the crowd on her side.

"I beg your pardon?" Phyllis hissed.

"You want forgiveness? God Victorious is the only one who can forgive."

There was that word again. Forgiveness? Phyllis, if she could be accused of any wrongdoing at all, had only given succor and human kindness to a sad man at the end of an alcoholic life, sad for having been married to a shrew like Anissa. Drinking himself to death had been the only liberation as Anissa doggedly refused him a divorce. She was cruel.

"Bitch!" Phyllis screamed, hurling the encased shotgun onto the sidewalk where it landed with a soft-buffered thud. The crowd took a step back.

"Mother Mary abhors you. She spits on you!" Anissa said, stepping over the gun, standing toe-to-toe with Phyllis, pushing her, forcing Phyllis back against the Jeep.

"You dirty coward, you frightful, rude, mean bitch!" Phyllis said, and then she slapped the older woman's face.

Anissa in true fighting form showed no surprise at all.

"You are a coward, a screaming bloody lizard!" Phyllis started to break down and swiftly, Roddy stepped in between the women and hauled Phyllis away, leading her, crying, by the arm across San Francisco Street into La Fonda.

"She asked for it. I had no choice," she blubbered, stumbling by people who tilted back to let her pass.

As soon as they were safely inside, they found themselves at the bar off the lobby. The room was half filled and immediately the waiter came up, already knowing what had taken place outside. He looked bookish, like a college professor, as his face was not weathered like the others she'd seen outside.

"I've been itching to do just that," he told Phyllis as he pulled out a chair for her. "They've been asking for it—intolerant and holier-than-thou—arrogant!" The conversational din subsided, people were curious about the upset woman and whispers passed with the finer points of the fracas.

Phyllis sniffed her gratitude and took the straight-backed chair at the round table. Roddy asked if they had any Scotch. "Sorry. It's the war. I have rum," the waiter said, pausing.

Something made him change his mind. "Hold on, let me see what I can do."

"Two, please. Make those doubles," Roddy said, looking at the man carefully when he returned with a half-filled bottle of Johnny Walker Black Label cloaked behind his back.

"Medicinal spirits," he said, winking at them. He appeared to be under thirty-five, right age for the service; so Roddy asked him about himself, where he was from, straining to hear his words over the clamor of an angry crowd pressing into the lobby, bellowing and stomping their boots. By this time the patrons in the lounge had resumed talking, raising their voices over the din.

"Born in Kansas—used to be a priest. Call me Jerry."

"Why are you here? What's so great about Santa Fe?" Phyllis asked, comfortable asking a priest to confess. "It looks poor."

"We don't need much," he said, pouring his light amber stash into their highball glasses. "Mountains, sunshine, good people, excellent climate. We've got all the local characters of any big town. What more could we need?"

As he spoke, the mounting echo of boots scuffling on the tile floors crowded in from the lobby, following Anissa still exuberantly speechifying, with the holstered shotgun in hand. The pack of people from the Plaza pushed in behind her. A second group of some ten or more dried up cowboys and muleskinners flanked LaBelle yelling, "*Puta, puta!*" They were halted by the clerk behind the main desk who came out, yelling even louder, "Quiet please!"

Phyllis looked over her shoulder in the direction of the disorderly pack and turned back to Jerry.

"What would I do here? What does anyone do?" Phyllis shouted.

"Hiking, fishing. I hear you have a shotgun."

"I fish. The gun's not mine. It belongs to Anissa Barclay. What an absolute bitch! I came all this way to bring it back to her." She asked, "Do you know her?"

The noise outside the bar grew strident. Jerry yelled his response. "It's a small town, we all know everybody."

"What happens if a new person moves in here?" She gazed up at the waiter assessing his celibacy. Why had he abandoned the priesthood?

"Always happy to have fresh blood. You'd be more than welcome."

"It's a pretty nonchalant place," Roddy offered. "The natives first served the Spanish soldiers a fine dinner in the sixteen-hundreds before being reduced to slavery by their guests."

His voice trailed off as Red-eyed Anissa stampeded into the bar aiming directly for their table, LaBelle and the mob trailing.

"Here's your gun. Get out of town." Anissa threw it on the floor missing Phyllis' foot. Jerry paid little mind to all of this, nodding at something unrelated.

"Who are these people?" Phyllis demanded.

"They're harmless," Jerry said. "Locals."

Roddy stood up, holding out his hands for peace. "Ladies, Anissa. Ladies," he bellowed. "Don't move, just everyone stay right where you are."

To retrieve the gun from the floor, he moved close to Anissa, bending down.

"It's yours," he said. "Please take it." Everyone watched, leaning into the argument—Jerry, the cowboys and muleskinners muttered under their breaths to each other. *Why won't she take it?*

"Keep the goddamned gun, you're the one who needs it," Anissa spat.

Which meant: "Get the hell out of town." More people crowded in, including a small, dark-haired policeman. He was young and unformed in the last of the leftover Pancho Villa pre-war outfits. Somehow he'd escaped the draft and was clearly a friend of the hotel. It did appear that the police officer and this ex-priest with a Black Market stash of Scotch had pull in these parts and neither had been drafted.

Phyllis smiled a weak victimized smile.

"Quiet!" the young police officer said, looking squarely at Anissa. He knew her temper and how she and that Edna Ballard had started several knock-down-drag-outs in public places and now he'd been summoned to throw cold water on teetotaling Anissa's first hot-blooded bar fight. He knew, they all knew, that the war had wrenched normal people to the edge of wrath. It replicated itself, stimulating fights. Men menaced each other in their vehicles, speeding on the dirt streets.

"Sit down, Ma'am!" he commanded Anissa. Another wooden chair materialized and Anissa was pushed down onto it and held by the shoulder.

LaBelle's face burned red. Even though LaBelle considered Anissa out-of-her tree *loca*, she moved in to defend her neighbor against the adulteress in very loud tones. For this, Anissa showed mild surprise.

"José, this *puta* took away Anissa's husband and got him so drunk every night that he rammed his car into a truck and killed everybody. She's *una arpía*."

"That's not what happened," Phyllis shouted back. "He was on a motorcycle, and so what if he was drunk?" But she could go no farther, and gazed up at the ex-priest for absolution asking him to champion her out of the present mess, put her in a better light.

Anissa slumped back in her chair, staring fixedly at Phyllis with pure disgust. José evinced no preferences as it was a clear stand-off between the two Gringa women, until LaBelle moved in to draw blood, accusing the redhead *puta* of sleeping with Anissa's husband, of ruining her marriage.

José certainly didn't care and Anissa seemed not to care—only LaBelle cared. Most of the people who had come for an afternoon drink had lost interest, now signaling for their tabs. The remaining few diehards moved their chairs and turned their back to continue drinking.

"This everlasting bitch refused to have sex with him, José," Phyllis said, standing. "You know her, she's a bitch!" She spaced each accusation dramatically with a short beat, then commenced the next. "She refused to sleep with him. She'd never drink with him, of course she refused to eat meat. You know how these I AM creatures are. She broke his heart." Now that she had the floor, Phyllis shot a disgusted glance at LaBelle and moved to put herself between the young officer and the meddling hysteric.

Phyllis was honestly startled at how badly it was going.

She had not considered that Anissa would be anything but reasonable and receptive.

"I have gone to great effort to return her bloody shotgun to her and you've seen how she attacks me!" Phyllis inhaled deeply. She could do no wrong, she was young and adventurous and she was in the right. And she looked like one of them in her fiesta skirt and ruffled blouse. She looked like she belonged. Anissa, the sorry loser, was dressed for the premature burial in some white religious kit.

"What about the Battle of Tripoli?" Roddy asked. "I thought he died in battle?"

Phyllis shot from the hip. "That was after. He died in battle <u>after</u> Anissa wreaked havoc with his life and ruined his self-confidence." She realized she'd slipped up.

"Officer?" she called for help.

"Spare me these lies," Anissa muttered. But at some small signal from Jerry, José took Anissa firmly by the arm and with a strained smile began to pressure walk her out of the bar past the front desk and out to the exit. He had confronted her often enough over her daily ruckuses hawking God on the Plaza. She was not the type to loosen up, so she shouted over her shoulder, "And stop playing that vulgar music!"

After Anissa dropped the last word, she found herself out on the street declaring herself the winner. LaBelle, also on the street, agreed. But Phyllis dusted herself off and claimed victory.

"They—these I AM types—are a pain in the butt," Jerry said. "Drinks are on the house."

"She is exceedingly rude," sniffed Phyllis, vindicated. "Raised in a bloody barn, I'd say, thank you very much. Is she always like this?"

He made a sweeping gesture to everyone presently in the bar. "She may have been at her best today. She always puts on a good show."

Roddy seemed preoccupied. Turning to Phyllis, he asked, "Are you and Anissa both referring to the same man, your late husband?"

"Of course not, she can't tell the truth even with a gun pointed at her. It's all lies."

"May I bring you another round?" Jerry asked, standing now. She nodded, looking up at him. It galled her to be treated so badly. None of it should have happened.

"You have to take into account what sort of bitch she is," she muttered, nodding for another drink.

"We see this every day on the Plaza. She interrupts everyone with her insane proclamations," Jerry said, moving away. "The Official Church does not recognize Saint Germain."

Phyllis caught his arm. "Did you take a vow of celibacy?"

"Parish priests only take a vow of obedience," he said, examining her carefully. "But we have some house rules." Then, he left to bring more glasses with ice.

Roddy, getting steadily drunk, drained his old one, and longed to be back in the common sense cockpit of his fighter plane. He'd named it the Red Hot Mama for the new Vargas dish on the nose—she was all he needed.

"Did you get a room for the night?" Phyllis whispered. Roddy made a comical spiral gesture with his hand, pointing upstairs. The room had been secured.

"I didn't take a vow of poverty, either," Jerry said, setting down the drinks. "That means it's okay to leave a tip. But tonight, drinks are on the house."

"You don't have to do that," Roddy said to him.

"The front desk told me you're with General Doolittle. You're one of Doolittle's Raiders."

"Then they must have a first class counter intelligence operation there in the lobby." Roddy winked and reached for his glass. Jerry did not react to this, but pulled up a chair to sit face-to-face with one of the most famous team of pilots of the early war. One of sixteen.

"So, it's a fact you're one of Doolittle's Raiders? You bombed Tokyo?" Roddy grinned back and nodded.

Phyllis was paying scant attention to Roddy in favor of the more promising Catholic priest.

"Jerry," she said in a low voice interrupting Roddy as he began to relate his famous bombing run over Tokyo—a raid they said could not have been done, "I need more Johnny Walker."

"Roger," Jerry said, standing. Behind him, the men in suits sat at the bar, never more than three of them in one cluster. Later, another entered, a slightly older man; he whispered something and they all paid up and left.

"Yes, get one for yourself and this time, I'm buying," Roddy slurred. "We get hazardous duty pay." So far, they'd polished off the one opened bottle of Johnny Walker and then to Phyllis' astonishment, a replacement had been found, simply because Roddy was one of Doolittle's Raiders. She looked at Roddy, it was getting late.

"Okay," Jerry said. "I'll join you." He nodded to the bartender who had already turned the jukebox low, swiped the tin covered top of the bar with his rag and was preparing to close by turning off the brighter lights. When Jerry returned he was more interested in men's talk than in anything Phyllis could come up with.

"Tell me what it's like to be a Raider," he said.

On the train, the Colonel had made allusions to Roddy's association with Doolittle. But in her mind, he'd been shot down and was falling fast.

She watched Jerry now, how he moved. She liked his smile and was surprised that Jerry seemed to be on the QT about everything. He was a good man to have around. He definitely had his finger on the pulse of the place, that and a key to the larder.

"Roosevelt decorated us personally," Roddy said.

"Live and learn," she muttered. There were better men for her.

"Yeah, I was with crew number eight, I was assigned Tokyo. The others went to Yokohama, some to Yokosuka. Miracle that we even made it off the *U.S.S. Hornet*."

"I heard about that well after the fact," Jerry said. "Choppy seas with the Japs on your tail. But you did it. You still managed to bomb Tokyo and got even."

"But isn't Tojo still alive?" Phyllis asked.

"Oh Baby, I know this stuff bores you and when I tell you that we have no idea if we caused any damage at all, you're going to think we're all a bunch of lying bastards. When we high-tailed out of there, all's we saw was big smoke and clouds behind us after we dropped our payload. The Chinese wanted us to bomb the Emperor's Palace, but the Army said no."

"The damage wasn't exactly the point," Jerry turned to explain to her. "It was more for morale, to punch them back after Pearl Harbor and Clark Field. They didn't think we had the range to even get there, much less being able to land somewhere. And, they were right. When they sank the *Hornet*, there was no place left to land."

"Tojo's still working on a reprisal. They'll come up with some last gasp," Roddy said. Phyllis shook her head. She'd not followed the conversation well enough and Jerry frowned.

"You lost all sixteen planes?" That much had become clear.

"So, you're saying that Doolittle just dropped bombs and crashed the planes?" Phyllis repeated. It sounded to her as if they'd bungled everything and she was being ignored. The two men were only interested in each other.

Roddy put his hand on her knee, squeezing it. "We had definite targets, and some of the bombardiers tried to take photos, but it was all smoke and the Japs claimed we were wide of their oil refineries. What do I know? I can't swear on anything and they sure as hell won't tell us. G-Two Picked up nothing."

Phyllis was barely listening as she searched through her pocketbook for a cigarette and a Zippo. When she found them, she purposely interrupted them.

"For instance?" she said flatly, snapping the lighter open, stroking the flint wheel.

"Doolittle proved two things. One was that he was a genius and could get a B-Twenty-Five twin engine fully loaded off an aircraft carrier, and the other was that he could fly in a fog. He didn't even need to see where he was going." Roddy continued talking after he had glanced Phyllis' way and reached for his lighter.

"Please forgive me. Here," Jerry interrupted, hunching over to Phyllis. He lit her cigarette.

"Used to be we flew by the seat-of-the-pants, and Jimmy Doolittle said well, hell, just paint my windscreen over and I'll show you how to fly blind. He's quite a guy." Roddy took another drink.

"What we gave them was a hellacious, surprise attack right on the Jap's mainland, with sixteen B-Twenty-Fives—we still call 'em Billys—and boy, were they surprised! Now they're getting even by sending thousands of those damned *Fu Go* balloons."

"That was over two years ago?" she interjected gloomily. Jerry looked at her and nodded that it was about time Roddy finish his drink and get back to bombing Tokyo. If bombing was what it was all about.

"Yeah, well, you should have seen what seriousness the Japs did to the *Hornet*. They hit the aircraft carrier with bombs, then torpedoes and two Kamikazes and whoosh! She was gone. The Navy guys were trying to save their own aircraft before the *Hornet* went down. We couldn't get back; we had no place to land. Some of the Raiders ended up prisoners and the Japs shot 'em."

"You get caught?" Jerry asked.

"I made it. Bailed and swam. Destroyer picked me up. Me and my crew. I'm grateful to the Merciful God who saved my sorry ass. He saved me just for you, Phyllis baby." He smiled sweetly. Plaintively.

"You were shot down by the Japanese Zeros?" she asked. *Zeros and Aces?* She wasn't following the story at all.

"We bailed out at eight thousand feet, parachuted off the coast of China when the Billys ran out of fuel. We had to let all sixteen planes go. *Sayonara baby!*"

He took another deep drink to wet his whistle and started in on the full story, arm gestures for punctuation. "The day before we were supposed to take off, we got clear warning that the Nips had spotted us. Doolittle had a choice—shove the planes loaded with bombs overboard so's they'd not explode on the *Hornet*, or get the hell out of there with a range of only two thousand miles. He says *we're getting out of here* and, man, did we run for our planes! We didn't even get dressed; we just took off and put those babes in the sky so the other fighters could be brought up on deck to dogfight the Japs. All our B-Twenty-Fives were fully loaded with bombs. We dropped 'em and hoped to make it to China where we had a deal to turn over the planes to the guerilla forces."

"They lost every plane," Jerry said, then chugged his drink, relaxed and was completely at home. "Sixteen B-Twenty-Fives."

Phyllis looked at him quizzically. Hadn't he said the same thing several times?

"Yep, I gotta admit it. Scary having planes crashing into villages.

The Russians got one though and turned the crew over to the Japs who shot most of 'em."

Phyllis had drained her glass and was staring off into the empty barroom. The story was an old one.

"Where is Doolittle now?" she said, bringing an end to this war stuff.

"He's there in England with everyone else in Europe, lined up waiting for the invasion," Jerry said.

"My plane's ready. I'll go where my orders take me," Roddy answered, raising his glass to an imaginary flag.

"I, on the other hand, just might stay here for a while," she said, looking pointedly at Jerry. "How is it that you seem to know everything about Jimmy Doolittle?"

Jerry nodded. "I read the papers."

"Let's turn in," Roddy said slowly. "You ready, Babe?"

9
Santa Fe, New Mexico

The radio played while LaBelle sat at the kitchen table using her left elbow to shove away a congealing enchilada as she made space for her nightly letter to Melo. She had written every day since September 1941, often late in the evening when she found the time. It was now May 1944. During that time, she had received only three postcards, one stating that they'd be married the minute he hit Stateside. Two on the same day in 1942, saying they were waiting for cigarettes, beef and ammo. When the hush surrounding the POW camp condition broke free, LaBelle wrote even longer letters to sustain his courage, but they were returned as the Japanese Red Cross only allowed 25 words.

Still, all mail was sent to the Red Cross in New York, written on onionskin paper and took months to arrive; if it did in fact arrive. The pouches went via ships vulnerable to attacks by imbecile pilots, not to mention submarines, torpedoes and mines, so she was never certain which of her letters had been received. She figured the odds were good that he'd receive at least half of them. In place of the stamp, she wrote "FREE" and addressed it to him as "Prisoner of War" Philippine Islands and posted it.

Every morning before leaving for Woolworth's on the Plaza, she sealed her letter and placed it in the old battered mailbox nailed to the cedar-post gate outside the plain dirt yard. The same barren yard that for a hundred years, maybe more, had been stage to family gatherings, and birthday parties for generations of children—plus who knew how many *matanzas?*

Had Nicasia's grandfather even been born when the first deep pit had been dug in the ground to roast a *cabrito?* Or a *lechon*, the succulent small pig instead of a goat. An entire beef had been buried with the hot rocks at her wedding to Faustino. Although the yard was not large, it fit its purposes and after each celebration, the pit had been refilled and the yard pounded flat. As she placed her letter in the box, she prayed that Melo's and her first child would scrabble about riding a tricycle in figure-eights on the hard fenced dirt.

Then she walked to the Plaza to make the Frito Pies at Woolworth's.

She began that night's letter: *Querido, Mi Querido Novio que me haces tanta falta*, itching to regale him with a detailed account of Phyllis' freckled chest, her arrogance, her comic turquoise fiesta skirt with silver rickrack, and how Anissa exploded in fury for very good reason. Adultery. It would have been satisfying to remind Melo how she felt about adultery, but she was limited by the twenty-five word limit and the silent emptiness between them.

And it would have given her enormous pleasure to relate how crazy Anissa still believed in the Purple Sword and had given the harlot pure hell at La Fonda. But she knew that by the time he returned home, all the chicken-livered Anglos would probably be long gone, since they had come to Santa Fe just to hide from the war.

So, after her greeting and her promises to love him forever she had room for a small sentence or two and, mindful of the Jap censors, she tried not to write "Japs" but to use "Japanese."

Each letter would be censored twice: American first, next the Japanese. So, she was mum about how Roosevelt handpicked the news. She made no mention of how MacArthur covered up, and then whitewashed the truth of the whole Jap atrocity matter. Nothing about the three men who escaped from Cabanatuan where he and Senio and the others of the 515th were. No mention either of the camp where *Los Japos* were interned so close to the Fort Marcy stables where Melo had first learned to ride a cavalry saddle.

And what about our own pilots strafing the Japanese ships that were carrying the Allied prisoners to Japan to work as slaves in the mines? When the strain of silence grew too much, she'd blow off steam waylaying and lecturing strangers on the Plaza.

"Makes me gag!" she would announce loudly. "They call it friendly fire. Fifteen percent? Sixteen percent of our own men? We're killing sixteen out of a hundred of our own men!"

And then she'd indicate she'd give them a *tamale* if they purchased a war bond.

LaBelle had the day off the day following their ejections from La Fonda's bar and posting her letter, she went next door to collar Anissa. "You sure gave *La Puta* what for," she said, nodding.

Anissa had been up for hours and was dressed. "She's not worth the time," Anissa said, trying to shake LaBelle off.

"But that dame is shacked up with a Fly Boy—guilt written all over him. He's one of the so-called *Flying Aces* that's been sinking POW ships and firebombing POW camps."

"Someone told me he was with Doolittle. He's a Doolittle's Raider— a real hero." Anissa sounded impressed, unusual for such a rabid, anti-war zealot.

LaBelle refused to buy it.

"He's a national war idiot. If those guys with their precision bombing even got within twenty miles of their targets, the war would be over. All they do is tear up rice paddies while the Gooks are alive and hopping around like roaches, churning out more machine guns," LaBelle said. "They better both get as far out of town as..."

"Maybe I should take him away from her?" Anissa mused. "All's fair in love and war. This is war."

"What?" LaBelle was shocked.

"That's right. Say I seduce the Air Corps pilot? Soldiers are easy."

"He's even more stupid than the rest of this brainless country. Who'd want him? Anyway, you I AMers aren't supposed to fuck."

"Watch me," Anissa said quietly. "Just watch. It's like riding a bicycle."

"You're crazy. You don't make sense." So LaBelle left off exasperated with her and turned to leave in exasperation. She knew—everyone knew—that if Melo was still alive, it was because the incredibly demented and vain Air Force pilots could be counted on to miss their targets. She hoped that wasted Roddy-the-Airedale would take a nosedive right off the Aircraft Carrier—overboard, knife right into the sea.

"He looks like a drunk. You said you and Saint Germain hate drunks," LaBelle said over her shoulder, halfway out the door.

Staring off into the distance, Anissa did not speak.

"Oh yeah, just following orders," LaBelle went on, talking to herself. "Orders to shoot up Red Cross ships. Bomb POWs." She stomped out to the street.

"Anissa's whacko," she said, muttering to herself as she walked. Later when the two neighbors ran into each other under a tree on the Plaza, they both fixed on Roddy's Jeep still parked near the hotel. Anissa smiled and LaBelle glowered.

"He's still asleep," Anissa observed. She had it all figured out.

"Spare me. The kiss-my-ass Air Corps pilots, God's gift, jackasses. She, *La Puta*, was drinking at La Fonda bar, *bottoms up!*" LaBelle was going overboard, swaggering past a bench, gesturing with her arm. "Bottom's up, *Puta* Phyllis!" She circled back to where Anissa stood, keeping an eye on the Jeep and gave a wink to a wingtip geek near the Plaza. "Get a load of him. Someone said they're lawyers. Must be waiting for an accident." Normally, they hung out next to the Capital Pharmacy in their ridiculous suits and funny shoes with the tiny holes. He looked back at her and smiled.

"Don't you just wish," she mouthed, and shook her breasts at them.

Now that she had a whore for a new scapegoat, she could ease up on both Anissa and Saint Germain with his Purple Ray.

"What do you mean, asleep?" she said.

"He's not up, so he's asleep." Anissa said simply. "Drunks can't get a hard-on."

"So, he probably can now. It's halfway to tomorrow; he's been asleep long enough to get one. What if she gives him the crabs?"

"If you see him come out of the hotel, grab me. I want to give him this information." She held out the pamphlet with gleaming Saint Germain on the cover, radiating flawless youth. "I need to talk to him."

"Well, maybe you could poison him. Make his balls fall off, so everybody thinks she did it."

The Jeep stayed parked, and after too much time, Anissa went inside the hotel to investigate at the restaurant. Not spotting either Phyllis or Roddy, she asked the hostess if they had staggered in for breakfast. They had not.

Later, Anissa said that Saint Germain had inspired her and that Saint Michael agreed that instead of sugar, Log Cabin syrup would work quite well. She poured some into his gas tank.

LaBelle's back was turned so she missed it. She had been listening to some dedicated isolationist shouting out against the absolute control the government used on the media. She then launched into a heated argument about the same thing with one of the Bohemian artist types who had joined her on the bench, and so she forgot to watch for Roddy and the whore. She no longer believed anyone anymore, much less even Edward R. Murrow's radio voice when he reeled off the exaggerated statistics of the enemy's wounded, of their surrenders, of the huge might of the American Navy.

Sleeping past noon, Phyllis and Roddy woke to a perfect blue sky and warm sun, the sort of day that beckons people out of doors. The Cash and Carry on Palace had opened at 0800 in the morning and had been doing its usual lively trade, taking in dollars and passing on gossip, bread and milk. At 0900 a military personnel carrier was already parked outside the grocery flanked by two armed men standing at attention, security for the cluster of ten Japanese internees wearing cast-off fatigues who were inside the store buying cigarettes. The local patrons waited outside in the warming sun, waiting for the enemy aliens to clear out and free up the aisles. The usual logjam on Palace Avenue was gearing into high.

The wing-tipped dark-suited men milled around in pairs, eyeing vehicles parked on Palace Avenue across from the store and blocking traffic, causing a green bus to honk plaintively for some space near the curb to take on passengers. The men made no move to direct traffic, so maybe they really were lawyers. Palace Avenue, as it entered the Plaza, was a perpetual traffic snarl, sun-up to sundown. Something to do with the fact that every car passing through town, every bus and truck, passed by that corner.

At 0915 hours, the first Japanese internee took his purchases to the counter, ready to pay with the money given him for work inside the Internment Camp. They came nearly every day, in small groups.

"There's not one of 'em doesn't smoke," Tom Haskins said, young at the time to be working for his dad. Often he delivered the Japanese orders from the back of a little cart drawn by the remaining burro, Angelina. With Paco, her owner, they pulled up to the guard post and left everything off with Procopio. Once it was inventoried, Tom was given cash and he and Paco-the-Mexican were pulled back up river to the store. He and Paco both smoked on the way back to the Cash and Carry. He smoked Paco's cigarettes, of course, not his.

Paco had appeared in Santa Fe looking for work after Pearl Harbor. He had an old burro with him and the town, short of manpower, welcomed him. Since Paco spoke Mexican Spanish he fit in and got along. All the kids, Tom included, had words from the local lingo, an antique Iberian-Elizabethan Spanish, frozen since the Conquistadors. They joked and got along. When the camp phoned in their order, using any language except Nip, Paco was always paid to deliver it. Tom rode shotgun to do the talking.

His Dad liked Paco and figured he was hiding him from someone because something didn't stack up. Everybody agreed that since he was here, he might be called to serve and nobody thought he'd ever pass boot camp because you probably had to be able to read. All he did was hang around watching, taking odd jobs. By afternoon, he'd go up the hill for firewood to sell the next morning back on the Plaza. Besides Tom and his dad, Paco didn't seem to have any friends, certainly no wife or kids. But he was a good guy and no one wanted to see him hurt. He'd get creamed in boot camp. No question.

When the internees finally ambled out of the Cash and Carry with guards flanking both ends of their small file, they moved quickly to their vehicle. Both Paco and Tom turned their heads to watch their armored vehicle pull away to drive less than a mile to the camp. The jigsaw of wartime efforts was tight in the small town, placing the top-clearance scientists less than fifty yards from the dangerous enemy aliens, as a clutch of vehicles convened to fetch the tide of overdressed visitors to Oppenheimer's mesa to the west. Both groups were equally polite and courtly when climbing into their cars. "After you," they all said, bowing each in his own manner. Everyone with a purpose flanked the north side of the Plaza; only Paco loitered, observing both war dances.

By midmorning, the Plaza had grown even livelier with Anissa squarely installed, covering her own beat. LaBelle, the buxom beauty wearing a conspicuous apron tied tight around her waist, had scurried (late as usual) into Woolworth's and could be seen busily engaged cooking that morning's Frito Pie through the picture window.

At noon, Roddy's open Jeep had not moved and no one seemed to pay it notice. Anissa sidled up to it with a few of her pamphlets and tucked one under the top-hinged windshield wiper on the folding glass windscreen. She placed another squarely on the worn driver's seat. After making several passes around the vehicle, she piled more information here and there and penciled her phone number where both Phyllis and Roddy would find it. Several people strolling about glanced in her direction.

No one would have been surprised if Anissa had taken a baseball bat to the windshield instead of quietly inserting her brochures. Since their arrival en masse (some said it was an invasion), the I AMers were known to cause damage if taunted. All they talked about was That Purple Sword.

In recent memory, a band of I AMers dressed in their white clothes had decimated the offices of *The New Mexican* after it had published some well-deserved criticism. Their response to this was to storm the newspaper, carrying heavy objects to bludgeon the light fixtures. They overturned desks and broke chairs. The peace they preached was peace protected by a very strong arm. The locals learned to be leery of all I AMers; Anissa in particular was a one-woman show.

After the Japanese internees had been driven off, Paco stood near Angelina, lazily watching Anissa move around the Jeep. He noted that she looked strong, strong and blond, and taller than most women in the town. A European couple in poorly tailored suits, carrying worn leather satchels, caught his eye as they paused to enjoy the local color. He saw them glance appreciatively at Anissa and then move in the opposite direction towards the Indian vendors.

An hour later, warm in the sun and happy to take a walk in the mountain air on the way to his bar job, Jerry strolled past the Cash and Carry with a treat in his pocket for Angelina, the bad-tempered burro. He patted her rump and smiled at the men in suits. He then smiled at the visiting tourists and grinned to some fellow driving a Ford on the wrong side of the street. Jerry had heard that some British were in town.

"*Qué pasa?*" he greeted Paco, not looking directly at him.

"*Lá, ella?*" He pointed his chin toward Anissa who was pursuing someone, belting out names like God Victorious Accomplished and Mother Mary.

"*Como no?*" Jerry knew his Latin. His Spanish fell into place.

"*Hizo algo con el Jeep.*"

"*Ojo,*" he said to Paco, pulling on his lower right eyelid. "Keep an eye on her." Then Jerry sauntered off to run headlong into Roddy with Phyllis straggling behind him as they exited the hotel aiming for the parked Jeep.

Jerry nodded, but they chose to ignore him.

Phyllis talked as she walked. "The only reason I would even consider going back down to that godforsaken place might be for poor Russell's ashes. Otherwise, I intend to stay right here." Then she pulled herself heavily into the Jeep. "What's all this?" she asked, gathering up one of the pictures of Saint Germain.

Roddy extended his hand, but glanced down. "If that's your only reason, I can have an orderly deliver the ashes to you at the hotel," Roddy said, pulling the printed matter out from under the windshield wiper. He inspected it closely.

"Her," he said. "The one who has the big beef with you."

Phyllis seemed pleased with this sort of attention and smiled as Roddy bent forward to push the worn starter on the early model Jeep, cobbled together with used Ford parts.

"I'll never figure you out, not in a million years," he muttered. The engine turned over three times before it seized.

She lit a cigarette and took a drag. "I don't know why. I've been up front with you from the start. I am not *your girl*. It's that simple." She stared straight ahead, avoiding him, and then glanced up to see the face of a wiry native gazing calmly at her, his rough hand holding the lead rope of a donkey.

"Jeep's dead."

"It's picturesque here. I like it." She regarded the sunburned man and smiled, not conscious of the dead engine.

"This Jeep's not going anywhere," Roddy said. "And I'm not a mechanic." He sat back and took a deep breath. After a moment, he saw the phone number written large in pencil. "It's got to be her. Here, ask this happy chappy here to give you a ride to her house so you can confront her yourself. Jerry says everybody knows everyone."

"Señora Anissa Barclay?" she asked the expressionless man. "Do-you-know-her?"

"*Si, Señora, la conozco.*"

"Me ride with you?" She nodded wildly at him, showing him how eager and trusting she was and that she viewed him without prejudice. She would treat Mexicans as fairly as she would treat everyone else, Roddy included.

He nodded calmly and motioned that she was welcome to ride on the back of the animal. Climbing out of the Jeep, Phyllis tossed her cigarette butt in the gutter and stood next to the burro.

"I am quite able to care for myself," she announced to Roddy and loud enough to be overheard by the usual cluster of locals. Some were ready to translate for her in case Paco needed to communicate with her.

"How much?" she asked him, rubbing her thumb and middle finger together, not noticing Anissa at the back of the crowd.

"One-dol-lar," Paco said slowly, stumbling through the syllables.

"Fine," she said as she mounted the animal and proudly rode off, Paco jogging behind waving a willow switch. Anissa waited a few minutes then quietly slipped into the passenger seat.

"Remember me from last night?"

"Dames… Of course I remember you." He looked squarely at her. She was wearing lipstick and gold earrings.

"I'll buy you a drink."

He nodded, studying her cautiously. "I just need a phone to call for a ride."

"You can catch the Red Cross "Deuce n' Half" tomorrow," she said brightly.

"I want to get the hell out of here. She's the craziest dame I've ever met."

"I've got a spare room."

"I sure need something," he said.

"I mean it when I say she's a slut. She lies. She's not even a widow; I know."

"Nothing surprises me," he said, giving up pressing the starter. Swinging his leg out of the Jeep, he watched her curiously.

"Let's go. I haven't had a drink in a very long time. You wouldn't happen to have some smokes, would you?" Anissa smiled broadly at him.

"Yeah, I've got some left. Isn't that guy taking her to your house?"

"She can wait on my *portale*. Word spreads fast; the neighbors all know who she is by now."

10

Heads close together, they sat around a small table in the La Fonda bar. Anissa, Roddy and Jerry. "Shouldn't you wait on those other people?" Roddy asked Jerry.

"It's not every day we have a Doolittle's Raider here. If it's okay with you, I'd like a de-briefing, the scuttlebutt."

"I must say, Jerry, you're not invited." Anissa added, "You are a waiter, for godssake. Scram."

"I called in sick." Jerry said, a smirk on his face as he lifted a new bottle of Scotch from under the table.

"It's my party. Three's a crowd," she said. "Roddy and I are having a drink."

"You might not recognize just how good I'm being to you, No charge," he said, sitting heavily in his chair. "Free booze, no tips. Most people would kiss my apostolic ring."

Anissa took a deep breath and glared at him as the men locked into talk about the war. After every fifth sentence, they took a synchronized sip of Scotch.

When they finally looked over in Anissa's direction, what they saw looming behind her paralyzed them with surprise. Crashing into their comfortable scene and raging up to them stood a frenzied head of curly black hair over two sumptuous and heaving breasts and seething red eyes— LaBelle. Fertile and explosive.

Aggravated now and goaded into a fury, Anissa tried to stare her down before she swerved her gaze. LaBelle glared back at them as she dragged a chair over, slowly raising it over their heads. She heaved it directly at Roddy.

"You asked for it!" she yelled as the chair came bashing down. "Stupid Flyboy Bastards!"

As Roddy tucked his head under the table, Jerry jumped quickly to his feet; Anissa bolted up to help restrain LaBelle who was still wearing her red chile-stained apron, holding her meaty arms with an iron grip. The food on the apron from Woolworth's kitchen looked like very close to coagulated blood.

"Get your goddamned hands off of me," LaBelle ordered, shaking her arms free. She looked at Jerry; he had been a priest; he should know how to handle murderers. "This man bombs our own POWs, he's killing our own men."

Jerry shook his head. "There's some misunderstanding."

"Like hell there is. Do something. Get this asshole out of here. I can't stand his stupid face," LaBelle ordered.

"Jerry, just tell her to calm down," Anissa said. "Roddy can probably help us here."

Roddy offered a weak smile. Neither he nor Jerry spoke as Jerry pushed the smashed chair aside and pulled up another. Sliding it to the small table, he motioned for LaBelle to sit down. They'd all talk it out.

"What'll it be?" he asked the Latin tiger.

"His ass," she said, still defiant and pointing at Roddy.

"I surrender." Roddy raised his arms over his head. "I gotta get out of here. It's the women."

"LaBelle, my child, please sit down here and let us hear you out. Something is gnawing at you. Let's get to the bottom of it," Jerry said.

"Eating is the word. Chewing, eating, grinding and it's this stupid war where Gary Cooper here flies in the clouds, bombing POWs."

"What's this?" Roddy said.

"You heard me. You've been bombing ships with POWs."

"She's right," Anissa said. "We know all about that."

"Sit down, please!" Jerry said, standing behind the chair. "Right here."

Standing, LaBelle glared at Anissa with a confusion of disgust and renewed disbelief. "You're drinking Scotch?"

"Not normally. This Scotch is rare—see, it even says so on the label. Have some."

"You have Schnapps?" LaBelle asked brusquely.

"Forget it, bring me a beer." She dropped heavily onto the empty chair.

"If you'll promise to take ten deep breaths, I'll go down and find you some Schnapps," Jerry said.

LaBelle stared at him. "Don't bother, Father."

"Peppermint Schnapps I take it." He smiled generously. Her desire was his command. "I want all of you boys and girls to sit quietly here until I return."

"What POWs?" Roddy whispered to LaBelle, as Jerry left the barroom.

"The ones on the ships," she replied. "We're sure Melicio Garcia's on one. We're getting married if you'll let up and let him get home."

"Father says be quiet," Anissa said, calm and modulated.

"The Japs sent some to China and now they're taking a bunch to Japan to work," LaBelle said, refusing to wait quietly.

"I heard something about it," Roddy said and glanced up to see Jerry bearing down on them holding a clear glass bottle in his hand. Dutch Schnapps. "Where did you get that?"

Jerry smiled. "You were talking, boys and girls?"

"LaBelle says that her boyfriend is on one of the Japanese convoy ships."

"He was in Cabanatuan prison camp," LaBelle added.

"I'll keep my ear to the ground," Roddy said.

"You must hear lots of stuff here," Anissa said to Jerry. "All those people coming through."

"Which people?" he asked.

"The ones in the wool suits."

"So you've seen them, too?" Jerry asked, examining the bottle of Schnapps as he held it up to the light.

"I know all about it. It's top secret," Anissa said. "You'd have to pull my fingernails out first." He studied her directly and raised his glass to her. "I swore secrecy," she added.

"You've been preaching about the All Encompassing Sacred Fire. You tell everyone about the Violet Flame and the Circle of Fire. You must know what you're talking about, your story never changes." He toasted her again and signaled something with a nod over his shoulder to the bartender.

"No. I know what Oppenheimer is up to. But I keep confidences, especially when they involve National Security," she answered, no longer flattered by his interest in her.

"You spend all day in the Plaza telling everyone about fire and victory and how the war on evil is all but over."

"It is. God Victoriously Accomplished is about to end this war and nothing you do, or Oppenheimer does, or any of us do will end it. It will be ended for us. I've told him so."

"I'll drink to that," Jerry said. "You give people the impression that you're in on some classified information that we're not." He turned to LaBelle who had calmed considerably, but not enough. "Now, you?"

"Anissa here thinks that Saint Germain and his buddies are going to save Melo. He needs more help than what these bozos here, and I mean you idiot Precision Bombers, can offer." She raised her glass of Schnapps to Roddy and took a fiery sip. It unsteadied her.

"Just tell me where he is and I'll personally see that everyone gets the word. I have some pull. I mean, we can parachute food to him, we can rescue everyone who's left in his camp first. That's our job; we're here to save the POWs. Who the hell told you we were out to kill our own POWs?"

"So, who do you take orders from?" LaBelle asked.

"Basically MacArthur at the top, Nimitz. I've got pull. I can get word all the way up to them."

Jerry stared at Roddy with a "Good Luck, Buddy" expression. Anissa and LaBelle shook their heads, negative, negative.

At that moment, out of the corner of his eye, he saw Phyllis storm into the bar. He looked at her, then at Roddy. She strode right to the table.

"Well now, isn't this just the party," she announced suspiciously viewing them as traitors.

"Phyllis! Come join us," Roddy called out jovially. "There's more Scotch."

But she refused to sit.   Like a coyote to the campfire, Phyllis walked around the table and fixed on Anissa. She continued circling, standing apart. For several tight seconds, no one breathed. Slowly, Jerry managed to slide another chair over, avoiding the bits of the smashed chair.

"For you," he said, reaching for the Scotch bottle under the table as the bartender came from behind his barrier sink with a fifth glass. He took it and began to pour a double/neat. No one spoke. Slowly, as Jerry centered the glass on the table he calmly indicated that the chair, now between himself and Roddy, had her name on it.

Phyllis didn't move, her eyes were fixed on Anissa. It seemed she was forming a plan because varying expressions flickered across her face and she began to include Roddy in her vision, back and forth between the two of them, one then the other. Still standing, she opened her mouth, then closed it, took a deep breath, closed her eyes, opened them, expelled the breath and said, "You are a consummate bitch."

The tension dissolved; everyone laughed tentatively. No more hurling chairs, just a simple challenge to a woman quite able to care for herself and if not, she was flanked by LaBelle, the War Goddess. Phyllis had more than met her match.

Roddy didn't count. No one heard him as he half-stood, "Ladies, ladies."

"Drink?" Jerry said, extending the highball her way.

"Is *she* drinking?" Phyllis asked, glaring down at Anissa's strong profile. "I don't believe my eyes. Holier-than-thou is actually having a drink?"

"Why don't you sit down like a lady and we'll all toast to the end of the war when it's safe for you cowardly little brats to go home again?" Anissa said.

"Oh?" Phyllis said, sitting down. "You say the war is almost over? I plan to wait it out right here."

"It has to end, child. It simply has to," Anissa responded. "I hope you're not planning to stay anywhere near me."

"I've taken a furnished place on Palace Avenue," Phyllis said, looking directly at Jerry. "It's just around the corner, up a block or so. An old adobe, quite charming. The owner is in Cornwall with the rest of them, a colonel." This news was absorbed in silence. Anissa did not look up.

"Will I be able to count on you for a small stash of house-warming Scotch?" she asked Jerry.

That was a loaded question. The wartime inventory of booze was cause for suspicion.

Who really owned the Harvey's hotel? There had been rumors that a three-star general had a share, or that General Eisenhower (five-stars) himself had an interest. Five wartime stars was next to God. Five stars controlled the Yanks. Five stars could even give the devil orders and run the OSS, throw in the Black Market as a Christmas bonus.

"Tell her it's from the Japs," LaBelle whispered to Anissa. "Tojo sends it for his Fifth Column. Camp Japo." She then turned to confront Jerry. "Come clean, Jerry," she said.

"You kids! It's probably Black Market. How should I know? It comes from New Jersey, on the train, once a month with the beer. I just put in an order." He laughed at them. Boys and girls. Silly children.

"So, can you have some extra sent for me?" Phyllis asked. "I'm going to throw a bash!"

"Count me out," Anissa said. "Don't invite me."

"Let me get this straight," Jerry said, his hands up. "We've got a request from the lady in turquoise for Scotch and another request from our future Fiesta Queen for her boyfriend's whereabouts, right?"

The two nodded solemnly.

"And Mrs. Barclay here has said she's not playing."

"I want Roddy to walk me home, if that's copasetic with you, Father Jerry."

"Finish your drink first," Roddy said.

"She took it pretty well," Anissa said to Roddy as they walked along the north side of the hotel toward the Frankish Cathedral on the way to Garcia Street. "I think she's got her eye on Jerry. Hope it doesn't hurt your feelings, but she needs someone to pour her drinks every night."

"Easy come, easy go," Roddy replied.

"Something doesn't compute. Do you think Jerry's a draft dodger?"

"He's not running from anything. Yet."

11

The numbers: D-Day, June 6, 1944—80,000 men lost. August 18, 1944—The President declared victory in Europe. He said the real war was over.

Twelve hundred planes firebombed Tokyo regularly from February to April 1945 destroying war installations and residences. One hundred thousand people died in the first drops.

By the solstice in June 1945, 300,000 died taking Okinawa, the last strategic stepping-stone base from which to launch the final Allied invasion of Japan. Propaganda glowed with stories of the impending victory over the Rising Sun.

Meanwhile, on August 19, 1944, Roosevelt suffered a fatal stroke while posing in his Harvard tie for a watercolor portrait by Madam Shoumatoff in Warm Springs, Georgia.

Anissa chortled to herself, and the other I AMers cheered that Madam Shoumatoff's still life began as a life drawing, but once their delirium faded, they watched Truman carefully. And they were kinder to him. He seemed honest and appeared to have no grudge against the I AMers. All hopes were pinned to him.

They cheered again as the Allied forces took first one island then another in the Pacific, building runways and throwing up bases closer to the Japanese mainland. Without the close-range bases, any invasion of the

Motherland was strategically impossible and Okinawa provided the last airstrips.

By June, the sun finally set at approximately 2100 Mountain War Time; temperatures rose during the day and continued rising as the sun baked the dry brown earth. Nicasia closed her windows against the heat during the day, and at night they slept with the doors and the windows open, cooling the adobe house with night air. One day in early June 1944—the curtains drawn, the front door closed—there was a knocking, then a banging. Nicasia rose from her kitchen chair to find a young boy from Western Union holding a telegram. Her throat closed.

"Telegram for you. It's from the Army." He handed it to her.

"Go away!" she screamed even while she gripped the actual telegram in her hand. Her eyes could not focus; horror blackened her vision so that she could not pick out the three black stars on the telegram's envelope; the death stars on every telegram.

"Oh no! Please no!" she screamed, staggering backward into the kitchen. LaBelle dropped her fountain pen.

"Please no!" screamed Nicasia and fell into a chair, holding her head in her hands. "My God, No!"

"Melo, *Querido!*" LaBelle bleated.

"I know, *Querida*. I know." Nicasia said softly having now to comfort the younger woman because the moment she had steeled herself against had finally arrived. Melo was her last; she'd lost her husband and Franque, her eldest son. Now this was her baby, Melo. They had known this day could come. It had come for so many others.

Both women held each other and wept. They sat in the growing dark and would not eat. Sobbing, forgetting from time to time to breathe, then gagging and gasping for air. They did not try to stop weeping and could not. Nor could they sleep. At three in the morning, they railed and howled. "No, No! Take it back! It's not true!"

Opening a window, LaBelle called out to the sky, "Melo! Melo!"

The telegrams never said their loved ones had been shot in the back, nor did they say they'd been acked out by friendly fire. They always stated that their men had died a hero's death—until some witness ratted.

"I don't want to live! No, No!" They wept and howled as they held on to each other, walking into the black moonless night, weakened by the carpet of retreating stars.

"Take me instead," Nicasia moaned. "I don't want to live."

"Merciful God, make it not true!"

Anissa woke from a sound sleep and heard sobbing shrieks through her open window. Barefoot, she bolted next door in the dark, stepping quickly over pebbles and rocks that dug into the soles of her feet, knowing that the unbearable had finally happened. That the time they all feared had come.

The telegram lay where it had fallen—on the darkened side of the kitchen table. She saw it as she burst through the door wearing her bathrobe, and she cried for them and with them. Now she too loved Melo insanely, even though she had only seen his handsome picture in the kitchen shrine.

"Pray with me to the All Powerful God Accomplished and his Archangels Michael and Saint Germain." The two women joined her, falling to their knees on the brick floor of the small adobe kitchen, facing the small shrine in the corner. The only light in the room was the wavering votive candle, causing their pained shadows to sway widely.

> In the name of God, the Beloved I AM Presence, and in the Name of the Beloved Ascended Jesus Christ, I AM the Strength, the Courage, the Power to move forward steadily through all experiences, whatever they may be, by the glorious Presence with I AM.

> I AM the Commanding Presence, the Exhaustless Energy, the Divine Wisdom, causing every desire to be fulfilled.

Serene, I fold my wings and abide in the Perfect
Action of the Divine Law and Justice of my
Being, commanding all things within my radiance
to appear in Perfect Divine Order.

In the name of God, the Beloved I AM presence,
release Melicio Garcia from the jaws of a cruel
death and return him to the everlasting love of
his mother and his betrothed, LaBelle.

At the end of the prayer, Anissa rose from the brick floor and
ceremonially held the sealed telegram with both hands before her closed
eyes, offering it to Saint Germain, Mother Mary and all the Saints. "I call
forth Your blessings on these two faithful women, Nicasia and LaBelle, and
show them Mercy Abiding in the Circle of White Lightning of Your Love.
Grant them the Strength of your Heart Flame."

Then standing, she took a knife in her right hand and slit the
envelope open, moving toward the flickering candle to read it silently:
"Pvt. Melicio Conception Garcia is on the rolls at Fukuoka Camp Number
Seventeen stop Nagasaki Japan stop from Captain Rodney Barnes stop."

She shook at the wondrousness of it. Racked with sudden streams
of tears, she could not pronounce the word, alive. A word that was suddenly
too astounding, too frighteningly beautiful to utter.

"He's not dead," Anissa whispered.

Nicasia whispered, "He's…there."

Yearning to come home, alive and in pain. Alive and brutally ill-
treated. Alive.

"Breathing."

"Distant," said LaBelle.

"Silent."

On his next leave, Roddy arrived in Santa Fe wearing his Class A uniform and a hero's smile. Anissa and her neighbors stood around him, hugging and clutching at him like a maypole.

"And you were promoted to captain."

"We've got food for them. We've got Jeeps to drop. You name it. It's headed for Fukuoka Camp Number Seventeen as soon as we can get past the Jap's artillery. We're preparing for the invasion."

"How soon?" Three of them needed to know. Anissa, Nicasia and LaBelle.

"Two more months, three at the most," he told them. June 1945, though Truman had penciled in March 1946. "The men have been redeployed from Europe, the Air Force, and the Navy. We have set a huge operation in motion. The end is near."

The firebombing of Tokyo had been stepped up. Leaflets demanding surrender were broadcast from the sky, knowing by this time that the weakened Emperor sought to save his people but could not relinquish his throne.

General Tojo and the empire's military industrial faction insisted that they fight to the last man, woman and child which, starving now and armed with rakes and bamboo poles, meant sure death. So, Emperor Hirohito held on, agreeing to capitulate only if he kept his throne and his personal fortune. He asked for compromises, conditions.

Truman and Churchill in Potsdam maintained that the surrender must be "unconditional" and so the war dragged on an extra month while the West insisted on that wording. Those semantics cost 200,000 more lives.

The Allies were not deluded about their future risks. They'd lost Ernie Pyle among the 12,500 men on Okinawa, and the Japanese had lost over 100,000, plus 150,000 civilian Okinawans. The first assault on the Empire's soil would kill as many as D-Day had. The lives of one million soldiers had been budgeted for the final battles, half of the remaining Allied armies.

Roddy told them he'd heard how the POWs were barely alive, their time was running out. The attack had to come soon. "So's we can save all of them."

"You are a marvel," Anissa said, holding onto his shoulder. "Do you drop letters too?"

He told her he'd have a 55-gallon drum filled with green chiles, Clark Bars and tobacco just for Melo and when he got the go-ahead from higher-up, he'd drop it. Letters as well.

"We'll let them know they're not forgotten," Roddy said in a commanding tone. The women were in the palm of his hand.

"You seen anything bizarre in the skies recently? Like a giant balloon?" he asked in an offhand manner when Nicasia served him coffee from her dented aluminum percolator.

"Balloons? Anyone here seen anything unusual floating in the sky?" Anissa asked the two. They shook their heads. No one had seen anything, not even weather balloons. Anissa was always on the alert for Saint Germain's promised appearance… He had been expected for some time now.

All three shook their heads. "Sorry. No."

"And I'll keep a lookout for ten-foot-tall Ascended Masters, too," he said. LaBelle and Nicasia blessed him over and over as he was led next door to where Anissa had actually managed a roasted chicken herself. Roddy brought the Scotch.

"You really shouldn't drink, you know. Alcohol poisons the Sacred Flame of man's soul," she said by way of excuse when she held out her hand for the fifth of Scotch. "I know Phyllis would kill for this bottle."

"Tough," he said.

"Good," she said, leading him into her bedroom. She sat him down, took off his uniform, piece by piece, and pulled him onto her, overturning the sheets, herself, her rigidity, her convictions, and her self-importance until he was ready to explode in her. But it was too brief, only minutes. She had given so many hours of staging and design. Breathless and unsure of herself, she cadged a smoke afterwards.

And they shared a Scotch, neat in a milk glass, and she thanked him, trying to mask her yearning for him. She accepted only what he offered, not hoping for more.

"I don't know if I understand women, you least of all," he admitted. "But I sure like what I see." Statements like this distanced him from Anissa. She thought men and women were similar, that is, all decent and like-minded; that under the skin, they were the same. Both outpourings of the Great I AM Presence.

But Roddy felt that they were a separate species, ships diverging on a vast sea. He wanted her to explain herself; less about God Victoriously Accomplished.

She didn't know quite where to begin talking because she had the feeling that she had stepped out into a very real but unfamiliar world. The best she could manage was to ask questions and not interrupt, for once. She did know that she wanted to be with him after the war, to take long walks and ruffle his hair.

"What are you going to do when it's all over?" she asked him, slipping it in casually. He had the bottle right before him and the contents were evaporating. Anissa had let down her guard. She felt unprotected and the liquor was hot in her skin.

"What am I going to do?"

Having chowed down on the home-cooked candlelit dinner, Roddy took a satisfying pull on the Scotch. The liquor burned and he breathed in the cool night air through his mouth. "My buddies and me figure automobiles are just about to go big."

"Not planes?"

"A million men coming home will want their own cars."

"Not houses?"

"They've got houses, theirs or their mothers, so they'll start with cars. They'll cash their benefits for them. Most of 'em were shade tree mechanics anyway, farm boys with their tractors. It's cars. I know I'm right."

"I suppose banks will loan war heroes all the money they want, won't they?"

"Most of them are pretty fair with us."

She nodded. He was a fair, sane man; of course he'd be given what he needed. She reminded herself not to interrupt or preach. Why would The Divine Order or even The I AM Presence ever fail him? He could go forward with whatever ideas he had and if he failed, he'd pick himself up, just like the rest of humanity. None of this had massive consequences.

She rose to turn on the radio. "Are you thinking of a hometown?"

"Midwest, the heartland."

"Heartland," she agreed. "I've still got the old house in Chicago boarded up. It has a dock on the lake."

"Sounds real fine," he said and turned his glass upside down. She moved the bottle towards him.

"I can't get this thing about the balloons off my mind," he said. "Are you sure you haven't seen any?"

"Really, no. And there's been nothing in *The New Mexican* about them."

"No, it's under a blackout order. You might need to spot them yourself." She leaned into him, impatient for his kiss. Once the tubes inside the radio case warmed up, Vera Lynn was heard singing, "*We'll meet again.*" She felt her heart breaking.

"I love this song," he said.

"Dance?" She clung to him as they moved hardly at all.

"I saw the movie at the base," he said, taking her in his arms. Of course, she had not seen it; I AMers disdained popular entertainments, so she said nothing. Instead, she pressed her face into his neck, breathing him in. Slowly she was learning to allow Roddy just be. To let him be a man. To stop interrupting.

"So, are you telling me that you actually like that Junior Airman?" LaBelle had asked after the incident at La Fonda. "Is that what you're trying to say?"

"Yes. He says he'll help. He'll watch out for Melo."

"The only thing he'd be good for is the *kamikaze* academy."

Everything changed after his telegram. The Flying Ace turned radiant, golden, accomplished and marvelous in everyone's eyes. He would save Melo, save all of them.

LaBelle told Nicasia, "He has to be crazy if he even gives Anissa a second thought. She's built like a basketball player."

12
Fukuoka Camp Number 17 – Omuta, Kyushu, Japan, 1944

Fukuoka Camp Number 17, Omuta was the largest and most miserable of the Japanese prison camps and it was under the command of the vicious Colonel Fukahara.

Melo and the other survivors of the Hellship disasters were barely alive when they were off-loaded and cattle-prodded to Omuta, Kyushu, twenty miles away from Nagasaki on the far side of the bay. There the wretched POWs were used as slave-labor and forced to mine coal under extremely dangerous conditions in twelve-hour shifts, seven days a week. Before 1945, the mine had been closed for several years, declared unsafe by the Japanese themselves and not only unsafe, but nearly stripped of seams. Now the face was being worked by the prisoners as a last-gasp with weekly smaller cave-ins and a series of unpreventable accidents.

No one was pleased to be assigned to Camp Number 17, even less the Japanese soldiers overseeing the POWs. This bleak assignment was given to the discarded and wounded soldiers of a deteriorating Empire. To be assigned to such luckless desolate conditions was a humiliation. These pathetic Japanese soldiers were in ridiculed and consistently slapped and bullied by their own superiors, so turning to torture and tantalizing the truly pathetic POWs briefly assuaged their degradations.

One deaf Nip taunted the food-obsessed men, holding out a bite of fish, then snatching it back with a cackle, mashing it with no teeth.

The dregs of the failing army, these disgraced and maimed Japanese soldiers were now forced down 1,440 feet deep inside the mine where they stood guard and yelled orders at the prisoners chipping coal from fragile seams, a large number of whom stood waist-deep in chilling water unstaunched from an underground spring.

A mutilated Japanese soldier beat the prisoners with his prophylactic arm.

As maimed as the overseers were in this nasty godforsaken mine, the detested Lieutenant Watanabe belonged yet to another category—those still fit soldiers assigned to the mine because of probable crimes against the Emperor. He could have committed any number of unpardonable crimes, such as cowardice or balking when given an order to commit *Gyokusai* (redeeming and honorable suicide). If the Imperial soldiers were beaten for hesitating, they could be beheaded for balking. Watanabe's dishonor was his punishment and this dishonor made him vicious. And he appeared to stalk Senio and Melo, so they kept him in their sights.

"Me-lo!"

"Senio?"

"Over here." The voice came from an abandoned tunnel near the main gate. Melo stumbled toward Arsenio, whose voice he had known since childhood. With each careful footfall, gravel to slipped on the descending floor of the spent mine cavity; Melo fell and tried to stop his fall with his hands. Sliding, losing his footing, his swollen feet sent flames of pain. He stifled a howl fearing that he might alert Watanabe who was standing guard at the mouth of the working mine.

Larger rocks moved and echoed against the hacked-out walls. From inside the shaft, he had no way of knowing what ramrod straight Watanabe had heard. Even for a prison camp, this Japanese was exceptionally cruel and seemed to have the mandate of some Ancestral Ghost telling him that he, and not Baron Mitsui, owned the entire miserable Mitsui Mine. That the POW slaves were his alone.

Outside the dark of the mine, Watanabe stood his post, so Melo extended his hands feeling for Arsenio's torn undershirt. It was warm in the mine and he could trust Senio. If Senio, the acknowledged master thief, made off with a can of sweetened Eagle condensed milk, it was hoarded for the both of them. Ditto for Melo. They were one and the same. A blood brotherhood.

Melo stopped breathing. The air filled with dust. Arsenio was gasping for air through his fingers, knowing that a cough could bring the bayonet. He crouched in a niche where he'd cached something, some treasure. Melo knew it had to be *quan*, food to assuage his beriberi. The disease was worse in Japan than it had been in the Philippine camp. The men, all men here, including the Japanese guards now, were starving.

The Empire was out of everything—even rice. Gasoline had been blockaded from the start. Of course, there was no meat left for the scourge of starving prisoners, yet if they did not have some calories, they were useless, lying in sickbay's Zero Ward howling with madness and dysentery, some blind. If Japan needed coal to power the homeland, these prisoners had to be fed. The rice gruel they were served twice a day was so repulsive they ate it with their eyes closed. They hoped the occasional crunch was a cockroach, but it was more likely a rotten fish head.

Melo was fortunate to have the milder form of beriberi because of the deficient polished rice. Often the beriberi affected men's groins. One POW's scrotum had swollen to ten pounds and he had to hand-carry himself. Not Melo, the disease which painfully affected his feet left him marginally able to work. Other POWs had it worse; their extremities had swollen up and inflamed the nerve endings on their feet, crippling them.

Here in southern Japan, Melo and Senio were now forced inside the mine to eke out the scant remaining coal; they worked seven days a week, in shifts of 350 emaciated men.

Inside the abandoned tunnel, the two men held their breaths and waited for the danger of being discovered to pass. After some time watching the dust dissipate, Melo, trying not to stumble and spew loose rocks, again followed Senio's voice hoping for stolen food, for *quan*.

So far, Watanabe had not come to the mouth of the mine. Melo's bare scabby feet ached with hot jabbing pains as he groped for his buddy.

"Remember Tivo?" Melo whispered to Senio, holding out his hand for the food he knew was there. Senio put something onto his palm. *Quan*.

"Yeah, Tivo." Primitivo hadn't made it onto the slime ships; he had been left to die in the Philippines with 500 other godforsaken POWs, some too sick to move.

Melo remembered Tivo's trick: how he could ease hunger, truly eliminate it, not merely soften it. Tivo and the Virgin of Guadalupe actually *quanned* away starvation, but only for them, the *varones* from Santa Fe. Tivo and the Virgin had saved them back in Cabanatuan.

This is how: every night under a *nipa* thatch, they would huddle around him, silently swatting mosquitoes and flies from the open latrines, watching and waiting for the sun to dip and tangle with the green leaves of the jungle. Just before dark, Tivo would fall to his knees and begin by intoning his long prayer to the Virgin of Guadalupe. She was the dark skinned mother of God who talked to Juan Diego in Spanish and Tivo addressed her in Spanish.

This prayer began by calling the Virgin down and She always came to Tivo. From the prayer flowed the *quan* which always appeared to each and every one of them. Next came the cooking instructions.

"*Quan* a chicken with shiny feathers, a chicken about six months old," Tivo would repeat.

"Cut off its head with one blow."

When the beheaded chicken had stopped running in circles, it was time to pluck her.

"Pluck the beautiful white chicken." The men made quick order of this. Senio more often started the fire, and by the time the chicken had been gutted, plucked and dressed, the coals prepared from hardwood bricks were white with ash.

"Cook the chicken slowly," Tivo said.

"You forgot the gravy," a voice urgent, near tears whispered.

"*No te preocupas,*" Tivo said.

With just one chicken, *La Virgin* sent twenty starving men sleepily to bed. Drowsy. Bellies full.

"My favorite was the *cabrito.*" Senio said, remembering back then. "By the time Tivo throws in the garlic and oregano, I am already in the arms of the angels."

When Tivo was a part of them, food came as a miracle direct from the Virgin of Guadalupe. No one got beriberi, not the *varones* from Santa Fe.

Tivo was probably dead. Senio could say nothing more than that.

The POWs were numb to the fact of death. There were things they did not talk about—the death of a buddy, the number of steps descending into the crumbling mine. That Tivo would not be going home. No one talked about what Tokyo Rose had said as the end grew closer.

They always craved sugar, but this time the *quan* had been a rat—boiled, whole, rigid and firm. Senio had picked the slick skin apart and shredded the flesh off the bones in inch-long strips with his coal-encrusted fingers. Half the rat would sustain Melo for a few more days, delay the coming blindness from malnourishment; stave off beriberi with a bit of potassium, some scant minerals.

They were going to make it together or they would die together. Nothing else was valuable—not sex, not money, nothing but buddies, loyal buddies.

They had always been friends; they held each other up.

No woman could ever come between them. They'd made a pact. They stayed together—in life and in death. This rat would buy them time.

It was good that the mine was dark. Such a meal was best blind. Senio held out a strip of meat in his blackened fingers. There was no escaping coal dust at the Mitsui Mine. It was everywhere and the overseers threw it in your face just to bring a laugh among themselves. You just forgot about it.

Doc Matson said in moderation it was okay. Moderation. Eating it was better than breathing it but once you were half-dead from asphyxiation, you got carried out of the mine. That part was good, Doc Matson said. Something else would kill you anyway.

Lately though, the doc dropped his stuff about the poisoned air, dropped it because everything, every disease and pain paled in the face of the August 1 Kill-All. All prisoners were to be exterminated. Drenched in gasoline, set afire. In a pit they themselves had dug for the purpose. The Japs would have to cover it all up, stomp it smooth.

Just forget about the coal dust.

Neither Senio or Melo was able to contend with the August First order. The men were doing everything to stay alive, stealing *quan*, catching rats. If they thought about it at all, maybe cashing in before August First was the way to go. Maybe they should not even eat the rat.

Melo could not help himself; he ate.

"Tivo says this rat is a ham with pineapples on the inside," Melo said, sitting back on his haunches in the dark of the mine.

"Okay, it's a ham."

"I can't remember why they put the pineapples on the ham. I've got *rice brain*. Can't even remember the name of my sweetheart."

"LaBelle," he prompted, wiggling the meat over Melo's nose. "Here."

"She still on deck?"

"No mail is good mail. No Dear John. She's on deck."

"I don't know but maybe she can't write. Can't read either," Melo muttered. No one had received any mail for three and a half years, so it wasn't a true test.

The Red Cross was only allowed into the Philippines a couple of times. Chances were good that the Japanese had made off with the nine-pound mercy packages of sardines and tobacco after they'd been surrendered, but no one had seen them in a couple of years. Because the Nips flung the mail bags into bug infested shacks (maybe used the letters for cigarette papers), the men decided they were forgotten. Abandoned. Lost. It was good that the Japs screamed at them; it meant somebody cared enough to notice them.

"I hope she's fat," he added. "I'm going to bury my sorry face in her soft warm flesh. I'm going to eat her up."

"Since you didn't get a Dear John, everything's A-okay."

"So," Melo whispered, "you think my *mamacita* is teaching LaBelle how to cook?"

"She's a great cook, your mama." Arsenio fed his blood brother the last of the boiled rat waiting for Watanabe-san to leave for chow.

They walked out slowly because they could no longer run.

They had been POWs for three full years plus and everyone in the camp was starving and in dire need. Normally the men only spoke of food. The idea of sex when it came up at all died in the lassitude brought on by starvation. Sometimes vitamin B helped the throbbing of beriberi but nothing could quell the dysentery or the wind-blown stench from the slit trench. Food, not sex, was the dream of Stateside. Earlier, still starving and still alive after the Death March, the men spoke of sex for the last time. It was 1942, April to be exact.

Then they divided up into tribes for protection: Santa Fe against Albuquerque and Silver City. Army versus Navy and everyone versus the Texans, the British and the Dutch. But as time passed, and the men grew weaker, rivalry and hatred sapped that little life was left in the POWs and in their exhaustion, they reviled none but the very worst of the Japanese. This was because the soldiers of the Rising Sun were ravaged by starvation and disease as well, and everybody needs some slack.

The Empire scrounged seaweed for food. Cockroaches, cats, dogs (lots of dogs), birds, rats.

Now, with rheumy eyes, the GIs (gastro intestinal became their call letters), had rampant, low-grade infections, so they wasted no motions.

No one whistled. No one smiled, no one was curious, everyone dragged themselves along, starving, doing the least they could do. No more jokes.

If they talked, it was always of food, what they'd eat when they got home.

Tivo told them how to cook it. Tortillas, chile, beer. They talked about the good news: that Roosevelt was going to give each of them a brand new Ford when they got Stateside and that MacArthur had retaken Luzon and all their POW buddies from Cabanatuan were on R and R on Waikiki Beach. No one talked about the "Kill All" and what had happened at the Palawan gasoline-massacre. They spoke of custard and chocolate.

The following day, Melo dragged himself slowly along on his foul legs, ducking into the middle of the strung-out line headed for the mine, when Watanabe zeroed in on him. "Speedo, more speedo!"

Melo was slowing the other prisoners.

He winced (or was it a sneer?) at the Gook, continuing his bird-like limp at the head of the line of men entering the mouth of the mine. Suddenly, Watanabe was on Melo's back, fast, like a black widow. Gravity had no force against the small boned, buck-toothed, crow-headed man with a face like a yellow beak. He stood raging before Melo, slamming his rifle butt into the coal-strewn path.

"Out!" he exploded. Then he pointed with the gun barrel to the closest wall where railroad spikes had been driven, pegs for equipment. "Face!"

Melo rolled his eyes at the little weasel and muttered something colloquial which caused the men, all New Mexicans—Indians, Spanish, Anglos who comprised "The Battling Bastards of Bataan"—to chuckle, shuffling closer to the mine for the day's misery of chiseling and hammering.

A mile inside the mine, they stabbed at veins while forced to stand in waist-deep water slowly breathing gas and coal dust, praying their poisonous smothering death would be painless, but terrified nonetheless. They knew how death in the sunlight stacked up; slow asphyxiation beat digging a six-foot trench, being set afire, machine-gunned down and buried with stones and dirt still alive, gasping in agony for a last lung-full of stinking air, yearning for and calling death down, like what had happened at Palawan. Like what was scheduled for August First.

"Don't sweat it, it's almost the end." Senio had a tremble to his hand when he had spoken. The "August 1 Kill All" directive had been received in camp and broadcast by Tokyo Rose with her silken voice. She cooed and called them POW suckers, telling them that they were all to be annihilated with no traces left behind.

Senio thought of Palawan. Palawan times 100,000. They were all to be incinerated. They'd heard it over and over on their hidden radios in camp.

"Promise?" Melo had replied and vomited. August First was coming up or had it passed? Were they already dead?

"I might not make it to the party," Melo said, knowing how Watanabe was fixated on his ass. "I might not make it to the Kill-All shit-kicking shindig."

Watanabe barked a stream of high-pitched short Japanese words at him, forcing Melo to wobble and face the coal black wall. Another Nip appeared with a rope. Melo was hung against the wall, tied by his wrists, and beaten. He writhed violently as Watanabe used the butt of his rifle to smash his hands, but he was too proud to scream out. Provoked, Watanabe began with a new frenzy.

"Dogenza!" ordered Watanabe. *Bend down and honor the dirt I walk on.* "Dogenza!"

The overseers slowed the dismal stream of POW slaves as they plodded towards the mine to witness Melo's beating. Slowly, passing by, they'd seen all this before.

Senio scanned the crowd for any of the bestial guard's senior officers. Doc Matson too had been keeping a weathered eye on Watanabe, whom he called "a deranged criminal,"

"Doc, Doc?" The murmur grew. "Get Doc fast!"

Responding to their calls, Doc came out of the sickbay and pushed through the cluster of men. Rushing over to the wall, he pointed away from Melo's torturing. "The mine, the mine is caving in!" he screamed, pointing frantically. "Cave-in! Cave-in!"

Even the prisoners turned in panic, hanging back as more men turned, refusing to pass through the gate. Watanabe halted mid-swing baffled by the foreign words. But the prisoners picked up on the trick, screaming, "Cave-in!"

Doc's ruse worked. When Watanabe dropped his rifle and pushed through the files of panicked slave laborers bunched at the dimly lit entrance of the mine, Senio hunched into the wall space left by Watanabe and unhooked the rope strapping Melo's bloody hands to the peg. Melo slumped to the coal shard ground and was dragged off, semi-conscious and out of sight, the men sheltering the two friends between hundreds of scabbed legs.

The Doc bought time by continuing to point to the mouth of the mine, screaming. It was a drill that worked. The Doc had pulled it off before but this time it was likely for real. The Japanese and their prisoners were all jumpy.

"He got the wrong man," Melo groaned, still lying in the path of the bent prisoners. "He's going to pay..."and he looked to a patch of sky while the tag end of the hundred and more of men filed around him. Some he could trust to rescue him, others would just as soon rat on him.

"He's going to live to pay," Melo said, weak, spurting futile threats.

"Stay cool, *hombre*," Senio said. There was no one in Santa Fe, or from New Mexico who did not know Melicio Garcia for the street fighter he was. On the Plaza he had been *the law*.

But that was at home before the war. Before signing up to ride cavalry in the National Guard and be paid to ride for John Wayne, the only job for a young man in town. At the tail end of the Depression and riding horses and being extras in movies wasn't half bad.

That was until they got sold down the river. First to Fort Bliss, then as artillery meat at Clark Field, then buggered in Bataan, now double-fucked in Fukuoka.

Senio dragged Melo into sickbay and stuck him out of sight, away from Watanabe's nose. Doc Matson stood over Melo.

"Again," was all Melo could manage. Doc had pulled him through again, and he meant "Thanks." Thanks again.

"I guess I asked for it," Melo had to admit in a voice barely audible. "I'm a son of a bitch."

"I hope you don't plan to play the piano," Doc had said, steeling himself for the violent screams as he reset the kid's hand. There were no bandages left to protect his swollen and broken mitts. Nothing to ease the beriberi swelling of his feet.

"All I can do is a temporary fix," Doc said, his mind on the Kill All. "But you've got Senio for a buddy. That counts for a lot. Bigger medicine than anything I can do for you."

He was right about Senio. Senio would kill for Melo.

But he was wrong about Melo. Melo did not scream when his hands were reset.

13
Santa Fe, New Mexico

Because of the war, Santa Fe was dead. Hard, bleak times had come to the four-hundred-year-old town. Roosevelt had imposed a ban on travel for pleasure, the art collectors and tourists vanished and businesses were liquidated. Since the start, the able-bodied men, employees and proprietors had been drafted together. But the downturn had begun years before with the Great Depression and a series of dust bowl droughts, so those who could were siphoned away on Route 66 leading to dollar-an-hour war-effort jobs in California. The best you could make in Santa Fe was a quarter an hour, if there was work.

The W.P.A. which had fostered art in town and in the pueblos, had been disbanded, leaving the artists and others floundering in a dried-up market. Melo and Senio lied about their ages and joined the National Guard.

But the climate, the clean dry mountain air and dazzling light remained unchanged. Artists and consumptives alike both found New Mexico to be an enchanting retreat, glorying in the vastness of the open spaces. They loved the purple mountains and the sparse population. When times were hard, Santa Fe was advertised nationally as a spa, a rejuvenating, four-season destination.

And a quiet place to spend a war.

Jerry had been right. Santa Fe was an invigorating small town and calm, if one overlooked the logjam on Palace Avenue and the vociferous disagreements on the Plaza. But it was a poor town and homes sat vacant, so much so that Phyllis had no difficulty finding her place. And she was informed to expect a Western welcome—a *bienvenida* party until dawn, inviting the whole town, mixing all age groups, all levels of economic strata, the three dominant cultures, and adding a few more. Phyllis, the key in hand, was ready for revelry. And she intended to throw the party herself.

Because the irresistible Western cool blue light brought the dazzling vistas as well as people into clear focus, 100 or so European and American artists stayed to ride out the difficult times. Also staying, not leaving, were the eccentric remittance-men with their outside incomes who added considerably to the general fun-filled delirium. John Levert and his dude ranch played a part. Diversity and eclecticism ruled. The wilder the better, the more the merrier. In a small town, you made your own fun.

And there was the Code of the West: Never ask a fellow where he's from. Always treat Miss Kitty like a lady. A man's handshake was his word. People were taken at face value. What Phyllis could have done in Dawson Creek, she would do here—she would rise above her tatty family and rule the town like a redheaded queen. No longer would Mum remind her to remember her place in the scheme of society. She'd fashion a new level of being, one with Bohemian risky delights. Here, she had *carte blanche* to re-fashion herself; and if she went too far, well, she could always pack up and leave as others had done.

Meanwhile, from her first night in Santa Fe onwards, she felt refreshed by the cool air, and she saw herself reborn, aristocratic, clever and a poignant widow with means.

She was buoyed because it was so different from West Palm Beach and the insufferable weather. She figured that avoiding Anissa would be a cinch because she was prepared for a more playful and open life. Anissa was a God-bothering, teetotaling, pamphlet-carrying fanatic and Phyllis was the "It Girl." How could they ever possibly cross paths except dead center on the Plaza?

As she pushed through the hotel's north doors, the sounds of Glenn Miller's rendition of *Along the Santa Fe Trail* sifted down the corridor. The song had become the anthem of the place; and for all she knew, Glenn Miller kept horses in a Territorial house on the Santa Fe Trail like so many of the "lungers" from the Sunmount T.B. Sanatorium.

Phyllis asked Jerry, "Does he live here too?"

"No, not Glenn Miller, but if we didn't let them play it on the jukebox, there'd be mayhem."

"I like it. It makes me feel dreamy," Phyllis said. "Where do you want me tonight?" She fit in, looking like a longtime native, wearing a fiesta blouse and tight dungarees with the *concho* belt she bought in Albuquerque. Jerry had said she could be a hostess, provide conversation and meet new people. He meant "shill."

"Where did all the Harvey Girl Guides go?" she asked. The Fred Harvey group was famous for their intelligent women guides to accompany and inform tourists regarding the art and culture of the Indians living in the Southwest. The Harvey Girls were paid very well, more than the men drivers at times. The hotel had framed photos of the "girls" in their concho belts and Navajo velvet blouses standing alongside the open touring cars.

"Most of them went home and joined the Red Cross." The hotel concession still belonged to the Harvey Company. "No gas, no tourists, so no Harvey Girls."

"Will they return when the war is over?"

He shrugged his shoulders, not knowing.

"Sit over there in the corner," he told her and she winked at him. "I hereby pronounce you to be *La Nueva Chica*—The New Harvey Girl." She was to be as cordial and engaging as they had been and Jerry would pour her drinks. Within the first week she had been introduced to a large measure of local color.

Her house on Palace Avenue was near the Governor's Mansion. Hers was not a mansion, but it contained a respectable three bedrooms. The second day, thanks to Jerry, she befriended Gustavo, a one-name artist who penciled out an invitation list for her swinging, *Me-Bienvenido Bash.* Y'all come!

"Invite everybody! Big small, rich, poor, Texans and New Yorkers," he told her, allowing her to buy him another drink. "If they don't know who you are when they walk in, they sure as hell will know who you are when they try to walk out." He put her on to a still down in the *barrio* and instructed her to order several gallons of homemade rum.

"Tell the owner you'll pay in greenbacks," he counseled. Others bartered with chickens and automobile parts.

It pleased her to know that she had a new identity: she was an Anglo. "God made only three kinds of people for His planet, Indians, Spanish and Anglos, and most of them were Anglos." The Blacks, the Chinese, the Jews, the Europeans and Russians—Anglos one and all. She, *La Nueva Chica,* was welcomed in as a true member of the *Cast of Characters* at La Fonda bar before the end of the week. If you were a Gringo, that was not so good. *Guëro* even less.

She anticipated that, on his off-night, Jerry would ask if he might stop by her place with some housewarming Scotch.

By the time she greeted his knock at the door her passion had been simmering and she offered him what he'd come for. Her lust was contagious. Not overly surprised by this, he sank into her kisses, eating and being eaten by her, weakened and unable to pull out. The Scotch was still in its gift carton, but she wanted him first; not yet the clinking glasses and toasts.

He followed her to her bedroom with a growing hard-on and she made love to him on the master bed, which she had doused with perfume.

Fifteen minutes later, standing, he pulled on his shirt first, then his trousers while eyeing her tangled in the sheets. She, in turn, was assessing him. Her hair was still in place.

"Have you had many women before?"

"Not many," he said. "No."

"Can you try again?"

He leaned down and kissed her lips. "Later," he said.

"Were you still a virgin in the seminary?"

"No, there was one woman, when I was eighteen. She was older than me. She had plans for her life that did not involve a teenager."

"But don't you want to make up for lost time?" She rose out of bed and stood before him, soft flesh, silky to the touch, yearning. "You can make love to me any way you wish. I like it all."

"I'm out of your league," he said and continued pulling on his clothes. "But I'll take you out for *posole*—it's a local, traditional dish."

"You can't be serious?" she said. Tentatively and gently, keeping her at bay, he helped her dress by fastening her brassiere, teasing her with pairs of kisses on her shoulders, two on each side, then around again. Assuaging her.

The sun was close to setting. Taking her arm, he walked her down Palace Avenue and across the Plaza to a small family-run restaurant catering to hungry travelers, a place where he was lovingly greeted by the *dueña*. Next, he introduced Phyllis as a newcomer and she received a very warm *abrazo*. They sat at a corner table and with the others in the restaurant, ordered the specialty of the house, or rather, Jerry ordered it.

Posole took some explaining, he said. "We call it underwater popcorn. It cooks for hours to make the rich broth of pigs' knuckles, pork and red chile. Very nourishing."

"Don't they have wine?" She took a small revolting bite and paused, trying to assess what it might be.

"Sorry, Babe, no wine."

Phyllis looked displeased. "This tastes like lunch, not dinner."

"Look, there is something I've been needing to tell you. Don't expect more Scotch," he said. "The Scotch at the bar is reserved for VIPs. It's not a day-to-day drink. I broke every rule bringing you some."

"But why?"

"It's just policy."

He'd cut her off. At the bar and in bed. She could feel her pale skin fire livid. After he dropped her off at her house with a careful kiss on the cheek, she tore through the box to the Scotch, poured herself a belt and started obsessing to herself in the bathroom mirror. She was not the sort of woman to be denied anything. The next evening at five, she debated even going to the La Fonda bar. What was next? Beer? Well, she took her beer at room temperature, a northern sweater-clad temperature.

The historic adobe inn sat at the true end of the Old Santa Fe Trail where since the 1609s there had always been a *fonda,* an eating house, and as far as Phyllis knew, La Fonda was the only place in town to go to be seen. Still owned by the Atchison, Topeka and the Santa Fe Railroad and run by the Fred Harvey Company since 1929, the requirement for gentlemen to wear coats had been let slide and now the only requirement was for "reasonable" social habits, which the unruly artists in town pushed to the limit. The old timers called it The Harvey House with a certain reverence even though wartime rationing had cut into Fred Harvey's meticulous high standards and his methodically trained Harvey Girls had now been sent to Albuquerque to meet the troop trains. In Santa Fe, the classy "all-white" waitresses were now replaced by local Hispanic and Indian girls in colorful skirts and blouses who staffed the patio and dining room, a welcome switch from the 1880s. In Santa Fe, no form of segregation existed in this diverse community.

So, she stopped by La Fonda just to be generous and to allow Jerry a second chance. When she stood near the low entry wall marking the bar, he looked up and grinned, evidently completely oblivious to the slights he'd caused. Coming closer, he gave her hand a secret squeeze then selected the best seat and brought over a fleshy man, pulling out a chair for him. "This is Adrien—he's a most interesting Dutchman."

She looked squarely into Jerry's eyes and nodded that he owed her a drink, now and not later and that it would be on-the-house. He nodded yes. "I know he will find you charming."

She was warm to the middle-aged man, showering fascination on him, all the while watching Jerry out of the corner of her eye.

Adrien Hackman, the old China Hand, had learned his English with the missionaries in China. He'd done his French in The Foreign Legation in Shanghai and had picked up Mandarin with a smattering of Japanese. He had worked alongside his father running barges of oil and gasoline up and down the Yangtze. By the time the Japanese had taken Manchuria and set up the Puppet Government in the port cities of China, the Hackman family picked up stakes and Adrien moved his wife and two daughters to the safety of the high desert.

"The embargo shut us down," Adrien explained to Phyllis. "The Japs arrested the rest of the Dutch in Java, seizing their petrol."

"Before Pearl Harbor?"

"Of course, everybody was wise to what they were up to. The Americans were amassing a fleet to protect their trade routes, but it took the yellow buggers no time to ruin your Navy and crush your Air Corps and overrun the entire Pacific. They sent as many planes to bomb Darwin as they sent to Pearl Harbor—hundreds at a time."

Phyllis' eyes widened. He made it sound very dangerous and she leaned forward after a quick glance in Jerry's direction. "How frightful!"

"Indeed. Your MacArthur actually saved the Aussies, and they adore him. Now he's even managed to get the Philippines back," he reiterated. "You knew, didn't you, that the Japs had been lobbing torpedoes at Sydney and Brisbane from the start. When MacArthur moved down, they stopped." She'd known none of this and she noted that he seemed to think that she was American.

"It's hard to put the pieces together when it comes in bits and snatches," she said, thickening her brogue.

"That's right, you're a Scot," he said and she smiled.

"So when did you come to New Mexico?" Phyllis asked him, veering away from the war. She'd been talking to him for a good twenty minutes before Jerry set a bourbon and soda in front of her and turned to wait on other tables. He was holding to the lousy no-more-Scotch policy. She sniffed at it and at her first taste slammed it back on the table, refusing to touch it.

"Smells like vomit," she announced.

Meanwhile, Adrien continued to talk. "I've been here waiting things out for several years. My wife and I had to get out of China anyway or get locked in prison camp. It feels quite safe here, but I'll be damned if I know what we're going to do when it's all over. My daughters need to learn more about their home country, Holland."

"Is your wife here?" she asked him, scanning the room for Jerry again. The ruddy-faced Dutchman took a sip of bourbon from his highball glass, and he shook his head.

"My wife's home, tending to her victory garden, I suppose. I give myself a little treat when I come into town. We're about fifteen miles north. In the Nambe Valley."

"I do hope that you will bring your wife and come to my *Bienvenido* Party. I'm throwing myself a bash." Later, Phyllis checked and found that he—but not the wife—had been on Gustavo's list all along. When Adrien rose to take his leave, she tugged at the shoulder of her turquoise blouse to show more shoulder and wished him well, reminding him again of her party.

"We may not have the petrol for driving twice in the same week," he said. "But I'll give it a good try and if I fail, I hope you'll ride out to the country with a friend. Half of the town lives to the north where we bask in plenty with our horses, pigs and large gardens. It's quite beautiful. It might remind you of your own estates."

"How lovely," she said, the word *estates* pulsing its way into her memory.

Since she'd rented her place, she learned (because she asked) she needed a pair or two of blue dungarees, a couple of cowboy shirts, and a large brimmed Western hat. Once she was completely outfitted, she looked like she should be herding cattle. On the other hand, she wasn't keen on that broomstick Navajo look either. She was more appealing in pearls than hammered Indian silver.

"Is there a place where one can buy a dress? A simple dress?" she asked Jerry, fidgeting with her clothes now that the Dutchman had left.

"You didn't bring any?" He seemed surprised. "There's Henkel's on the Plaza."

"Did I not tell you that all my luggage—the trunks, the cases— were all stolen?" He looked surprised. "I must have forgotten," he shrugged.

"Well, what I need you to know is that this damned American whisky smells like dog vomit."

"Blame it on the war."

More flocked to the party than were invited; it was a huge success. All ages, every type of person, all happy to raise a glass and meet a newcomer. Jerry came through with some gin for martinis, but no more Scotch. He stayed only a short time before returning to La Fonda.

"Just play music and give them lots to eat and even more to drink," he advised her, so she was well supplied with gallons of homemade rum, plus the gin.

An old Victrola spun out the day's popular songs, like *Sentimental Journey*, one after another at 78 R.P.M. What favorites had not been in the cabinet when the owner of the house, Colonel Carlos Ortiz y Gambas, had shipped out for the European Front, were brought by the guests who came bearing several dishes of beans and *posole* (again), each insisting theirs was the best in the state. Other local dishes were made with corn and squash, beef and cheese and some cookies packed with lard. Phyllis greeted each guest with a florid graciousness, accepting the dishes like a queen.

"I'm here until it's safe to return to our family holdings," she informed all the varied Anglos and Spanish who flocked in. Most seemed to think that Scotland had been blitzed along with London, and she was lucky to have been pulled to safety. The rollicking party buzzed—laughter, singing and music, smoking and drinking, dancing. No one left before dawn. And Gustavo was right: by the end of the party, everyone knew damned well who she was.

The next day, her name was linked to the wave of hangovers sweeping the town. Gustavo had insisted on bartending, sloshing the rum, roaring with delight at seeing his friends there; and he was quite right, everyone now knew her name and they'd had a rip roaring good time the night before.

After answering the ringing phone, Phyllis shook herself awake, took three APCs and pulled on her clothes. Emma Gudman had called early to insist Phyllis join her for a bread-and-butter lunch and rehash the wild party. They were introduced early on at the party and she'd spent some time talking to Emma, learning that she had her cap set for a New Yorker. He was divorced, played the cello and kept dressage horses. And he sounded difficult.

Phyllis stood outside La Fonda's crowded restaurant, wearing the broomstick skirt, waiting for Emma who rushed up in a linen suit. On her right hand was a ring, nothing more. No Indian silver.

"I'm so glad you could join me!" she effused. "You and I have so very much in common." She signaled to the waitress and the two of them began to wend their way through the large dining room to a table on the far side. "Where we can talk."

"I never know how to dress," Phyllis said, admiring Emma's outfit.

"Nonsense. Here you dress as you choose. Wear what you feel like. This is New Mexico." Emma took her seat and Phyllis followed. "No one cares what you do here, but they'd appreciate hearing all about it the next day."

"Still, I need something better to wear."

"First, kudos on your party last night. That was quite a gathering. Now, everyone in town is going to show up for the next one. I'm just sorry that my good-looking beau, Bruce Hillman, was stuck in Nambe, some problem with one of the horses. He said he hated to miss it."

"Adrien did not come either. Do they know each other?" she said. Emma nodded that they did, of course. "Interesting people live here."

"A great mixture," Emma agreed. "Quite a number are fleeing the war. Good company for the most part. A large majority are educated and well traveled. Then there are the artists and the traders, some of whom walk about looking like Indians and staring at the fireplace. Then there are, of course, the dumbest sons."

"Dumbest sons?" Phyllis asked.

"It began as a joke, but it's the men, women too, whose society families want them well out of the way. They're the ones with money, of course."

"I quite love renegades—are there enough of these creatures to go around?"

"Yes, a good number. Look for Anglos with small ranches on the outskirts of town, playing polo and throwing *mariachi* parties. You had a few over last night."

"Bachelors?"

"Some, there are more men than women here." Emma said. Phyllis glanced around the restaurant to sight single men while she savored this news. "Some homosexuals as well."

"Do you have many Spanish friends?"

"The Spanish are very political. But when they come in the evening, they bring guitars and sing. It's quite marvelous, but there's not a one of them unmarried." Emma put her hand over Phyllis'. "And...without exception, and they all have frighteningly jealous wives."

"I've met some of those, a LaBelle somebody, big as a house." Phyllis said, and then she changed the subject. "Your ring is beautiful. Are you engaged?"

"That's a charming thought! This ring is all that's left," she told Phyllis, holding up her hand with its six-carat diamond. "And it's paste."

"Take my advice, you don't have to tell people." Phyllis gazed at her. She was beautiful, in her late thirties, probably Jewish. Phyllis had met very few Jews.

"Ahh, but you see that's my point. I've lost every one of my family to the Nazis, my entire family."

"My God," Phyllis said. "I keep hearing dreadful war stories here."

"I've told my tale of woe so many times in this very gossipy town. As I said, *No one cares what you do here…* People vie for outrageousness."

"Is your story outrageous?"

"No, but in the beginning everyone bent over backwards. Now they're weary of the whole thing and all they can talk about are the POWs and the atrocities committed by the Japanese. Well, that is nothing compared to what my family suffered. Dachau." It was Phyllis' turn to put a freckled hand over Emma's.

"How did you get out?"

"When the Nazis began confiscating property around nineteen-thirty-seven, my father had my mother's jewelry copied in paste. She put the good pieces on a ship to send to a New York bank. Her collection was celebrated, of course, so no one would ever have suspected that mother and I were wearing the fakes. By the end, it was simple enough to tempt a ridiculous guard and remove what he believed to be an exquisite sapphire necklace from my neck. I make it sound easier than it was, but in the end I was able to leave Germany."

"And your parents?"

"My mother chose to stay with my father. Forgive me." Emma cast her dark eyes down, then closed them for a moment. "I cannot…"

Phyllis did not believe a word of it, as she had not believed Russell Barclay had lost his finger in a hunting accident; and she was now deeply envious of Emma and her compelling drama. Her stolen wealth and power, her noble bloodline and the unspoken need for tenderness and charity all irked Phyllis. It was an audacious cover-up, and she'd been thoroughly trumped. So far, all she'd managed was a flimsy allusion to some "family holdings". She'd have to work harder to be in Emma's league..

"Your family must have been wonderfully rich," Phyllis said, making notes regarding this scenario for herself. Phyllis began to begrudge that Emma had lost more than anyone else had even thought of possessing. And that she was beautiful, not only that, but she was beautifully dressed.

"Wealthy, not rich," Emma corrected and continued in a slightly superior manner: "These Americans are so *naïf*. They know nothing of war, of being a refugee." She took a sip of the iced tea and continued. "But they are kind people."

"The ship bearing my jewelry was torpedoed by a U-Boat and all was lost. A month later, I followed by ship, completely unaware of the disaster. Now I'm here waiting for the insurance to reimburse me so I can start a new life."

Phyllis shuddered, conceding now to the brilliant construction of dandling the promise of huge wealth, and being able to discuss it like the weather.

"Until Lloyds of London pays, I am living hand-to-mouth. I feel very much alone sitting here, waiting. I need to start again," Emma said.

"But, you've already got a beau, a man."

"I've known him from the first when I arrived here. Of course, I want nothing more than for Bruce to recover from his messy divorce so we can start a life together."

"You were right, we do have a great deal in common," Phyllis whispered, then stopped. "So this is a good small town to find a husband in? I met my last husband in a small town in Canada."

"Better than many places during these very trying times."

"Do you think I could find a man with a small ranch, a dumb son with some bank accounts? A chap like that would suit me," Phyllis confided. "My husband who died was an exciting man. He adored me and left me fixed, but I don't intend to be alone."

"You're a widow? I'm so sorry," Emma said. "Please don't count on finding any man coming home from the war who is mentally stable. You should look very favorably on the ones that are here now. What about Jerry?"

"Jerry's not the marrying sort. No money to speak of."

Emma produced a knowing smile. "I've never thought he cared for women. It's odd that he wasn't drafted into the military as a chaplain of some sort. He could manage to do quite a bit of good. More than being just a bartender."

"He just doesn't know what to do with women, he's very much just a boy so I'm having to bring him up, so to speak. And in the meanwhile, I fancy giving him a big sinful burden to confess if, as he says, he returns to the priesthood."

"He's probably not just a simple waiter. There's something in his back-pocket." As she spoke, the music blared from the bar and she was forced to raise her voice. "Are you certain he's not homosexual?"

"He's just a greenhorn with women," Phyllis said over the noise. "Practice will help."

"Ahh, there's that *Rum and Coca-Cola* song again. It's lascivious but even you and I are dazzled by the Yankee Dollar, are we not?"

"They play that song all day and night," Phyllis said. "That and *Along the Santa Fe Trail* number. Even the small band in the bar plays it continually." When she looked up, she found Adrien standing nearby in search of Phyllis. He'd been sent to the restaurant's farthest corner.

"Emma and Phyllis, how lovely to find the two of you together!" he exclaimed, insisting that the both of them spend the weekend in Nambe to meet his wife and daughters. Phyllis quickly accepted, providing that Emma and Bruce agreed.

"I hear all your homes are grand," she added.

"Adrien's gardens are absolutely gorgeous," Emma said and smiled up at Adrien who seemed impatient to get on with things.

"Look, I'll take you home. Just throw a few things in a bag and come along with me. Rita is anxious to meet another cultivated European, so we'll hack up a few goats and have a party. I don't mind telling you that I have a small still and my Aquavit is the only reason anyone even bothers with me at all!"

Phyllis immediately accepted the invitation with the full hope of getting Jerry's goat. "Did he say goat?"

"Goat," Emma replied and laughed. "They throw a *matanza* at every opportunity. Particularly for weddings."

"And do they serve that *posole* too? With the goat?"

"If it's a *matanza*," she said, nodding her head. "The word means butchering, so you may think of it as a 'mixed grill.'"

"I think that I should only go if you come too."

"I look forward to it." Phyllis took heart from this and got up from the table slowly.

After saying goodbye to Emma, she ducked into the bar searching for Jerry so she might broadly announce that the invitations were beginning to pour in. "I shan't return until Monday, most likely."

"Monday's my day off," he said somewhat offhandedly. "May I come by for a drink?"

"Call first." And she rustled out of the bar, silver rickrack glinting.

"Are you absolutely serious about eating goat?" she asked Adrien, as he helped her into his parked pickup truck. She could see he'd been hauling something large like an automotive engine sitting on wooden blocks in the back bed of his very used truck.

"A local specialty, *cabrito*. Tastes nothing like veal if you ask me, but Rita rather likes it."

"Are you absolutely certain she wants guests?"

"Of course. She's been going batty with the kitchen radio delivering only questionable news."

"What's that?"

"Just the usual bombardment about the crumbling empire. Between that and the continual traffic, it's quite bad."

She directed a green-eyed curious look his way which caused him to laugh. "Once we get on the road, you'll see the problem—buses, trucks, taxis, Jeeps, everything massing up. It's like the goddamned Far East." He cut the engine to spare the petrol and coasted into a parking space in front of her house.

"No rush," he said.

She ran in to grab her clothes, make-up, comb and toothbrush and quickly reappeared at the truck. Assuming of course that Adrien was trying to put the hustle on her, she pondered whether Rita were a jealous, dangerous wife like the Spanish ones. Emma had said nothing about the woman.

She swung into the cab as he started the engine. They climbed a long hill before Adrien turned off the ignition and coasted down the other side in neutral. Once they were out of town, past Tesuque and the San Juan Ranch, the vistas of red cliffs and *barrancas* came into view, the vital red colors intensified by the iridescent blue sky. She thought that if she stared at such bare-boned beauty, she might go mad enough to pack it all in and actually stay in New Mexico. When she thought of trees and foliage, Aberdeen and Florida came to mind. This desert was sere and distant, fresher.

"Does anyone paint this view?" she asked as the truck rumbled along, the heavy engine occasionally shifting with a deep metallic *thunk*.

"There are certain scenes almost impossible to render," he said. "Most attempts appear amateurish." They were on a two-lane, rutted interstate road headed north when they passed one of the green buses she'd seen converging on Palace Avenue pulled over now and to the side with people spilling out.

"I'm not stopping for them," he declared. "I can hardly lug the load I have in back."

A cluster of men in military uniforms lined the side of the highway, all shielding their eyes from the sun as they examined the sweep of sky. "What are they doing? At first, they looked to be saluting."

"It's been weaving back and forth up there since yesterday," he said solemnly. "I'd have thought it'd be gone by now." Phyllis craned to look out the windscreen, squinting.

"A basket, it's got a basket. Like the Montgolfier brothers."

"You know about them, do you? Well, all I know is that it's hardly a pleasure craft—it's for espionage."

"How thrilling. Look, do you think you can pull over up there, so we can have a look at it? See, there's another car pulled off." Adrien checked his rear view mirror and thrust his arm out the window, signaling a right-hand turn. They veered off the road and came to a stop not far from to a small knot of men in three-piece suits lining the shoulder of the road. They seemed to shrink away from Adrien's dusty pickup, shuffling closer to their own sedans. But one of them recognized the redhead from the bar and smiled as he approached her, offering a look through his pair of binoculars.

Taking them, she asked, "What on earth is it?" squinting through the lens, turning her back on the man for a few seconds. He cleared his throat. Removing the binoculars, she did a double take. She'd seen him as well. And hadn't he stood near the drug-store often with another man, smart in his dark suit too?

A fire truck pummeled past, exceeding the regulation thirty-five miles an hour, before he answered her.

"Dirty Japs," he said. "Thousands of *Fu Go* flying bombs. Love letters from the evil emperor."

"All the way from Japan?" she asked him, noting that the other men were more concerned with tracking the object than discussing it. Just then, three more fire trucks careened past, this time with sirens blowing. So the fire departments had been alerted; where was the Army? She turned to focus on the chap who had loaned her the binoculars. "In miles, how far is it from Japan?"

"Six thousand plus, farther than any carrier plane can fly."

"But it's drifting backward, over that mountain range."

Adrien muttered, "It's right over The Hill, that military setup, the place with people in barracks. Can't help seeing all their lights at night, lit up like Paris. That's exactly where it's been headed for the past day."

"For security purposes," the young man said, looking at her intently enough to memorize her freckles, "please keep this to yourself. There will be widespread panic if the public catches wind of these balloons. Not only that, if it ever gets out, the Japs might know that their dirty little business succeeded. Please keep it zipped." He swiped his finger across his mouth and smiled at her.

"Okay," she said. She meant A-Okay. *Loose Lips Sink Ships*. Zip. He was certainly attractive and what with his dark suit, a bit more conservative than she.

"Right-O," said Adrien. Back in the truck, he started it up and they continued north toward Nambe and Pojoaque to the sound of beating pistons. They chugged past more vehicles pulled over along the side of the road. "You know who those chaps are, don't you? The one you found so charming?"

"So good looking they should be in the cinema," she said, still transfixed, gazing at the sky.

"FBI. The town is crawling with FBI and CID, all doing separate counter-intelligence, never sharing. Each has to begin again at zero to report back. When he told you to keep it zipped, and why, he meant that you and I are now under surveillance."

"Sends tingles up my spine. Really." She gave a frisson. "They're on the Plaza, looking for spies?"

"They are spies themselves, looking for other spies. The CID are military spies and the FBI are a cut way above, dressing like they do because J. Edgar Hoover wants it known that they are superior both in education and intelligence. I was pulled over once and they had a go at me. It was not pleasant. All because being Dutch, I know some Japanese. Most of the Dutch in Java know Japanese. The Dutch are good at everyone else's languages simply because no one is interested in ours."

"Do you think they'll pull me in?"

"See just what questions Jerry has for you when you're back. I'd be interested to know."

"Jerry? Why Jerry?"

So much for the pleasant weekend in the country. The house in no way resembled a Scottish manor house, being one story, and so low and rambling that it was dwarfed by the cottonwood trees. Bruce, Emma's beau, wore Navajo jewelry on both wrists, as well as dungarees and a cotton shirt, and if he was as rich as Emma had hinted, there was no indication of it. Phyllis considered herself far more elegant in her own dungarees and concho belt than he, but she could never out-match the masterful Emma.

By the end of the two days, the ever-present Aquavit had burned the inside of her mouth. And the goat *matanza*, which was indeed a butchering, caused Phyllis high distress. In fact, she was disgusted by it. Being so overcooked, the guests pulled it apart with their greasy fingers and ate from their fingers. All in all, it was a messy sort of thing, leaving Phyllis unsettled.

Afterwards, the Hispanic neighbors held a pony race. They bet heavily and at the end of it all, no one paid up. They clapped each other on the back and lost interest in anything other than getting staggering drunk, etched on the Aquavit.

Emma took it all in stride and said she'd write a bread and butter note for the both of them. "Thank you," Phyllis said. "I wouldn't know how to find the words."

"Hi Babe, how was your weekend of gracious hospitality? Did they have a mariachi band to serenade you?" Jerry asked when he dropped by her house on Monday evening, failing to call first.

"Splendid," she said, closing the door behind him. "One interesting thing did happen though. Have you heard of *Fu Go* bombs?" He let her close the door, then took her by her arms, binding her, buried his face in her hair.

"Oww! Not that tight," she whispered. "Hurts."

He put his tongue in her ear and spoke each word slowly. "Weren't you asked to keep your lips zipped?" He kissed the side of her face and loosened his grip. "For security purposes."

She pulled away and stared at him. He had started giving orders again. Always telling her what she may and may not do.

"Who told you that?"

He dragged her into the living room and pulled her down like a child onto the loveseat. He was stern and her redheaded temperament quickly expanded to steam. She recalled she'd been treated like this before.

"Phyllis, you are a guest of the United States and if you cannot heed even the simplest request, I assure you, the government will make things exceedingly unpleasant for you."

"I don't understand how you seem to know about the *Fu Gos*. You weren't even there."

"Do you understand what I just said?"

She nodded and set her jaw. "Look," she said. "I don't know who you are in cahoots with but you tell them for me, will you? Tell them that you don't cut the mustard and I presume you get my gist!" She stood to show him the door.

After she slammed it behind him, she watched him from a window, seething as he looked back, turning several times to see if she'd relent and beckon him back. But she had her pride. When he was out of view, she slumped on the love-seat and beat an angry rhythm, pounding her fisted left hand with the palm of her right and enumerating aloud the few choices she might have remaining to her.

She could still continue on to Santa Barbara. Meanwhile, for tomorrow, the following day and next week she needed diversions. And bars. There must be more bars than just one. Jerry had misplayed his cards, and Phyllis chose not to hold down a chair at La Fonda bar just to be a pal to some moral virgin. She had not agreed to play hostess for him simply because of the drinks. She had other fish to fry. More people to meet.

The next step was only too obvious. Unfinished business. She had unfinished business. Anissa. Taking on Anissa.

14
Fukuoka Camp Number 17, Kyushu, Japan, 1945

Melo and Senio were alive after the harsh winter with no clothes, no blankets and thinned rice. The death rate from starvation and disease climbed, and compounding the prisoner's jeopardy was the authentic fear now of being bombed by their own countrymen. From February onward, the US Army bombers raced overhead in huge formations, systematically bombing the mainland. Dogfights and explosions thundered overhead whenever the visibility permitted. Raid after daylight raid pocked the skies, and the Japanese Zeros gave earsplitting chase. If there was cloud cover, the bombers went elsewhere and the immediate fear of a shock-induced cave-in declined in the deep mine. Night duty was always more relaxed.

The Allied strike force was priming to cripple the Japanese war machine by softening the Empire for the land battles when the Allied infantry invaded from the south. In Nagasaki, the Mitsubishi Arms Works was a major target for the fighter planes to scream down to 1,000 feet with sights set for a direct hit before pulling up and out. The prisoners were wretchedly aware that more often than not these bombers were appallingly wide of their marks, frequently miles off-target. Being twenty air miles from Nagasaki still left them living in a kill zone. "Precision Bombing" was a joke.

When the B-24 Liberators were first spotted groaning overhead toward the Mitsubishi munitions factories, everyone cringed, the guards as well as the POWs. Even if it was too exhausted to be strategic, the Mitsui mine itself was a probable secondary target. And in the beginning, when the men at Camp Number 17 first saw clouds of smoke and ack-ack puffs black against the southern horizon, they cheered and swaggered in spite of the knowledge that their presence was invisible, uncharted and forgotten. But when they were sent into the dark unstable mine, their hopes were overcome with terror. The longed-for liberation would follow the demolition of any of the several Mitsui mines, each with a day shift of 350 men buried alive by their own American and Allied pilots. Any explosion, any tremor or concussion would domino that cave-in and the soldiers and POWs would be buried alive. Death by this means could take a week.

Two days after Melo had been beaten by Watanabe, there was an air raid siren quickly followed by an *all-clear*. The clouds were patchy on August 9th, by the calendar—a Thursday—but the men had grown too listless to keep track of the days not marked by some startling event. Once it had been determined that August First had passed and they were still alive, they passed the "Kill All" off as more of Tojo's oriental chickenshit.

Most dates did not matter, even the dates of deaths. Deaths did not matter either. Like the pilots above them, if a buddy did not return, no one indulged in speculation. Mourning was unemotional, silent; soldiers had long ago ceased asking, *Why not me?*

Melo and Senio walked numbly past their barracks from the mess hall, oblivious to the sirens. Air raid warnings were often confused with the smelter factory whistles and the whistles for the shift change in the mine, so this one siren passed unnoticed. When the *all clear* sounded immediately on the tail of the first warning, the danger of attack dissolved. Probably some trigger-happy guard pushing the wrong button.

All-clear, forget it.

A hole opened in the cloud cover overhead and since neither Melo or Senio was below in the mine at that time, they might have spotted the two B-29s droning overhead at 30,000 feet, glinting splinters of sunlight. And later, they believed they had. It was 1053 hours. Most air raids had a terrifying swarm of fifty and sixty fighter planes thundering low overhead, skimming the hilltops, then pulling up to storm north with a payload of firebombs. Their combined droning was enough to cause small landslides.

The two planes above the clouds pulsed without great notice.

All Clear.

When the *all clear* sounded, the clouds were scattered and Senio remembered shrugging. These B-29s were too high. With luck and prayers, they were two reconnaissance planes with photographic equipment. The POWs had taken rocks, strips of underwear, anything they could lay their hands on to spell out *P-O-W* in the dirt and on the roof of the largest barracks. They hoped the cameras had picked them up. Someone needed to be made to give a damn; no one knew they existed.

Arsenio squinted up and hollered, "This is a godforsaken POW camp. Do you copy?"

But Melo was in no condition to smile and he doubted bitterly that anyone cared about their presence. What seemed like ten minutes later they both saw a fireball in the direction of Nagasaki; saw it hover in the sky and turn into a giant mushroom, its stem churning and boiling red on a bed of black smoke, a fire burning in the cloud.

Moments later, they were rocked by a ground wave, which brought paralyzing fear for the lives in the shift below. Melo and Senio stared at the fiery core and caught their breaths, shakes wracked their bodies.

Below, the men in the shafts were terrified by an underground lurch that echoed the sounds of rock hitting rock down the warrens of abandoned shafts. Everyone froze, above and below, both the prisoners and their overseers; all had been forewarned that the mine was poised to collapse, direct hit or not. And not only was Nagasaki a prime target with its weapons manufacturing plants, but the workers were POWs, and if the fire was a bomb, the other prisoners had been hit.

Deep in the mine, the lights flickered. The men closed their eyes, tried to breathe through their panic when the lights faltered a second time. Then they went out completely and the men were paralyzed with a compounding dread.

A haze formed over Nagasaki.

Meanwhile, as Melo continued to drag himself, and to be dragged slowly toward the POW sickbay, both he and Senio kept a suspicious eye to the south where a rising viscous black smoke obscured the light. The murky pall spread thickly throughout the day, dropping the temperature and blocking out the sun. Later, they learned that Nagasaki was on fire.

Over the next few days the wind drifted in random streams across the bay as Nagasaki burned. The fires pushed by the coils of moving updrafts swallowed the breathable air. By the fourth day, cinders fell like snow and no more fighter planes cluttered the sky. They simply stopped coming.

A hollow silence.

Because of his hands, Melo stayed in sickbay and avoided *tenko*, the roll call which starred Watanabe at his most perverse. But like everything in prison camp, and like the US air strikes, everything had a double edge. Every benefit drew a penalty. In sickbay, rations were cut to two servings of rice per day. Men able to work were given a second runny spoonful before the leftover watery rice slops from the early shift were hauled over and delivered in buckets. But only after the able prisoners had left for the mine carrying their cold rice *bento* box lunches.

For ten hours, until 1630, Melo would receive nothing to eat. Then only a chunk of bread, a bowl of watery rice. The bread always petered out before the weak and crippled saw any.

Melicio was not a malingerer; he had been spitefully bludgeoned, and he lay quietly and silently on the wood slats recreating Tivo's magic in his mind. While trying not to burn what negligible calories he had, he created a full-blown *matanza* in his head with a skinned baby goat dressed in wild onions and herbs. He wrapped the carcass in wet burlap and slow-cooked it overnight with hot rocks in a four-foot deep pit. Of course they drank too much beer watching over the *cabrito*; they drank themselves blind. Of course. All this in his mind wild with pain.

Later, Melo dragged himself off the slats to queue for food in the mess, sullen and riddled with pain, injury, beriberi and hunger. His useless hands braced his bowl. Afterwards, Melo kept to himself and walked to his pallet.

No more speaking; Melo had already muttered greetings to his *compadres* lying on all sides of him when he'd arrived. They all had broken each other's arms and legs in order to escape being crushed in the inescapable cave-ins. The overseers allowed them out of the hell pit mine because of their tortured howls, relieved to turn them over to Doc Matson.

When Melo snailed back from the prisoners' mess, he did not acknowledge them, for they weren't the first and they certainly would not be the last to mutilate themselves in this camp. Many burned themselves with battery acid and kept the lesions festering—that was something you could do for yourself. Getting your legs broken with a shovel was done by a buddy, often for a couple of rations of rice. The five who had mutilated themselves did so because they had been commanded to hack away the very pillar of coal holding up the ceiling of the deepest tunnel. Anything would have brought it down. Above ground now, on their backs and unable to walk, they too felt the concussion from Nagasaki. Or had it been an earthquake? Bombs caused just a single concussion; they were favored for that alone. Earthquakes were a succession of frequent rumbles and shakes, one after the other. And then came the after-shocks. The mine could not withstand such a series.

Which was it?

After the baffling jolt, the men below waited, not breathing. The overseers and guards grew faint. An hour later, the mine still held, but there was no electricity to run the cars for them. Shaken, they were shoved ahead by the guards to start the long climb out on foot. Their cap-lights faltered, so they palmed the walls and pushed each other out like blind men, crawling up the roller-coaster steep slope to the light. Hours later, all 350 men had made it out.

A chilling silence and no after-shocks followed. The nightshift on August 9th was not cancelled. Filled with trepidation, Senio knew that after the 1630 bowl of slop he would be forced down into a weakened mine where the power had been cut for the cables sliding the iron train cars 1,440 feet down the steep chute into the foul, cloying heat. The electricity had failed, they were issued battery cap-lights and sent down, stumbling until the guards themselves balked and turned back.

Topside the terrible smoke was spread by the wind. It stained the skies and the next morning when the shift stumbled in, their watery rice was ladled out under a deepening black sky in a darkening mess hall. Senio, exhausted and anxious, covered in coal dust, came by sickbay to check on Melo. The prisoners' hysteria over a possible mine collapse had slackened and he had *quanned* half a sweet potato which he held in his hand.

"Something's up," he said, leading Melo to the latrine where he could devour the stolen potato unseen and hidden by a wall and sheltered by the stench.

"Food all over the place. Best estimate is some of the Nips were called to fight the fires in Nagasaki. Factories, homes, everything is burning."

"Says who?"

"The guy I got the *quan* from. He also told me Watanabe's been drinking. Wait until the shift's down and check it out. Watanabe's real shaky."

The morning after the fires started, Watanabe had stood his post guarding the gate to the main Mitsui mine. Exactly as Senio had discerned, he looked troubled. The rod he had up his ass had been removed and he could barely stand. The man known for his cunning and malice now leaned against the black wall, listless, the shoulders of his uniform covered with accumulating mottled dust. He looked beaten. Mauled. His soft hat and insignia were covered with the particles as well.

Melo noted all of this and dragged himself back to sickbay to report that Watanabe-san seemed half-dead, or possibly he just had his first real case of the GIs like the rest of them.

But still on duty after noon, Watanabe held himself together long enough to bully the prisoners climbing from their truncated shift to daylight. Even under normal operations, after the men were hauled up by cables to the base, they arrived exhausted and short of breath—panting and wheezing from their final climb topside. Friday, they stumbled, close to asphyxiation.

Without the deep-mine cars, the laborers dragged themselves along for hours in order to reach the great tunnel for the grueling final climb up the unending steps. "What you don't know, can't hurt you," everyone said and no one wanted to know how many steps they were forced to negotiate in and out. Twice a day.

The steps were jinxed. Word was that anyone who was stupid enough to count the steps into and out of the mine would die. Double-jinxed if he counted the punishing number of risers in *Nihongo*, then he and his group of ten would all die in certain, unavoidable agony. This meant that counting *ichi, ni, san, shi, go* would bring on US Flyboys for a bombing that would crush the mine in on itself and exterminate the entire shift, buried in a black hell, a mile inside the earth. Slowly. But as long as the number of steps remained uncounted, their odds of survival improved.

Senio came out of the mine into the semi-shrouded smoky light and knew better than to roll his red eyes at Watanabe, so he kept his head hung, trying to assess the guard's current frame of mind. In the mess hall the afternoon before, he'd heard the various accounts of the POWs' panic that morning. When the jolt struck, the men related how they broke off hammering and were paralyzed with terror as clouds of coal dust and flammable gases rose. They froze where they were. If they were not in the waist-deep seepage, they tried not to breathe, trying not to stir more dust as the thick patch expanded in the available air.

Then all lights went out, the air pressure began to drop and they gave up waiting for a car to roll them out as the guards pushed past the prisoners in their haste to be first out. With their cap-lights fading, the men started out on foot in the coal-laden air, guiding a stunned-to-silence Gook ahead of them following the track.

Any spark could have ignited the gasses and blown them all to bleeding hell, they related, incredulous to have made it out alive. Once the air had cleared enough, the men filed silently, slowly, walking softly with their faltering lights, following and no longer prodded by their bayonet-jabbing overseers.

"Tomorrow, no mine," Watanabe-san announced to the stragglers at the tag end of the next day's file. Ears pricked. Maybe today was Saturday? They all knew that the Mitsui Mine in Kamioka on the West Coast above Nagoya had been given Sundays off for the past year, or what felt like a year. Here, at Camp Number 17, they were allowed but one day off in ten, never more.

Something was up.

"No go," Watanabe said, keeping the glint of his gold front teeth hidden. He did not move his sallow face except to squint.

Senio started the rumor: Watanabe had been fired and made to grovel, to execute a *Dogenza* before his superiors with his head in the dirt, or to perform *Gyokusai* in the form of *hara-kiri*, or to disembowel himself by completing the prescribed *Seppuku* which would require a clever follow-up ritual, *Kaishaku*—the sacramental beheading with a Samurai's sword in order to put the poor bastard out of his suffering. The important steps of *Bushido* were all set out and prescribed and the POWs spent hours getting matters like this straight. They could wish nothing less for Watanabe. The rumor that he was drunk because of this took hold. It was the warrior's way. The honorable way. *Gyokusai.*

"*Domo arigato-gozaimasu*," the file of men muttered and bowed, keeping away from the brooding guard, watchful, grateful for the next day off, while wishing the man ill. Senio's story spread through the barracks. The night shift had been cancelled as well.

"Hold onto your hat," Senio told Melo when he shuffled into sickbay on the way to the POW mess. Melo lay on his side with his back to the open door.

"I don't have a hat," he replied, turning to face Senio.

Flies from the *benjo* buzzed and dive-bombed the miserable men. It was either stifling hot or bitter cold, nothing in between. Because of the filthy haze, today it was cooler, a break from the forecast for an endless hot, muggy and fetid summer. It was cooler, but overlaid with the smell of burning chemicals and wood from Nagasaki.

Hearing friendly voices, Doc Matson came into the large room.

"*Qué tal, Señor Arsenio Lujan. Cómo andas?*" He liked Melo's buddy. Doc was from Las Cruces, a large flat town at the base of the Organ Mountains best known for violent dust storms and chile farms along the meandering Rio Grande as it shambled on south to Old Mexico. Melo and Senio owed Doc their lives. Never deserting them because they were New Mexicans. They stuck together. And because he was a doctor, he mothered them. And on the sly, the Japanese soldiers came to him with the clap. What could he do? Sugar pill placebos was all he had and the suffering bastards said it worked.

The Doc had been with all of them through the fighting, through the Surrender, in the Death March, Camp O'Donnell and then to Cabanatuan. He was with them on the *Mati-Mati Maru* (Wait-Wait Hellship) zigzagging north to Japan, caring for the dying and constantly bargaining for more rice to be lowered into the ship's hold where the men were packed in like animals sliding on their own shit. He was always with them, arguing for medications, asking for leniency, reasoning with them and foiling both sides of the camp with placebos. His trick—what he'd done for Melo, he'd done time and again—saving a man by distracting the guards, rigging an argument over some trivial matter or just screaming that the sky was falling in. He had a bead on the Japanese mentality: since the enemy soldiers were trained to obey, they never questioned an order, any order. Two conflicting demands threw them into confusion. Controversy made them powerless and so they yelled back, screaming.

Doc said, "They are wholly unable to scream at me and beat you at the same time." Doc Matson was as close to a family member as anyone could have been. His boys needed him, disgraced and abandoned first as cannon fodder, then dishonored by being surrendered and now as godforsaken POWs.

"No work tomorrow. The mine is not open for business on Sunday." Senio could not contain his relief.

"Tomorrow is Saturday," said the Doc. "If I were you, Melo, I'd get the hell out of here and back into the chow line." Doc glanced past Melo to the five suckers who'd mangled themselves a few days earlier. "That goes for you guys, too."

"Scram," he told Melo, fully expecting him back, weak on his wooden pallet after the insufficient meal.

Melo followed Senio to the chow line. The usual prisoners who worked in the mess were incredulously slopping unmeasured scoops of rice into their bowls.

Word spread fast: the soldiers and guards were off base. The guard posts were empty. The doors to the storeroom with the bags of rice were unlocked. Things were in disarray; the harsh lines of order had been ignored. And then they found the storage room filled with quinine, morphine and all the medicines the Japanese had kept locked away from them.

The POWs' mess supervisors had not shown up, so their portions were up for grabs and the men ate themselves sick. They tore through their old and undelivered Red Cross packages searching for cigarettes but there was only canned milk, prunes and raisins—Yankee foods the Japs could not stomach. The mail they yearned to read had been rubbished back in the Philippines, but they had food now and they had medicine.

"It is a trap," Melo said.

Sunday became a holiday, then Monday, and Tuesday, and the prisoners were afraid to go beyond the empty guard towers for fear of being massacred. Tokyo Rose said that they might be spared if Truman and MacArthur surrendered unconditionally. Otherwise, the scheduled Kill All was in effect.

"Who's Truman, again?" Melo asked, tapping his head. "Rice brain."

"New American President. He wants this war over," was the answer. A stronger short wave radio had been assembled out of pilfered parts by the artillery engineer, a Master Sergeant, and late at night a station in San Francisco came through. The war was close to its end, but it sounded like so much propaganda. Like a sick and perverse Tokyo Rose.

Senio Lujan, the consummate thief, threw caution aside and led a raiding party into the Japanese Officers' mess and returned with *sake* and canned mushrooms.

"Get these out of sight!" he commanded, hiding the supplies in a trashcan.

Later that night, the moon still darkened by particulate matter from the burning city, they requisitioned the hoard and the men got drunk, dulling the pain of their approaching deaths. Everything pointed to the massacre, above all, the fact that the entrance barricades were ajar and the guard towers empty. Loaded rifles had been left standing in the guard posts, a sure indication that the Camp Commander expected *Kaishatsu* (honorable action) before he had to give the order to have all of them machine-gunned or set afire as human sacrifices, sacrificing their last hoard of gasoline on the emaciated prisoners.

Major Fred Smith called all of them out of their barracks to advise the men. "They expect you each to take the guns. It's their way." Each man was expected to kill himself. According to their strict code, only cowards needed help dying.

"My bet is that they are right outside, ready to cut us in half the minute we crawl out," Doc Matson told all of them.

"Exactly like what we did to them on Iwo Jima. Each surrendered Japanese came out of their caves unarmed, their arms over their heads. They expected to be shot."

"And?" Senio said.

"We did. We killed 'em," Doc said under his breath. "Had to."

"Bottom's up," Melo said, holding a *sake* bottle between his wrists. "Cuts the pain. And makes you bold." No matter how drunk they got, no one dared leave camp.

On the seventh overcast and silent day, General Hitachi entered camp with eight men, each beneath him in rank. He called for the prisoners to fall out. He called for *Tenko* (roll call). It took some time for the order to be delivered to all the barracks but finally at least half of them stood in a line, chests raised over stomachs distended from devouring heated cans of sweetened condensed milk.

Next to General Hitachi's flank, the ragged captured officers formed a line, facing their POW soldiers.

Having graduated from UCLA in physics in the early 1930s, General Hitachi spoke a flawless English. He had been given a high position in the Mitsubishi plants in Tokyo and, as a member of one of the powerful *Zaibatsu*, he had been in direct communication with the military through which Tojo rigidly controlled the Empire, able so far to override even the Emperor himself. And he was a friend of Baron Mitsui, a man richer now for the work of these POW slaves.

The POWs knew him as a man who was impatient by nature. Now, showing little of his usual irritation, he stood quietly surrounded by eight brooding officers.

"Attention!" he commanded. The men straightened their ranks and fell silent. Those who had been roused from one or another type of stupor straggled into the back row to avoid a beating. The prisoners had learned from sad experience that Top Jap Brass did not tolerate any swaying or twitching in formation, and that the very act of walking in a zigzag was unacceptable and punishable by swift decapitation.

But here the General waited for the shifting to stop without ordering it stopped. He had long since given up demanding that the prisoners dress suitably; they had no clothes, nothing, even though their officers were a little better off.

In his finest uniform, full ribbons and metals garnishing his chest, General Hitachi stood before them elegantly at attention. His hair had been closely shaved and his hat sat squarely on his round intelligent head. The insignia shone as he waited. Occasionally, he whispered something to one of his uneasy subalterns.

Then he examined the rank of prisoners and estimated that the full complement should be but a percentage fewer than 1,700 men because of the dying in Zero Zero Ward. Today, his officers reckoned that a collection of less than 1,100 had fallen in before him. General Hitachi let it pass.

"Attention!" he called out. Then, suddenly his mouth went dry and he faltered, unable to speak in English. All he could manage to utter were two Japanese words to the POW officers closest to him before he turned on his heel and left the camp through the opened gates, followed by his junior officers.

He had said: "*Senso Owari*."

Few even heard him; fewer still knew what it meant.

"No war," one of the Dutchmen whispered. "It means the war is over."

This was greeted by silence. The men held to their lines without movement and no one spoke except to pass on the translation. "*Senso Owari* means that the war is over."

"Great," Melo said, standing and staring ahead, his throbbing hands held to his heart. "Who won?"

15
Santa Fe, New Mexico, 1945

P hyllis took long, determined strides from her house to the Plaza, counting her steps as she nursed her anger at Jerry. Two hundred seventy-six steps from her front door to La Fonda. The important number, she noted, was 276. She continued without counting now as she skirted the hotel looking for Shelby Street where Jerry had told her ladies could buy dresses. "Henkel's," he had said and when she found it, was just opening for the day. Several nicely dressed manikins in church-going clothes had been placed in the window and next to the door was a small sign, "Help Wanted." That sign triggered a reverie in her mind about the restaurant in Dawson Creek where Russell had fallen for her. He made her feel truly loved for the first time in her life.

A little bell sounded as she entered, and a Latina girl with tightly curled persimmon colored hair came forward to greet her. "Good morning, I'm Mona."

They stared at each other's hair. Phyllis' mass of curls was a deep copper, less raw than Mona's thick carrot head. "I got it from my dad, they call him Red. He's a POW," Mona offered.

"Is he okay?"

"Yeah, he's coming home with the men who were liberated in the Philippines. All the men from Cabanatuan are finally being shipped back. My mom is real nervous. She says she doesn't know how she's going to feel being a wife again. She's afraid he's going to take away the car. Before, if she wanted to drive somewhere, she always had to ask him first."

Phyllis' mind went back to her Lincoln Zephyr and the sweet house with the sea grape arbor. A wistful yearning washed over her until she remembered why she'd been eager to leave Florida. The weather, the deplorable neighbors; if she had to return, it would only be to sell the house, collect the money and think about moving to Spain.

"I know how she feels about the car," Phyllis agreed.

She ended up with a yellow flowered rayon dress, not too long out of date, that had a nipped waist and padded shoulders. The skirt came to just below her knee.

"Since the war began, they got shorter every year," Mona said. Though rayon was not strategic and silk was. Ladies stockings were still unobtainable. Silk had been inventoried in preparation for the land invasion of the Empire, enough silk to drop several hundred thousand parachutes. All of this slated for March 1946, a year away.

"May I leave my khaki shorts here for a few hours?" Phyllis examined herself in the dressing room mirror. Then she placed her hand on her stomach, inhaling to expand her chest. The yellow floral dress had large white Lucite buttons securing the front. "I'll need white pumps."

"You'll find a good selection at The Guarantee, next door. A huge shipment from I. Miller's arrived yesterday."

"Oh?"

"Rationing is coming off, bit by bit. We've been seeing more inventory," Mona observed. She was curious about Phyllis. "Do you live here? Are you looking for work?"

"I've just moved here from my family's estates outside of Glasgow. I'm an asthmatic." And she smiled at Mona and thrust out her hand. "I feel so much better here. The air is so invigorating."

"I hope you get well soon. Come back any time."

"I could never take a job away from a war widow," Phyllis said, smiling. "Does someone sell Black Market Scotch here?"

"The Capitol Pharmacy sells liquor. They're just down on San

Francisco Street, past the Paris Theater. Why does it have to be Scotch?"

"Every good Scottish lassie pours herself a few fingers of Scotch from time to time to keep away the castle's chill. It's impossible to heat the whole pile of rocks. No one has that kind of money anymore."

"That dress is very becoming. You look more like a pin-up than a princess."

"Thank you," Phyllis said, her mood high, positioned to settle scores. She strode out into the bright sunlight, over to Washington Street and the Plaza, scanning it for Anissa. To the right, she counted fifty-odd blanket-wrapped Indian vendors mothering their wares under the long *portale* of the Palace of the Governors. They were stoic and philosophical, for in their four hundred years, many wars had come and gone; this one was but one more.

A couple dressed in gabardine bent over one display, and the dealer turned to answer their questions. The Santo Domingo jeweler's face was rounded, lined and serious but not troubled, and her dark hair had been drawn back in a traditional native chignon. Otherwise, the *portale* was as sleepy as the early morning Plaza stretching out before it. The burro on the corner of Palace and Washington was asleep on her feet, twitching ears as big as fruit.

Around the corner, the Cash and Carry was pushing out people carrying groceries and welcoming in others. The Japanese had come and gone.

The clock in front of the First National Bank read 10:21. A thin scattering of people milled about the Plaza under the elm trees; several drunks were still prone on the best benches. A few early housewives purposefully cut across the square to do their shopping on San Francisco Street, and in the very far distance, Phyllis saw two chaps dressed like pallbearers in their dark suits standing side-by-side. She hoped that one of them might be the handsome chap who had offered her the binoculars. Far more attractive than Jerry and he was probably not impotent. She remembered that he had recognized her from the bar—a promising sign.

When she thought of Jerry, she clenched her teeth, shook her head of hair, and planted her foot heel first as she began to count steps again.

Now as she felt the soft fabric brush across her knees she saw she was in luck, the binoculars-bloke was right there in her sights.

"Say, there," she said, approaching the good-looking fellow in the three-piece suit and wingtips. "Hey," she said provocatively. "Remember me?"

Most other men wore cowboy boots, or work boots, not polished black shoes.

He gave her the once over, rubbing his lower lip with his thumb. "You promised to maintain security."

"It was hardly a secret—Jerry already knew all about it," she said, watching him relax slightly. His partner—in the same get-up—stiffened. She looked directly at the both of them.

"You were warned not to reveal what you had seen."

"Can we go over there and have a cup of coffee?"

"I'm on duty, but in your case, we'll call it a debriefing. I know a place." He signaled to his colleague with a nod then headed down San Francisco Street, holding Phyllis' elbow firmly. The De Vargas Hotel was around the corner, off San Francisco Street and had a restaurant usually filled with somber Indians, either eating or talking, rarely both at the same time.

"You and I both know I'm not the only person here who knows about those bloody *Fu Go* balloons," she said in a low voice as they fell into step beside each other.

"No. A number of people as well as the population of Nambe and Pojoaque are onto them. Some three thousand Firefly troops are tracking them. The one you saw hovered for two days before it fell to the ground. The point was to keep it out of the papers."

"So, did it get into the papers?" she said as they entered the restaurant and took a table far from the window. The silent waitress stood above them with a pad in her left hand and a questioning set to her mouth. Only the sounds of cutlery scraping the ceramic plates filled the large room.

Phyllis, aware of her own effect, surveyed the clientele to determine if, when she entered looking like a movie star in her yellow dress, they thought she was a movie star. The diners had indeed stopped whatever they had been doing to study her.

"It has not been in the papers," he said. Such a serious young man just a few years older than herself.

"So, what have I done to your little project?" she asked.

"You breached security," he answered.

The Indians were silent, leaning on their tables possessively. "What's with them?" she wanted to know.

"That's just their way," he answered. "They are customarily quiet."

She needed to speak confidentially, so she leaned across the table to whisper.

"Everybody here is so spooky," she said suddenly noticing the waitress looming above their table.

"Two coffees," the man said, glancing up. Then he turned to her and in a monotone said, "I'm Horace. I know that you are Phyllis MacAndrew from Aberdeen and your father retired as a bookkeeper clerk before he passed on, leaving your mother a widow with very little to live on."

Phyllis examined his somber face, annoyed. "I was switched at birth," she stated for the record.

"I also know you take cream in your coffee." Then he continued. "You are an only child. You do not have a brother and he was not killed in the war. And that unfortunate matter back at home should not have made news. It should not have turned out the way it did. Mr. Roger Steward and the headmaster were aware that you were under age and..."

"I find this exceedingly boring."

"You left for Canada soon afterward, citing asthma as the medical cause."

"And your family, Horace? Were you born in your ridiculous three-piece suit?"

"May I continue? Much of this was taken from *The Aberdeen Times*."

"What if I said no?" She barely moved her lips when she spoke. He had turned on her in the same manner as Jerry had. And because of Jerry, she had cut herself off from La Fonda Bar, the virtual Anglo center of this defunct town.

"You lived with an older man named Barclay who died in a one-man accident under the influence of alcohol."

"What about your shoes? You actually look as though you might be a bloody spy yourself. You actually do, if you ask me." She looked up coldly at the waitress hovering above, two cups in hand.

"Thank you," she spat.

He immediately moved the creamer to her side of the table.

"Thank you," he said next, taking his mug and reaching for the sugar. "I'm just repeating what is in your dossier. May I review your last train ride and how you got yourself here?"

"Why are you doing this to me? I only came to chat, to thank you for lending me your binoculars on Friday." Before she checked to see if they were being overheard, she looked first at him. "I have done nothing to warrant an attack like this."

She rose, leaning over him. "You're a good-looking man."

"And you are a real dish. But our assignment is to be aware of people who blab things they should not."

She placed both hands on the table's wooden surface. "You hardly think that I am really a spy, now do you, Horace?" She was eye-to-eye with him, determined to bring him to bay.

He could see down her dress. "Nice dress. It becomes you," he said suddenly, confidently blowing cool air between her breasts.

"Thank you. Will you do me a favor?"

He shrugged and smiled, flashing an *all-clear*. "Just ask."

"Zip your lips," she said, placing a finger on her mouth. "My past is top secret. I was switched at birth as I told you and, being a baroness now, I am roaming the countryside looking to bestow favors. Are you ever off duty?"

He leaned nose to nose with her. "What do you have in mind?"

"High altitude exercises," she replied, flashing a brittle smile.

"I know where you live," he mouthed the words.

"Just to be safe, phone before you come," she said. "There's someone I have to jilt first." She winked. He winked.

"On second thought," she said, turning away, "forget it."

Leaving him at the De Vargas, she decided he was too hide-bound government; that he'd never do.

Humming now and headed for the central obelisk, sunlight blazing off her red hair, she stalked across the open space and drew a bead on her target. Horace was her first duck; the next was coming across her sights, close at hand.

Anissa was seated in the dappled sun on a vacated bench, gleaming in her whites and deeply intent upon arranging a stack of printed material. She did not glance up when Phyllis slid beside her onto the empty bench.

"I've come to apologize," she said. Anissa looked up startled.

"You?" Anissa shimmered in her saint's white uniform, but in the main she looked uninterested.

"I owe you a huge apology. I've been rude."

"Rude? Just rude?" Anissa turned back to her task, head down.

"You're right, more than rude." Phyllis suspected uneasily that Anissa was again actually prepared and ready for this confession because she remained steady. Phyllis had prepared as well, suited up for it, so she stood now.

"Correct." Anissa returned to making order of the pamphlets.

"I should have just said, no."

"For what?"

"To Russell. When he asked me to marry him. I should have turned him down flat. He was already married to a beautiful woman, far more beautiful than I." She was idiotically fishing for a return compliment. It came out cockamamie.

"Russell? You think I miss that drunk? He was a hopeless sinner and it is the desire of Saint Germain's that mankind not poison itself with alcohol but that each soul reside in the Fullness and Oneness of his own God Presence."

"Jesus drank wine."

"The Violet Flame can release the planet from its burdens of evil. Russell was part of the Evil. Alcohol is the Corruption that brought us the war and keeps it burning."

"I mentioned Jesus..."

"Jesus was the Real God Presence. He was the Oneness of God. He cast out devils. There are many Ascended Masters and He was the Greatest of them. The Fires of our Hearts glorify Jesus," Anissa said. "Are you trying to accuse us of not accepting Jesus among the Great Manifestations of God? Jesus? You must know that we also accept the Lord Shiva."

"You agree that he drank wine?" Phyllis' voice carried a certain insistence.

"He cast out devils, don't forget. He also drank with publicans and sinners in order to show them that he had become man. Alcohol is vulgar. And it hurts me to have to say it. You are vulgar." Anissa stated this simply. "That's not to say that even you don't have a Higher Self; we all do. Somewhere."

"I come from a very fine family with large country holdings. I am here because I'm seriously asthmatic. I've also come to personally apologize to you for Russell's behavior and for not being able to keep him either sober, or alive." At the end of this, Phyllis took a breath. She meant to force Anissa up out of her trench.

Anissa said nothing.

"I'm glad that you now own Dawson Creek," Phyllis tossed off.

Anissa looked bored and for a long while did not speak and when at last she broke the silence, she was resigned. Some twig had snapped.

"I prayed for you," she began slowly. "I prayed that the Flame burn your heart and connect you with the God Presence. I prayed you'd be purified and walk in the Light of Christ. That the God Presence bring you three things: Power, Wisdom and the Love of God. Same things one always prays for." Anissa paused, beaten, silent now as though trying to recall the exact order of her prayers. Cosmic Law was about to saddle her with the very soul she had saved. The tables had been turned.

Phyllis, unnerved, felt for a moment that perhaps she had just received the start of the apology she had elicited.

"I'm touched." Had she really, through some added twist, triumphed in a war against a woman dressed in immaculate white and who believed herself avenged by sword-bearing angels? The victory would be large in that case.

Anissa sat shaking her head, staring off toward the treetops. She said nothing as Phyllis stood facing her, seeming to hover, waiting.

To break the silence, Phyllis said, "Please just accept my apology."

"It was never my intention to become your friend. I only prayed for your conversion," Anissa said, humbled. "I am a laughable victim of my own arrogance. I thought so well of myself when I prayed for you. I felt superior praying for my enemy, something we do as an everyday practice." She looked defeated: Phyllis was her personal prodigal, a POW needing feeding, care, and if she could be believed, medical attention—perhaps even an iron lung for her sham asthma.

Long Scottish Presbyterian sermons jogged Phyllis' understanding. Anissa's moral crisis had historical subtleties. Once you pray for your enemy, and he is converted (or apologizes), Jesus suggests that you rejoice and kill a fatted calf. She thought immediately of Adrien's dreadful *matanza*, that traditional New Mexican butchering and feast, followed by dancing and barrel races on horseback. She wanted to discourage Anissa from feeling beholden to host a barbeque.

"If it makes you feel better, I have no intention of *not* drinking."

"The decision has already been made for you. With the Violet Flame, you will lose yourself and spin into the Ascension itself. Such is the power of Saint Germain."

"Please believe me, I have in no way made such a decision!"

"You might feel a loss of something that is not real, but the matter is out of your hands. You have been saved."

"Nonsense. I fully intend to meet people at night and be social. Drinking and smoking. I don't want to live like you, condemning fun, turning my back on sex."

"Saint Germain will never allow his precious ones to slip away in the night. No use pretending that He does not exist in your life. Once you have responded to His call, you will be cared for. Forever."

Phyllis instinctively stepped back.

Across the Plaza, watching the two women warily, LaBelle emerged from Woolworth's with a dark foreboding. She trusted neither of them. Folding her arms over her apron, hitching them under her breasts, she stood staring at the two Anglo women, saying nothing before she returned to the business of making lunchtime Frito Pies. She knew that those two baffling Anglo women did nothing but create problems for themselves and everyone around them.

They'd have to sort this one out themselves, she decided, and turned in another direction.

Meanwhile, Phyllis was growing visibly upset. She felt Anissa was trying to consume her. "I am very afraid that you have got the wrong lassie," she said, wrenching herself away from Anissa's vise-like missionary zeal.

All she had asked was to be accepted as an equal. But Anissa had catapulted off into some wild reverie. When she broke out of it, she whispered, "Well, so, I fully give you Russell. I mean in my heart, I gave him up long ago."

Phyllis shifted on her feet, smoothing the yellow flowered dress against her thighs. "Would you please not treat me as though I were your child?"

"My child? That's rare. Let me think about it," Anissa said, turning again to her stack of pamphlets. "I have the box with Russell's ashes at my place. Roddy left it off. It's yours if you want it."

"It's empty."

"Yes, I know. Because he was buried in West Palm Beach and he stayed in the ground. Only Ascended Masters are able to rise bodily." Anissa looked up suddenly, her face creased with grave concern.

"It is impossible to resist the coming Golden Age. Allow the Violet Flame to move through your body. At first you might feel dizzy, so telephone me any time of the night. I may be able to help."

"Not bloody likely," Phyllis said under her breath, smiling as if she'd just been fitted with new teeth. Phyllis was being sucked unwillingly into some Army of God. What she had come for was not this. She'd wanted Anissa to apologize for having underestimated her and for calling her names.

She had only wanted Anissa to eat crow. Crow tacos. Consume crow salad at La Fonda. Not to consume her.

"What do you really think of me?" Phyllis conjured an imaginary exchange.

You are very pretty. I like your dress.
But what do you really think about me?
You are a good person.

Phyllis thought she could be mollified if Anissa would say something like, *I think that you are very beautiful and elegant. And a good person.*

In response to this acknowledgement, Phyllis would then realize that she thought of Anissa as her mother. Do second wives feel this way? How could they not?

Do you love me?

If she'd been drinking, feeling liverish, that was one thing. But she had not had a drop. It was simply that time had gotten away from her, so she simply went to bed and woke well before dawn after a wave of assaulting nightmares. Nightmares about herself, not those old ones of Russell's bloody death. In the dreams, she was buried in a dangerous helplessness, a vengeful bomb burst overhead, vaporizing the fortunate. Dead fish carpeted the sea. In the dreams, she had been drafted and sent into the real war.

Anissa had said to call no matter what hour. "I read your literature. War is evil. I can see that now," she confessed to Anissa. War was no longer seductive, visceral, sexual, uninhibited and mesmerizing. In its throes, Phyllis had been captivated. She was not alone. Nations were still enticed by it.

"This war must end."

"I'm glad you called. I know that I frighten you," Anissa said.

"No, you threaten me. I don't want to give up drinking just-like-that. Smoking either. Or sex either. I don't want to. It's not for me." In her mind's eye, Phyllis saw Anissa rising from her expensive sheets, wearing a blazing white nightgown. "It's just that suddenly I can see war for what it truly is."

"You have come face-to-face with Evil. And it is immense. Rely upon Gabriel, the Archangel who rolled away the stone of Christ's tomb. He will take your hand. Sleep then in His protection." Anissa spoke softly with total assurance about the powerful cleansing ray that would bring Phyllis into the White Lightning of God Victorious.

"Alcohol, tobacco, sex and meat have given you up, they have abandoned their hold on you," Anissa whispered. "You will go home to your true home."

"What if I don't want to go home to Scotland?"

"I prayed to Saint Germain and Gabriel the Archangel; they will bring you home, Phyllis. Do you believe me?" Anissa asked softly. "To your real home."

"Tonight has been my first night with no booze or sex."

"Trust in the Awesome Power of the Flame," Anissa said. "Go back to sleep and your dreams will be fused with love." She spoke like a mother but she did not call Phyllis *child*.

Theirs was a professional relationship: Missionary to Infidel, Temperance Worker to Drunk. "Good night," Phyllis whispered, putting the receiver back in its cradle. When she awoke the next day, she felt brand new.

"I've forgiven her," Anissa announced to the incredulous LaBelle who had lain in wait. "I prayed for the Violet Flame to purge her. Even she has a higher self."

"You are stupid."

"No, she's young and wants to join the Abundance of the Great White Brotherhood. I had to forgive her."

"You are an idiot."

"She agreed to give up sex and liquor," Anissa said.

"She's a landmine. Get her out of my way!"

"She really wants to join The I AM Presence."

"The day *La Puta* gives up her goddamned booze is the day I stop swearing." LaBelle said. "That's a flat out promise."

16

"They played that song and I cried," Melo revealed after they had heard *Sentimental Journey* on the radio in the small Garcia adobe. Until this crack in his silence, Melo had refused to reveal anything about the war and what he'd been through. It was hardly that he had put it all behind, as the nurse had said, but any inkling of what he'd been through would have drowned him. Senio had come by as usual to smooth things over for him, to cover for him.

"We didn't even know Doris Day from a hole in the ground," Senio added. "Really."

"The guys on the base couldn't believe we didn't know the song," Melo chipped in. It was well after ten in the morning and they were all hunched around Nicasia's kitchen table, drinking coffee and eating sugar donuts from the bakery on the Plaza.

"It's dark in here, turn on the lights," LaBelle said, walking in with more donuts. Never pausing in her stride, she pulled up a chair next to Melo and breathed all over him. "I got the sugar ones for you."

Melo, a coyote by nature, was suffocating under the continual observation. He couldn't help how his mother watched his every move but LaBelle took up too much space, but Senio was always welcome.

Anissa barged into the house whenever she felt like it, quite often with Roddy. This time, Roddy was not with her. Later in the morning, the entire neighborhood stopped in with casseroles, cakes, *biscochitos*—the whole schmeer. "Eat, eat!" they screamed at him.

The place had become a free-for-all. LaBelle decided Melo wanted the scratchy music turned lower.

"No, you can leave the radio on," Senio said, catching LaBelle as she rose to switch it off.

The day before Melo was released from Bruns General Hospital was her last day at Woolworth's. She followed him everywhere, trying to reason with him. She had been instructed to say, "Just put it behind you." But she knew better.

They had hired all the taxis in town to parade them home from the Bruns General Hospital on the morning Senio and Melo were released. Cars, trucks and taxis honked, revved engines, and radios blared. Hundreds of jubilant New Mexicans stood outside weeping grateful tears, crying, "Our boys are back!"

Senio, the triumphant and able thief, had stuffed his duffle with a lifetime supply of filched APCs and Band-Aids and was now riding shotgun in his dad's Chevy home to his house near the Governor's mansion on Palace Avenue. He was flanked by no less than three very pretty girls he'd known in school.

Anissa found the welcome triumphant and moving as, honking, she drove her car to escort the cab taking Melicio Conception Garcia to Garcia Street where he did not want to go.

Past midnight late the night before, he had shaken Senio awake. "I don't want to go home."

"Hey, man, you gotta go see your *mamacita*."

"LaBelle is a bitch." The hospital did not hold the men captive; they could spend the day at home if they chose. Anyone could leave. Their first stop had been Letterman in San Francisco and then at Bruns in Santa Fe for nutritional and psychological follow up. Melo's hands had been surgically reset (this time with anesthetic) and the casts removed a few days before. "I'm being straight with you. I do not want to see LaBelle."

"Yeah, I'm with you," Senio said. "She's hard to shake."

"She won't listen to anybody." He was standing in hospital pajamas, scrawny, pale, describing his frustration at simply trying to make her listen. "Tried to talk to her. It's been four-and-a-half years and she won't go home."

When he threw a fit, Nicasia had reasoned in LaBelle's favor. "There's no jobs in Trinidad, except for the railroad. So she has to stay here."

"'But LaBelle thinks we're *novios*. She wants me back and she wants me to buy her a house." He remembered how she even tried to usurp his bitterness surrounding the surrender. She could not stay away from his private secrets, combing his mind with those spike fingernails, overwhelming his humiliation and uncertainty.

"If I ever get my hands on the Gooks that did this to you, I'll tear their hearts out!" she said when she first laid eyes on him.

"Hey, the war's over," Melo told her, not wanting to talk about the past.

Neither Melo nor Senio were able to cope with all the well-intentioned mauling and interrogating. They tried as best they could to conceal their whereabouts from their families—not to go home, trying to avoid dealing with the postwar hysteria.

Talk and reason could not erase the deep disgrace they felt. They knew they had dishonored their country, humiliated their families and shamed themselves. They had surrendered the flag of the United States of America to the enemy, and because of this they deserved to die. Nine hundred of the 1,800 men from New Mexico were bones beyond anguish. They were dead and at peace, including Melo's father, Faustino, and Franque, his elder brother.

But as long as they clung to life and survived, Melo and Senio, two buddies since birth, two *compadres* were responsible for their part of the fucked-up mess they had made of the war.

"Do not dishonor your flag," Senio's father admonished the twin boy-soldier cousins before they were loaded onto the back of the convoy truck in 1941. Boys whose blood seethed with Inquisition Arab justice, fiercer than the Spirit Warriors of the Empire, fierce with pride—a legendary eye-for-an-eye pride with raging hearts, they yearned to take the law into their own hands. The direct opposite of the Nip's simple animal obedience to an idiot emperor. The Spirit Warriors of the Empire were nothing more than suicidal robots. Melo and Senio were macho fighters with a pure sense of justice.

In spite of this, Arsenio and Melicio had been forced by orders to dishonor the flag and at bayonet point had been force-marched with 70,000 captive slaves along the road sixty-eight miles from Bataan. A bayonet in their backs, they had stepped over Franque howling in pain and walked on. Too terrified to help his own brother. But maybe it was somebody else's brother.

"You didn't do it. MacArthur did it," Senio repeated, trying to slither out from under the degradation. "We were surrendered, we did not surrender."

But there was no real honorable discharge for either of them.

Late the night before they were to return home, Melo sat on the edge of Senio's bed, refusing to be dragged home. The semi-dark ward held twenty beds. The night nurse's desk released a soft warm light for the eight hours from 2200 hours to 0600 that the nurse was on nightmare call. She had been counseled not to touch the shrieking patients, only to coax with a small voice, calling them out of their recurring and nightly slagheap.

"It's okay, it's okay," she cooed. "Just try to put it all behind you."

Melo stared at her. Did she think it was supposed to be easy?

"You guys okay?" she asked in her tiny little-girl's voice.

"We're gonna stay right here."

"Lots of GIs say that. You can always come back here," she offered. "Just take it slow, real slow." Smiling over her shoulder, she said, "Try to put it all behind you." And she returned to the desk under the sole light.

"Never say surrender, say were surrendered."

"We took it. We took everything they gave us. They never cut us slack and we took it like worms. We took everything they put on us."

"You're right, they treated us like scum, and we took it."

"We are still scum balls. We're not worth shit," Melo insisted, unable to face being seen again on the Plaza where he'd raised all kinds of hell before the war.

"We could go back to the Philippines. They love us in the P.I."

"They surrendered too. What good is it when it's scum that says you're great?"

"When we got off the plane from Nagoya? I thought they'd go crazy screaming like they did just seeing us alive. For sure they thought we were goners, the way they fell all over us."

"They already knew all about the August-First-Kill-All Order. They thought all hundred thousand of us guys in Japan had gasoline poured on 'em and were set on fire, screaming human bonfires."

"Yeah, well, in my worst dreams, that happens. Every night, I dig a slit trench and they make me stand in it and pour gasoline all over my body and I can't get buried while I'm still screaming. They won't put out the fire even to bury me alive. And they make me set Franque on fire. Dirty Japs."

"Me too, same deal."

"As I see it, the Nips didn't want us, but we surrendered." Melo looked up to watch the night nurse treading softly back between the rows of beds. "MacArthur didn't want us. Nobody did."

"We were surrendered. There's a difference."

"Not that anybody'd notice, there's not." Melo smiled at the nurse.

"We were shit and chickenshit."

Tentatively, she laid a hand on Melo's shoulder and checked to see if he was about to become violent.

"Tomorrow's your big day. You need some sleep. I'm telling you, there's going to be nothing but parties for you guys. Believe me. So get some shut-eye. "

"Santa Fe's going all out for you guys," she added like it was a good thing.

"The only way I'm going is dragged." Melo whispered to Senio.

"Nobody, but nobody's going to come between us. Not LaBelle either. We're sticking together."

"You got it," Senio agreed. "You can come stay with me. We got a shed."

"Who's Tara? I thought your name was Anissa?" Melo said, pushing the broken donut around on his plate. On a scale of one-to-a-hundred, she was low; she rated about a thirty-one in his book.

"I am. I'm trying to tell you about a goddess and how I think she can help you with your nightmares and your depression, Melo."

"Goddess?" He was suspicious of both LaBelle (nine on a scale of a hundred) and Anissa. He remembered going all the way with LaBelle four-and-a-half years earlier when she wasn't so huge and menacing. This Anissa was new on the scene, but she practically lived at Nicasia's. She came across as some kind of religious fanatic/psychiatrist. Plus, she was trying to screw up his brain; she was on his case.

LaBelle wanted to get married, have an FHA house, and she wanted to have babies too. He didn't know if he even could fuck anymore and he sure as hell didn't want to try. He was used to lying low in camp. There nobody ever did anything they didn't have to do, like laugh or jerk-off.

Only Tivo ever talked. Every night he'd talk about *quan*, he'd give cooking lessons, a real one-man *matanza*.

Looked like Tivo didn't make it home.

His mind was drifting. He saw his *mamacita* trying to get his attention. He felt stuck with her, too.

"Tara. She's a white goddess, like a lady Buddha. Her mission is to ease human suffering. She can help you, Melo *Querido*," Nicasia said.

"Listen to her, Melo baby. She's a good person and she wants to help you."

But it was too late. Melo had had it. Screaming and howling, he shoved his cup across the table, splattering hot coffee on Anissa's white clothes, before he stomped out of the small dark house and slammed the door behind him.

"It's too much!" he screamed at Senio. "Too fucking much! They're like fire ants, crawling all over me, biting and burning. Nobody leaves me alone, not for a minute. I'm going crazy!"

"It's okay, buddy. It's going to be okay." Senio took Melo's arm and walked him out of his home and onto the packed dirt yard in front of the faded blue painted door. "The first week's supposed to be creepy-strange." He steered Melo towards his Chevy.

"So, this Anissa who moved into town and won't leave," he said. "She's here every goddamned day. It starts at about sunrise, all these people with their *cazuelas*, their fucking potluck coming to the door and saying, *No se molestan!* when they're waking us up all the time, never letting us get into the shower, or take a shit before we have to sit down and start eatin' again. You know what it is?" He bellowed as they walked downhill toward the Plaza, "it's a goddamned wake! They are bringing food because they think I look like I'm already dead!"

"I don't think so, *primo*. I think they're bringing you food to celebrate that you are fucking alive!" Slowly, the two walked out of the yard headed for the Chevy parked on Garcia's dirt street. It was reparked a few blocks away on Palace Avenue where Senio had grown up. An identical parade of tamales waited at the Lujan's but Senio didn't fight the giddy town. He had returned home.

"Come on, buddy." Senio said, slamming his driver's door. "You're staying here with us."

Melo stopped in the center of an upturned concrete square where tree roots had dislodged the large pieces of sidewalk. He was still shaking with anger and frustration, not ready to bang into Senio's and give everyone an *abrazo*, or touch them, or be touched.

"Come on, hombre. You'll be fine shacked up at our place."

"It's the questions." He moved his head slowly, side-to-side, and his mouth went slack.

"They won't…"

"No," Melo whispered. "They're talking A-Bomb. Nagasaki A-Bomb. 'Did ya see it?' they keep on asking? Anissa, she's the main one. When she looks at me, it's like lightning flashes out of the sides of her eyes, but I'll never tell. I'll never tell her we saw the bomb. I'm telling you, lightning comes sideways out of her eyes."

Senio put both hands on his buddy's wracked shoulders and gazed into his shattered face. "Melo, it's called battle fatigue. You have battle fatigue. *Yo tambien,* I have it. We have battle fatigue. We've been through atrocities we can't even talk about. We're war-damaged. Deeply wounded."

Melo rocked on his feet, smiling like an idiot and rolling his head one way, his body the other. He was flotsam on the tide, rocking, and he rolled his head back and forth, humming something indistinct.

"What is it, man?" Senio pressed. "You're scaring me. What is it?"

"No," Melo said. "It's not battle fatigue, it's radiation poisoning. You and me are fried *chorizos,* we're warm inside and crispy on the outside. We've been cooked by the A-Bomb, the wonderful *Hijo de Puta* A-bomb."

"Who said that? Nobody ever said stuff about radiation poisoning."

"Well, there's Captain Roddy, he's a pilot. He came by and asked if I felt anything yet. Do you feel anything yet? He kept on pushing at me, and Anissa said, Tara, the Goddess could set me up and I'd be okay enough to have children. Children? Kids run from me, they don't want me either."

"We've been poisoned?"

"First your balls shrivel, but that's not as bad as when your whole body is filled with cancer and you can't even die. They're gonna tell you to shut up when you scream too loud an' they're gonna tell you you're gonzo-nuts and there's no such thing as radiation poisoning."

"You're not making this up?" Just hearing Melo talking crazy left Senio short of breath.

"No and if anybody says, *just put it behind you,* I'm gonna go crazy."

Down the block, a redhead dish came out of a house, smiled, *Buenos días* and turned to walk toward the Plaza.

"Hubba Hubba!" they said under their breaths. Unconsciously, they both reached for their balls.

"This guy Roddy said it was 'A Top Secret SNAFU.' They never thought the bombs could kill way after the fires are all put out and the bodies carted away."

"Just come with me. Stay at my place."

"Naw, I don't want to see anybody." Melo said and turned to walk away. But not to the Plaza.

"Tell 'em to get the hell out of here," Melo said, thrusting his head out the bathroom door. LaBelle, Anissa, Procopio and Nicasia were at the oilcloth covered kitchen table, speaking in whispers and trying to allow Melo the sleep he needed.

"Up all night." Nicasia closed her eyes and crossed herself.

"It's okay, really. It's quite okay. We understand completely. Please, it's okay," they repeated as they pushed in their chairs, took a hasty sip of the weak coffee and made for the door. "Let's give him some time to get back to being himself."

Nicasia was exasperated because she, for one, was desperate to talk to somebody, anybody. She wanted them all back to know if his behavior was normal for the survivors. Most people said there wasn't any normal, nothing was normal. Then why was Senio easier?

"He's smarter, he just hides it better," was the reply.

At times, she asked the blue and white statue of the Blessed Virgin if Melo was really on the earth, not a ghost from hell. He acted like he was Satan on parole and nothing she said helped. The V.A. confirmed that it was like this with all the survivors. Roddy went farther. He said they might be dying. "Just give 'em whatever they ask for."

"But what's the matter, *Hito?*" Nicasia howled. "Just tell me!"

Everything was terrible now that he was back.

"Don't ask so many questions!" Melo screamed back. "You're always asking too many goddamned questions. And don't call me *Hito*, it sounds like Hirohito." He came out of the bathroom stark naked, dripping water on the kitchen floor.

"Who was the dame with the red hair I saw yesterday? You know her, she's been around."

"Phyllis? *Muy amiga de Anissa*. They go back." Nicasia studied her son in horror. So thin, not slim—skinny. His shoulders were broad but stooped and the muscles on his bony arms looked like stretched cords, ropes, ropy. His back was scarred—lashings, like a *Penitente*, a *Hermano* who had thrashed himself with leather straps, asking for expiation, reciting sins, then begging forgiveness.

His crumbled re-set hands were stiff as claws.

"*Hito*, please put on some clothes," she said, tears staining her sallow cheeks. "Please." His maleness looked diseased, dangling flaccid and lifeless. Just when she'd been told that his balls would shrivel, he paraded them before her.

She sobbed.

"Whose house is this?" he demanded.

"My father's, your father's, mine, yours."

"Tell 'em to get out. All of them, or I'm going to stand here like this and throw their *posole* right back in their faces. And tell everybody that if I ever see rice again, I'm going to puke all over the table!"

She threw herself on the floor, clutching his naked knees, face-to-face with his wet penis. Her head nuzzling his thigh, her arms holding him against his madness. "*No se haces asi*. Please no."

"Get LaBelle out of here. Put her on a bus back to Trinidad."

"Please, Melicio, *Querido*, please do not do this!" He pulled himself from her and she toppled forward.

"Isn't there anybody you listen to?" she wailed. He put his skinny arms out like wings, dropped his hands on his cadaver hips. "The dame," he said. "The one with the Rita Hayworth hair."

Nicasia felt addled. "Who?"

"I'll get my pants on but you gotta get LaBelle out," he told her. She needed help getting up off the brick floor and until he realized what he'd done to her and extended his hand, she knelt in the wavering shadows of the room, lit by the flickering votive in the corner shrine. The votive was still there. She kept it lit against his homecoming and Melo had not yet returned.

17

"Don't say it, it's jinxed! Nobody was stupid enough to count the steps out of the mine."

"*San-byaku go-ju shichi.*"

"Oh man, you counted 'em? Three hundred fifty-seven in Nip? Do you know what that means? Excruciating death. I'm serious, there's no way out. You remember, it meant that everybody was going to die."

To Senio, breaking the rule meant that both he and Melo were doomed. They had been topside together when they saw the *Pika-Don*, the flash/boom; they had been cooked with radiation together.

"*Pika-Don* was a fucking birthday party compared to what's next."

"Shit," Senio said. "Shit."

Melo slumped over the bar at Famous Coney Island Club on West Water where Julio was standing them both to drinks. He'd given up. The guilt, the disease, the pressure to be normal and get a job so he could buy a house, get married and be forced to screw so he could have children, or have to confess to the Padre why he didn't feel like doing it.

If the Garcia's house had been big like an airplane hanger, like the Lujans' he could have hidden from her, but it wasn't. In his house, it was either him or LaBelle, not both.

"Hair lacquer, cold cream, deodorant, curlers—stuff all over the place!"

"Hey," Senio said, accepting a free beer. "I'm not a war hero," he said it again to Julio, the *cantinador*, the bar keep. "We're from Bataan, and nobody gave a damn, so you don't have to give us drinks. We can pay."

"I gave a damn, I've always given a damn about both the Two Hundreth and the Five Fifteenth," Julio insisted. It got so that neither could force himself to look Julio in the eye. He refused to understand how gutless they'd been. Too spineless to die, chickens who could not fall on their swords.

"I hear you guys even barbequed MacArthur's horse," Julio said, trying for a laugh.

"Yeah, you said it. Not enough to go around, being as we were about eighty-thousand troops on Luzon, but the Two Hundreth all got a slice." Melo rolled his eyes and rubbed his stomach which was distended and gaseous from buckets of *posole*. Neither could talk about how, at the end, before the surrender, they left nothing for the Japanese to eat. They burned everything to rubble, and then demanded that the Japanese feed them.

The door to the street swung open. Both men craned, watching it close behind the hottest chick in town. She was built, wearing all white, and she cocked her head at them.

"Hubba-Hubba," Melo gurgled. She was one fine pin-up and the only one who could make him forget about the radiation. It was hard not to know precisely who she was. Senio was hot for blondes, not redheads, but that didn't stop him either.

"Felice," Senio said, flirting with her, trying to steal her heart. "Do you mind if we call you Felice and not Phyllis? *Felice* means happy."

"Felice," Melo iterated, then reiterated and then again until Phyllis stared at him with obvious concern. "*Bebida?*"

"I don't drink anymore," she said, meaning it. Melo knew instantly who had arm-wrestled this gorgeous babe into teetotaling captivity. She had also gotten her hammer-hold on Nicasia and was trying for a half nelson on LaBelle. The woman, Anissa, spread panic and terror, even putting the grip on Melo about his continual drinking—drinking to forget. It was prescribed.

"I've seen you both up the street from me."

"Yeah, Palace. Senio lives on Palace."

"And, Melo. Your mother is a close friend of Anissa."

Melo shot her one of the stupefied looks he'd last used on Watanabe-san. "Close?"

"Coke?" Julio asked. "Sit down. We were talking about the war."

"It's over," Phyllis observed, unable to take her eyes off of Melo. "There can never be another war. The bomb ended war forever. Saint Germain and Gabriel have given Their promises. They never fail. The Violet Flame has cleansed evil from the earth. You don't need a crystal ball to see how true it is."

In spite of the drivel, both men snapped to life.

"I remember when they dropped the coke cases on Fukuoka Camp Number Seventeen. It was *epantoso*. We shit bricks." Senio said, encouraging Phyllis to take a sip of her coke. "A fifty-five gallon drum of catsup broke open by the slit trench."

"What's a slit trench?" she said, laughing.

"A *benjo*, bathroom."

"How come you stayed in camp for another month after the armistice?" Julio pressed them. Both men looked down at the bar, *yeah, well*, they muttered. "Some guys busted out of camp, grabbed a passing train and threw all the Japanese off. They just rode the trains, stealing food, getting drunk until they ended up where somebody spoke English."

"Those were the guys who believed we had actually won the war."

"Nobody knew anything. The guards all ran off and there we were with bags and bags of rice, bottles of *sake*. Senio spent the first week stealing everything he could find, razors, combs, *futons*. He snuck back and forth stealing, hiding things that belonged to the Japs. We already had everything we'd dreamed of stealin', like food."

"That was the first week," Senio said. "We didn't feel too great either. We still had hard lumps remembering our buddies who didn't make it, and there we were, eating ourselves sick."

"We didn't know anybody knew we were alive. We heard nothing for three years. *Nada*. We figured the whole thing was a trap," Melo muttered, hunched over his beer, walling it in with his arms, prison-style.

"Relax, it's not going anywhere," Julio told him, meaning the beer.

"But when the plane came over with American flags flying out the bomb-bays, we knew we'd been located. They dropped cigarette packs with notes saying, *We shall return*."

"We thought it was a sick joke," Senio said.

"LaBelle told Anissa she wrote you every day, every single day," Phyllis interrupted. "The letters went through the Red Cross."

"*Nada*," said Melo, looking strangled. It was a lie, anyway. More of her made-up stuff.

"Every day," Phyllis stated. "Three-and-a-half years. That's something like a thousand letters."

"So what's it to me?" he demanded. "I got the first ones at Clark Field, before we surrendered to the Japs. I wrote back. Cold shoulder. Like we say on the beach, *and that's all she wrote*."

"Look," she said, placing a hand on Melo's arm. He jumped. "You guys are heroes. You had a huge float in the parade at Fiesta."

"Not me. We were still in the Philippines. We liked it there, except they eat rice." Her hand was still weighing his arm down and it felt hot. She was making no move to lift it.

"Did you kill a lot of Japs?" Julio interrupted. Neither responded. "Say! I'll bet you gave them living hell," he said. "I'll bet you killed millions of 'em."

Both buddies took a swig from the bottlenecks and looked away. "No, not me," Melo said.

Phyllis simply watched them in the long bar mirror.

"Me, either," Senio said. "We didn't want to kill any Japs. We just wanted to get out of the camp. We didn't want to go home either, we just wanted out of camp."

"Come on, you hated the slant-eyed slime. I know you did. You wanted to slit their yellow bellies," Julio said, a confidential set to his eyes. Phyllis noticed how unnerved both men had become, but it still didn't compute. Everyone hated the Japanese, war was war. She remembered the old saw about the stamp where the GI told his mother to steam it off and underneath was, *they have cut off my tongue!*

War hatred survived the surrender. No one was ready to forgive and forget as the paper reported that large groups of the men from Jap Trap demanded repatriation, going home to their bombed-out Empire. They hated the *round-eyes* now.

"I'd like to invite you to my place," she said, changing the subject.

"I don't hate the Japanese," Melo mumbled, looking at Phyllis.

"See their guts hanging out like that? You didn't leave 'em squealin' like pigs with their guts dragging on the tarmac?"

They stared at Julio as if he was the enemy.

"Come on," Phyllis said, pulling at Melo. "You're right, the war is over." She stood to leave, looking pointedly at Julio.

"War is never over," Senio replied. "It lives on until the last man is gone."

"Come on." She tugged at Melo's arm. He had stopped being so edgy and followed her into the eye-aching sunlight. Senio's permanently requisitioned car was parked on the street. Melo piled in behind Phyllis, and Senio steered the old Chevy with his left hand and left the engine running when he dropped the two off in front of Phyllis' house. She asked Senio in as well but he had no interest.

"No, that's okay. I don't like being indoors during the day," he said. "We're used to jungle places with holes in the roof." Melo caught him checking things out in his rearview mirror as he drove away. He felt lost without his buddy. But once Phyllis had urged him inside her place and left the door ajar, he relaxed.

"You're safe," she said. "I won't lock the door."

"Not bad," he said, bobble heading, trying to look impressed as he surveyed the house. He figured she'd figure out that he could not concentrate for more than a few seconds anyway. *Rice brain.*

"My lease is up in a couple more months." She was conscious of the difference between this airy house and Nicasia's small Garcia adobe Melo had grown up in. His was typical, dark against the summer sun, and practical with low ceilings for warmth in the winter. Subsistence mud homes, functional and enduring.

"I don't have any beer," she confessed, sitting down on the loveseat and patting the cushion beside her. "I hope that's okay?"

He said nothing, remained standing.

"You probably want something to drink?" she said, judging that he'd already had enough. He nodded and made a little spiral with his finger.

"Back," he said, heading out to find a package liquor store.

"You don't talk much," she said when he returned thirty minutes later.

"Nothing to say," he offered and pulled the cap off the bottle with a small tool. "*Abre-latas*, opens cans and bottles. Spanish lesson."

"*Abre-latas*," she repeated, smiling. He tipped the bottle up, filling his mouth; he finally swallowed and burped. She could see him getting looser.

Later, because he could not bring himself to talk much, she took him into the bedroom. But he would not sit next to her on the bed. He sat on the floor which left her sitting above him on the edge of the bed. She began rubbing his neck.

"Yeah," he told her, "the Navy dropped whisky wrapped in mattresses and Doc Matson gave each of us a spoonful of whisky and we threw the mattresses out because we were used to sleeping on slats, wooden slats. I don't feel safe on a mattress."

"Can you tell me why?" she asked, purring into his ear as she traced the scars on his back. She was the bigger-than-life princess who roamed the countryside looking to bestow favors. If she succeeded, it would be the first time she wasn't three sheets to the wind herself when she granted favors.

"Four years we slept on slats, me and Senio next to each other, guarding. I can't sleep without him no more." He was getting smashed. Phyllis had had plenty of practice handling drunks. This one was over the edge and limp, so she left him propped up and slipped out to make a phone call.

"Anissa, it's me," she said. "I've got Melo here. Tell Nicasia he's in good hands."

"Don't drink. I told LaBelle you were really sober, honestly and truly on the wagon. I told her you were straight as an arrow so she'd stop swearing. The bet was her idea anyway, not mine."

"I'd forgotten about that. I'm a good girl now—a very good girl. Even without alcohol." Phyllis paused. She reflected that her sacrificing booze and praying to the Violet Light to restore World Peace had been an historic success and she took no small credit for this.

The flip side was, of course, now that peace had been signed on the *Battleship Missouri* and the ink was dry, her lease was up. It was the right time to either go home or stay put. (Florida didn't count. She planned to celebrate the sale of the Lantana house with four fingers of Scotch, maybe more.)

Why the bloody not?

"Senio doesn't like LaBelle either," Phyllis whispered into the phone to Anissa. "In the car, he said she was lewd, crude and obnoxious."

"That's typical GI talk. She's not rude-crude-and-obnoxious. She's sane, and right now she's really spitting tacks. She's hurt and angry, so she can't do anything but howl."

"He said she was pushy."

"Sure, she might be pitching a fit, but she's finally packing," Anissa said. "Nicasia had me drive down to the bus station to buy her a one-way ticket back to Colorado, said she was happy to pay for it. Everyone knows Melo wants her out."

Phyllis hung up and then relayed this information to Melo who was still sitting on the floor using the bed as his backrest. When Phyllis related that LaBelle was packing, he whistled through his teeth.

"Maybe for the short haul. She said she'd be back. Wants a job here with the V.A., getting paid to tell men what to do and when."

He took a slug of the beer. "*Cerveza*," he whispered.

"When's the last time you got it up?"

"My dick?" He had to think. It was before the surrender.

"Nothing since the surrender. I can't handle anything since the surrender in forty-two."

"Let me help you. Trust me, Melo. I'm very good at this," she coaxed him. She was Tara, the Compassionate Goddess of the sideways lightning eyes who eases suffering. She kissed him, stroked him, whistled tickle-breath along his spine. She rolled him over where he was, onto the rug, onto his back. And she teased him with her dragonfly soft touch, a caress no stronger than a breeze. When she floated above him, hanging, he was forced to rise up to meet her. When he could stand it no longer he came, splintering.

She watched him go crazy, fly out of his mind, and it was at that moment she understood that under threat of extinction, the species grows more potent; it can procreate an entire generation, populate a whole continent in order to preserve itself.

The beheaded dandelion bursts into seed and scatters in the soft winds before it withers. Once spent, it desiccates, lying on the shore where seas of dandelions will spring up.

Afterwards, Melo slept for ten stretched hours, dreamless and without screaming. He gave her seed enough for a thousand nights of copulations. He could not save himself from her, and she would conceive a son because so many men had died.

T wo days later, when Phyllis and Emma met for lunch, again at La Fonda, Emma Gudman immediately sensed a change in Phyllis.

"It's nothing more than hormones," she said, shaking her head. Phyllis then whispered how fulfilled she felt, she used that word fulfilled. She said she felt truly whole and like a woman for the first time.

"Oh my dear, this will never do." Emma knew that the mismatched affair was doomed. "You've got that insanity that comes over pregnant women."

"I've never felt more myself," Phyllis said, very pleased with herself.

"It won't last another week. I've got a doctor who can help."

The second woman to learn of the pregnancy was Anissa, who shook her head, mystified at how Phyllis seemed oblivious to her own stupidity.

The word spiraled out like chimney smoke over the small town where Nicasia was helpless to deal with the issue.

"Just let it be," she told LaBelle. "It's God's will."

LaBelle raged, tore up her bus ticket, unpacked her suitcase and flung her clothes everywhere. "*Hijo de Puta!*" she bellowed, convinced it was a boy.

Was this just another stall, an excuse? Nicasia wondered.

"No, goddammit, it is not from God, it's from Saint Stinking Germain and all the chickenshit they've been loading on us about God's Victorious Shit!" Nicasia said nothing about the swearing. Phyllis had only vowed not to drink or smoke, or so she had said.

LaBelle paced the kitchen like a bull. "It's like the Mormons too! All holy, no drinking, no coffee, but can they fuck like rabbits!"

"Men will be men," Nicasia suggested.

"Ever since he got back, he's not the same. He looks like Melo but he's not. He's part dog, part devil. Something, somebody ripped him apart, mutilated him. Listen to what I'm telling you." She looked straight down at Nicasia who cowered on a hard chair in front of the kitchen table. "She's got the clap and now he's got it."

"I told him she's not even a Catholic. I warned him. I said, maybe she's changed?"

"She's still a whore."

Nicasia continued, and then faltered, "It only happened once." She tried to make it sound like a small error.

"Says who? He told you that? He's a slimy worm. He's been

screwing her over and over, every chance he gets. Don't believe she's packing to go back to some place it rains all the time. Goddammit! I'm going to run her out of town on the back of a burro and he's going with her. Mary and Joseph. I hope they sleep in a cesspool. Their baby's deformed."

"After all you've done, all those letters." Nicasia knew LaBelle's suit was hopeless, that LaBelle was another exhausted casualty of war. They all were and the situation was very difficult. Mothers love their sons; women came and went. Sons stayed. Once you have a son, he's yours for life.

"Unless he's a gringo," she muttered silently. Gringos push their children out of the nest like Jack-in-the-boxes. Up and out. Bottle-fed, off to school. Get a corporate job, make money. She could not do that.

"That slut has my baby. She has stolen my baby!" LaBelle raged, enlisting her own private logic. "My baby…"

"But Melo has battle-fatigue. He is very sick, too." Nicasia tried to soothe her.

"That makes it worse. If he has the poisoning like Roddy said, then I was going to have his baby quick, to give to you." She stopped swaggering and rested her hand on Nicasia's sagging shoulder. "I was going to bathe him, powder him and bring him to you. Your baby."

"*Querida.*" Nicasia reached out to touch the abandoned *novia*. She took her moist hand and held it.

LaBelle dropped to her knees, shifting weight because of the grit on the brick floor, closer, face to face with her tragic *mamacita*. "Too many losses. He has dropped me. Now he's walking out on you."

Nicasia understood what LaBelle was trying to say, but she knew that Melo would always come back to her. But not to LaBelle, not now. Even if the baby was half-gringo, did she think Phyllis could steal the baby away from his *nana*?

LaBelle was right. The hard truth was that yes, Phyllis would never bring the baby to his *nana*. Nicasia began to weep.

"And I was the one going to give you Faustino and Franque back." LaBelle sat on the floor at Nicasia's feet, sobbing. "I made that vow—that I would make your world better. Back like it was."

Listening, Nicasia burst into sobs. Of course it was true. In her mind, she traced evidences of how LaBelle showed her furious loyalty to Melo—how she'd grown fertile and fat. She was ready. She was abundant enough to give birth and nurture her babies. She was an intimidating queen bee able to do what only queen bees do.

"*Querida*, you take too much on yourself. Some things are too broken to fix." Nicasia sobbed. LaBelle had offered the overpowering ability to restore her losses with the gift of new life, clean life. Nicasia had not understood. She had treated LaBelle as a foreigner—as an occupying army, a Nazi—when the woman's mission was to save Melo for his agonized mother; she prayed for him only, she lived for the Garcias—present past and to be born.

Her mission was to save both Melo and Nicasia. To hell with the others.

LaBelle had insisted that God keep him alive, which gave Senio a free ride on Melo's bus. She had no other intention in life but to preserve Melo's life, because Nicasia had already lost so much in this War Against Evil.

"If she has his baby, it will stink. The blood will be piss-yellow." LaBelle seemed to bluster, but it still rang true. "*La Puta* is polluting *La Raza.*" *Raza* meant everything deep, valuable, intelligent, strong and fierce about her people; it was their culture, their gift to the world. It was who they were. Their very being and heritage; their love for their land.

"Come," Nicasia said. "Come to my bed."

LaBelle followed, wracked with outrage and loss, and together, arms wrapped around each other, they lay entwined on the sagging bed, the *cama matrimoniale* Faustino and Nicasia had slept on as young married lovers, dreaming of making their world together. LaBelle, three times the weight of Nicasia—no, four—moved her arm to support the old woman's head.

"I didn't understand. I just never understood why you were here, why God had sent you," Nicasia said, contrite and riding the sorrow of her losses. "You really wanted to give me back Faustino and Franque?"

"How could I say his name and not make you weep? I saw Tojo pounding nails into his skull, torturing him and torturing you. So I said nothing so maybe you could sleep at night. I screamed for you. What could I say that would not make you cry?"

"You came here to save my family?"

"I wanted to fight for you, for Melo. I wanted to lift you up to the sky like the *Padres* with the communion host—hold you up in my hands and honor you."

"Why?"

"I saw it from the first. You have *gracia*, you are kind and excellent. I cannot watch everything turn bad and not fight." *Gracia* did not translate; it was rare, beyond grace. What the Virgin has. *Full of gracia.*

"I wanted to see you restored," LaBelle whispered.

"When Melo brought you home, those years ago, did you see the future? Everybody was alive, Faustino, Franque, Melo. We were all together, alive."

"No, *Mamacita*, I could not see the real future like it turned out when Melo was in the National Guard. But he saw it coming, the draft, the war."

"How do you know he saw it? You were young then, children, *novios*, sixteen years old."

"He knew it, because the war was in him and he knew it because it was so huge and dangerous. People know about their lives, what's important. If you look deep, you know when you're going to die."

"The war is his life?"

"Life, yes. Not his death, because I said, *no.* Melo was the one man who had to live."

"How?" Nicasia had understood, but she needed proof.

"He promised he'd come back to me. I made him promise."

"But I prayed that the Virgin keep him safe, I believed that God would protect him." Nicasia had not wanted to allow LaBelle this much power over her family, for she had prayed incessantly; she had devoted herself to her own men. Thinking on it, Nicasia considered that LaBelle's faith was arrogant.

"Me, not God. I protected him. God wants to snag souls, pull them up before they can mess up. Melo was headed for trouble, all that stuff on the Plaza, whose bench was whose. You remember, always in trouble?"

"You surprise me, *Hija*. I don't know what to say," Nicasia admitted to her strange almost daughter-in-law. "You astound me." A heavy veil had been lifted; LaBelle was a beautiful birthing *madre*. She was a Warrior Mother, not a bully. And she was arrogant, but Nicasia saw that it was just because she was young. Twenty year olds always think things are easier than they are, and swifter.

"I know I'm pretty loud and gross, but I never said anything that wasn't true, and I never got burned up on stuff that didn't need fixing. Only I didn't ask somebody else to fix everything up for me, like Anissa calling up Saint Germain and that God Victorious to do everything for her, like her personal servants. I can fix damage by myself."

"So, now what can you do when Melo has gone *loco*, out of his gourd?"

"I'll come up with something," LaBelle said softly. Her fists were clenched, her breath short; she couldn't think and talk at the same time—not about the heavy stuff.

18

Mesmerized by the campfire of memory. Melo screwed himself up to check out the Plaza, skirting it like the coyote he was. For him the Plaza represented the centuries of the town itself; the center of his youthful being. He went alone to survey it from a distance, always able to turn back, to duck into the dark of the Famous Coney Island Club bar.

He walked past the Cash and Carry on Palace headed towards Washington Street and nodded to Tom Haskins, the owner's kid who was old enough to shave now and did not remember him. Tom stood in the doorway talking to Paco in Mexican; both men turned to watch him as he passed. It seemed to Melo that Paco peeled off and trailed him because when he turned his head, there was the Mexican guy walking too close, so he shot him a scowl. But when Melo halted at the corner of Palace Avenue and Washington Street, the crazy Mexican loped past. He was the last of the faggot vendors with his flea-bitten burro tied to a lamppost.

Watanabe would have had him for lunch.

Melo realized that maybe he'd overreacted. Maybe the guy wasn't walking too close, but he didn't like anybody standing too close. Not LaBelle either. So he paused to say something friendly.

"Do I know you?" Melo tried to smile.

The woodchopper shrugged his shoulders and put his hands up with a good-natured smile. "Paco," he said.

Mexicans are something else, Melo thought. This town had been settled by fierce Moors who'd just as soon kick you as kiss you. And here was this *tipo* with his gentle Mayan blood, the meek kind that incited the conquistadors to sack and massacre. Poor bastard. Before the war, he said to himself, the guy would have either learned to stick up for himself or been beaten up. The Plaza had a pecking order and it looked like Paco wasn't even in the line.

Melo patted the burro's dusty head and wove across Washington where he stood with his hands on his hips, satisfied that the Plaza looked the same as it did when he left with the National Guard in 1941; only he had changed. The Plaza was still okay but he had cratered, been bombed out.

Trees—the same elms. Obelisk in the center. From the north side sixty Indians passively watched life go on. For Melo, they had never really counted; they never crossed the street to where he sat on his bench.

He counted them: thirty benches, some on the center diagonals, some rimming the outside in the shade. The *primo* bench now faced the manure littered spot reserved for the much-photographed Paco and his burro. The same buildings were there and all the same streaming traffic rolled past. If you wanted to go from here to there, say from Garcia to the post office, you had to go by the Plaza, by this bench. Say, you went from Galisteo to Chimayo on Good Friday on your knees, Melo would spot you as you crawled past.

He walked slowly by the benches, remembering how it was before the war. There were actually four *primo* benches with the great front row view. And every car that passed knew to salute. Arms waved, guys hooted, girls smiled.

Now that it was fall the Plaza was dappled with turning leaves, the religious freaks had vanished, and the screaming pamphlet-pushers (the human litter) was pretty much gone. Melo walked slowly over to the bench he liked, his bench. But it was not empty. A kid sat on his own personal bench.

Melo took inventory. One bench over, a drunk slept with a

newspaper tented over his face. Two women with thick ankles had grabbed the farther bench and were talking quietly to each other, their feet apart, holding their purses on their laps. Nothing he could do about that; they'd yammer for a while and move on. Farther down was an empty bench.

Melo hung back, apart, watching when the burro let out a bray and delivered a steaming pile of burro shit which Paco-the-Mexican (after removing his sombrero) swept up. There were always burros on the Plaza when he grew up. Now there was just this mangy one left.

Two benches occupied and the third bench, the one Melo liked best, was cooling the butt of a teenage thug, hair slick with styling grease, pegged pants, combat boots, black clothes with a switchblade on a chain attached to his belt loop. The fourth was empty but it wasn't Melo's designated bench. The third bench had his name on it; he had always set himself up on the third.

He shook his head, took out a cigarette and looking down, lit it. Then he raised his head, blew out the smoke and swaggered to his bench, facing the *pachuco* kid. Sixteen giant steps, rhythmical, swift paced and deadly.

"Off!" he said.

"Huh?" The smart-ass kid was ready to argue.

"My bench. You are on my bench. Beat it. Scram."

The jerk stuck out his lower lip, sneering. "Says who?"

Melo hated to do it. No question but that he was forced to do it. Was he being unreasonable? After all he'd been through and now there was a snot-nosed kid right there on his own private bench, the bench that had been marked for Melo Garcia, street fighter and son-of-a-bitch mean-bastard.

All of this history had taken place before Paco had wandered into town to sell wood from the back of his burro. He should have figured out the deal because he'd been standing right near Melo's bench when the fight broke out. Maybe Paco was too dumb to be a reliable witness, but he'd seen it all and he should have known that Melo was completely in the right because the third bench was sacred.

Paco could have said something to José, the cop, when he appeared suddenly wearing a more reasonable cop's uniform. And he could have said it in Mexican. José should have gotten the straight story from the Mexican witness.

But no. José acted like a zombie cop and grabbed Melo by the back. He yanked him across the street and made him stand next to a fresh pile of new burro shit while the facts of the case were counted out. Meanwhile, Paco claimed to understand and to agree with Melo. Then Paco turned around and agreed with the fag *pachuco* and the whole thing went right down the drain.

"*Sí, sí. Cómo nó,*" the Mexican said.

"I could tell he wasn't from here," Melo explained to José the cop, no longer dressed like Pancho Villa. Anyone from Santa Fe knew which bench belonged to Melo and as a sign of respect to leave that bench empty. The Mexican seemed to confirm that it was like this South of the Border in small towns. But that the *pachuco* had been hanging around and sitting on that bench for about a year or two.

"That doesn't cut it," Melo announced.

"Melo, I gotta say…" José was trying to be reasonable.

"You said he was from Española. They got their own ratty Plaza."

"Melo, I don't want to book you. But…"

The ambulance arrived and the kid was loaded in and hauled off. "I went easy on him," Melo stated for the record. "He better *never* come back here."

"Melo, now listen to me. The war is over, you hear me? There's no more beating up people just for the hell of it," José said while extracting a pair of steel handcuffs off his belt hook.

"Jerk wouldn't move. There's an empty bench right over there. I had no choice."

"All the benches are empty now," José said. "You're scaring the bejesus out of everybody. This is a public place." The cuff opened like a coyote trap and the cop moved to snag one of Melo's wrists. "I don't want to do this."

Melo threw a punch to his gut that doubled him; José fell groaning to the ground, rolling onto his side madder than hell. Melo would have taken it from Japanese, but he wasn't going to take it from a guy who was in grade school when Melo was the Big Man on Campus, when he was The Law. Besides, he was no longer starving and bullied by little short Japs like before and his *rice brain* was starting to clear up. There was something to be said for three squares a day—*posole*, beans and beer.

José was on the ground and Melo stood over him, looking down, when a backup cop appeared on a horse and put Melo on the ground with one swift kick. Melo knew horses; he knew that lying between the four long legs of a quarter horse was not good placement. Still, he had been away and waited more than four years to get back home to give 'em hell.

Paco untied the burro and led her off. If LaBelle had been spooning out Frito Pie at Woolworth's, she would have come out, picked him up like a sack of chiles, and saved him some jail time. But it was his idea to make her quit her job and go back to Trinidad. Senio was driving that Chevy of his dad's all over the place, sharing smokes with some blond, cruising with one hand on the horn and his arm out the open window. He was otherwise occupied.

Nobody was around to take custody. So they called his ma.

In the police station, Melo was forced to sit on a wooden chair with his hands cuffed in front of him. His most serious offense was attacking an officer and he was booked for unruly behavior, disturbing the peace, and resisting arrest.

"José's not an officer, he's a smart-ass sergeant," Melo said. Men standing around the precinct cleared their throats and said nothing. Anissa, the exact person he did not want to see, walked in. He looked sideways at her because for some screwed up reason she had forgotten to leave town with Edna Ballard and the rest of her congregation in search of the New Jerusalem. No one could figure why she hung on, unless it was because of that flyboy in Albuquerque. Or to get under Melo's skin.

"What's going on here?" she demanded. It was none of her business.

"Where's Nicasia?" someone asked her. They all knew big-mouth Anissa from her scraps on the Plaza and if anyone was disqualified as a character witness for Melo, she was it. Her latest holier-than-thou mission was to clean up the Plaza by yanking drunks off the benches and making sure no one pissed on the grass.

Cleaning it up for whom? It was a public space. Drunks, children, widows and politicians used it. They were the citizens, they loved it here. All they had to do to get free speech restored was to kick all the I AMers off it and the first and last step was Anissa herself. And until Melo returned from the dead (so to speak), the Plaza was reserved for diversity, all nationalities—French, Lebanese, Spanish, Indian and Anglo—and all religions, all lost souls. Mounted police on pretty horses clustered in the sun chatting in the three serviceable languages, switching back and forth like radio dials.

"Get her out of here," Melo muttered. "Where's my *mamacita*?"

Anissa stumbled over the answer to that question. She was sleeping like the dead cuddled up with LaBelle. The door was wide open.

"Taking a siesta," Anissa replied.

"Why didn't you wake her? You knew Melo was in here." Everybody within miles knew now.

A reasonable question, hard to answer. She had been afraid to wake her and it looked like the bus had already left without LaBelle. Big trouble, she surmised, so she just shook her head.

"She was not alone, she was with LaBelle," Anissa said later and immediately regretted it. Melo strained at the cuffs, stood up and kicked the chair over. His howls were indistinct, difficult to transcribe.

"Whoa," Captain Sanchez said, "get back down, Buddy," he ordered and slammed Melo back onto a second chair.

"Get your hands off of me!" Melo spat. "Get Felice then. Here's her number."

"Phyllis MacAndrew is out of the country," Anissa said.

What were the dumb-asses talking about? This made sense to no one.

Melo addressed Anissa. "Bitch."

"She went to Mexico."

"Negative," Melo said. "I saw her last night."

Anissa did not elaborate as she all but fled the precinct to try again to wake Nicasia from what on the surface had all the trappings of a suicide pact, or a strange irregularity. She returned and nervously crept through the open door.

Both women were out of bed, alive and slumped over their elbows on the kitchen table—but not talking. When she entered, they barely glanced at her as they sat silently drinking coffee. The room was still littered with the worldly belongings of LaBelle, lying where she'd heaved them in her fit. From their grim faces, Anissa guessed that they knew about Melo's bullying the kid downtown and that someone had told them he had been booked.

"If you'd only answered your phone!" Anissa complained, coming through the door. "He wants to see you." She was relieved that they were at least functioning. "He's at the precinct."

Neither spoke. They exchanged glances, and each time the glance became more loaded with significance. With the last volley even Anissa could read the fact Nicasia and LaBelle knew Phyllis' little secret and Nicasia was in LaBelle's corner of the ring. She could see that both women were incensed and that perhaps sleeping arm-in-arm was a Spanish warrior's way of preparing for battle.

Good news, bad news. "Do you want the good news first?" Anissa asked. She knew just how to fix everything—just the word "abortion" would help.

"No," LaBelle announced, resentment shooting out of her.

"Do you want the bad news then?" Anissa had the car ready to drive Nicasia to the police station. Tradition dictated that mothers of prisoners bring tortillas to feed the incarcerated. We'll just swing by the Cash and Carry and load up.

"No," said Nicasia. "We've had enough bad news, right *Hija?*" Anissa was baffled at the new bond between them and remembered weeks ago having driven, cash in hand, to the bus station for LaBelle's one-way ticket to Trinidad, Colorado, at Nicasia's insistence.

Over the years, the ups and downs of these two women had defied all Midwest common sense. It was enough to give Anissa headaches. She remembered in particular the time she'd been roped into driving the two of them to Chimayo to pray for the POWs. LaBelle had masses of curls then, not to mention an intimidating set of breasts and a definite Latin dazzle. Now she was simply big and surly and her eyebrows seemed to have grown together. But her nail polish never chipped.

At Chimayo, she'd refused to get down onto her knees and she disrespectfully told God to get Melo back PDQ, and Nicasia never corrected her. Clearly LaBelle had no respect for authority. No manners, no grace. Just animal determination.

"Melo needs you," Anissa said, trying not to alarm them through any inflection in her voice. She was curious about the clothes plastered all around the room, but said nothing.

"He can wait," Nicasia said. "We waited years for him." Anissa was puzzled. She resolved to listen to them, to heed them. His mother would have gone to the stake for the kid. Why not today?

"He's being taken to jail, Nicasia. He needs you to bail him out." Nothing hysterical to incite LaBelle. Anissa downplayed Melo's violence. "I'll give you a ride."

"Good," LaBelle said. Anissa remembered the night at La Fonda bar when LaBelle had set out to protect her, splintering a chair and missing Phyllis, the tramp who had stolen her husband, Russell. LaBelle was known to brood upon injustice and to claim the right to personally administer against it. And just the word *adultery* was enough to throw her into a rage; she could be counted on to fling more chairs. She'd be a great stand-in for Melo rattling the bars and yelling obscenities in the slammer.

"They can have him," his mother said.

That figures, Anissa thought, considering how everyone was

running LaBelle out of the State of New Mexico. She even looked bitter, vengeful. It was evident that Nicasia had asked her to stay. But why?

"Tell him to keep his pants buttoned," his mother said.

"Come on, Nicasia, you're his mother," Anissa said.

"That boy has been nothing but trouble since he got back," his mother said. "He could use some time in the cooler."

"He's war damaged, Nicasia. Roddy said he'd be this way for a while and to just give him what he asks for, no questions asked. You remember?"

"That was before."

"And now? Now he's not suffering? He's just hunky-dory fine and dandy?"

"He could use some time in the slammer." Nicasia folded her skinny arms around her caved-in chest. "With his pants on," she added.

Anissa knew that given enough time, Melo would get himself into deeper trouble with the police. No one wanted any truck with him. She could not help him; she was out. He'd already drawn lines that Anissa could not cross. Not to mention LaBelle's being out in left field. Phyllis just drove off, probably too chicken to deal with him too. Everybody was holding out for Nicasia to take over and reason with her son.

"Nicasia," Anissa said, taking a chair at the table. She brushed away some crumbs from the oilcloth *mantel* and waited until her next-door neighbor, the woman she had grown to cherish and revere; the woman who had suffered more than most from the useless damages of the war, was ready to listen and to actually look at her.

Nicasia and LaBelle had pursed their mouths and stared off toward corners of the room, refusing to speak while the votive candle wavered, then steadied. It wavered again and with a sizzling whisper, went out. A scent of burning string filled the kitchen. It was the only smell; no beans, nothing simmered on the cook stove anymore.

"Nicasia," Anissa began again, knowing that the dead candle bode badly for Melo's bail. She was pleased that it had quietly gone out by itself before LaBelle had violently strangled the wick.

"Melo needs you to come and settle him down, or the police are going to be hard on him. He started a fight on the Plaza. Beat up a kid from Española because he was sitting on the wrong bench."

"Back to the same old thing," LaBelle announced. "This is where I came in."

"Okay, so it seems that you are both really down on the guy, but if just one of you posted bail it would help. Captain Sanchez says he needs Nicasia."

LaBelle shot a glance at Anissa and whispered to the older woman, "She doesn't know." It looked as if Anissa had tuned out Melo's latest outrage.

Nicasia took a breath and spoke. "Melo has to marry your—what did you call her? Your doxie friend, Phyllis."

"Oh my God, that's all taken care of," Anissa dismissed their feelings. "That's my good news!"

"If he stays in jail, he can't chase her down and get married." Nicasia knew logistics. "I want him kept there."

"It's for the best," LaBelle said. "The only solution."

Anissa knew that with one word she could turn the tide and have them back in Melo's camp. She took a breath and plunged. "She's already had an abortion." Anissa had not wanted to break confidence, but the postwar world was vast and dazzling and Phyllis was ready to take it on in spades. This breach of confidence could only help because, if anything, Phyllis was ready to ride now, and if she meant what she'd said about making Anissa come around, well then she'd gotten what she had come for.

"No!" both women shrieked at the same time. "*Dios mio, no!*"

"That's my baby, she's killing my little boy!" screamed LaBelle.

"*Pobrecito. Pobre, pobre, pobre,*" Nicasia simpered, dissolving into a pitiful state.

Anissa was no fan of abortion, but she had a practical side to her and the two women brought her up short, surprising her.

"Abortion is murder," LaBelle said unambiguously

"Get me the little baby," Nicasia said. "Why didn't she think of me?"

"It's too late," Anissa said. A woman like Phyllis would never go through nine months of pregnancy, not to mention childbirth, just to be generous and demonstrate her high principles. Phyllis was on the move; she was on the make for another man like Russell Barclay, a man who might save her from herself by gifts and careful flattery.

"She could stay here. We'd take care of her until the baby comes," Nicasia said. "No one would care. No one would see her." If the baby were handed over it would be theirs, not a runaway selfish Gringo child. If it were raised with them, he would stay. And it was a boy.

"You're right," Anissa said. Everyone was right. But Phyllis, short on most virtues, at least knew herself and what she was running from; all she desired was a first class ticket out, and in her covenant with luxury, lugging around a half-breed boy was a roundtrip back to the wrong terrain.

For Nicasia, a child was more life, and she hungered for the two children LaBelle had offered.

Anissa could only put up with the women's noisy heartache a short while when she had to get out in the clean air. After that she was too conflicted and depressed to return to the police station and explain that they might as well give Melo a washed set of pajamas and lock him up.

The phone rang off and on all through the dark night. Neither woman cared; the only call they would welcome was from Phyllis, contrite.

"I'm afraid something has happened to your mother," Captain Sanchez informed Melo.

"Get me out of here!" he howled. His cell was small. The ten lights overhead turned everything grey and his eyelids were so thin he couldn't sleep under the blazing wattage. There was no dark, no relief, and he railed and rattled the bars and screamed. The Captain sent someone the next morning to give Nicasia a ride, but she turned it down.

"It's better he stays where he is." She knew his rages.

"I'll go," LaBelle offered.

"No, *Hija*, not yet." So LaBelle drew herself up, combed her curls and set out to put a note on Phyllis' door, but she was helpless to leave Melo to himself and showed up in the precinct anyway.

"He does not want to see you," they told LaBelle. She knew this but she could not stay away. He was upstairs in a room with a small window and a view of the sky but not of Senio, who stood below outside on the sidewalk ruminating over his buddy's mess. He tossed a coin to decide whether or not to tell Melo about the baby. The dame must have been about one minute pregnant. Not much more. It had to have happened that night after the Famous Coney Island Bar.

"Please turn the lights out at night, so he can sleep," LaBelle asked as she turned to leave. "You know what he's been through."

With the lights out at night, he slept until he woke everyone in the building with his terrifying nightmare shrieks. His body had been set afire again. The screams echoed against the hard adobe walls.

When Phyllis returned home and read the note on her door, she realized she should have told him something, certainly a lie. The pregnancy was hers, the upshot of hazardous duty, and it did not concern him. She had tempted fate before and skirted it. Now she had been caught short. So what? Still, she should have listened when Emma had clearly warned her about the jeopardy of dealing with these passionate Spanish. "They fly off the handle at the slightest thing," she had been told.

"Best never to bring our little secret up. God only knows what will happen," Emma cautioned her as they rode back across the border in a Mexican taxi. The procedure wasn't ghoulish; the doctor spoke English.

"Sorry I left without telling you," she said to him when he was brought downstairs and seated before her at a hacked-at, carved-on piece of desk the size of Nicasia's kitchen table. He was wan and his eyes were red. "Very rude of me."

"Where did you go?" There was a frantic look overwhelming his face. No one in the jail had hassled him; they all knew what the Japanese had done to him and he'd come out half hero and half beast.

"Emma and I went over the border to Juarez. It's a charming place."

"For what?"

"Oh dear, you haven't heard of Martino's, a very fancy place where you can get lobster and steak, surf and turf—like the Stork Club in New York."

"A restaurant? Which one did you have?"

"Both, darling. Of course, I had both." He stared at her in disbelief.

"Both surf and turf? You went there for that?"

She could see that this confused him; that she was talking to a *rice brain*. Of course he had not heard of the Stork Club. The very word might be a trigger to something else, so she dropped it fast.

"I hear you got into trouble on the Plaza," she said. His hot blood was no surprise, but the fact that no one had bailed him out was curious. These Spanish families were tight.

"I gotta get out," he said. "Senio told me that Mama knows something. He wouldn't say."

Phyllis sensed danger, froze and then turned to the Captain, "How much does he need?"

"Two grand," Captain Sanchez said. "Cash."

"Oh, dear. How long does it take for a Florida bank draft to clear?"

"Ask the bank," Sanchez said. "Ten days, two weeks."

"And you won't take a check?"

"Felice, look. You don't have to do that. Senio's my buddy. He always comes through for me," Melo said. She smiled, relieved that she might just walk out and avoid dealing with this fiery man.

"He's outside, camped out on the sidewalk, guarding you. Okay if he comes in?"

"Is the Pope a Catholic?"

She stood and gave Melo a weak smile. First she had to get out of this jam, and she left the small jail easily buying her way out by trailing promises behind her.

She'd been bestowing favors on the wrong people; she had harmed him. And she had essentially harmed herself. She'd been lured into a strange cult and into an even stranger culture, all because she was weak and lonely and mad at stupid Jerry. Hiding behind her charade, she could not accept any blame or rejection even from idiots. She would do herself a favor if she went straight to La Fonda, pecked Jerry on the cheek and ordered a double.

"Melo wants to see you," she told Senio as she came out into the sunlight from the jail. "He's in bad shape."

"Did you tell him about the abortion?"

"It is not his concern. It's mine." She smiled lightly and walked up the block in the direction of the Plaza. She might send for her Lincoln Zephyr, and once it arrived she'd no longer be walking. Like an idiot, she started counting her steps.

They still played the same *Old Santa Fe Trail* song. Nothing was new; things were still lively at the familiar old bar. Conversations came from various corners of the main lobby, and off to the left, the bar was filled.

"It's Saturday," the hostess explained.

"Is Jerry still here?" Then she saw him at a distance, facing a very large gesticulating woman. After waving for a few seconds, she managed to catch his eye.

"Hello! A face from the past!" she called out. He did a double take, immediately breaking off from what had been so absorbing that he practically tripped running to greet her.

"What a coincidence." He kissed her cheek. "Come."

When she moved to follow, she saw that he'd been talking to LaBelle who last heard of was being rocketed up the highway to Colorado in a grinding bus. Phyllis sensed a land-mine when Jerry waved LaBelle over and he pulled out three chairs from around a small table. The heat from

LaBelle's fury preceded her, but Phyllis was certain that the news of her plans to return immediately to Florida would departure plans would calm the poor rejected woman down.

"Oh dear, I'm interrupting something between the two of you," Phyllis said, not wanting to sit, never thinking that she was on the line.

"No, no," Jerry insisted, taking her by the arm.

"I thought you were about to move on!" Phyllis said. "I'm planning to leave as well. You and I have that same thing in common. Be sure to tell Anissa and her clique that I'm on my way to better things."

They were both outsiders and trying to get in deep with the locals. This town had formed alliances over the past four hundred years—strong alliances. Closed associations.

"It's a tough town."

"I don't give a rat's-ass what you do, *Puta*," LaBelle said flatly. "Father Jerry and I say that abortion is murder."

Phyllis took a deep breath. "What business is it of yours? I don't meddle in your life. You bloody well can stay out of mine. I just came to tell you I was leaving."

Jerry put his hand over Phyllis', both to console her and to pin her to the table. "This is a very Catholic community, and to them, abortion is a grievous mortal sin. But…"

"You are judgmental, condemning, petty-minded people and you can bloody well mind your own business. People have abortions all the time."

"Not here."

"That's exactly why I had to go to Juarez. But the doctor there said that since the war he's seen women from here every month, all the time." Phyllis misread their serious looks for interest; they were not listening.

"Why aren't you cheering?" she demanded, shooting looks at LaBelle. "I thought you wanted to marry the chap. Well, take him. He's all yours!"

"Phyllis, child, sweet thing," Jerry began slowly. "Will you let me state the problem from a completely different point of view, one you've never considered, I'm sure?"

"If I have to stay and listen to your preaching, I'll need a stiff drink."

He laughed. Of course she could have a drink. He waved to the bartender.

"One Scotch on the rocks and one beer," he called out. Not a word passed until the drinks had come. He kept one hand pinning Phyllis' arm down, the other on LaBelle's wrist. She had gained so much weight over the past year he had hardly recognized her when she had bristled into the bar. He was relieved that the chair under her still held. The story had poured out from LaBelle the minute she marched into the bar looking for the ex-priest. "We've got to talk," she had said.

"A cigarette too?" Phyllis reminded him.

When they were served, he put his head down, closed his eyes and invoked some unnamed assistance. While he fussed with his preliminaries, Phyllis wondered why he'd stayed on after the war. Was the CID still creeping around, listening for conversations at the single most likely place, the communal well? Who was paying him now?

"LaBelle," he began, still bridging the two of them with his arms, "is upset because you did not offer her your baby, if you did not want it."

Phyllis was unprepared for this. "Me?"

They both nodded.

"If I went on and actually gave birth to the pathetic thing, I'd want to keep it for myself," she answered. "It's a lot of trouble."

"So, no baby," he surmised.

"Exactly," Phyllis said. "Like war. No one has won this one." She took an initial tentative sip to see if he'd brought her the good stuff, and then a hungry pull on the highball glass.

"Melo's a basket case," she added. "He's in no position to be a half decent husband."

LaBelle gingerly took a taste of her beer and drew in a deep breath, obviously unsure where to begin.

"May I discuss that point?" Jerry said. "LaBelle is in love with Melo.

She's loyal to him. She says that she pledged to care for him and his mother for better or for worse, and this is worse."

"Why?" Phyllis said. "Enough is enough. He could not care less about her, she's fat."

"He doesn't know what he wants," Jerry said, looking at LaBelle whose face was now streaming with tears. Phyllis felt sorry for the poor flailing thing. What other options did she have? Was there anything more than poverty and cold winds in Trinidad, that train stop to and from Chicago? No one ever got off in Trinidad, if anything, they all boarded the Atchison, Topeka and the Santa Fe for Los Angeles just to get the hell out of Trinidad, and now LaBelle was being run out of Santa Fe, the one place with bright lights.

"So, you and LaBelle know what's good for him?" Phyllis asked.

"You have the floor," Jerry said, encouraging her. After she took another sip of her Scotch, memories of a bright past came to her, memories of dancing with handsome men. Memories of new dresses, her lime green peignoir and orchid corsages. She remembered her car, her house, her sea grape arbor, the concert halls in Aberdeen, her schoolmates laughing, and she wondered why she had ever turned away. Everyone said it was the war, but was it really just the war? No, it was the grey petty minds of Aberdeen, so she ended the war not victorious, but more lonely and estranged.

If not home, where could she go next?

"I'm leaving this place better than I found it," she began slowly and although LaBelle wasn't listening, she did not interrupt. Phyllis wanted to insert something about how her conversion and alliance to Saint Germain did indeed end the war, that she played her part, but she thought better of it.

"I'm a good person; I did well by all of you. I brought Melo out of his shell. I showed him that he is not impotent. I did what I do very well, you have to agree."

LaBelle had met her match. She might be brought around to allow Phyllis her personal success if she'd get out of town and leave them to lead their lives as before, without fancy Anglo ways. But misery directed her and she needed to tighten the wires and make herself as wretched as possible, though she knew the answer.

LaBelle asked the brash redhead, "Do you love him?"

"Let me just say that I accept the fact that men find me very exciting."

Jerry had to agree and hoped that Melo stayed in place. "Phyllis is packing up and going off. If he follows her, he'll get lost."

"He's going downhill in jail," LaBelle said. "He can't be left there very long. He's already dying."

"I'll front the bail," Phyllis said. "I don't really care anymore."

"Dying?" Jerry asked.

"Radiation poisoning. He was exposed to the atomic bomb. Senio too."

Jerry pursed his lips together and shook his head. "That's nuts," he said.

Phyllis stood to leave. They were all mired in demoralizing problems, and any brush with these POWs and their families was depressing—everything was a battle; the war fed upon itself, eating its own tail, then doubling back for seconds. Phyllis wanted out. Anissa was packing too.

"He heard about the baby," Captain Sanchez told Phyllis when she arrived with the cash. "I thought he was going to rip the place apart." The bills were not new and crisp as she laid them out on the desk.

"Why did you have to tell him? It's none of his business," she said, returning the envelope with the cash to her purse. "Can't anyone ever have a secret in this place? Does everybody have to know everything about everybody?"

"I don't remember who told him, but I sure know how he took it."

"What is it to him? Why me? I have a good mind to leave him right where he is," she said. Again, the princess wandering the countryside bestowing favors. "I want him to stay locked up right where he's supposed to be."

Senio came into the office. "I heard Anissa fronted you the cash."

"She did."

"If he follows you out of town, we're keeping the two grand. You only get it back when he goes to trial," Sanchez warned her.

Melo was brought down, his hands uncuffed. "You got that Melo? You stay in town until you get to trial."

"Hey, Felice," Melo said, "you don't have to do this."

"I rather seem to. But please, don't jump bail."

"LaBelle's still there. I can't handle house arrest."

"She's *buena gente*, Melo. Just take it a day at a time. Put it all behind you."

Melo blasted Senio with a helpless look.

The three of them walked out onto the street. Melo looked around and said nothing. They continued walking. She remembered an earlier conversation.

"When is it ever going to be over?" she had asked Melo in the Famous Coney Island Club—the night she turned him inside out.

"It's over when the last man is dead," he had said.

She'd been caught into a self-perpetuating downward spiral and the only way she could manage to have any fun at all, to laugh again and flirt, was to find a more likely place with people more like herself. London might be perfect.

It was November 1945. The war had been over since the Feast of the Assumption on August 15th and some of the wartime Gringos had packed up and taken a lot of the excitement with them.

The leaves on the Plaza were yellow, red and falling, the clear blue mornings were crisp and the late sun warmed the benches now crammed with locals, some still drunk. On the mountain, the aspen had finished turning into a dazzling display of golds, reds and heart-quickening yellow before their dormancy. The war was splendidly ended now. Gasoline was available, and picnics were packed for short trips. Harvest ceremonials in the pueblos were over; deer and buffalo dances had taken their place. Snow was coming.

Paco, the old Mexican, arranged to buy his first pickup truck. This event was a technological advance for any wood cutter's career. By this time, everyone outside the Cash and Carry agreed that his picturesque useless burro was just plain stubborn. A new one was needed because Angelina balked, wheezed and refused to go anywhere without being tirelessly beaten, He'd named the burro Angelina—a sweet name in spite of her reminding him of big LaBelle, the gal who used to make the Frito Pie across the Plaza; both had their own minds. But buying another burro was unthinkable and he also knew that LaBelle would never leave either. And like the burro, beating her would be foolish.

She absolutely refused to go to Trinidad; she did not want to go anywhere, hadn't Paco heard all about it? Seems she called Santa Fe her true home, and refusing to leave even when she was given a free ride, she had picked up her strewn clothes and re-hung them in Melo's small *guardarropa*.

He heard too that Melo got out of jail and went to his friend's house and took over the shed. Then he heard that Adrien Hackman was selling his pickup truck.

The war finally over, it was true that the Hackman family was giving up their hideout in Nambe and returning to the Far East, but the two pretty daughters preferred to finish their studies in Holland. They were selling everything, and the last thing shucked was the old truck. But as he told Paco, it had been faithful and true. During rationing, it ran on *posole*, goat-flesh and Aquavit. Paco agreed that a docile pickup was the perfect solution to his dilemma.

"*Bueno, bueno*," agreed Paco seeing an opening to branch out into the delivery business—wood and groceries for the men home again with back pay. The postwar fever had taken him in as well.

Adrien Hackman cut the engine out of old habit and stepped

down from the cab of his pickup truck to begin the negotiations with Paco advanced. No longer would everyone pick their way across the hot piles of burro shit with their noses in the air. Everything was changing. For the better.

"Amigo," he said confidentially putting his hand on the Mexican's shoulder, "you point it and it goes. No arguments."

"*Es un bueno troque*," Paco agreed and pulled out a wad of bills from the bottom of a kindling basket. "*No te quieres Angelina?*"

"No," Adrien said, shaking his head and patting the rump of the maligned animal, raising puffs of dust. Seventy-five dollars in bills—cash for the 1930 Ford pickup. He stepped up to Adrien with the crumpled bills and swapped them for a single key.

Eventually Paco asked him to turn the truck around to head in the opposite direction, making the excuse of wanting to see all of the tires in action. There were scratches and gouges on the bed of the truck, a few dents but no rust. Four tires. *Bueno, bueno.* When Adrien started it up, the vehicle was noisy and set frightened Angelina to braying.

The two men shook hands.

Paco did tap dances to calm himself and with a flourish, he coaxed his burro up onto the bed of the truck.

"It can't be difficult," he announced with a happy shout. "Even women can drive." He called out an *adios* to Adrien, and turned the key and pushed the button. The truck shot ahead, shooting from standing still to twenty miles-an-hour, scattering pedestrians. When he slammed on the brake, the engine choked, and frightened Angelina brayed harshly, skidding to the back gate. But Paco had fallen in love with the pickup.

"Even idiots can drive these," Paco announced as he started it up again, careening around the Plaza and off to College Street where he knew enough to remember to feed the mechanical beast with some red leaded gas. What with the stopping and starting, Angelina's life was endangered. But as fond as Paco was of her, her useful days were over; the future lay with technology and this very truck was the future. If she managed to get herself home alive, she'd have to be content with a pasture.

He zigzagged down the street, the engine cutting out each time he applied the brakes, until he could make a broad turn off Old Santa Fe Trail, across Manhattan ("*Cuidado, Cuidado,*" he screamed) onto the last block, aiming for the corner gas station. In fits and starts, he arrived. When he accidentally hit the accelerator not the brake, he plunged straight into the gas pump, knocking it off the island and shattering the glass bowl. Gasoline bubbled, belched and pulsed out of the tank onto the pavement. He hit the brake this time.

The truck skidded on the slippery spill and Paco ran over the glass. The left front tire was punctured and the truck came to a stop perched on the island, resting on mangled parts of the former pump. His tire whistled slow air. Gasoline boiled out of the pump, gushing like an unstoppable mistake.

"Nobody smoke!" the station manager screamed, running out of his office. "Help!"

"Shit," Paco said in perfect English.

LaBelle heard this as she came out of the station, shoving a pack of Chesterfields into her purse. She had been buying cigarettes for the past month, smoking, not eating. So far, so good. She was down twelve pounds.

The truck was dented, one headlight looked bad, and the station was awash with gas. The burro had been hurt, bleating, bleeding.

"Oh, Paco," she said in Spanish. "Where did you get that truck?"

"Adrien Hackman sold it to me," he replied in *la idioma*. "Young boys drive them. *Borrachos* can drive them. People who are sick drive themselves to the hospital. When people are not driving them, they park, French kissing in the moonlight.

"It looked so easy." Paco had crinkly lines around his eyes and his face was tanned leather, but he looked like a naughty kid. This time it was English.

"You've got to get the burro out," she said as she went to the back gate and opened it. A panicked Angelina knocked hefty LaBelle down into the overflow. The contents of her purse spilled into the pooling gas. The package of cigarettes was now a *Fu Go* weapon. Paco gallantly leaned over her, wringing his hands in despair. He appeared to be more embarrassed than worried about the expenses he'd brought on himself. The squandered gasoline at fifteen cents a gallon was only a beginning. In fact, he was more concerned about LaBelle than the truck. If he had been an Iberian Moor like most of the town, he'd have kicked the tires, accused the truck of mutiny and fed it buckshot. Instead, he took a deep breath and helped her to her feet.

"I'll get you another pack," he said again in English.

LaBelle looked at him in disbelief. So he was a part of it too! Most likely he was someone's counter-intelligence, Army, Navy or Air Force. Paco was just another spook on the Plaza hired to spot the passing of folded scraps of nuclear information between Commie sympathizers and Russian scientists whose war had just begun. She'd guessed this by filling in the blanks. Packs of men loitering, leaning against the walls of the Capitol Pharmacy dressed like lawyers who were paid by J. Edgar Hoover with his fetish about wardrobe. Then there were the Indians watching, Jerry pouring drinks in the bar, the entire staff behind the reception desk at La Fonda—all listening and placing phone calls. And there, right under the eye of the Manhattan Project next to the Governor's Palace, local-color-Paco, the illiterate Mexican, dragged his burro Angelina around with little stacks of hand-cut wood on her back. Ratting on people, a plant for someone, but not with the FBI counter intelligence looking for unannounced spies. Whoever he worked for now was still operating.

She stared at him again, seeing that Paco smiled when his burro turned and trotted off, favoring one of her four legs. The fact that he was bored with his donkey confirmed her insight.

"It looked so easy," he wailed, wringing his hands. In an emergency, he spoke in *puro Americano*. No sing-song accents.

"Your burro!" LaBelle said, pointing to the animal's disappearing hind quarters.

"She'll go home," he said, watching Angelina limp off in the direction of the hill where she was stabled. "*No te preocupas.* She's a lot smarter than this pickup."

"I'll drive you home," she offered, fanning her drenched skirt behind her. The station manager had turned off the gas and was spreading ripped shreds of newspapers to sop up the spill.

LaBelle, in the meantime, climbed into the truck, slid on the worn upholstery, and complained of a vicious headache from the fumes. She turned the wreck on and slammed it into reverse, backing the truck off the island, hitting the overturned pump again. Then she got down to pitch in with the paper. They worked as quickly as they could, using a wide broom to accumulate the packing.

When the left front tire was fitted with a retread, Paco reached into his deep pocket and fished out a ten-dollar bill for the gas. He agreed to replace the pump and within a half hour, order was restored; the truck was damaged but still it rolled out of the station and up the dirt road to his place. Behind the wheel, LaBelle was speeding with the mind of a teenager, cutting school with a bale of hay in the back bed in Trinidad, Colorado. A plume of dust followed them.

"Like riding a bicycle," she yelled into the wind, her face out the window. Paco stuck his face out the other, not wanting to breathe the gasoline fumes from her clothes. As she piloted the rattletrap up the Garcia Street hill, she wondered where he actually lived and if it was paid for with surveillance funds. Why not? He wasn't going to return to Mexico anytime soon and he probably wasn't even Mexican. Mulling the facts over in her mind, he seemed crafty enough to be a Colombian.

"Your Spanish is Colorado Spanish," he noted. "Different."

"I went to high school in Trinidad. I was a cheerleader," she said. "Where are you really from?"

"Bolivia. My family owned tin mines," he said. "We had drivers." He nodded to her as an explanation. "It looked easy, even idiots drove cars there."

"Where'd you learn English?"

"A military academy in Miami."

Interesting, she thought, looking down at her shoes on the floor of the truck. She'd forgotten how much body-English these trucks required as she demonstrated the use of the clutch. She stalled only twice when her timing was off, downshifting.

"This is where I live," she told him as they ground past the Garcias' adobes lining the dirt street.

"I know," he said.

She stared at him, trying to figure out how she had never copped to what he had been up to. She always took him for an illiterate woodchopper. The fact that he looked so utterly honest and simple was probably because he was short. And he was polite.

He asked her a question about Melo, but she passed it off.

He asked her a second time, "What's the matter with Melo? He's not right in the head."

She said nothing, because she tried never to think and talk at the same time. She was protecting a plan bubbling up in her brain and she had to remember it, step-by-step.

When they climbed up Apodaca Hill where most of the woodcutters lived, he pointed to a tidy small cabin. There were healthy piles of firewood, cut and stacked, and the windows were draped so she could not see inside. The burro was already there, her head down, grazing on the chamisa.

"What did you study in Miami?" she asked. "Tin mining?"

"I didn't like geology," he said. "I switched."

"To science, right?"

"Yeah, physics. How did you guess?"

"Okay," she announced to him the next morning when she drove his truck back to his place so she could take him back to the Plaza. "Truth or dare."

"That game?" he said, standing near the truck on the driver's side. It was wild, she thought, the difference between how he looked—poor from the way-the-hell-and-gone Sierra Madre Mountains—and how he spoke, as if he'd been around big cities like Paris, France. Not too different from Anissa, and then there were his manners. Gentlemanly good manners!

"What happens with radiation poisoning? Truth or dare."

"Is this your game?" he asked, putting his face into her open window. "Why do you need to know?"

"Melo."

"Yeah, Melo. He's a case." Paco nodded to indicate that he understood something of the heartbreak. Then he turned to the back of the truck and began to heft small logs into the bed. They hit the bed with a metallic echo.

"He says he got radiation poisoning at prison camp, twenty miles from Nagasaki as the bird flies," she called out to him. More noisy pieces of wood flew from the neat pile to the bed of the truck, and observing him, she figured he wasn't the guy who had carefully stacked the cord in the first place. He probably didn't work alone.

In between armfuls, he paused. "That was a fifty-thousand kiloton plutonium bomb, radiation was right under the mushroom cloud," he replied, waiting for her to push the start button. "So, that's why he's so crazy?"

"What?"

"The fight on the Plaza. He's running scared?" He opened the passenger door and climbed in but she did not push the start button.

"That's one explanation. The other is that I'm making him marry me but he hates me," she said, trying not to sound desperate.

"No, it's all the same. People are afraid of radiation, men especially."

"Paco, who says that?"

"Oppenheimer. He's gone berserk over the effects of the bomb too. He's already delivered a talk saying that mankind will curse the names of Los Alamos and Hiroshima. He's carrying on with his hands shaking, insisting about using only peaceful applications of atomic power. Everyone knows how he feels and that Truman won't listen to him. Truman wants the bomb all to himself, but he also wants it kept secret."

"Everybody already knows all about the bomb. Hiroshima and Nagasaki." She leaned her head on the steering wheel and pressed her eyes shut.

"Not all about it, yet. *New York Times* said there's no Disease X under the bomb and MacArthur wants the whole thing kept quiet. He says he won the war, not the bomb and if it left radiation poisoning, then that's Truman's personal public relations mess." He could see that she seemed calmer, and he gave her time to stop shallow breathing.

"So, it's all shoved under, like everything else. Covered up. What about Melo and Senio?" When she did turn to talk to him, she looked confused, trying to reconcile how smart he was when he talked in English— unable to shake her old idea of him.

"If he and Senio were in the fallout pattern, it will show up like leukemia in their blood cells. Their platelets will not coagulate."

"How big's the fallout pattern??"

"No more than ten miles, generally. They tracked it at the Alamogordo test site."

"What happens if you're in the fallout? What happens?"

"You can scuff it up, or brush it off your clothes when it's still glowing. It's in the ashes."

"But how much ash can you handle?"

"No one's sure yet."

"What should we do?"

"Just have them test his blood at Bruns Hospital. They can do it pretty quick. Lots of red blood cells, plenty of white: no leukemia. It's a simple routine."

By the time she and Paco got the truck to the Plaza, the tightness in her chest had gone, LaBelle could breathe without taking deep breaths. She was no longer afraid of Melo's resentment. She was ready to take him on—for his own good, of course.

"Hey Paco, what's your real name?"

"Francisco Ricardo Velasco y Suarez. Why?"

"What do you know about the *Fu Gos*?"

"Amazing feat. Who'd have thought it'd work? Six thousand miles!"

"What are they for?"

"Oh, very crafty scheme, really. At a certain point, the balloons were to drop and start fires. And it worked what with this long Western drought. They started a forest fire in the Northwest and a munitions factory too. That's when the Firefly Troops were formed."

"Why's everything always secret?"

"The Japanese did it to get back for Doolittle's raid, which we did to get back for Pearl Harbor. We never learned what damage the raid did, and we don't want them to know that the thousands of silk fire balloons did actually do what they were supposed to a couple of times. So, it's still classified."

"Goddamned national security."

"No, national pride."

19

Santa Fe, New Mexico, March, 1946

"Hey, Tivo made it back," Senio announced.

Melo perked up. "Tivo, eh? He's alive?" Primitivo Lucero was the one reason any of them were still alive. It was Tivo's idea. He was the one with the connection to the Virgin. Senio even cut short his nightly raids stealing stuff in Cabanatuan to get back in time to hear Tivo lull them out of their crippling hunger. During the worst of the prison camp days, Tivo sat like a Gook, down on his haunches, butt practically in the dirt. He fluttered his hands, pointing as he rocked rhythmically back and forth on his skinny legs, leading them through the sacred rites of the kill and then teaching them respectful preparation of their dinner. Everything was preceded by grace, by calling down the Virgin's blessing on Her lowest of the low, Her pariah POWs.

And the *matanza* itself? For the prisoners it was a prayer as well, a centuries-old ritual, The Last Supper. They lived their Gethsemane clawing for life. Their souls had been too crushed to rise up and ask to be saved. They had only the body shell struggling to endure and the *matanza* bought them time. Guadalupe spread her bounty over them, bringing both sacrament and prayer.

"Tonight, our *quan* will be lamb chops with butter and parsley," he would begin. "First you find a nice, fat little lamb and tie it up. Careful when you slit the throat because we don't want the fur to get messed up. In a few days, we're going to save it for a blanket when it's soft and ready."

Melo and Senio would have eaten their last bowl of *lugao,* watery prison camp rice, as early as 1600 hours, or 1630 if they were at the end of the chow line. By the time they'd tried to sleep the hunger pangs would start hammering hard at them in the thick mosquito dark.

Then, after sunset, just as misery poured over them, Tivo came on. But it was really the *La Virgin de Guadalupe* who spoke through him saying that She felt so bad for the POWs that She even let Tivo lie about being a chef at La Fonda. Every night, Tivo and the Virgin rocked them into a contented sleep like milk-sopped babies. And the Virgin knew that their survival lay in keeping them alive not with brotherly love but with enough sustaining anger to fuel their will to live and so she filled their bowls and let Melo's rebellions simmer.

At Tivo-time, each *matanza* began with an invocation and prayer to La Virgin, and after a brief silence for reflection, they butchered the gifts she sent them, their entrée, the centerpiece. The rite of butchering took most of the time and Tivo, always merciful, went gently and slowly, especially one night when it was a full-size grass-fed beef.

"Take the time to cut it properly," he sang out. Then, wasting nothing, Tivo set aside the tenderloins and roasts for his twenty-odd New Mexico buddies and he saved the tail, hooves and ears for the gelatin-rich base for the next day's *posole.* "Take your time."

Slow-cooked delicacies delighted Tivo while Senio would have pan-fried the whole damned bull in red palm oil just to gorge himself; his hunger could not wait for ceremony. There were times Tivo almost lost patience with him. Almost, but not quite.

"Rocky Mountain oysters are cooked over very low grey-coated coals," Tivo explained wearily to Senio again. But he caved in and allowed him to toss the gonads on impatiently the red hot coals. "Keep turning them; try to grill them without burning the hair too much. Slow, keep it slow.

"Too much heat makes them tough," Tivo repeated, reaching out with a stick to check them. The gonads being his own favorite, Tivo called out meticulous instructions in his low sing-song voice.

"Here, Melo. You spell him now." And he motioned for Senio to move to the side of the huddled group. Melo, suffering from *rice brain*, seemed to have infinitely more patience, and more often Tivo allowed him to tender-cook the oysters—hair singed but not burnt black. "*La Virgin* likes them easy-to-chew."

Senio's true art was his masterful procurement. Often when Tivo left out an essential ingredient, one of the men gently reminded him what was missing (salt, green chile, garlic) and Senio would be sent to *quan* it. *Anis*, chocolate, onions, a soup tureen, Senio had a handle on it all; he could filch a handful of Chimayo red chile for tomorrow's leftover stew as easily as soy sauce and fish bones.

For Thanksgiving, (out of clean air) Senio produced a plucked turkey.

But he had divine help.

God, it smelled good. Real good. Every night when the sun dropped low, they huddled under the *nipa* shelter crouched on their emaciated legs, ready to spend the time stirring and serving the meal before they stuffed themselves, enjoying a Chesterfield afterwards. Always a Chesterfield.

The poorest of Her poor, *La Virgin* gave them what she herself liked to smoke.

Once, Tivo got dysentery bad, and Senio took over but it never tasted as good. Maybe he had left out *el comino*, the cumin. Something was missing.

But in Melo's mind his feelings of utter comfort and peace spread like butter when he heard that Tivo was back alive. They owed him their lives and at least a thousand dinners.

"So, we're going to throw a bash for him, cook a *cabrito?*" Melo offered. They both knew how to cook a baby goat by burying it in a pit; or they knew how Tivo cooked one. Nicasia had her old family recipes but this was not a woman's show. It was all Tivo's. A man's *matanza*.

"It's so great he's back." Senio said. "*Muy bueno gente.*"

"Hey, *Primo!*" Tivo bellowed the next day on the Plaza, his hand up for slapping. Melo was relaxed, seated one leg over the other, arms stretched back across the back of the bench. He leapt up and whacked Tivo's palm and they stepped back to check each other out. Both had shaved, both were fat in the middle, skinny on the ends, like brownish tropical bananas.

"I went to your house but your mama said you moved in with Senio. What's the matter, you guys turn queer or something?"

"Naw, it's just that LaBelle hogs my old bed."

"So you and Senio tooling all over the place in that old Chevy? I seen him cruising the Plaza with a bunch of *chicas*, radio going full blast."

"Well, if you saw that, you forgot to look here at my bench. I hold office hours all day. Unless it rains."

"No kidding? Same bench, isn't it? You stay there waiting for job offers?"

"Not me. I'm just here, keeping the peace."

"Peace, that's cool, really cool. Like a deputy?"

Melo smiled. "You remember Bouncer Gurule?"

"Man, he was something else." Tivo shook his head, grinning.

"Yeah, so Sanchez and José and the police all pay him for keeping things quiet, being as he raised all kinds of hell all the time and he knows who does dope, who's clean. They gave him a job."

"A-Okay! That's great!"

"So, now they're putting him up for judge, saying he knows the law better n' anybody, so he can be a judge. Pay's way up there." Melo surveyed the Plaza, glad the burro was gone. A beat-up truck stood in its place.

Tivo shook his head in amazement. "Man, you lucked out. For sure he'll go real easy on you."

"If he knows what's good for him," Melo said and Tivo's face broke into a huge grin.

"It's real good to be back. I don't know why I got so messed up about coming home."

"Me too. We were all scared shitless," Melo said, remembering that they had talked about going back to the Philippines and running cigarettes in the Black Market. Buy 'em in the PX, sell 'em in the streets. Big bucks. Scotch and cognac too. The girls were small and cute.

"You come and help me cook a *cabrito?*" Melo was hopeful.

"Why not? Let's throw a bash," Tivo nodded.

"My place?" Melo meant the pounded-flat yard on Garcia Street.

"But the way I operate, you remember, I never touch the meat. I just talk."

"You jerk!" Melo said and gave the guy a huge *abrazo*. "You fuckhead!"

"First you dig a hole, maybe four feet deep," he began. "Then you get the baby goat. It's got to have silky fine hair, a real pretty little goat, still sucking its Mama's tits."

"If you're talking about my yard, we'll need a post-hole digger just to get through the dirt. Man, it's like bloody cement."

"Hey, *Hito*, how are you?" Nicasia came through her little door when she heard the pounding outside.

"We're throwing a *matanza*. Tivo's going to cook a *cabrito*. "He raised the single handle of the posthole digger over his head and brought it down to the ground with as much force as he could muster. The blades went in about an inch each time. At this rate, he would be busy for days. The baby goat would keel over from stringy old age.

"When?" she asked. She knew not to react—not to say anything. She was content seeing him, even if she was walking on eggshells. He raised the implement over his head again and brought it down with a reverberating *chunk*, then pressed the blades together to scrape through the solid caliche earth.

There was a movement inside the kitchen; through the open door he caught a shadow passing by the table. It moved on and he returned his attention to the unyielding dirt. He raised the tool and let it drop.

In the house, a small curtain facing the yard moved slightly.

He raised the digger over his head again and brought it down. The handful of dirt he'd dislodged could have been swept up with a broom. All through the war, Santa Fe had been in the grips of the same drought that hovered over the entire Western United States. The earth was like a crusty sieve; water sponged down and was gone. It started with the Dust Bowl way before the war. Had to end sometime.

Someone was watching from the curtained window. The votive light was still out, the room dark beyond the open door.

He raised the five-foot implement and let it drop again. *Thump*. This time, he had chipped another small square of dirt. His hole was four inches deep and no more than a foot wide.

He did it again with the same results. "How deep does it have to be?" Nicasia asked.

"Four feet deep by about six feet," he replied, glancing at the figure behind the curtain.

"Tell her I can see her."

After a minute, LaBelle came to the open door and stood behind Nicasia, surveying the small dent. "I have an idea," she said and left to return with a kettle heavy with water.

Water turned the grit into mud, but slowly, an inch, then two, but never more. Melo continued with his overhead motions and LaBelle poured water into the hole. Nicasia was on her knees, pulling out mud with her hands. By the end of the hour, the hole was a foot deep and wider. It had been hard going and no one spoke. They'd also pulled out a few hard bones, white and porous from *matanzas* past.

They stood back surveying their work, hands on hips, the tops of their heads hot from the fixed sun overhead.

"More water," LaBelle said, turning. She filled the hole six times and let it soften.

"*Mis padres* used to butcher out here." Nicasia spoke of at least five generations before hers. That explained the growing chips of bones being pulled out of the dirt. Years passed and the yard was compacted over the *matanzas* of long ago. One femur was long enough for children to make a stumpy stilt. They needed one more.

"Now, I got to get a goat," he announced.

LaBelle stood in the shade of the wall and lit a cigarette, saying nothing.

"If it's a *matanza*, a real one, we got to have some horses. Races up and down the street. Prizes too," he added.

"I'm seeing Paco tonight. He'll get you your goat," she said, taking a deep drag and not offering him one.

"You been riding his burro?" Melo said with disgust.

LaBelle looked better, and she'd done something to her face, it was less mean. He judged it to be something about her eyes, like she'd plucked her eyebrows. When he thought of the pretty delicate Filipino girls, he was wistful. They weighed about a hundred pounds dripping wet and they laughed at everything he said. Even if it was sad.

"Paco? That dumb Mexican?" Melo blurted. He studied her more carefully. Her hair was shorter. She was either taller or thinner.

"First, he's not dumb and second, he's got a pickup truck," she said, inspecting her cigarette, transfixed by the curling smoke. "Give me some cash and I'll bring you back a goat. The burro's free."

"Paco's an idiot," he said, craving a cigarette.

"He'll give you the burro for free."

"Kids ride them, they don't eat burros."

"Nobody eats burros," she said, smoke filling her lungs again.

"We did before the surrender. We ate everything, even MacArthur's horse." He scrutinized her face and realized that she had never bought his story about MacArthur's horse.

"Smoke?" she offered. Politely, he accepted.

Still bleating for its mother, a silken, milk fed goat was tied two days later to a stake near the deep cooking pit. A fire had been started at the bottom with faggots Paco had dropped off, and rocks had been thrown onto it to be heated. Thirty people milled around, each with his own idea about how to cook the animal. Since *cabrito* was a community event, they'd brought shovels, faggots, and a handful of hay for the promised kid dinner. A few children came by to stroke the silky offering. Killing it would be orchestrated by Tivo alone.

Wives and aunties were at home cooking up a storm because the *cabrito* was not big enough to feed all the people who were coming. *Matanzas* were a traditional sixteenth century Come-and-Get-It. They were a community event as important as weddings and births.

"Tivo only said to get one goat, but it had to be perfect."

A keg of beer had been emptied, another was on its way in the back of Paco's truck with LaBelle in the cab, listening to the radio and talking like there was no tomorrow.

"I'm thinking of running for Fiesta Queen," she told Paco. "By Christmas when they do the judging, I'll be back down to my regular weight."

"Remember," he repeated. "I don't talk much. Okay?" She was a strong woman, trustworthy, so he decided, "You'd be a good Fiesta Queen."

"Don't worry." She lit him a cigarette and put it between his lips and she watched him as he drove, shifting now ever more smoothly.

"Let the clutch out all the way. Don't ride it," she said.

Anissa had heard the comings and goings and took a break from packing up four years of stuff to put on a huge straw hat. She came to stand around and watch on her last full day in Santa Fe.

"*Hola*," she said. Everyone nodded. When it came time to kill the little animal, she would cover her eyes and run for home, claiming she was still a vegetarian.

"I heard you are going back to Chicago," Melo said, not looking at her directly. He took a deep pull from the jam jar warming a half head of beer. In the winter the coffee turned cold instantly. In the summer, the beer got hot. Everyone blamed the altitude.

"I am," she said and moved right next to him standing on his shadow, too close. She had learned much about life and loyalty and the strength of family ties from the few short war years living with the Garcias. "I'll always remember you."

He stared at her, hoping that Chicago had big meat hooks that could reach down a thousand miles and grab her back to its Swift and Armour heart before today's sun had set. She didn't really belong. And vegetarians were all way off base.

"Phyllis says she's going to miss you, too," she said carefully. Phyllis was a risky subject given Melo's volcanic moods.

He gazed at her, dumbfounded. News traveled like lightning. When he was in jail, the whole town knew why Melo was there and that the Gringa woman he picked up got pregnant and had to go Old Mexico for an abortion, and they heard about Nicasia and LaBelle's outrage about the whole mess and how they would not bail him out. And because no one was able to keep even a small secret, they could sure zero in on one poor bastard and make him look like a huge horse's ass.

"Nobody here's going to miss Felice," he said, hoping the word got around.

"We're actually both leaving tomorrow. Roddy's dropping Phyllis off at the train station and then we drive to Chicago." Melo's *rice brain* intermissions gave her plenty of time to finish what she was saying and even granted her more in case she had anything else to say. So she had time to idly watch the community of neighbor women fussing with the plank table, stacking plates and counting forks before she spoke again.

"So, LaBelle said we could come by and say so long and farewell. She said that a *matanza* was our *despedida*, a so-long party." With that, she excused herself by putting a hand on the top of her straw hat and turned back to the other Garcia house she'd rented next door. He caught her arm.

"Here's the deal, if you come to our *matanza* it means you promise that you are really going. It's a Goodbye thing."

He wanted it to be ceremonial. If you agreed to a *despedida*, you agreed to get the hell out of town or get a Papal Dispensation to come back.

Anissa nodded. She really was pulling out of town. He'd decided that it was **either** them or him—someone had to leave town.

On the way back to her house, Anissa whispered something to LaBelle, which needed some time to soak in and register. And when it did, she screamed out louder than a bull.

"I don't believe it," LaBelle shrieked in laughter and she leaned down and said something to Paco.

Melo was convinced that it had to be about him, something derogatory. Maybe she'd called him an asshole. He ambled over slowly to set her straight. That LaBelle could not look at him confirmed his suspicions. Red-faced, surprised, and nervously giggling, she dropped her head and with the back of her hand rubbed her glistening eyes, still shaking and snickering, like some idiot teenage girl. She'd slipped into convulsions.

"So," he began, "this is Tivo's party. It's more than a *despedida* for the Gringa bitches."

LaBelle glanced away and squeezed her eyelids together, stifling snorts like being helpless in church.

"LaBelle," he said firmly. She needed to listen to him, to follow his words. Finally she looked at him and shook her head in happy astonishment. He could see it. She was being evasive, covering up something she thought he was too stupid to handle.

"It's an everything party," she said. "*Bienvenida… Despedida.* War's over and guess what? I'm not supposed to tell you, but Anissa gave me her car for keeps. She gave me her two-door Ford!"

"She did?" he said, instantly jealous. Really jealous that the green car with the tan upholstery and two doors and a radio had been given to the one person who was not supposed to be here. The one who should have been tied down and carried away in a bus headed north.

"She gave it so you can go back to Trinidad?" The question barely masked his disappointment. He'd lost a girlfriend, a baby, his family house and now a car. Some accidents were considered frozen—things that should not have happened but could not be changed. They were always abnormal. But stuff came out of them; stuff that should never have happened now made everything afterward veer off course. This was one.

"No, Melo. Sorry, bro. I'm staying." For a fleeting second, she smiled at him, but too quickly she slipped away mentally, as her eyes jigged to the gate on the street and fixed on Senio's Chevy.

Melo followed her gaze.

As Senio cut his engine, Tivo stepped out. His hands were empty. Senio left the car parked in the street with room enough on the dirt road for other cars to edge by. Chances were good that, by sundown, the street would be entirely blocked with trucks and pre-war cars held together with bailing-wire. Whatever still rolled. After dinner, they'd have a barrel race right there on the street. It was going to be wild. Real *matanzas* were like that.

Melo spoke to LaBelle. "Why did she give you the car?" He suspected that this was a trick, a huge joke. He could not bear to look at her, so his eyes followed Tivo as he came closer to the house.

"Someday I'll tell you what she really said," LaBelle said as she walked off, jingling the car keys in her hand. What Anissa had said was that the car belonged to both of them, but if he wanted to drive it, he had to ask her. It was okay to make him beg.

Nicasia and LaBelle greeted Tivo. "A beer, please," he said and walked over to examine the pit where the dying embers had warmed the rocks.

He squatted down, rocking on his crouched legs like any Asian waiting for a bus. The small group pressed in closer; no one spoke—Melo, Paco, LaBelle, Nicasia and some skinny wiry cousins from down the street. Eventually Anissa and Phyllis strolled over with Roddy and when they did, Tivo stopped and looked up having no idea who the *Güeras* were, so he stared.

Phyllis sucked all the attention to herself, all talking stopped. It was some trick of hers, something redheads could do and that's the way she wanted it. No one else existed, only Phyllis.

Nicasia was vaguely aware that Roddy had come and was standing close to Anissa, but she could read Phyllis' very thoughts: *Hey look at me! Hubba Hubba.* Damned woman.

When Melo looked up, Phyllis was standing by the fence, and a formless panic rose beyond his bone thin ankles to past his groin. On top of everything, she had shamed him by bailing him out. He had not laid eyes on her after that, and down the line she got the cash back from the judge.

She didn't like it either—men lavished on her, she did not spend money on men.

But Emma had warned her that the POWs returning were war-damaged. Too late, she understood that Emma was European war-savvy. Like she had said, the veterans are not "mentally stable."

So Phyllis had to buy her way out and because of it, she knew it was time to leave town. There were just too many hard luck stories. Bye, Bye, Blackbird.

She could not crack this town.

Still, she stood like a magnet, pulling everyone's attention to herself. And no one fixed on Tivo during this time. A few minutes of this and she reddened, knowing that the heat from Melo could blister. She threaded her way through the group, touching one on the shoulder, another on the arm. She stopped at Melo. "Take care of yourself," she said, looking straight into his eyes.

"We need to talk."

"No, I have to get back to where it rains. I'm going home. Roddy's dropping me off at the train," she told him loud enough for Nicasia and LaBelle to hear.

"Be good." And she leaned over and kissed him on the cheek, a cool kiss with firm lips. *These people are so passionate,* she thought. She could not escape soon enough, but she had nowhere to go but back to West Palm to face the music, whatever it was. Aunt Marjorie was already seasick on a transatlantic ship, headed home.

"All I did was take him to bed once and now he thinks he owns me," she had explained to Anissa in the little house next door. Roddy had to laugh. *Nothing had changed. Phyllis was still making the same mistakes.* Some were small like being dead wrong about Anissa, others not so small.

Things changed. Not only was Roddy sold on Anissa by this time, he was driving her to Chicago the next day to help her open up the house, the one with the dock on Lake Michigan. It was near his automobile dealership.

Almost at the same time, Phyllis and Anissa agreed that it was high time to pull up stakes. Santa Fe had been a refuge when they needed it. Anissa for one would remember even the smallest detail of Nicasia's world, while in the long run her presence would be just a memory for the Garcias, a story with different endings over the years.

Certainly Melo, if he regained his sanity, would get mileage out of all of them, herself, Phyllis and Saint Germain.

Tomorrow, after a final lunch at La Fonda, Roddy would drive the three of them out of town. The War was over, and the battle wins and losses still debated. Standing near the window, they popped open a bottle of champagne and toasted themselves and their futures, glancing from time to time from the window at the doings next door.

In the dirt yard, more neighbors gathered for the ritual *matanza*. The life of a young goat would be sacrificed to restore the mind and soul of a POW, to return his brave heart. The long-awaited *matanza* would welcome Nicasia's loyal son home to his land, his people. *La Raza*. A *matanza* also to bring the dead back into new vivid life of legend and memory.

"They take everything so very seriously," Anissa observed, glimpsing from time to time past the curtain. "I can't quite figure out what they're up to over there."

"They are hot blooded; they'll die for an idea, any idea." Roddy emptied the last of the booze in the cabinet into their glasses as they continued to pack the books and a collection of Indian pots. The shotgun leaned against Anissa's suitcases. It had been accepted as an apology.

"Or they can refuse to die, too, like Melo and Senio," Anissa speculated.

"He scares me to death," Phyllis said blowing her last kiss and closing the door on the adventure. In her mind it began with a *bienvenida* party she'd thrown and ended with this *despedida*. She had work to do and places to go and she raised her glass to seal her future.

"Sing it again, Tivo. Sing for us," Senio called out in the dry afternoon.

They could hear a clear voice calling out a prayer to the Virgin of Guadalupe. Tivo sat back on a stool and repeated his chant, the prayer for mercy and well-being. His voice was crystalline and floated out in all directions. LaBelle's contralto joined in and against this came a low throaty murmur from the bowed heads of guests with closed eyes, a rumbling sound like distant thunder against the Sangre de Cristos floating above the small town. Thunder itself being another invocation.

Tivo's long fingers pointed to where the goat with its fine silky hair had been tethered. "Take a tender young goat and render it unconscious with a merciful swift blow to the head," he began and Senio stood to administer the easeful death. No one spoke while the blood was cupped and the goat skinned. Occasionally LaBelle chose to look away until she saw that Paco, too, was transfixed.

Occasionally she had to remind herself to breathe.

"Rub the flesh with garlic, oregano and mint," Tivo chanted in Spanish, waving his *brujo's* hand over the pink and firm and perfect meat.

"Place it in a moist burlap bag, washed clean especially for the meal."

Melo never took his eyes from Tivo. The sound of his voice carried him back in time. He felt as if he hovered several inches above the ground, swaying and pitching from foot to foot as he flew back to Cabanatuan Prison Camp and the *nipa* hut where night after night, the captives leaned in to hear the Virgin's voice promising motherly love and nourishment as She sang out through Tivo's bent frame.

She chanted about the earth and the herbs and medicines and the bounty from the sea. She called forth harvests and farmers kneeling over each scallion, each carrot. And the farmer's daughter with sunshine turning her hair to satin as she pulled watercress and mint from the beds closest to the well.

She sang of wheat fields waved by the wind and a pretty Filipina in a conical hat, singing in a *Tin-a-kling* voice as she set out shafts of sprouted rice. "Planting. Rice. Is ve-ry nice."

"Lower the goat into the pit and sprinkle it with herbs, throw in garlic, onions, oregano and mint. Heap beautiful herbs on the suckled baby goat."

One by one, the ghosts of Japanese soldiers rimmed the yard, watching. Watanabe clutched his chest and performed a *Dogenza*, kissing the dry dirt of the foot-pounded yard. Dead buddies swooped down, a fly-by from the sky. Faustino and Franque walked through the crowd, proud to belong, generous fragments of their love for Nicasia pulsing in everyone's heart. They poured their souls out over Nicasia, kissing her. *Gracia*, so full-of-grace.

Then damned if Doc Matson didn't walk in, grinning and taking credit for keeping them alive—for the whole shooting match.

Melo heard Tivo call for ten more drenched burlap bags and he watched LaBelle break away from where she stood to bring them. Melo heard the Virgin singing out to the daughter who wove the blankets, to the Indian mother, spider woman who spun life and wove civilization into being, calling for more beauty, more weavings.

He heard LaBelle answering back, "Here I am, call me!" And he suddenly saw this young woman's power to create and give life. He saw the gifts she could heap on them, all of them.

And he saw that he belonged to a place and it was a place that claimed her as well. And he relented because he had seen how life blessed itself and made more life.

Tivo sang out: "Lower the *cabrito* into the pit, cover it carefully with burlap cloths and when you have done this, shovel in the earth you have set aside."

Melo's face was wet with tears. He was no longer angry; he no longer needed to rage and storm, to bellow his fury alone in the dark. Truths this significant are borne through sorrow. They can only come from pain.

The afternoon had grown cooler and was passing and the *cabrito* was lifted out and peeled from the burlap and set upon a long table outside the door to the small house. Eighty people had gathered with their votive lights. When dinner was ready, another prayer was called out.

"Lord, we thank you for this bounty which we are about to receive," they said. "Thank you for bringing our men back to us."

Sixty, seventy guests formed a line to serve themselves while Melo sat apart from the crowd, the setting sun coloring his face crimson as he looked up. LaBelle stood above him with a candle in her left hand, the other holding Nicasia's small one. They both gazed directly at him, through him, and he flinched.

"Why me? What'd I do?" He accused her of attacking him again.

"So, did you?" LaBelle wanted the answer. "Did you get covered with that atomic ash?"

"Yeah we walked in it, and it crawled up our legs and into our balls," he said. "But we were too good. We were too great. Nothing can hurt us. Neither Senio or me."

"Paco says chances are good you're going to make it," LaBelle said flatly.

"The V.A. says we don't have leukemia." He looked up at her and saw her shining. She was even beautiful. If she wanted to be Fiesta Queen, well, maybe she could, but she'd have to be married to one of the original families. Nobody got to be Fiesta Queen just because they're stacked and have a great smile. He gave his mother a weak nod.

"Just because you got a car, you think you can be Fiesta Queen?" he said to LaBelle.

Kneeling in the dirt, she put her candle down and took his hand while his mother stood.

"Let's go back to the beginning. Let's start again. You are home," she said to him. "This is your home."

"I am your mother," Nicasia said.

LaBelle said, "I wrote to you every day."

Melo stared at her. Had they met a long time ago?

"This is my home," he repeated. He still had *rice brain* but he was getting better at remembering. So much had happened.

One by one, the guests passed by Melo with their candles and he blew them out.

One by one.

Author's Note

Everything was the war. Occasionally, someone would change the subject but otherwise, my parents and their friends drank too much and rehashed the war.

As children, we learned to swim at the Hotel del Coronado at Coronado, California, with our young anxious mothers waiting for the return (or the black-starred telegram) of their husbands from the Pacific theater. After the jubilation of V-J Day on August 14, 1945, my widowed mother married Admiral Foote's newly discharged Aide-de-Camp, who after the honeymoon, moved us to bomb-flattened Japan to set up the Coca-Cola plants for *our boys*. To my Texan stepfather who had been D-plus-one-hour on Omaha Beach, they were all God-fearing, high-minded coke-drinking boys and they needed their comforts.

General Douglas MacArthur was soon installed as the Supreme Commander of the Allied Forces in Japan and Korea with the purpose of establishing a democratic constitution that outlawed war and at the same time retained the Emperor, granting him immunity from war crimes.

The Occupation of Japan began with the Seabees building bases, barracks, housing, Quonset huts, schools for the dependents, and Bachelor Officer's Quarters, as well as the plants for Blue Seal reconstituted milk, and Coca-Cola in green glass bottles.

MacArthur's offices were on the top floors of the Dai Ichi Building with a view into the Imperial Palace grounds. The General's daily arrivals and departures were theatrical. A large crowd awaited and stood in respectful lines overseen by the Military Police at attention in white gaiters and carrying billy-clubs. Flying flags with his five-star rank, his mirror-polished car would appear and the great man, tall, dignified, a garden of ribbons on his decorated breast, would step out of the car, the door held open by an orderly in full dress. The Japanese bowed to him, the foreigners clapped. This is how I remember his staged office arrivals: they were aristocratic, important and subtly underscored by the shadow of the Japanese Emperor sequestered nearby in his Palace.

In 1946-47, everyone lived at MacArthur's pleasure. He was the Supreme Allied Commander of Japan and South Korea. Every passenger manifest came across his desk. When my grandparents came to visit us, he sent a telegram to the Imperial Hotel two blocks away from his headquarters. Addressed to them personally, it said, "Welcome to Japan. Stop. General Douglas MacArthur."

The Press Club was on a side street off "Avenue A" in Hibiya near the Palace moat. My parents lingered long hours in its bar, reexamining the war. Survivors of the Bataan Death March would pass by. One, Bob Broadwater, an ambling skeleton, chose to stay in Japan and was joined by his wife to work for Coca-Cola. There were British from Hong Kong and Singapore coming through, all of whom had been interned by the Japanese. There were other Allies, the Australians and the White Russians, one of whom was my riding master, always overdressed and carrying a riding crop, buttons shiny.

It was bleak, and the reconstruction progressed slowly. There were profiteers, Black Marketeers, spies, thieves, missionaries and the occupation families who lived separated in their own Americanized housing areas. We rented a series of houses owned by Japanese who could still not afford to heat them, and the Occupation had a special department to set rent scales. In the beginning coal heated the homes and operating trucks had coal converters strapped to their sides. The air was foul from it.

Tokyo Bay was an obstacle course with hundreds of rusting crucifix tipped masts and conning towers rising from their salty graveyard. My parents' close friend, a Dutchman, had salvaging equipment. One of those sunken ships was thought to hold a million dollars worth of the Philippine gold ingots sacked by the Japanese, and my stepfather purchased shares to reclaim the treasure. He fronted $10,000 for his portion of the bullion, rather than risk the money for a large share of our neighbor's burgeoning radio shop, Sony.

"MacArthur is leaving," my brother and I were solemnly informed, and we joined the mounting crowds outside the Dai Ichi building. That April morning in 1951 when he and his family left Japan, I lay in my bed, gazing up through the window to see waves of planes flying in formation as a final salute to their Supreme Commander. He was irreplaceable, no one else had the right stuff. The talk was all about him, and fifty years later, I can still recall our desolation at his departure.

But for small interruptions, adults simply drank and talked endlessly about the war. My brother and I led our own dissolute life, cutting school and mastering Pachinko at the machines lining the entrances to the subway stations. We were outside the law, not Military police, nor the Japanese police could take an American civilian into custody. One American businessman shot his wife and there was no one qualified to write him up.

Bombed-out Tokyo was a desperate city. Charcoal hibachis were fired up every noon and evening, adding to the murky haze riding the rooftops. Mount Fuji was never seen floating on the horizon. The Black Market flourished, the FBI granted clearances, and both the OSS (precursor of the CIA) and CID knew everybody's business.

By 1952, we moved to Okinawa, a noodle shaped coral island with clean air, 68 miles long and four miles wide at its widest. Of course, the house was on Hacksaw Ridge, where 70,000 Japanese soldiers and cave-holdouts were gunned down and set afire and 12,500 Americans and 150,000 Okinawans were killed. Almost a quarter of a million people. Caves with rusting machine guns and rat-attacked bags of spilling rice rimmed our 13 acre property. Spent ammunition and unexploded grenades lay in the grass six years after the last battle. "Just our kind of place," said my younger brother. We gathered thousands of skeletons of dead Japanese soldiers.

"Home at last," my mother said. We were to live a normal American childhood with fresh air, sailboats, a swimming pool. Plus an Army brat school in Quonset huts on a South China Sea beach.

"Don't go into the caves," she warned. Too late. We'd been pillaging them from the start. We melted candles on top of skulls like Horatio in the Lawrence Olivier *Hamlet* and we extracted gold-capped incisors, intending to drill them for stringing.

"There seems to be a problem with the help," my mother observed when we came in with another skull. There was a problem—they were outraged. The caves were soon cemented over by the Okinawan government. We shrugged. Nothing more than that came of it.

Fueling the active social life on the Island, Gilbey's gin cost a dollar a bottle, Scotch, bourbon, rum as well. Cigarettes were a dime a pack.

When my step-father was promoted to vice president of Coca-Cola International, we moved to the Philippines, where Manila was riding her postwar boom with businesses restored and huge new fortunes. My classmates had been interned in Santo Tomas, some even born in the women's prison camp. I was mad for a handsome *mestizo* (Half Filipino, half Scot) who had grown up hidden in the jungle, strafed in the rice paddies by the Japanese.

And then, the divorce. "Too much drinking," my mother said as she soon married a former Nazi Youth with German dueling scars and my stepfather married a Japanese, all of which added new input to the continuum. The two pairs of newlyweds were inseparable. Houses never very far apart, they had lunches and talked about the War. I was encouraged to travel because travel made a person interesting.

Santa Fe was remote, small, foreign-feeling. One-third Native American, one-third Anglo and one-third Hispanic. It seemed so historically remote—overlooked and safe.

I was astounded when my neighbor, Luis Sena told me that he spoke some Japanese and recited his vocabulary from in prison camp. In the beginning, he did not talk about the Death March or being starved, and beaten, but he often limped and his back pained him. The War again. As time went on, I heard more stories and we talked about the War, a subject I seemed to know by heart.

In this retelling, I hope I've properly honored their courage, their traditions and fierce intelligence. My small effort is insufficient to express the gratitude we feel for their having endured what was truly the unendurable.

I am especially grateful to Luis Sena and Vicente Ojinaga for giving me long hours; appreciative of Jeronimo Padilla, director of the Bataan Memorial Military Museum and Library; grateful for Paul Fussell's, *Wartime*, an examination of American behavior during WWII; to Gavin Daws for his important close accounts of the GIs lives in his *Prisoners of the Japanese*; to George Weller, the Pulitzer Prize-winning reporter who was the *First into Nagasaki*; to John A. Glusman for his eloquent *Conduct Under Fire*; and to Nancy Bartlit whose continuing research for *Silent Voices of World War II* illuminated the conflicts over the Japanese Internment Camp in Santa Fe. The list of remarkable sources is very long.

My appreciation goes out to many. To Jim Smith of Sunstone Press who said, "I love two things: stuff on World War II and novels about Santa Fe." Music to my ears. And to Major General Jasper Welch, USAF ret., my charming and encyclopedic brilliant historian, many thanks. To David Tett, postal historian; to Eugenia Wilkie; Jerry Delaney; Ken Lincoln; Jonathan Carleton; Judy Wilson; Les Daly; Bethany McQuaid; Kay Hamilton; Jane Ann Welsh; Elise Phillips, the Santa Fe Writer's Workshop; and my daughter, TC. for reading and re-reading this.

The title of this book, *Now Silence*, was inspired by General Douglas MacArthur's speech on the battleship *USS Missouri (BB-63)* after the peace had been signed. "Now the Guns are Silent." He ended his delivery with, "Your sons and daughters are homeward bound. Take care of them."

Suggested Readings

BOOKS:

Mary Austin
The Land of Little Rain
Sunstone Press
Santa Fe, NM, 2007
First Published by Houghton Mifflin Co, 1903

Everett M. Rogers and Nancy R. Bartlit
Silent Voices of World War II: When Sons of the Land of Enchantment Met Sons of the land of the Rising Sun.
Sunstone Press
Santa Fe, NM, 2005

James Bradley
Flyboys:
A True Story of Courage
Little, Brown and Company
Boston, MA, 2003

Dorothy Cave
Beyond Courage:
One Regiment against Japan, 1941-1945
Sunstone Press
Santa Fe, NM, 2006

Jennet Conant
109 East Palace:
Robert Oppenheimer and the Secret City of Los Alamos
Simon and Schuster
New York, NY, 2005

Gavin Davis,
Prisoners of the Japanese: POWs of World War II in the Pacific
William Morrow & Co.
New York, NY, 1994

Thomas J. Friedman
The Lexus and the Olive Tree
Anchor Books, Farrar, Straus and Giroux,
New York, NY, 1999

Erna Fergusson
New Mexico
Sunstone Press
Santa Fe, NM 2009

Paul Fussell
Wartime:
Understanding and Behavior in the Second World War
Oxford University Press
New York, NY, 1989

Paul Fussell
Thank God for the Atom Bomb and other Essays
Ballentine Books
New York, NY, 1990

Nora Gallagher
Changing Light,
Pantheon Books
New York, NY, 2007

John A. Glusman
Conduct Under Fire: Four American Doctors and their Fight for Life As Prisoners of the Japanese, 1941-1945
Viking Penguin, The Penguin Group
New York, NY, 2005

Paul Horgan
Lamy of Santa Fe
Farrar, Straus and Giroux
New York, NY, 1975

Sandy Hotchkiss, LCSW
Introduction by James F. Masterson
Why is it Always About You
The Free Press
New York, NY, 2002

Donald Knox
Death March: The Survivors of Bataan
Harcourt, Inc
Florida, 1981

John Pen La Farge
Turn Left at the Sleeping Dog
University of New Mexico Press
Albuquerque, NM, 2001

Ruth Laughlin
Caballeros, The Romance of Santa Fe and the Southwest
Sunstone Press
Santa Fe, NM, Revised 1945 edition

Philip A. Lunday and Charles M. Hampton
The Tramway Builders: A brief history of Company D 126th Mountain Engineer Division
Copyright 1994 by Philip A. Lunday and Charles M. Hampton

Richard Melzer
Ernie Pyle in the American Southwest
Sunstone Press
Santa Fe, NM, 1996

Patrick K. O'Donnell
Into the Rising Sun
The Free Press, a division of Simon Schuster
New York, NY, 2002

Eleanor D. Payson, MSW
The Wizard of Oz and other Narcissists
Julian Day Publications
Royal Oak, MI, 2002

Kai Bird and Martin Sherwin
American Prometheus: The Triumph and Tragedy of J. Robert Oppenheimer
Alfred A. Knopf
New York, NY, 2005

Hampton Sides
Ghost Soldiers: The Forgotten Epic Story of World War II's Most Dramatic Mission
Doubleday
New York, NY, 2001

Gordon Sumner, Jr.
Marching On: A General's Tales of War and Diplomacy
Red Anvil Press
Oakland, OR, 2004

Henry J. Tobias, Charles E. Woodhouse
Santa Fe, a Modern History 1880-1990
University of New Mexico Press
Albuquerque, NM, 2001

Otto D. Tolischus
Tokyo Record
Reynal & Hitchcock
New York, NY, 1943

Frederick Turner
Of Chiles, Cacti, and Fighting Cocks
Owl Books, Henry Holt and Co.
New York, NY, 1990

George Weller
First into Nagasaki
Crown Publishers
New York, NY, 2006

Gordon Thomas and Max Morgan Witts
Enola Gay
Stein and Day
New York, NY, 1977

VIDEOS:

The Liberation of Los Baños
Directed by Martin Gilman
Narrated by William Lyman
Produced by Greystone Communications for the History Channel
Copyright 2004, A&E Television Networks

The Conscientious Objector
Produced and Directed by Terry Benedict
Written by Terry Benedict and Jeff Wood
A Chaparral West, Inc. Production in association with D'Artagnan
Entertainment, C.2004

ARTICLES:

"A Deliberate Dissonance"
By Elizabeth Cook-Romero
The New Mexican, Pasatiempo
p. 46, April 27, 2007

"America Faces the Atomic Age: 1946"
By Dr. Lloyd J. Graybar, Ruth Flint Graybar,
Air University Review
January-February 1984

"Weeping Moon over Mountain of Exile"
By Paul Weideman
The New Mexican, Pasatiempo
Santa Fe, New Mexico
April 27, 2007

"The Day the Emperor Spoke in a Human Voice"
By Kanzaburo Oe
The New York Times Magazine, May 7, 1995

MOVING PICTURES:

The Best Years of Our Lives
Directed by William Wyler
Written by MacKinlay Kantor and Robert E. Sherwood
Staring: Dana Andrews, Myrna Loy, Frederic March, Virginia Mayo and
Hoagy Carmichael

LECTURE:

"This History of New Mexico"
By Thomas Chavez
Former director of the National Hispanic Cultural Center, 2006

Printed in the United States
124367LV00003B/163-195/P

Lucasville Legends is published by Lucasville Media
an imprint of JL dub Media, Inc.
9255 Towne Centre Drive, Suite 500, San Diego, CA 92121

For information regarding permission, write to
JL dub Media, Inc.
9255 Towne Centre Drive, Suite 500, San Diego, CA 92121
www.Lucasville.com

Lucasville is a registered trademark of JL dub Media, Inc.

Printed in the United States of America

Editorial Credits
Jean-Marie Van Lancker, President UIM Pleasure Navigation
Sarah M. Crookston, Reading Specialist
Photo Credits
Degiorgio, Melvin. 6-7(pilots), 12b, 13a, 23b, 30b
Guillerno, Marcello. 21c
GoPro. 10, 15, 17bc, 18-19a, 21b, 27b, 28b
Henderson, Sarah. 12a, 22a, 32-33
Moorkens, Peter. 8-9, 16b, 26ab, 27c, Back cover
Runza, Roberto. Cover pilots, 14, 16cd, 17a, 22b, 23a
Overlaet, Karel. Cover boat, 2-3, 11a, 16a, 21a, 31ab
Sammut, Claude. 5, 13b, 29b
Scerri, Dennis. 6-7(background), 30a
Sieveke, Sven. 18b, 19b, 20ab, 24-25abc, 26c, 27a, 28-29a

Publisher's Cataloging-in-Publication data

Wilson, Janet L.
   Nigel and Michael's ocean race boat / Janet Wilson.
   p. cm.
   ISBN 978-0-9834110-3-1
   Series : Lucasville Legends.

1. Motorboat racing --Fiction. 2. Motorboat racing--Juvenile fiction. I. Series.
II. Title.

PZ7.W6843 Ni 2011
[Fic]   2011906759
The publisher does not endorse products whose logos may appear in images in this book.

Nigel & Michael's
Ocean Race Boat

Janet Wilson

LUCASVILLE
Legends
ON THE EDGE

Hi! My name is Nigel Hook.
I am the throttle man of the #77 Lucas Oil boat.
The team has just built a new race boat.
It is called SilverHook.

6

Hi! My name is Michael Silfverberg.
I am the driver of the #77 Lucas Oil boat.
This is a story about the first Grand Prix
with our new SilverHook race boat.

Ocean

Two Engines
Type: **Sterling**
Model: **Class 1**
Horsepower: **725 each**
Fuel: **Petrol - 2 tanks**
Capacity: **260 gallons**

Air Scoops
used to force air into
the engine compartment
to cool the engines

Rudder
used to turn
the boat

Two Propellers
used to push
the boat forward

Two Trim Tabs
adjustable flaps used to
balance the boat when racing

Race Boat

Safety Cockpit
Restraint: **5-point harness**
Oxygen: **2 SCUBA tanks**
Canopy: **reinforced roll bars**
Windshield: **1-inch thick**

Hull
aerodynamic design and built very light for top speed
Model: **SilverHook GP48**
Material: **carbon fiber**
Length: **50 feet**
Top Speed: **120mph**

OIL.

77

Boat racing is the only motor sport that requires two people to race the vehicle. The racers are called pilots. One pilot is the driver and the other pilot is the throttle man. There are no brakes on our boat, so working together is an important part of boat racing.

The race course is built using huge buoys that float in the ocean.

White buoys are used for the start/finish line. Yellow is used for right turns and red is used for left turns. We must keep yellow buoys to our **starboard** side and red buoys to our **port** side.

One lap is almost five miles. This course has one left turn.

This **Grand Prix** is two races. The first race is the Sprint Race and the next day is the Endurance Race.

11

**Race Day 1
Sprint**

Today is the Sprint Race and the ocean is rough. The crew checks the engine compartment and tightens the nuts and bolts.

The boat weighs over 12,000 pounds. A crane is used to put the boat into the water. These are the wet pits.

Our crew puts a red tape up for each lap.
Today's race is the start plus 10 laps.

Each time we finish a lap, we pull off a tape.
This allows us to see quickly
how many laps are left in the race.

Soon the race will begin. Michael and I
wonder how our new boat will perform.
Will all of the crew's hard work pay off?

Michael and I put on our safety equipment. Our helmets have radios so that we can hear each other over the engine noise. We will talk to our crew during the race.

These are fire-resistant suits. The life jackets will inflate if their cords are pulled.

15

Green flag! I hit the throttles. Wow!
The sea conditions are rough. Here we go!

The acceleration is fantastic!

We are at the first buoy. I throttle back (just a little bit) and Michael turns the wheel. We must work together to get around the corners.

I hit the throttles and say, "Nice driving!" The crew tells us that we are five seconds ahead of the next boat.

The gauges are hard to read. This rough water has everything inside the cockpit rattling like crazy ... including our eyeballs. Hang on! Full speed to the next buoy!

Nine more laps to go. Can we win this race?

Race Day 2 Endurance

Our crew chief reviews the lap speeds from yesterday.

Great news! SilverHook had the fastest time in the first lap.

During our team meeting, the crew talks about the work they did to repair the boat. SilverHook is ready to race today, and so are we.

Michael and I pose for a photograph.
Nice ... but we are thinking about the race.

Race officials told all of the teams that
there are 6-foot waves in the ocean today.
That sounds like a great challenge for us!

We are confident as we head out to the
starting line. We know our crew
has carefully prepared the boat.

Green flag!

24

We are in the lead!

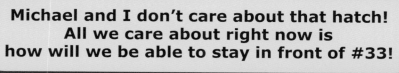

All of the hard work by the crew was worth it. SilverHook has won her first Grand Prix!

The crew is waving and cheering for us!

We do TV interviews. Michael explains the vibrations and how the boat was running.

We sign autographs on the way to the podium.

The podium! This is the best place in the world.

Michael and I are very happy!
We cannot wait until our next race.

Vocabulary

acceleration [ak-**sel**-uh-**REY**-shun] - to gain speed

aerodynamic [air-oh-dahy-**NAM**-ik] - designed to reduce drag caused by air flow or water flow

anxiety [ang-**ZAHY**-i-tee] - a tense desire; eager

anxious [**ANGK**-shuhs] - feeling worried and excited at the same time

capsize [**KAP**-sahyz] - to turn bottom up; overturn

fire-resistant [**FAHY** ri-**ZIS**-tuhnt] - something that is totally or almost totally unburnable

Grand Prix [grand **PREEZ**] - a very important competitive event

horsepower [**HAWRS**-pou-er] - a unit to measure the power of an engine

inflate [in-**FLEYT**] - to expand with air or gas

port [pohrt] - the left-hand side of a vessel, facing forward

starboard [**STAHR**-bohrd] - the right-hand side of a vessel, facing forward

vehicle [**VEE**-i-kuhl] - a conveyance that transports people or objects

vibration [vahy-**BREY**-shun] - the feeling created by something shaking